DEMONIC

DEMONS DOn 1 DATE

HANNAH WALKER

DEMONS DON'T DATE

Commander Bo'saverin Hevalis, head of the Cobalts, is trying to recover from the injuries he sustained in battle. The enforced downtime is giving him too much time to think, torture for a man of action. The trouble in their sector is weighing heavily on his mind as it seems to be getting ever closer to the demon homeworld.

The only good thing is the strange green-haired man he rescued constantly stealing his attention. There is something about Ari that pulls at Bo in a way no other ever has.

As the two get to know each other, there is no denying the attraction between them. Bo longs to show Ari a life that he's never had a chance to experience before.

Held hostage by his mother, Ari grew up locked away from everything and everyone, only experiencing the world on his compcube and longing to explore what is outside the walls that trap him. Now, living with the demons, he's free to find himself and live his own life and find his passions.

Even as feelings grow between Ari and Bo, enemies lurk in the shadows, slowly working to take down the demon leaders and send Ari back to his controlling mother. Bo will face down any danger to prevent Ari being taken from him, allowing them to start the life they both deserve.

COPYRIGHT

DEDICATION

To the other half of my soul – I love you.

There are so many people who work with me in getting my books ready for release, I could not do what I do without them.

Emma and Meghan, thank you, for everything.

To my betas, Laura, Michelle, Kris and Bradley, thank you.

Cody, thank you for taking the time to talk and to help me get certain aspects of Ari and his biology right.

My editor, Jessica McKenna.

www.facebook.com/JessicaMcKennaLiteraryEditor

liteditor.com

My cover designer, Kellie Dennis.

Cover art by Kellie Dennis @ Book Cover by Design

www.bookcoverbydesign.co.uk

www.facebook.com/bookcoverbydesign

TABLE OF CONTENTS

CHAPTER ONE

Bo'saverin Hevalis shifted about on the med bed, trying to get comfy. Was it too much to ask to just be able to sleep? He hated not lying on his back, but the medics insisted he not use that position while he was healing from his injuries after the ceiling collapsed on him and Aridien. A metal girder had fallen across his back as he'd protectively caged Aridien below him. They'd gone hunting for Caris, Dasa's love and, at the time, an ambassador for the Barin Alliance. He'd been kidnapped from his ship while returning from Landran, where he'd gone to see the Avanti. Bo couldn't help but smile. Between Caris and Ari, they'd rescued themselves. He refused to even consider the fact that Veris had helped. The Red demon may have helped them, but it was his fault they were there to start with.

He remembered waking up to Ari beneath him in a full blown panic. At the time, despite how severe his injuries were, guessing from the pain in his back, his only focus had been on calming the man below him. Every protective instinct he'd ever possessed flared to life to coalesce in a desire so overwhelming to protect the man below him it overrode every pain receptor in his body. Ari had been his only focus. He remembered cupping Ari's face, his thumb tracing back and forth over the soft skin of his cheeks. When Ari cupped his own cheek in return, a sense of serenity had invaded him. Memories of the beautiful green blush that stained Ari's skin blazed in his mind and he'd wanted so badly to kiss him. Of course, his brother, Dea, and best friend and prince, Dasa, had chosen that moment to rescue them. Oh, he appreciated it, but damn, their timing could have been better. A minute later and he would have tasted Ari's lips.

So now here he was, lying in a med bed, back on Kenistal, fed up and cursing the fact Mac was his roommate. Oh, he liked Mac well enough, he even liked his family, but Kery'alin, Mac's wife, attempted to mother him at every opportunity.

"Just go with it, Commander." Mac sniggered at the look on Bo's face. "Seriously, I gave up long ago even attempting to stop her. It's less hassle if I just let her get on with it. Plus, I've long since realized it's better for my own sanity if I let her have her own way. Life at home is not pleasant when she's in angry demoness mode."

Bo continued to scowl. "But you're mated to her, I'm not."

Mac threw his head back and laughed. "That's not stopped her before and unlikely to stop her now. Seriously, Commander, she's worried, compensating for the fact I'm injured. I know it's not my position to ask anything of you, but try to go easy on her, please?"

Bo groaned. "I think you've been taking lessons from her. You know just the thing to say to make me relent. *Fine*. She can mother me and I won't say anything."

Mac laughed at the put upon look on his commander's face, regretting it the minute he started to cough violently.

"Frek. Mac, are you alright?" Bo reached up to tap his comm link, but his hand froze as Mac waved him off.

"I'm fine." Mac's frustration leaked out into his words.

Bo snorted. "You're as 'fine' as I am. Which is to say, totally not fine, and thoroughly fed up with being stuck in bed. Both of us are Cobalts. Demons of action. It's wrong to keep us confined to bed."

"Now, the two of you can stop all this pouting right this minute." Kery'alin stood in the doorway of their room, one of their demonlings on each hip, and one clinging on to her pants.

"Papa!" The eldest demonling ran across the room, stopping short at the side of Mac's bed. Since the first time he'd hurt Mac clambering up, he always waited for permission.

Bo bit back his laugh as the demonling bounced from side to side, his arms flapping about, a massive grin on his face as he waited for his father to lift him up.

9

"I don't know what you're laughing at, Commander. You get to cuddle one of these two while I get food out for you both." Kery'alin narrowed her gaze at him. "No complaints either. Not if you want my parinka in hobrin sauce."

Bo sighed dramatically, and held out his hands for one of the demonlings. Kery'alin had him and they all knew it. Parinka was one of the specialty meats of Kenistal and considered a real delicacy. Smoke cured, spicy and rich, the slivers of meat were often accompanied by a robust sauce. Kery pulled out a box and Bo's eyes lit up. Xozi squares. These were made from grains and similar to the rolls commonly found on Alliance worlds, but these were lightly spiced and melted in the mouth. They were the perfect complement to parinka.

"Mac, I just might have to steal her from you. If you get treats like this, then you are one of the luckiest demons in the Cobalts. Mind you, I wouldn't go telling them— or you'll always be having visitors." Bo was already trying to steal the bags from her to get to the parinka, avoiding the hands she batted at him.

Mac grinned wide as Bo suddenly had his arms full of a squirming demonling.

Bo nuzzled the young Pau. She was a rich golden color, her tiny horns and fluffy tail making him smile. Looking over at her brother Loas, he saw how identical they were, apart from the fact that Loas was lime green. Mac's eldest demonling, Welin, was a rich copper color. "Kery, your demonlings really are beautiful."

Kery blushed at Bo. "Thank you, Commander."

"Less of the commander. Your mate may be under my command, but a beautiful demoness like you should only ever call me Bo." He winked as she blushed deeply.

"Commander, are you trying to hit on my mate? I may be injured, but I'm sure I'll find a way to challenge you. Either that or I'll whisper to Caris…"

Bo scowled at Mac. "Fine. But I may just take you up on that challenge one day."

Mac snorted. "No chance of that, Commander. It's going to be a long time before I'm even able to move about by myself in a chair. Walking? *If* I can, that's going to be a long way off. I'll never enter the ring again."

Bo tucked the demonling firmly against his chest as he leaned forward. "You listen to me and listen good, Warrior Mac'likrit. *You are a Cobalt.* You will be up and about. Will it take a while? Probably. But you *will* walk. If I have to find a way to fly Corin to us, it *will* happen. I'll go and retrieve him myself personally if it comes to it."

Mac's eyes widened at the stubborn determination in his commander's voice. "You would do that for me?"

"If he doesn't, I will." Prince Dasa grinned from his position leaning against the doorframe.

"Your Highness." Kery attempted to drop into a curtsey while juggling a demonling and bags.

Dasa smiled at her as he shook his head. "No need. Here, let me take little… Loas, isn't it?"

Kery's eyes widened at the mere thought of her prince knowing the name of her demonlings, her throat working as she attempted to speak. Giving up, she nodded and passed her son over, marveling at the ease with which the prince handled him. Loas gazed up at Dasa and patted his cheek.

Dasa leaned down and nuzzled the little demonling. "I came to see if you two wanted some company? Caris and Ari are chattering away next door."

"Now, are you saying do we want Caris and Ari's company, or yours?" Bo stared his friend and prince down.

"Me, of course! Those two are gossiping like crazy. I need some—"

Dasa was abruptly cut off by Caris' voice. "You better not be about to say you need some manly, warrior type company."

Dasa's gulp was visible, his eyes wide, gaze darting to Bo as if he would help bail him out.

Bo just laughed as his prince stuttered.

"Caris, mek iban, I would never dream of saying something like that."

Caris, finally in view, narrowed his eyes at his demon mate until he caught sight of the demonling. He held out his arms and Dasa sighed, relinquishing his hold.

Bo's attention, however, focused completely on Ari, who was hiding behind Caris. Ari looked stunning. As always, his green curls were tumbling about his head in carefree abandon. His amber eyes intrigued Bo. They shone with happiness when Ari simply interacted with Caris and any young demonlings. The slight tilt to them captivated him. His pale, creamy skin was such a contrast to the vivid blue of his own skin. One of his favorite dreams saw Ari wrapped up in his arms, naked, laying skin on skin. He shook those thoughts off; the last thing he wanted was for anyone to notice that he reacted physically anytime Ari was around him.

"Ari, would you like to say hello to this little demonling?" Bo kept his voice gentle, not wanting to spook the skittish man.

Ari all but ran over to Bo. His nerves were playing havoc, being around so many demons, but for some reason, he always knew he was safe when Bo was nearby. He looked around for a seat, but they were all taken. He knew his blush was staining his cheeks green, but Bo was lying on his side, shifting about on the bed, being careful not to hurt his back, patting a space beside him. He shook his head, but the look of sadness on Bo's face saw him quickly scramble up. Damn demons always made everything so big. He almost had to jump up, which of course made him blush so much more. He smiled at Bo, trying to dampen down the color that always rose in his presence as he took Pau from Bo's arms. He snuggled the little demonling, loving her rich golden color. She giggled at him and grabbed one of his curls, winding it between her fingers.

Bo bit back a wave of jealousy. He wanted to be the one who had his hands wrapped up in Ari's curls. He longed to see the green against the blue of his skin. "Pau loves you." Bo nodded at the way the demonling was staring adoringly up at Ari.

"I like her." Ari traced a gentle finger down her cheek. "I've always loved children. They never judge someone based on what they were born with. They love equally." Ari never noticed the look Mac and Caris shared, both of them knowing his history wasn't pleasant.

Caris leaned into Dasa, whispering, "Please tell me you've managed to make progress on granting him full asylum here."

Dasa nibbled on Caris' ear. "Father has almost finished everything. It will be done by the end of the day. Once we have that in place, we can start talking to Ari. I want to know how he ended up on that ship in the first place."

Caris' face turned into one of molten fury. "I want whoever hurt him punished. He's sweet and innocent. He deserves looking after. Once Mac is better, I fully plan on taking Ari out with me, exploring things. I want him to get a chance to discover who he really is. What he likes, and hates."

"You have to know Bo is going to hate that." Dasa chuckled gleefully at the thought of his best friend, Bo, being driven to distraction by Ari happily exploring Kenistal.

"And you're not? You're going to be just as protective." Caris quirked a brow at Dasa, who simply growled, not bothering to respond otherwise. Both of them watched as Ari almost leaned into Bo, silently seeking his support.

Ari looked up at Mac and Kery. "Your demonlings really are gorgeous. I long for the day I can have children of my own."

Bo's pensive gaze rested on Ari as he talked to Mac and Kery.

"So, Bo, how are you feeling?"

Bo jumped as Dasa's hand settled on his foot. "Not too bad, the back is getting there. Still, the doctors say it's going to be a couple of weeks before I can get fully back to normal. Which makes me worry. Who is going to keep an eye on your sorry ass?"

"You mean who is going to keep beating you at the rings?" Dasa smirked.

Bo spluttered. "Oh, just wait, the minute I get the all clear from here, I plan on meeting you in the arena. Only this time, I'm thinking we should go for the Pik'dorin."

Ari's gaze shot to Mac as he choked on his water.

"You plan on challenging our prince to a Pik'dorin match? Has he ever actually lost one?" Mac stuttered out.

Kery tsked at him as she tried to clean him up.

"I am not one of your demonlings. I can wipe myself up, you know." He scowled at her, before blowing a kiss to take the sting out of his words. Kery just laughed at him. "Kery! I'm a Cobalt, for frek's sake." Mac scowled, but dragged her into a kiss anyway.

Ari was watching the back and forth with interest. This was so different from the way his parents were with each other. His mother was a force to be reckoned with. She ruled the home with an iron will and determination that saw her succeed so greatly in the trading arena. His father was a meek man who bowed to his mother's wishes and demands every single time. When his mother had packed him off… He shook off those thoughts, determined not to let anything bother him while he was around his new friends.

"So what is Pik'dorin?" Ari was pleased Caris asked the question as he wanted to know as well.

Bo grinned. "Pik'dorin is a training session with ceremonial poles. The poles are longer than us. Where we are about eight feet tall, the poles are about ten feet long. We battle with them, twirling them, using them both to attack and act as a defensive mechanism. It's graceful, full of thought. The moves are precise and it's spell-binding to watch. Prince Dasa here is one of our reigning champions, although I'm inclined to say it's because no one ever dares to really try against him." Bo winked at Ari, who promptly flushed again.

"Is it dangerous?" Ari's voice was quiet, too used to being told to shut up and that his opinions were neither wanted nor needed.

"There are injuries, but there tends to be lots of bruising, rather than anything more serious. Why, Ari? Are you worried about me?" Bo's heart beat faster as Ari's head dropped, hiding his reaction behind a cloak of hair.

Caris took in Ari's move and promptly changed the subject. "Mac, what have the doctors said about your injuries?"

Mac groaned. "It's both good and bad news. The good news is they've been able to repair the damage to my foot. It was almost twenty hours of surgery, but they managed it. The bad news? It's going to take a long time to fully heal and they doubt I'll ever be able to take on a full Cobalt role again."

"Oh, Mac, I'm sorry." Caris moved to Mac's bed and hugged him tight. "As far as I'm concerned, the most important thing is you're still with us. You saved a lot of lives, Mac. You will always be a warrior in my eyes. I can only apologize this all happened because of me, because of who I am."

"No, Caris. I would have happily given my life to save yours and you know it." Mac scowled at Caris, angry at the mere idea of Caris believing he was responsible. "I just wish I'd been able to stay on as your bodyguard."

"Who says you can't?" Bo cocked his head to one side as he studied Mac.

"It's going to take me months to be able to walk and who knows if I'll ever be able to do anything properly." Mac's gaze was hooded, but Bo could clearly see the anguish in his eyes.

Bo waited, forcing Mac to meet his gaze before he spoke. "Sure, it might take a while, but there is no reason you can't still be part of Caris' team."

Caris hit Mac upside the head. "Even if you aren't my official bodyguard, you are still my friend and I would love to have you as an assistant. I need someone to help me wade through the political and social quagmire that is Kenistal. I cannot think of anyone I would rather have in that position than you. So I'll have none of that feeling sorry for yourself behavior. You are important to me and that

15

is not going to change, no matter what your physical condition ends up being. Do I make myself clear, Mac?"

Mac grinned widely. He'd almost forgotten just how feisty Caris could be when he wanted. "Yes, Caris." Mac reached over to grab Caris into a hug.

"Hey!" Dasa scowled, but Caris simply grinned.

Bo quietly rested his hand on Ari's back, moving closer to whisper into his ear. "How are you doing? Have you fully recovered from everything?"

Ari's back heated at Bo's touch. He found himself shifting closer, into the warmth. "I'm still a little sore, but I'm doing well. The doctors are pleased. You didn't have to do what you did, back then, when things happened, you know?" Ari blushed as he realized how convoluted his words were. "I mean— you didn't need to protect me. I'm not worth risking your life over."

Bo reached out and cupped Ari's face with his free hand, turning Ari's face so he could meet his gaze. "I don't want to hear you talk about yourself in that way. You are *just* as important as I am." *If not more so,* he whispered in his own mind.

"Why do you say that?"

In Bo's opinion, Ari looked adorably confused. "Ari, you're remarkable. To survive on that ship by yourself is impressive on its own. But, when you add onto that helping Caris escape, then the way you piloted that pod, well, it all adds up to one remarkable package."

Ari was completely stunned. No one had ever really complimented him before; apart from Bo the only person to do it was Caris. Certainly no one in his family ever had.

Bo let his words sink into Ari's mind. He didn't want to overwhelm him, but there was no way he was going to be anything other than completely honest with him from the word go, which meant compliments, among other things.

Pau suddenly let out a blood curdling scream, startling everyone in the room. Kery groaned and went to take her from Ari, but he

16

shook his head. "What's up with her?" His voice was whisper soft, as though he was still shy talking amongst so many people.

"Her first set of scales are starting to form and it can be painful." Kery tilted her head to one side, thinking. "Umm, the closest I imagine you would liken it to is toothache."

"Ah." Ari gently shifted Pau so she was on his knee. He held her gaze before crossing his eyes and sticking out his tongue. She let loose a hiccup and cough combination. He kept pulling faces at her until she calmed down. Then, making sure she was secure on his knee, he started to bounce as he sang softly to her. Pau's gleeful giggles echoed around the room. Then he grabbed her tight, smothering her little golden cheeks with kisses. She tried to return the favor, but drooled all over him.

"Oh, my, I am so sorry, Aridien." Kery ducked her head, rooting through a bag for a cloth.

"Just Ari, and I love children, so I'm perfectly happy being drooled on." He smiled indulgently as Pau grabbed hold of his finger and squeezed, her face scrunched up tight. "Oh, tiki, does it hurt?"

"Tiki?" Bo went to scratch at his back and scowled as Ari knocked his hand away.

Ari blushed, his cheeks going incredibly green. "There's no direct translation, but it basically means beautiful little one."

"Well, Pau is beautiful." Bo grinned wickedly. "I'll bet she'll have lots of young demonlings after her as she grows."

Mac grabbed a pillow and went to throw it at his commander. He sighed as he took in his demonlings all around him and stuffed the pillow back behind his head with a mutinous scowl on his face.

Ari gently smacked Bo on the arm. "Don't be mean." His eyes widened as he took in his arm as it lay on Bo's arm. He went to yank it back, but Bo laid his own hand on top and kept it there, winking as he did so.

Bo shifted back slightly on the bed, giving Ari more room. Watching Ari with Pau, he didn't know for sure what captivated him more, the sight of Ari alone, or Ari holding a demonling. He caught Dasa's gaze and narrowed his eyes at the speculative smirk his friend wore. He could see it now. He would get no end of teasing if he pursued Ari.

CHAPTER TWO

Kery carefully lifted Pau from Ari's arms. Ari was fast asleep, curled up against Bo as he held her. Bo himself had succumbed to the pain meds he'd been given and had snaked his arm around Ari protectively.

"Ari certainly seems to have taken a liking to Bo." Dasa studied the pair of them.

"I would say the feeling is mutual, considering how protective Bo is being, even in sleep. Then adding in how he protected Ari during the attack…" Caris let his words trail off, a speculative gleam in his eyes.

"What do you have planned, my little dynamo?" Dasa tweaked Caris' ear.

"Well, Bo is going to need company as he recuperates. There is Mac, of course, but, Ari also needs to get used to demons. You've seen how he is around even the most mild-mannered of demons. He shrinks into himself a little, keeps quiet, and worries on his bottom lip. Who better to help Ari overcome his fear than Bo?"

"And while he does, you hope they fall properly for each other?" Dasa's tail whipped about before curling around his legs. "You know… your plan has merit."

"No need to sound so surprised, you know," Caris drawled.

Dasa's answer was to simply grab a hold of him and kiss him senseless.

Kery and Mac where chuckling away quietly as she readied the demonlings. Brushing a quick kiss over Mac's lips, she cupped his face. "I'll be back later, once I have them settled. My sister will look after them."

Mac cupped her face in return, holding her in place. "Don't tire yourself out. I love spending more time with you, but looking after those three…"

"Mac, look at it this way… I nearly lost you. Let me hover for a bit. No matter how tired I get, I need to reassure myself that you are here, still with us and whole."

"But I'm not whole, am I?" Mac gestured down at his leg.

Kery whacked him over the head. "I won't stand for any of that talk, Mac'likrit. So you hear me now and hear me good. You are here, back with us and alive. Yes, you have some physical problems to work through, but… You. Are. Here. That is the only thing that matters to us. I would have been devastated if we'd lost you, so deal with me hovering for a bit and enough of this pity party or I'll be bribing your commander with xozi and parinka to make your life hell."

Mac groaned. "Damn, woman, you can be so mean."

Kery just smiled sweetly. "I know, but you love me anyway."

"That I do, my treasure, that I do."

"What do you want to do about Ari?" Dasa nibbled at Caris' jaw.

"Leave him here to sleep. He's had some nightmares lately and he looks happy and comfortable there. We can let the doctors know. They can check on him."

"He does look remarkably comfortable there, doesn't he?" Dasa took in just how relaxed both men looked. Ari looked so small in his friend's arms, but there was a peacefulness to his features that spoke of a deep, healing sleep. "I'm going to take you back to your bed and then go and see my father."

"I want to come with you." Caris' chin jutted out slightly, his face a mask of stubbornness. "Before you say anything, think about it. I know I'm not a demon, but politics and negotiations are my thing. Trust me. I want to make sure everything is perfect for Ari. I don't know everything that went on with him, either when he was taken, or back on his home world, but I want to make sure he is fully protected. I need to know he is safe. He risked a lot to help me."

Dasa's face softened. "Alright, but if you get too tired, you must tell me."

"Thank you." Caris snuggled into Dasa's arms, content to simply be close to him.

Dasa and Caris walked into Vict'arin Kan'erkit's office. Vict was the king of Kenistal and Dasa's father. Yet, Caris found he got on well with him. He was gruff and regal, but he held little doubt the king cared deeply for every demon in his charge. The smile Caris was wearing for Vict slid from his face as he took in a stunning purple demoness sitting in a chair opposite him. He watched as she looked him up and down and apparently found him completely lacking.

Dasa squeezed Caris' hand tight. "Caris, I would like you to officially meet my sister, Princess Alenska Kan'erkit. Alenska, this is my mate, Caris Dealyn, the former ambassador from the Barin Alliance."

Alenska sneered. "Only you, brother, would join with a no horn."

Caris recoiled from the venom in her voice. His hand slipped from Dasa's as his man charged forward, hauling his sister out of the chair and pinning her to the wall by her throat. His scales were at full hardness. Her scales hardened a few seconds later.

"Do. Not. Ever. Insult. Caris." Each word was punctuated with a squeeze of her throat. "Caris has done more to help this world then you ever have. Do not try me on this, Alenska. You *will* be civil, you *will* be gracious and you *will not* use the term no horn to me, or to

Caris, ever again. Or meeting me in the rings will be the least of your problems."

Caris hadn't realized he'd grasped Vict's hand as he stood watching the demon siblings. If Caris wasn't mistaken, Vict was standing protectively beside him. He realized it wasn't to interfere with his demonlings, but to protect Caris.

Vict lifted Caris' hand and rested it on his arm, patting it affectionately. "This, I'm afraid, is not unusual. Those two have never really gotten on well. They are too different. Alenska should know better, both with her disgraceful words and at risking challenging Dasa. Ah, well, that's my demonlings for you. Now would you like some ruinsk teo, or tea, as you call it? Or some davroc?" Vict couldn't stop the chuckle at the look of disgust on Caris' face at the mention of davroc. "It really is the perfect pick me up drink, you know."

Caris scoffed. "It's thick enough to be tar, sour and incredibly bitter. Trust me, it is *nothing* like my coffee. I'll take a ruinsk, I think."

Vict led Caris over to some chairs. "So, tell me as much as you can about young Aridien. I'm guessing you have already used your contacts to find out information."

"He's Aducian, which is a race from a planet in the Cherion sector. As you know, he was held captive on the Loperis ship when I was taken onboard. He went out of his way to help me as much as he could. Not because he thought it would help him, but because that's the type of person he is. From what I know, his ship was attacked, his guards killed and he was taken. I get the impression he considered the guards friends— that they, more than anyone else in his life, had been nice to him. He'd overheard the Loperis talk about selling him to an upmarket breeder, or auctioning him off."

"A breeder? But he's male." Vict flicked his eyes over to his two demonlings who were still arguing in the corner. He rolled his eyes and refocused on Caris.

"Aducians have three sexes. Male, female and lenis. The lenis are essentially male, but they have the ability to bear children.

22

Outwardly, their anatomy is male, but internally, they carry both male and female parts." Caris shook his head. "It's not something they talk about commonly. They are highly prized in their society because of their rarity, but also badly treated. They suffer a lot of prejudice, often live very lonely lives, some in seclusion away from most of the population. Others are not so lucky and are bartered, sold and traded. They are sent to medical centers to be studied and experimented on, or used as sex slaves and to carry babes."

Caris took a deep breath. "Anyway, he was scared, he's young and has obviously led a very sheltered life, probably because his parents kept him isolated, or at least that's my best guess. He's convinced his family will disown him after this. He says they will believe he has brought shame to the family name."

Vict studied Caris. "But, you don't think so?"

"No. It's obvious he has led a sheltered life. I'm not saying his family cared about him, but for whatever reason, they kept him well looked after. It makes me believe they had plans for him."

Vict's face contorted slightly. "What sort of plans?" he growled out.

"I'm guessing you have an idea. But, I think they were planning on selling him themselves. Either that or using him to their advantage some way. His mother is some sort of big trader on his world."

"Sadly, that makes sense." Vict grimaced. "From what you've said, I'm guessing his ship wasn't a random target. She could have been sending Aridien as some part of trade deal, and the Loperis found out about it. But, there is also the fact Veris and Jari'nik were involved in all this. I want to know just how big the connection is between them and the Aducians. I've spoken briefly to Veris, who is surprisingly open about his involvement in all of this. I don't know what happened up there between you three, but I would be inclined to say that Veris is changing."

"I guess it is one thing to be against me, a puny Terran, an ambassador from the Barin Alliance, and another thing to become involved in murder, abduction, assault, bribery, corruption, and treason. You know I have never liked Veris, that much is obvious, but he did everything he could to help us. I don't for one minute believe he was responsible for my abduction."

Vict grimaced, almost unhappy at the news, desperate for there to a reason behind everything. "I have to say that's the impression I got when I interviewed him. He's a typical Red, out for whatever advantage he can get, but, he wouldn't risk hurting Kenistal as a whole. He may not like you, but he wouldn't do anything to hurt you, Dasa, or all of us on Kenistal. Besides, he risked everything sending that file to Dasa while onboard the ship. You were still missing, he wasn't doing it to curry favor, or defend himself. He thought you'd fully escaped and was trying to warn us."

"Still, it will probably be best if we talk to him some more. He may know more about why they wanted Ari." Caris pursed his lips as Dasa once again had his sister up against the wall.

Vict had finally had enough. "If you persist on behaving like little demonlings, then I shall treat you like little demonlings and send you to your room, with no evening meal and no access to anything."

Both Dasa and Alenska shot one last evil look at each other before taking seats. Dasa turned sullenly to his father. "Why does she need to be here for this? I'm inclined to wonder how much she knew about everything. Jari is one of her closest friends, after all."

Alenska's eyes narrowed and her scales hardened. Before she could so much as twitch, Vict smacked her leg with his tail. "You will sit." He roared. "You lost the right to be angry when questioned when you took up with those friends of yours. You were never one to listen to a cautionary word and your actions are now returning to twist your tail. You will sit, be quiet and accept whatever judgment I pass. Now, I want to know exactly what you had to do with Jari."

Alenska drew a breath and held her father's gaze. "We were friends, nothing more and nothing less."

"Even though you knew that being friends with her would bring the royal family into disrepute?" Vict pursed his lips, his tail twitching rapidly against his leg, and unless Caris was mistaken, there was a small wisp of steam coming from his horns.

"I'm fed up of always having to live in his shadow." Alenska sneered at Dasa. "Just because he is the first born male, he gets everything. I would be a better ruler than he is."

Dasa snorted. *Not a chance.*

Vict let out a long-suffering sigh. "Alenska, you are my demonling and I love you, but… be sensible. You are far too selfish, far too self-serving and you become far too bored too easily with diplomacy and politics. All you want to do is become a warrior, fight in the rings, in the trials and challenge other warriors. There is nothing wrong with that. But… you cannot turn around after you have cultivated such a lifestyle and expect to be accorded the same respect politically and diplomatically as your brother does. Don't think I don't know that Jari was chasing after Dasa here. There is no way I would have allowed the match, no matter what anyone thought. Jari was not someone that would have been suitable for Dasa, the royal family, or Kenistal. I have no doubt you had some sway in her chasing after Dasa. So how about you come clean and tell me everything you know?"

Alenska's scales rippled as she fought for control. "I know nothing about Jari, her trade deals, or kidnapping. I'm going to go and see mother." She stormed towards the door to Vict's study. "At least I know she will be pleased to see me."

Vict let his head fall against the back of his seat. "Your sister always did have a flair for the dramatic."

"I still think she knows something." Dasa's scowl lingered on the now closed door.

Vict studied the door for a moment. "Agreed, but right now there is little we can do other than force her to reveal what she knows. I fear that would cause more problems than it solves. So, putting her to one side for the moment, let's continue discussing Aridien. I have all the documents completed and I simply need you to look over them, Caris. They need to not only stand up to our judges here, but the scrutiny of the Barin Alliance. The last thing I want to happen is for someone to be able to pull him away due to paperwork. Sure, we are not part of the Alliance, but I would rather not cause a full scale diplomatic incident getting this wrong. Besides, with the connections the Aducians have, and the sheer volume of trade they operate, things could be made very tough for us here if we aren't careful. The one thing I need is his full name." Vict turned towards Caris expectantly.

"We shall go and ask him. Besides, it's about time Caris was back in bed resting." Dasa held up his hand in an attempt to shut Caris up. "No, I just got you back, safe, but not whole. You're just going to have to cope with me being a little more protective for a bit."

Caris' nose wrinkled, his distaste obvious, but he let Dasa take control.

CHAPTER THREE

Ari woke to the sound of quiet murmuring. Slightly disoriented, he kept his eyes shut, trying to work out where he was and why he was so safe and warm. Then the weight over his waist twitched. *Twitched?* He wriggled against whatever held him slightly and the reverberations of a chuckle ran through his body. Which meant this was a person. *Bo.* It meant it was Bo.

The thought thrilled him and scared him in equal measure. Never before, apart from with Caris, had he stopped worrying about things. Caris was like a brother to him. Bo was something completely different. He wanted to make Bo happy, to kiss him, to do all the things he'd only ever dreamed about with someone he wanted, not someone he was forced to be with.

He may have been sheltered by his parents, but that didn't stop his guards being as kind to him as they could. They'd sneak him things in, especially books and a compcube. It was his greatest treasure and he'd been upset to lose it when the Loperis took him. He'd learned everything he could on the device, having access to all the Aducian databanks. Even those files that were protected, he'd learned to bypass security measures early on and read everything. While most people just used two of the cube's four view screens, he tended to use them all, his fingers flying over the controls on the two input sides easily, manipulating the data faster than his guards had thought possible.

He remembered helping Kolean to source an extremely rare song for his husband. Ari spent weeks tracking a copy down, but it had been worth it. Kolean had been so happy. He'd tried to insist on bringing Ari a gift, but he didn't want one. He was just happy to see his friends happy.

Pushing thoughts of his past to one side, he snuggled deeper into Bo, uncaring who was in the room. Bo would keep him safe.

Bo grinned down at Ari, who was burrowing deeper into his arms. It thrilled him to know the man who was rapidly becoming an integral part of his future was content in his arms. His eyes shut, he ignored the voices of Mac, Dasa and Caris whispering on the other side of the room.

"You have to admit, that's adorable," Caris said as Ari turned in Bo's arms and snuggled deeper. Bo's tail wrapped around Ari's legs, one arm cradling his head and the other his waist. Bo's nose seemed to burrow its way into Ari's curls as Ari's hands rested on Bo's chest, right over his heart.

"Come on, Caris, you need one more night of rest here before the doctors will let you go." Dasa started to lead Caris out the door, ignoring the grumbling and pouting. He wanted Caris healthy and whole. He would do just about anything the doctors requested.

Bo lay dozing, listening to the rise and fall of Ari's breathing. He'd given up trying to work out why he was so drawn to him; instead he was simply going to go with it. The problem was he got the distinct impression that Ari was innocent in many ways, which meant he would need to date him, court him. *But Demons don't date.* He scowled. *I guess this one does. After all, there isn't much I wouldn't do for Ari, if he'll let me.* He lay there, happily holding Ari, thinking of all the things they could do together. If he could get out of the damn med bed first.

Ari was happily humming to himself as he ate breakfast. He avoided looking at Caris. Every time he did, there was a knowing glint to his eyes. He chose to ignore it, hoping the next time he looked up it would be gone.

Caris smiled behind his mug of teo, the smile dropping suddenly when he knew they needed to talk. "Ari…"

Ari's eyes widened as he looked up. "What is it? I can tell from your tone of voice it's something."

Caris reached out and grasped Ari's hand. "I need to ask you some questions."

Ari closed his eyes, his stomach sinking and resignation filling him. "I knew this was coming. Go ahead."

"What's your full name?" Caris watched a moment of anguish cross Ari's face.

"Aridien Gerosa Kelotian. Son of Agota Kelotian, the renowned Aducian trader. You know, she isn't as her name suggests." At Caris' questioning look, Ari explained. "Her name means good-natured. That's the last thing she is. My father is Xerves Kelotian. He… well, let's just say my mother rules the family. He does as he is told."

"Your mother is *the* Agota Kelotian? High trader for the Aducian Empire?"

"She is, and trust me, it's not something I am proud of. I am well aware of her reputation amongst the Alliance. It is *definitely* deserved. She's hard, forceful and determined. She will beat anyone into submission verbally, come at them from all angles until she gets what she wants. She regularly investigates her enemies and those she chooses to do business with. She will use every little thing to her advantage."

Caris tried to relax back into his seat. "How will she react when she finds out you've been taken?"

Ari snorted, before blushing, his hand briefly covering his face. "She'll already know and angry wouldn't do her reaction justice. Some of her assistants will have been fired and most likely expelled from the city for failing her. Those left will have cowered in fear. She's been known to beat people who fail her."

Caris drew in a sharp breath. "She's that bad?"

"No." Ari rapidly shook his head. "She's worse." He scrubbed a hand through his hair. "What is it you want to know?"

"King Vict'arin is putting the final touches to the paperwork to grant you full asylum here on Kenistal. And, should you choose to accept it, honorary citizenship. He just needs to document reasons for it. It's a formality, but one to protect you should anyone choose to contest it."

Ari's breath was speeding up. "The king would do that for me?"

Caris squeezed the hand he still held. "He would. You have to remember you brought Mac and me back to him."

"And Veris."

"Well, I'm not exactly sure Vict was especially excited about that, but yes." Caris smiled softly. "Ari, I told you, I would make sure you were safe and could stay here, but I need you to give me reasons."

Ari started to panic. Thoughts of outlining everything his mother had done, had said, subjected him to, kicked his pulse into hyperdrive. His breathing came out fast and hard.

"Ari, Ari! Stay calm for me. Frek! Dasa!" Caris screamed, hoping he could be heard through the two open doorways into the corridor.

Seconds later, Dasa sprinted through the open door, Bo following behind him at a much slower pace, batting away the hands of med staff trying to stop him. He swept straight past his prince, and ignoring the twinges in his back, scooped Ari up into his arms. He sat down in the comfy chair Ari had been in and tucked him in tight. One hand grasped the back of Ari's neck, the other traced soothing circles over his back. "I'm here, Ari, it's alright. I've got you." Over Ari's head, Bo was scowling.

"What happened?" Dasa watched Ari break down with a frown.

"I asked him if he could give me reasons for the citizenship and asylum forms." Caris walked tentatively over to Ari and squatted down beside him, reaching out with a finger to stroke his cheek. "I'm sorry, Ari."

Ari sniffed, finally calming down now he was safe in Bo's arms. "No, it's me. I'm just not feeling very brave at the moment and the thought of going over what I went through is scaring me. Promise me I don't have to go back? I don't have to stay here, just don't send me back to her."

Bo tightened his grip, his soul hurting at the prospect of what Ari was going to tell them. "Ari, I promise you, you're safe here. There is no way I, Dasa, Caris, Mac, or the king will let anything happen to you. The king is doing everything he can to make sure you're safe. If you can't trust him yet because he's done nothing to earn your trust, then trust in Caris, trust in *me*. You *know* I'll keep you safe."

"I do trust you. I trust all of you here in this room." He looked around at everyone, seeing two guards by the door. The look on his face prompted Bo into action. "Warriors Kek'tobrin and Ep'robal, stand guard outside until I summon you."

Both warriors nodded and left the room quickly and quietly.

Caris poured the demons davroc, and a soothing oplin teo for both Ari and himself. "Go at your own speed. I know this will be hard, but the sooner we can fill out the forms the better. Whatever you say to us..." He gestured around the room. "Is private. We will tell Vict only what we must to secure your citizenship. Or, if you don't want new citizenship, you are still welcome to asylum. Vict wanted me to assure you, whatever *you* want is what is important here."

Ari shifted on Bo's lap, sighing with relief when he refused to let him go. "The best way to explain would be with a little history lesson about Aducians. Overall, the odds of a child being lenis is around an eighth, but the chance grows with each subsequent birth to any couple. It's why most families stick to having one or two children. I used to think my mother and father had five children as a status thing. But, I found out when I was around twelve galactic

31

cycles that it was deliberate. They'd kept going, *wanting* a lenis child."

Ari held Bo's gaze, with his own haunted eyes. "They'd always wanted a lenis child as it was the ultimate bargaining chip they could use in negotiations. Aducians have no issue with sexuality and so she wanted to use me to effectively sell to a wealthy businessman or politician."

Bo never let up the gentle caress over Ari's hair. "Are you saying she deliberately had you so she could use you in a trade deal?"

"That's exactly what I'm saying."

Bo sucked in a harsh breath. For a parent to do such a thing to a child was bad enough, for the child to know about it? That was cruel. "What was your childhood like?" Bo hesitantly asked, not sure if he honestly wanted to know.

Ari took a deep breath, tucking his head back into Bo's chest, not wanting to see the looks of horror, sympathy and compassion in the faces of his friends. "My brothers and sister let me know from an early age that I wasn't wanted. I thought it was purely because I was lenis, but I know better now. They taunted me regularly. When I was five I was isolated to my own suite of rooms, forbidden to have anything more than the most cursory interactions with them. I had a rotation of guards on me at all times. There were four in my suite, two outside. No one was allowed in or out without permission."

Ari paused to take a sip of teo, using the moment to steady himself. "I was schooled, not in the same way as other children though. My lessons consisted of looking after children, caring for a home, a basic education to get by in life. On top of that, I was taught the intricacies of party planning, hosting events, and some diplomacy. I was clothed, but they were little better than rags. Even the servants wore better clothes than I did. Kolean, one of my guards, smuggled his husband in one day. His name was Felexy. He was so kind. He taught me how to mend my clothes and how, when they were too threadbare in places, to cut them up to make new ones. Occasionally he would have Kolean smuggle in some cloth so I had something new to work with. Those two men were more like fathers or brothers to me than guards. They even smuggled me in a compcube one day. It was how I learned to pilot spaceships on a simulator." He smiled at the memory of piloting the pod when they escaped from the Loperis.

Caris swallowed past the bile in his throat. "You were taught all of that from the age of five? They kept you prisoner?"

Ari snorted. "They didn't say that, of course. It was apparently for my own protection. I rarely saw my father. He wasn't allowed to visit me after he snuck in some treats. My mother, well, all she would do was issue orders. So the only friends I really had were my guards. But, I lost them when I was taken by the Loperis."

Bo tenderly cupped Ari's face. "I don't want to dredge up too many bad memories, so why don't you just go ahead to everything that happened recently."

Ari's soft smile of thanks sent warmth spreading through Bo's chest.

"The first I knew things were changing is when my mother was happy. She was never happy. But, there she was, planning an expansion to the mansion we lived in. She planned on another two wings to be added, one to become almost state-like. Grandiose and totally ostentatious. There was talk amongst the guards about why. Rumors had it that she was bribing someone in the Barin Alliance to look the other way at ports when her shipments came in. While it doesn't seem like much, trade ships can be delayed for anything from a week to two galactic months in port. So you can imagine if all her ships within the fleet were instantly passed through ports, the extra routes and trade deals she would be able to negotiate with the time saved would be huge."

Caris' anger started to bubble to the surface. So many times as an Ambassador, planetary governments had tried to bribe him, thinking he was corrupt, a status that was attributed to far too many politicians with the Alliance.

"It was Threeday night and I'd been summoned to the family residence, not mine, theirs— it was never really mine. Anyway, they were all in such good spirits and I had no idea why. There were a couple of men there. I know one was from the Barin, the other, I have no idea. They looked so pleased. I should have known. I should have run… not that there was anywhere I could run to. All the way through the meal, the two men were looking at me like I was a piece of meat on display at the market." Ari shivered at the memory.

"My mother considers it rude to discuss business at meal times with guests, so I listened to her talking about how I was gifted at party planning and making people feel welcome. She made me perform that night. I wasn't sure what she was doing, but I did what she asked anyway. You did not ignore a 'request' from my mother. So I pretend I was the host and ran that evening meal. Every time I walked past my brothers, they would subtly try to trip me. If my mother had known, she would have gone crazy. Not because they were doing it to me, or that I could have hurt myself, but because it would have embarrassed her to see this paragon she'd built up falter."

Ari brushed angrily at a stray tear that dribbled down his cheek at the memory of the treatment he received at the hands of his siblings. "As soon as the meal was done, I was made to serve them drinks. It was there that I discovered what was going on. I was being sent as little more than an offering to a senate member from the Alliance. I think it was one of the hereditary Founder senators."

Caris sucked in a shaky, stunned breath. "Who?"

"Renauld."

Caris' jaw cracked from the force of clamping his teeth together. The air was coming out of his nose in fast bursts as he struggled to control his anger.

Dasa attempted to calm Caris. He shared a look with the other demons, oblivious as to why the name would make Caris quite so angry. "What's so important about Renauld?"

Bo stroked a finger down Ari's nose, loving the way it wrinkled as he watched Caris' reaction.

Ari shook his head. "I don't know. I actually know very little about him, other than he is a senator and likes men for liaisons."

Caris called on all his training to calm his temper and control his breathing enough to talk. "Renauld is indeed a hereditary Founding senator. He's a direct descendant from one of the original five. He's… he has a reputation for being arrogant, controlling, domineering and violent, especially in bed. There are rumors of ex bed partners being made to disappear one way or another, not that anything has been proven." Caris winced at the look of horror on Ari's face. "He's also seventy galactic years old. He's not Barinian, he's from Gosterin, their average life span is double Barinians."

Ari couldn't stop his body shaking at the images filling his mind— what he would have been subjected to, what he would have been forced to endure.

"I've got you, you're safe, I promise."

Bo's words soothed him like nothing else could and Ari clung even tighter to him.

"I'm sorry, Ari, but your life would have been torturous had you made it to him. I can only imagine how he reacted when he found out you were missing." Caris winced as he asked his next question. "I'm sorry to have to ask this, but will your family, your mother, have reported you missing to the Alliance, or the Aducian council?"

Ari turned around while still keeping tucked into Bo, loving the feeling of security his arms held. "She would." He smiled sadly at the collective sigh of relief from his new friends. "But only because the deal she made would have been dependent on me being delivered into Renauld's hands."

"Are you saying she wouldn't care that you were missing?" Mac hissed.

"She wouldn't and if she finds me and Renauld refuses me, I will be returned to the family in shame. I will be cast out and no longer considered part of Aducian society."

"You will *not* be going back there." Bo growled.

Ari tenderly patted Bo's arm where it rested around his waist. "I have no desire to go back, but my mother has a way of making things happen if she wants them badly enough."

"That's why Vict is doing everything he can to prevent it from happening." Caris held Ari's gaze, letting him see the truth in his eyes.

"You have to know there is no way my father will allow you to be returned and face that future. You saved the most important person in my life and therefore one of the most important people in his life. He considers— we *all* consider you a hero, Ari. You're going nowhere, you are one of us now, whether you like it or not." Dasa winked, trying to bring a smile to the young man's face and reduce the stress and anger pouring through his friend. The connection between Bo and Ari was as obvious as it had been instantaneous. He couldn't be happier for them both, if they acted on it, that was. Of course, it wouldn't stop him teasing Bo about it.

"I'm going to make a couple of discreet enquiries with some of the contacts I trust within the Alliance, see if there has been any reaction from Renauld. One thing concerns me though. Did the Loperis just happen upon your ship by accident, or… did someone sell your mother out?"

"I don't know. I honestly don't know." Ari shrugged.

"Well, we have everything we need for the forms." Caris turned as the door opened.

"Sorry, Your Highness. Commander Bo, the doctors wish to see you." Warrior Kek'tobrin stood in the partially open door.

"Send them in." Bo nodded his thanks.

"Well." Doctor Amkdren smiled at them all. "Caris and Aridien, you are completely free to go, but come and see us if you have any problems. Commander Bo'saverin, I'll let you leave on the provision that you are restricted to light duties and absolutely no using your scales until they heal, or wielding a sword."

Bo went to argue, but thought better of it. At least this way he would be out of the med center. He nodded his agreement.

Amkdren turned to Mac. "I'm sorry to say, Warrior Mac'likrit, you will need to stay here a couple more days. I want to make sure the bones and scales are fully set before I let you return home."

Mac sighed, but knew it was for the best. He nodded. "At least you get rid of me, Commander."

Bo's eyes sparkled. "If you think this lot is going to leave you to wallow down here, you'd better think again." Bo gestured to Caris and Ari, who grinned widely.

Mac grabbed the pillow behind him and pulled it over his head, hiding from the laughter echoing around the room.

CHAPTER FOUR

Ari couldn't stop fidgeting. His head was lowered and he was peeking through his curly bangs. The only reason he didn't run was because Bo was in the seat next to him, his arm casually slung over the back of Ari's chair. Ari didn't think Bo even knew that he was twirling one of his locks around in his fingers.

"Ari." King Vict'arin's voice was soft. "Please look at me. There is nothing to be nervous about."

"But you're a king," Ari whispered.

"I am, but I'm still Dasa's father and still the man that gets told off by his mate, and trust me, that happens far too often." Vict winked, smiling when Ari giggled softly.

Ari lifted his head and looked around the king's study. It wasn't imposing the way he'd expected it to be. Instead, it was tastefully decorated in warm creams and wood. The chairs were comfy and there was a fire roaring, a gentle smell of citrus hanging in the air. They were all gathered there to make his citizenship official. As well as the king and Ari's friends, there was one of Vict's assistants, a stern man by the name of Leyok. Then there was Dasa's sister, Alenska. She scared him. The way she looked at him made him shiver. She definitely didn't like him, that much was obvious.

"I have all the documents worked out and as soon as we both sign it, it's witnessed and bears the royal seal, you will officially be a citizen of Kenistal. I have to check, are you sure this is what you want? You will always be welcome here, so don't feel like you have to do this."

Ari looked around at his friends, seeing them smile, but making no attempt to tell him what to do. They were letting him make the choice and he instinctively knew they would support him, whatever decision he made. "I'd like to sign. There is nothing for me on Aducia, and it's never felt like home. You have all been kinder, friendlier and more welcoming then I have experienced before."

Vict smiled and picked up an ornately carved pen sitting on his desk, signing the document with a flourish. He turned the page around and Ari leaned forward, taking the pen from Vict's extended hand with shaky fingers. His heart was beating rapidly, his breath coming fast as he signed his name. The second it was witnessed by Leyok and Dasa, Caris jumped up and grabbed him into a hug.

"I'm thrilled for you, Ari. I think we need to celebrate." Caris ignored the groans coming from behind him. "And... I think we need to do it without those two grumps behind us."

Ari smiled widely. "I would love to see more of my new home."

A thrill went through Bo at Ari calling Kenistal home. "If we can't be there, you must have some guards with you." Bo stared Caris down.

"I'm fine with that, but they don't get to choose where we go." Caris looked between Bo and Dasa.

Dasa groaned, but kissed the top of Caris' head. "Be careful, hey? I only just got you back."

"Always." Caris snickered at Vict who was laughing away.

Vict smirked at his son. "Why don't you take two of my guards. They will keep an eye on you and know how to avoid getting in the way, plus they can't be bribed by my son."

"Oh, thanks, father," Dasa drawled.

Alenska huffed. "I don't see why I needed to be here for this. Is there actually anything important or worthwhile for me to attend to?"

Vict stepped in before Dasa could react. "Alenska, behave. You still have a long way to go before you're back in my good graces. I personally extended the invitation to Ari to become a citizen here, not your brother. I suggest you bear that in mind before you start in on treating him badly. Know one thing, I will not tolerate him being subjected to taunts and jibes from your normal crowd. Do I make myself clear?" Vict held her gaze until she dipped her head, mouth pursed tight.

When he released her gaze, she grabbed her wrap, threw it around her shoulders and stormed out of the room. The tension dropped the minute the door shut behind her.

"So Caris, where do you plan on taking Ari?" Vict looked between them.

"Well, I was thinking of walking through the market to help him get his bearings and see the type of things on display, what Kenistal is actually like. Then I thought I would take him clothes shopping. He's been borrowing mine, but I want—"

Caris didn't get a chance to finish his sentence before Vict spoke, his voice muffled at first as he rooted through one of his drawers before holding up a bag. He walked around the table and perched on the arm of Ari's chair.

"In here are some smaller coins. You'll find it easier if you use these in the market." He then dropped a credit chip on a chain over Ari's head. "Here are some proper credits. I want you two to go shopping and buy absolutely everything you need and some things you want but don't need. No." He held up his hand stopping Ari from talking. "I won't let you refuse. Let me do this. I want you both to go and have some fun. You've both had a tough time lately."

Ari impulsively put his arms as far around Vict's wide chest as he could and hugged him, smiling when he got a very gentle pat on the back as if Vict was scared of hurting him. "Thank you. You've been kinder than my own parents."

Vict coughed as he pulled back, a serious mask slipping back into place. "Now get out of here and have fun. Son, you and Commander Bo'saverin can stay here."

Dasa slumped in his chair, perking up a little as Caris gave him a gentle kiss on his cheek.

Vict gestured to two warriors by the door. "Yavek and Deek'in will look after you today."

Ari studied the two imposing Cobalt blue guards and swallowed. Caris grabbed his arm and started to lead him out the room. His gaze sought out Bo.

"I'll see you when you come back. Go and have some fun." Bo winked at Ari, loving the immediate green blush— that color was fast becoming his favorite.

Ari was looking around the market wide-eyed. It was bustling with activity. Merchants were shouting out their wares, competing with each other. Constant jibes were flying back and forth. He avidly watched as two demons started a fight. One was orange, the other silver. Without taking his gaze off the pair he asked Caris. "What's the difference between all the colors? Are they just random?"

Caris watched as Deek'in whistled for two city guards to deal with the battling demons. "Their colors determine their clans. When a demonling has their twentieth naming day, they go through something called the Rite of Ferik. It's a guild selection process that determines where they end up. Demonlings will change color during the selection process to the color for their new guild. The only demons who don't change color are the royal family. They are born and stay purple. The orange color shows the demon belongs to the manual workers' guild. So they help to build houses, look after the land and so on. The silver demon belongs to the metalsmiths' guild."

"So all guards are the same blue?" Ari looked at the vivid blue of the guards discreetly watching them.

"You know, I'm not sure." Caris turned to Yavek.

"Ambassador—" at Caris' glare, he winced— "sorry, Caris, those who are the same blue as we are belong to the Cobalt Guard." He turned and gestured to the two guards breaking up the fight. "Those are the city guards and as you can see they are a lighter blue.

There are also guards who are a delicate blue – those are the temple guards."

Ari beamed. "Thank you, Yavek."

"You're welcome, Little Demon."

"I'm neither little, nor am I a demon." Ari pouted at being called small.

Deek'in patted Ari softly on the shoulder. "To us you are little and you are now a Kenistalian— you signed the forms this morning. Therefore, you are one of us. I shall call you Little Demon, a fitting name I think, as you certainly have the courage of a demon. We heard about the way you piloted the pod."

Ari's gaze darted about, everything demanding his attention at the same time. Deek'in grinned. "I know you need to buy new clothes, and there are a couple of good merchants we can go to. I'd suggest doing that first and sending what you buy back to the palace, or last and we can take it with us?"

Ari looked to Caris, overwhelmed and indecisive.

Caris chuckled. "Clothes first, then look around. There's a couple of things I want you to see."

Ari whimpered and stared longingly across the market. "Caris…" he whined, his voice soft and awe-filled, "It's a *tech* store." He blinked rapidly. "I know I can't get anything, but can I at least look?"

Caris grabbed Ari's arm, guiding him across the market. "Even if there isn't enough credit on the chip Vict gave you, and I *really* doubt that, I have plenty of my own. You can get anything you want. I don't want any disagreements either. You deserve spoiling and it would be my honor to be the one spoiling you."

Ari squeezed Caris' arm. "I keep needing to say thank you today, yet the words aren't enough. I need something bigger."

Caris hugged Ari quickly. "All the thanks I need is a smile on your face."

Deek'in grinned as he opened the shop door, beckoning them in. The proprietor, a Grey demon, smiled as they entered. "Welcome to Tink's Emporium, my shop. Is there something in particular you were looking for?"

Caris watched in amazement as Ari stepped forward, totally confident, his normally shy personality gone.

"Do you have an Aducian compcube by any chance?" Ari's hands itched to get his hands on some of the equipment on display. There were so many things he'd seen over the years that he wanted to try out but couldn't get a hold of.

"I wish I did," the Grey demon replied. "I've seen them, but never owned one. I've tried to tinker something close to it, but never got it quite right. Forgive me for asking, but you're Aducian, aren't you?"

Ari grinned. "I am, and while I've never built a cube, I've made enough adaptions to my own in the past that it shouldn't be too much of a hassle for us to work it out. I'm Aridien." He held out his arm in the traditional Aducian greeting— fist closed, forearm extended, the inner part revealed.

"I'm Opink'ik, tinkerer and owner of this fine establishment." He extended his own arm, mirroring Ari, laying his own arm over Ari's before sliding it back and tapping their fists together.

Ari smiled widely before looking at all the tech on display. "You have some incredible things in here... Oh, is that a Zevki 1000? Those are impossible to get hold of!" He moved over in front of a long, slim device that looked mundane to anyone not knowledgeable in the tech world. He turned to Caris. "These are incredibly rare. If I remember correctly, there were only around two hundred even made."

Caris peered at the device. It didn't appear to be anything other than a long, slim rectangle of polished black marble-like material. "What is it?"

Ari whirled around to look at Caris, mouth agape. "You really don't know what this is?" When Caris shook his head no, he looked at the two guards who shrugged. "How can you not know?"

"I'm guessing none of us, bar Opink'ik here, are as fond of technology as you," Caris teased.

"The Zevki 1000 is a holographic device that is capable of mapping brainwaves and rendering a life-size representation of any item. The problem with it is the Zevki was only capable of reading a handful of races— those who had activated a certain area of their brains through evolution. It's incredibly rare to see one outside of the Pegasus sector." He bit his bottom lip. "Is it okay if I spend some time here?"

Caris smiled widely. "Of course, go on ahead, there are some chairs over there where we can sit and wait."

Ari's grin nearly lit up the room. He looked at the display case in front of Opink'ik. "You have some remarkable devices in here. Some I recognize, some I don't."

"Call me Op'ik. I think we are going to be firm friends. A lot of what you see here, I have made myself. As a tinkerer, we have a natural aptitude to creating devices, modifying them and well, tinkering with things." Op'ik lifted a metal box with gears and links worked into the lid. When he opened it, the box was filled with gears slowly turning, as though they were powering up. He flipped a switch and a small screen rose out from a concealed slot at the rear of the box. Slowly, the screen flickered to life and the startup screen of a comppad appeared. From the bottom of the device, a mechanical keyboard slowly slid out and rose up, fitting over the moving gears and locking in place. 'Welcome, how may I be of service today,' a slightly mechanical voice sounded from a grill on either side of the screen.

Ari traced the brass gears on the side of the box, careful not to interrupt the mechanism. "It's fully operational?"

Op'ik grinned. "It does everything a normal comppad does, but it is self-powering. The gears are weighted in such a way that each turn increases the power reserves. There is also a hand crank." He pointed to a tiny area on the front of the box, an ornate cylindrical pipe nestled against the detail. Op'ik unlatched it and gently slotted it into a hole in a gear. "You turn this, and keep turning for two galactic minutes, and it will give you enough power to keep it running until its reserves build up."

Ari's gaze traced over every part of the ornate device. "Op'ik, this is incredible, the mastery on this, the intricate work, I'm stunned. It's both a work of art and a genius invention. Too many worlds rely on their power reserves and would be lost if they couldn't use their tech. This would be incredible for those worlds that have power issues."

Caris picked up on parts of their conversation. "Did I hear right? You have a device, a comp device, that works without power? What about interference from various external sources like dampening fields?"

Op'ik narrowed his eyes for a moment as he considered the question. "Realistically, the parts are all mechanical, apart from the screen, so I can't see it being influenced by any dampening field."

Caris' mind was spinning and there was only one thing he could focus on: Landran. He turned to Deek'in, cursing the fact he'd yet to get his own comm implant. "I need you to contact Prince Dasa and have him meet us here immediately."

Deek'in's eyes widened ever so slightly, but he nodded. His fingers reached up to his link, connecting to the main comm center. "Patch me through to Prince Dasalin please. I have an urgent message from Caris Dealyn."

Caris watched his eyes narrow, as though whoever he was talking to him was questioning his request.

"I am well aware of what the punishment is. Now, put me through before you're the one who will face the consequences."

Less than a minute later, he was connected to Dasa.

"This had better be important."

Deek'in winced, but stood ramrod straight. "My Liege, Caris is requesting your presence as soon as you are able. We're at Tink's Emporium."

"Is there a problem? Are Caris and Ari in danger?" Dasa's demand came through the comm link so loud, Deek'in winced.

"No, Your Highness, I'm not sure what it's about, but Caris seems insistent you are here."

Caris walked up to Deek'in. "If I talk here, can he hear me?"

"Hold on." Deek'in switched the external voice nullifier off. "Talk now."

"Dasa, get your horns down here now. It's important. I think I know of a way to help out our *new* friends." Caris was careful not to say too much. He had no idea how secure the link was.

"Warrior Deek'in, tell him we're on our way."

Deek'in didn't have a chance to respond as Dasa cut the link. "He's on his way." Deek'in shared a look with Yavek. "Have we missed something? Is there a problem, Caris?"

Caris shook his head. "Not at all. Something those two were talking about made me think of a problem Dasa and I have been mulling over. I just want him to see this. You guys are doing a great job. I miss Mac, but I couldn't be happier to have you two as guards. You're not all stern-faced and fully accepting of the fact we aren't demons."

Yavek scowled. "That's not true."

"What isn't?" Caris' nose wrinkled as he thought.

"You *are* both demons. As I said earlier, Ari is a little demon now and you are with our prince, therefore you are our little prince. You're both demons as far as I'm concerned and anyone who wants to insist differently can meet me in the ring. Too many stuck up Reds have been saying that I'm guessing." Yavek's tail was whipping back and forth, a testament to his anger.

Caris laughed. "Does anyone actually like the Reds?"

46

Deek'in and Yavek shared a look. "The other Reds." Their voices rang out at the same time, making them all laugh.

Ari was still deep in conversation with Op'ik, but they both looked up at the laughter. Ari shrugged and went back to chatting about the devices Op'ik had made. "So that one's a comppad and this one is a security console?" The device in question was a sleek design with rounded edges and a well of moldable gel in the center.

"It is. You slide your fingers into the gel and then manipulate the commands on the screen. On my travels, when I worked on one of the Kenistalian spaceships, I met several races that didn't have the traditional hands most humanoids have. They often had one digit, or something similar. They always found it hard to work any universal equipment. I know even the Barin Alliance doesn't make adjustments for these races— they are simply not offered the jobs where they need multiple fingers, no matter how gifted they are. This console can be attached to any piece of equipment and provides a secure link and interface for those races to use standard equipment. I'm still trying to work out some of the glitches in the programming on this one though."

"I would love to help on this, or any other project you have going." Ari bit his lip, nervous, and desperate for Op'ik to say yes. This was a dream job to him. Something he'd never have considered possible in even his wildest dreams.

"If you aren't too busy with any other responsibilities, I would love to have any help you offer. I can tell you know what you are talking about and seem as interested in this stuff as I am." Op'ik's tail was wrapping around his legs before spinning out and back again.

"Are you so desperate to be away from me then?"

Hot breath washed over Ari's neck, making his curls sway. *Bo.* He turned, his nose rubbing against Bo's arm as he looked up. "What are you doing here?" His breath hitched at the sight of Bo in dark trousers, his chest bare to let the wounds breathe and heal. *Damn man is too gorgeous for his own good.*

"Caris requested our presence." Bo nodded to Caris who was off to one side, as Dasa crouched in front of his seat. They were whispering frantically.

"Is everything alright?" Ari rubbed at his nose before trying to blow a stray curl out of his eyes.

Bo tenderly brushed the curl away and tucked it behind Ari's ear. "You tell me. You were the one here."

Ari peeked up through his eyelashes. "I got distracted talking tech with Op'ik here."

Op'ik bowed slightly. "Commander Bo'saverin."

Bo dipped his head. "Tinkerer Opink'ik."

"So you weren't paying any attention to what was going on around you then?" Bo grinned as his hand rested against the back of Ari's neck, his thumb brushing back and forth gently.

"I love all things tech and I never got much of a chance when… well, in the past. When I saw this shop, I wanted to look, and Caris, he, uh… well, he insisted that I could look for something to get and if there wasn't enough credit on the chip the king gave me, he would use his." Ari ducked his head.

Bo shared a look with Op'ik. "Anything he wants, he gets. If I have to leave before he chooses, then bill it to me. Contact my assistant and she'll send the credits straight over."

Op'ik grinned at the look of astonishment on Ari's face. "Of course, Commander."

"Bo, you can't do that!" Ari looked up at him. "Why would you want to anyway?"

"Because seeing you smile makes me happy and I know being able to have tech of your own is a dream of yours. It's one that I will take great pleasure in fulfilling for you." Bo kept up the gentle strokes on Ari's neck.

"But why?" Ari blinked up at Bo, creases forming on his forehead.

Bo used his other hand to smooth out the wrinkles. "Because I want to. Because you are a remarkable man, Ari."

"I'm nothing special. My mother made sure of that." Ari swallowed back the feeling that he wanted more with Bo. It wouldn't do him any good; he had nothing to offer such a kind, strong, hardworking, and deeply gorgeous man. Bo needed a strong demon, someone who could stand tall by his side, who knew what they were doing, knew the demon world and the politics. He needed someone who would complement him and, most importantly, someone who knew what it was like to lie with someone, who knew how to pleasure a demon like Bo. None of those things were him.

Bo pulled Ari in for a gentle hug, kissing the top of his head. "I don't know where in your mind you just went, but I don't want you to go there again. You are a greater man than most. You have more courage, faith, loyalty, resilience and perseverance than anyone I have ever met. Hopefully, in time, you will learn to see yourself as others see you. Until then, I'll just have to think those things for you. And you, Ari, are an incredible man. Now, are you ready to choose something, or do you need more time?"

Ari's gaze darted around the shop, focusing on one thing after another. He went to reach out for a comppad, not the special one Op'ik had shown him, but a standard one. Then he went for a kit that would help him design his own. His gaze kept darting back to the ornate mechanical device Op'ik had created. Bo could tell he was completely torn. He was about to tell Op'ik they'd take both when Dasa stepped in.

"I'd like to buy the mechanical device for Ari here, and commission you to make a couple more just like it." Dasa ruffled Ari's curls as they joined them at the long counter.

Bo glared at Dasa over Ari's head, his eyes narrowing further when Dasa simply smirked. "I'll take one of the kits for Ari, unless one isn't enough? You'd better make it two."

Ari turned, his gaze darting between the two demons. The guards behind them were trying to hide their sniggers and Caris was flat out laughing as he walked up and dragged Ari off to one side. "Typical competitive demons."

"What's going on?" Ari whispered.

Caris moved in closer. "I'll explain when we get back to my suite— it's more private. We can't really talk here."

Ari nodded, watching Dasa playfully shove Bo, who quirked a brow at him. Soon enough they had packages all wrapped up. Bo strode over to Ari and squatted down in front of him, his hand immediately cupping Ari's cheek.

"I'll see you back at the palace. If there is anything you want, and there aren't enough credits on the chip the king gave you, tell the shopkeeper to bill me and have it sent to my offices. My assistant will sort it out."

"I can't. You've already got me a kit." Ari shook his head so much his curls bounced all over the place.

"Two." Bo grinned. "I got you two. I was serious when I said I wanted you to have things, Ari."

"Why? Why are you doing this? Why are you all being so nice to me?" A single tear trickled from the corner of his eye and he went to dash it angrily away, but Bo beat him to it.

Bo gently wiped away the tear, caressing the damp skin left behind. "Because you're special, Ari, don't ever forget that." When Ari went to respond, Bo covered his mouth with a large blue hand. "No, don't say anything. Just accept it." He leaned forward and gently kissed Ari's forehead. "I need to get back before the doctors realize that I'm gone. I'm not sure this is what they meant by taking it easy." Bo grinned, completely unrepentant.

Ari's hand fluttered against Bo's back. "You didn't hurt yourself because of me, did you?"

Bo lifted his other hand, completely cupping Ari's face. "I'm fine. Nothing happened. Now, go and have some fun with Caris. Make sure you get some clothes, and not just tech, hmm? You could even try out some tep'rink trousers." Bo's pulse sped up at the thought of Ari in the traditional demon attire. He could picture his pale skin, and with his chest bare, he would be able to see how far that blush extended. He ruthlessly pushed the thought to one side. His uniform pants didn't leave much room to hide an erection.

"You don't want to come with me?" Ari's voice pitched low and trembled, as if he was worried about asking.

"Not this time. I would love to, but if I come with you, the demons will be on their best behavior. It's probably best you see the market at its worst so you know what you will have to deal with if you live here. Demons are loud and boisterous, they push and shove each other as a matter of course. There is nothing aggressive about it normally— it's just the way we are. Demons are big, noisy and brash, but that doesn't mean they aren't caring, it's just that you need to be in the right situation to see it. I want you to be comfortable here. I want you to feel you can walk about the city and not be worried. I want you to relax and get to know people. I want you to explore and find things you like. But most importantly, I want you to fall in love with... my world. I want you to feel like this is home." Bo reached around and squeezed Ari's neck gently. "I'll wait for you back at the palace."

Ari leaned into Bo's grip, soaking up the peace and serenity Bo always brought to him. "Will I have to leave the palace now I'm out of the med center?" It was the one thing he'd been worried about. He didn't want to be anywhere his new friends weren't. They made him feel safe, secure and loved.

"No. I thought you might like to stay in the second bedroom in my suite so you are near one of us. Besides, no one really wants to be around Dasa and Caris. They can be fairly noisy." Bo waggled his eyebrows, making Ari blush.

"I'd like that. I feel safe when you're around." Ari's soft smile made Bo's heart lift. Getting a smile from him brightened his day, made his soul soar. Oh, he was in so much trouble. He was deeply attracted to him, but Ari was innocent in so many ways he would have to go slow. Slower than slow... he would have to court him, and wasn't that the problem... Demons don't date, they fuck.

"Where did you go?"

Ari's voice broke through Bo's musings.

"Sorry, my mind drifted a little there. It, err… must be the, umm, lingering effects of the meds they put me on." There was no way Bo was going to admit he'd been thinking of fucking Ari.

"You're sure you're okay? Not in pain?" Ari looked over Bo, his heart racing at the wide expanse of blue chest he wanted to touch.

Bo's eyes lit with fire. Ari was licking his lips as he assessed him. It looked like Ari was definitely interested. "I'm fine." He stood and gently pulled Ari up with him. "Now, go and have some fun with Caris." He gently tapped Ari's ass, making him squeak.

Ari scowled indignantly at Bo, making him laugh. He caught Caris' gaze as he watched them speculatively and blushed. Oh, how he hated blushing. It was the bane of his life; he could never hide his feelings with it.

Caris took pity on Ari, grabbing his hand and walking to the door of the shop. "Thank you, Op'ik, for indulging us. I am quite sure we will end up being regular visitors here if Ari has anything to say about it."

Op'ik laughed. "I look forward to it. Ari, you are welcome here anytime. I would love to work with you on some of my ideas. I may be part of the Tinker guild, but none of the other tinkerers share my love of devices from all over the galaxies. The chance to share my passion with someone who understands is a dream come true."

Ari walked back and gripped Op'ik's arm, saying goodbye in the traditional Aducian way. "Thank you for welcoming me. I will definitely take you up on that offer." Walking back to Caris, he waved goodbye, squinting slightly as they walked back into the midday brightness of the market.

With a quick kiss of his cheek from Bo, Ari watched as both he and Dasa walked off, leaving him alone with Caris and their guards.

"So… clothes?" Caris grinned at Ari's wrinkled nose. "Come on, it will be fun."

Ari narrowed his eyes. He wasn't enthusiastic. The demons were all huge, so what clothes could there possibly be that would fit him? Then again, owning his own clothes, getting something because he simply wanted it, sent a thrill for him and he smiled up at Caris. "Lead on."

CHAPTER FIVE

Ari sank into the seat outside the little restaurant that Deek'in and Yavek had suggested, his feet aching from walking around the market and shopping for clothes. He'd fallen in love with the tep'rink trousers. They were different from anything he'd ever worn and were so luxurious against his skin. They made him feel good about himself.

He'd been surprised by the variety of food on offer at the restaurant. They sold a mixture of foods from around the universes. There were delicacies like the planet Treykon's seelis on the menu. Seelis was a shellfish and, if cooked right, almost melted on the tongue. Caris had opted for something he said came from Old Earth. It was some form of roasted red meat with what looked to be roots and a thick sauce covering it all. He wasn't sure it looked appetizing, but as long as Caris enjoyed it, it was all that mattered.

He'd opted for hablini, an Aducian soup, which he'd been amazed to see on the menu. It was closer to a stew, by traditional galaxy standards. There were several combinations of meat in it, with lots of blue vegetables which were his favorite. It was too sour for most palates, but he adored it. Back home, one of his guards had been married to the head cook. They knew it was his favorite and did everything they could to make it for him on a regular basis. He smiled as he took his first spoonful. He groaned as the tastes washed over his tongue. "This is amazing. It's close to perfect in taste."

"Just close to perfect?" A new voice grunted out behind him.

He jumped, his spoon clattering to the table.

"Who are you to insult my cooking?"

Ari's troubled gaze darted to the floor. Out of the corner of his eyes, he could see Yavek, stand up, his chair scraping on the stone floor beneath them.

Yavek's cobalt skin immediately shifted to scales. "Watch what you say, Ulkrit. Aridien here is a personal guest of the king, and that is Caris, Prince Dasalin's mate. I would not be picking a fight with either of them if I was you."

Ulkrit growled. "I don't care who he is. He doesn't know what he's talking about if he says my hablini is only close to perfect."

Ari took a deep breath. *Ari, this is the start of the rest of your life. If you want to live here, you have to learn to hold your own in situations like this. Be brave. Imagine Bo is standing beside you.* He stood and turned towards the mint green demon currently glaring at Yavek. Deek'in stood protectively beside him.

"Your hablini *is* only close to perfect. I stand by that and, yes, I would know. I *am* Aducian, after all. This is certainly no way to treat your customers. As for the hablini— you're missing one of the spices. You don't need much, but it makes *all* the difference to the taste." Ari stared the demon down, but registered the look of shock on Caris' face beside him.

Ulkrit blinked a couple of times. "You're Aducian? I don't believe it." He scoffed.

Yavek grabbed him by the neck and slammed him into the wall behind their table. All around them, demons were watching. It wasn't often the Cobalts got riled up. "You're on your last chance to learn to be respectful. Choose to be disrespectful one more time and we'll see what Commander Bo'saverin has to say on the matter."

Ulkrit refused to break Yavek's stare, not wanting to back down, but risked a glance around him to see who was on his side. His eye's widened as he got a good look at Ari. "Y-you, you're Aducian."

"I am." Aridien stood there with arms crossed in front of his chest. "Although it matters little. Whatever my heritage, you should not be so insulting to customers. I would also say, whatever my heritage, you should simply not be so insulting. So I'm smaller than you, I have pale skin, no horns or tail. Why should that make me less? Why should my genetics make me less? You remind me of people on my world who believe those differences are a race's weaknesscs and should be bred out."

He was of course referring to his status as a lenis, not that he would say that out loud. "Differences, whatever they may be, should be celebrated. After all, is it not the differences in food you celebrate here? You have dishes from many worlds across many universes. I would have thought that would have made you appreciate the variety."

Ulkrit slumped as much as he could while still pinned to the wall. "I am sorry. I didn't… I'm sorry."

Ari studied Ulkrit, making sure his comments were actually sincere. "Apology accepted." Sitting back down, he calmly went back to eating his soup. It was very good, even with the missing spice, and he wasn't about to pass up enjoying one of the few nice memories he had of his birth planet. He refused to think of it as his home planet anymore. *After all, you're a little demon now, aren't you, Ari?* He smiled softly to himself at that thought.

Caris shook himself out of the slight stupor he'd fallen into watching Ari defend himself. Oh, he wished Bo had seen that. It reminded him of the Ari he'd seen on board the Loperis ship when he stood up to the Loperis guard, Quasi. There, Ari had been full of fire and protecting himself, Caris and Veris. While Ari was mostly shy, there was definitely a core strength to him.

Yavek focused on Ari, making sure he wasn't upset or offended. Seeing he was fine, he dropped Ulkrit unceremoniously on the ground. "Watch your manners in the future." Holding Ulkrit's gaze, he let the words sink in as the demon squirmed. He eventually returned to the table and his davroc.

"Are you sure you won't have anything to eat?" Ari gestured to the davroc in front of both Yavek and Deek'in.

"We shouldn't even be having this, but Caris insisted." Deek'in sat sniffing at his second steaming cup of davroc.

"Why shouldn't you?" Ari took another spoonful of hablini, letting the memories drift by him.

"Because, Little Demon, we're supposed to be alert for every moment. Always on guard, ready to defend you both at a moment's notice."

Ari took hold of his drink, a sweet, tart juice, and as he went to take a drink, he deliberately let the glass slide out of his fingers. Deek'in's hand shot out and grabbed the glass, setting it gently back on the table.

"So drinking davroc stops you reacting, does it?" Ari gestured to the glass.

Caris burst out laughing, surprising some nearby demons eating in the restaurant. "You have to admit, he has you there."

Yavek narrowed his eyes at Ari. "Where is the shy little demon we got this morning? What have you done with him?"

Ari snorted, slapping a hand over his mouth and nose, mortified at the sound. Caris' laughter just deepened.

"You didn't see him up there…" Caris tipped his head, gesturing to the sky. "He was strong and brave, courageous and smart."

Ari, having recovered, dropped his hand. "Only because you were there with me."

Caris shook his head. "Don't diminish what you did. You saved my life."

"And you saved mine." Ari beamed.

Deek'in and Yavek shared a look. "We have *got* to hear this tale." Deek'in's tail curled lazily upwards, brushing accidently against Ari's arm, who jumped, making them laugh.

As Caris told the story of his capture by the Loperis, meeting Ari, and their subsequent escape, Ari sat demon watching. They were in a little courtyard. It was circular with only the one entrance which they were sat opposite. On the right was what looked to be a working pottery barn. He could see a couple of mint green craftsmen working at wheels. Another was pounding clay. Fascinated, he watched intently as a blob was thrown onto the wheel. Foot pumping the lever rhythmically to spin the wheel, the craftsman splashed water onto the clay and started to shape it with his hands.

Slowly, the clay began to take shape. The demon slowly pushed into the middle of the mound, first with a finger, before eventually his whole hand, hollowing it out, smoothing out the lines as he did so. Ari watched avidly as the bottom was pushed out into a bulb shape, before narrowing and flaring out once again until there was a pronounced lip. He watched as the craftsman took a long, fairly thick sliver of clay and attached it to one side. *Oh, it's a goblet, or a tankard.* He wasn't sure what the demons actually called them. The silver ones Dasa and Bo used were goblets, but they didn't have handles.

The craftsman let the wheel come to a stop before he worked on the design. Slowly but surely, what looked like an animal took shape. He couldn't be sure, but the handle definitely looked like a tail. He sighed as a couple of demons blocked his view.

Looking around, he focused on a shop on the left. It sold underwear. He would definitely need some of those. Maybe he could get some nice ones, rather than having to make his own out of scraps of old clothes. And there he went again thinking of his previous life. *No, stop, Ari. That life is done, you're safe. You're no one on Kenistal. Stop thinking and start living.* He took a deep breath and relaxed. He was going to go over to that shop and buy some underwear. He wouldn't worry about the cost. He wouldn't go for the cheapest ones. He would look around and choose ones that were soft, comfortable and colorful.

"What's got you smiling?" Caris' words interrupted Ari's musings.

"I know we talked about going… home after this." Ari's face broke into a beaming grin. "But can we go over there, and there?" He pointed to both the underwear shop and the pottery barn.

"Of course we can." Caris smiled as he sipped his juice.

"You want to go to the pottery barn?" Deek'in checked.

"I do, it looks amazing. I want to watch."

Deek'in shared a look with Yavek. "You see the Mint Green demon working on the left? That's Oz'ki, my sister's mate. I'm sure he would be happy to let you try it out."

Ari vibrated in his seat. "Really?"

Deek'in nodded. "Really."

"Oh wow, I love this planet. There is so much I can do and people are so kind. Thank you, Deek'in." Ari's smile was huge, joy shining from his eyes as he looked at Caris and the two demons.

Caris took Ari's hand, smiling away, Ari's happiness infectious. "Anything you want to do, we do." He looked at Yavek and Deek'in. "Are you guys happy being our guards?"

Yavek burst out laughing. "Of course we are. You guys are fun, we get out of the palace, we don't have to guard corridors or politicians. Trust me, if you guys wanted to get rid of us, we'd be begging you not to."

Caris sobered slightly. "When Mac is healed, one way or another he'll be with us."

Deek'in dipped his head. "We will do everything we can to help him. He's a hero, make no mistake, he is well respected amongst the Cobalts."

"I don't want him to ever think his role as a warrior and a Cobalt is over, not because he defended me. I was the reason he was hurt in the first place, the reason so many Cobalts died, or were injured. I will never be able to repay them."

Yavek laid a gentle hand on Caris' arm. "It is what we do. Most of us would do it each and every time. I know you don't see it, but you are important to Kenistal. You've made our prince happy. You've given us a secure enough future with a strong leader to come. You are respected."

"Even if I'm not a demon?" Caris prompted.

Ari listened intently. If Caris had problems because he wasn't a demon, he certainly would too.

Yavek sighed. "There will always be some demons that won't like the fact you two aren't demons, but they are a minority."

"Why do I matter in all of this?" Ari scrunched up his face.

Deek'in and Yavek both stared incredulously. "Is he serious?" Deek'in's stunned gaze focused on Caris.

"I think he is." Caris chuckled.

Deek'in leaned forward so he was level with Ari's face. "Ari, all of us know that Commander Bo'saverin has taken an immediate liking to you. Anyone gets too close— the look warns us off. Word quickly spread around the Cobalts that you are under the protection of our Commander. In the Cobalts, that is sacrosanct. We protect everyone; we are there to protect the royal family. But he is *our* commander. He's one of us."

"I don't understand. He was just doing his job, I thought?" Ari questioned.

Caris wrapped a gentle arm around Ari. "You were carried out of the pod by Bo when it was on fire after we crashed, and he didn't put you down until he had to. He stayed with you when the attack happened. He refused to leave you alone. When everything collapsed, he protected you with his body. When he was hurt, it was the thought of you being in trouble, of you being in pain that brought him round. I don't know exactly what he feels, but he's drawn to you. He tracks you with his eyes, he wants you near. Ari, my friend, the commander of the Cobalts is intrigued by you and is attracted to you."

Ari blushed the deepest green Caris had seen. "I'm attracted to him too. He makes me feel safe. I feel like I can be myself around him and not be judged. But I'm too inexperienced for him. I have nothing to offer him."

"You have everything to offer him. You are quite a man, Ari, and experience doesn't matter. You captivate him just the way you are. And trust me, when he sees you in those tep'rink trousers, his horns will steam." Caris winked and the demons laughed.

Yavek patted Ari's arm. "Trust me, we all see it. Our commander is yours for the taking. Just don't make it too easy on him, hey? It's only fair to make him work for it."

Ari looked from one to the other. "Really?"

"Really. But, only if you want him, Ari. Please don't feel pressured into anything just because we mentioned it."

"Oh no, I want him, I just never thought I had a chance." Ari grinned shyly.

"Well, you definitely do. I can't wait to see his reaction when you walk in wearing that." Caris studied Ari. He had on a pair of rich green, super soft tep'rink trousers that complimented his pale skin and green hair. While the trousers were wide and flared out around his thighs and calves, they tapered to fit close against his ankles. His top was a pale gold and fit snugly, showing off his lean physique. On his feet were a pair of golden shoes. He looked amazing.

"You want to go to the shop first then? Before we go back to the palace? I would suggest changing back into your old clothes if you want to work on the pottery. You don't want to ruin your new things." Deek'in gestured to the potters who had splatters of clay all over them.

"Good idea." Caris winced at the idea of getting clay out of clothes. "I'm sure the shop won't mind us changing in there." He got to his feet. "Come on then, Ari, more shopping." He grinned wickedly as the two guards groaned.

CHAPTER SIX

Stunned at the variety of underwear on display, Ari had no idea where to start. A slim Bronze demon walked up to him, smiling. "It's not often we see non demons here. Please tell me I can help. I normally only get to sell boring things to boring demons." The demon pouted.

Ari laughed. "I need help, if I'm honest. I've never had anything but boring undergarments."

The demon rubbed his hands together. "I'm Perik. We're going to need to work on your choice of words, but we'll get there. Okay, let me look at you…" Perik slowly walked around Ari, assessing him. Then he moved on to Caris.

"Oh, no, we're just here for him." Caris held his hands out.

Perik shook his head. "No, you as well, Mr. Ambassador, Little Prince. I've seen the way you dress and I longed to get you in here to appreciate my fine stock. Trust me, if both of you choose some of my pieces, Prince Dasalin and Commander Bo'saverin won't know what's hit them."

Ari did a double take. "What about Commander Bo'saverin?"

Perik chuckled. "Oh, come now. This isn't that big of a city. We've heard the rumors that the Commander is completely smitten with a green-haired stranger. That has to be you. So how about we find you some things that will send his tail into a spin." Perik winked.

Ari may have been blushing profusely, but he was nodding vigorously.

Caris shrugged. "I'm game. Anything to tease Dasa with."

Perik laughed. "Oh, I like you two." He beckoned them over to a long table. "So here we have all the styles and fabrics. It looks daunting, but once we work out what style you like, we can start choosing fabrics and colors." He started at one end. "Here we have what most of the warriors wear. They are designed with their muscles and scales in mind. They help with the muscles, keeping them warm so they don't seize up and cramp, and the cloth matrix helps the oxygen flow through the body. As you can see, they are very tight. All the better for appreciating a package." He waggled his eyebrows. "Obviously, these types are designed with demons and scales in mind, but we do the long demis like this in general fabrics."

"I think I want something a little sexier." Caris snorted as he held a pair up to himself; they went past his ankles.

"Good, we can bypass them. How about these?"

Perik held up what looked like a pair of tiny shorts. They looked like a band of material rather than anything else. It looked like they would sit on his hips and barely cover his ass. They were skintight and would leave little to the imagination.

"Now these are remarkably comfy. They keep everything in place and are practical while the choice of materials and colors can be quite decadent."

"I really like those." Ari picked up a pair and held them up against his body. "Everything I've had was baggy and boring. These look like they would make me feel sexy."

Perik nodded. "Oh, they will and you'll look sexy too. They suit your body type." He turned to Caris. "What about you? You want these, or maybe these?" Perik held up what looked to be a pouch with barely there string holding it together.

Ari shared a stunned look with Caris. "What *are* they?"

Perik laughed and moved to a plastic model on the end of the table. "These."

Ari stared, barely blinking. Whatever they were called, it was little more than a bag holding the model's bits in. It looked like the bag was tied with a thin elasticated ribbon designed to hold it in place against the hips.

Ari shook his head rapidly. "I'll stick with this style." Caris turned his back on the dummy and gestured to the shorts. "Definitely those."

"Perfect choice for you both. You're slim enough to carry it off. Now for the fun part, choosing the materials. There are plenty of variations. From your average every day laxin cloth which keeps its shape, to dainty, barely-there lace ones. How about I bring over a selection of them to you? While I'm getting them, I'll have my assistant get some davroc for your guards. It looks like they need it." They all looked at both guards who were stood in front of the window staring resolutely outwards. All three burst out laughing.

Perik came back with a selection of the shorts. "First off, have a look at these." He passed over some simple black ones. Ari held them, marveling at how soft they were. "These are general everyday ones. They have some elastic in them, so they keep their shape and are extremely comfy. Plus, they make your ass look great." He winked.

Next, he passed over another black pair, only these were slightly decadent. They had vertical stripes. The stripes were solid black but the mesh in-between the black stripes was a dove grey. They would give hints about what was underneath. Ari blushed furiously.

Perik grinned. "These are designed to tease your lover. The mesh isn't as transparent as you would think. They end up just giving a barely-there hint of what's underneath. I promise you, wearing these will intrigue your demon. Next we have these. This is sinka lace. As you can see, it's made from the thread from sinka spiders. The threads are woven into the web-like patterns by seamstresses. They are extremely delicate, but incredible to wear for special occasions. Very few demons can resist the sight, whether the sinka lace is worn by men or women."

Ari's face lit up as he gently ran a finger over the fabric. "These are incredible. I bet wearing either of these pairs, you would feel so sexy."

Perik leaned forward conspiratorially. "Trust me, you do. I love wearing these. Now, if you are feeling more adventurous… how about these." He held up another pair.

Ari's mouth dropped open. He realized the shorts had been getting more provocative. Perik was holding up a pair which appeared to be little more than mesh. Only this mesh was thinner than the other pair and almost fully see-through. The waistband was a strip of thicker material, similar to the paneling on the striped pair. A ribbon with a bit of mesh sticking out of it was in the center. Ari's forehead creased as he studied them. "What is that?"

Perik laughed. He stuck his fingers in the middle of the mesh and waggled it about. This is where—"

"I get the picture," Ari hastily blurted, his eyes wide.

"If this doesn't get your man desperate to be with you, then nothing will."

The corner of Caris' mouth kicked up. "Oh, I have got to get some of those." At Ari's stunned look, he explained. "If I ever get in trouble with Dasa, those are so going to get me out of it."

Ari frowned as he thought, before whispering, "Would any of these help me get Bo's attention?"

Caris put his arm around Ari's shoulders and drew him close. "Trust me, between any of these and your new clothes, poor Bo won't know what hit him." He turned to Perik. "It looks like we'll both be taking several of each. Now, let's talk colors."

Back in the clothes he'd borrowed from Caris, Ari was laughing at Deek'in. Despite sending most of their new clothes back earlier, he was laden down with bags. Yavek had explained it was better one of them was free to react and defend their charges. Deek'in had lost the bet and was now grumbling about being a krafic— a pack animal used to transport goods to the more remote villages.

As soon as they were close enough, Deek'in called out. "Oz'ki!"

The mint green demon's head snapped up. "Deeks, what you doing here?"

"I have a new assignment." He gestured to Ari and Caris, grumbling when one of the bags caught a gust of wind and slammed into his privates. "Ari here," he stuttered as he winced, "is fascinated by the pottery barn."

Oz'ki turned to look at them both. "Which one is Ari?"

Ari shyly stepped forward. "I am. I've never seen anything like this. It's fascinating."

Oz'ki blinked a couple of times. "You've never seen pottery being made?"

"I've led a sheltered life." Ari ducked his head, trying to fight his shyness.

Oz'ki shared a look with Deek'in. "Well, here." He threw an apron at Ari. "Put that on and come over here."

Ari quickly put on the apron and was surprised when Oz'ki pushed him onto the stool. He moved his half-done piece to one side and threw a lump of clay onto the wheel. Squatting down, he positioned Ari's foot on the pedal. "Pump that a couple of times to get used to it."

"You want me to…" Ari gestured to the wheel.

"I do." Oz'ki nodded.

Caris was cheering. "Go Ari!"

Ari gingerly pumped the wheel a couple of times, laughing when a couple of drops of muddy water splattered against his cheeks. "Oops."

"Perhaps a little too fast." Oz'ki laid his hand on top of Ari's foot and gently guided him to the right speed. "So, this is the clay. You need to keep it moist as you work. Every now and then, reach forward, dip your hands in that trough and sprinkle water over the clay."

Ari copied the move Oz'ki mimed.

"Now gently rest your elbows on your knees and let your hands hover over the clay. I want you to wrap your hands around the clay, squeeze slightly and pull upwards, so you're bringing the clay with you into a pillar shape."

As Oz'ki spoke, Ari followed his directions. His tongue peeked out as he concentrated.

"Good, now push down until you have a thick disc." Oz'ki leaned over and checked how Ari was doing. "Wet your hands a little more."

Ari grinned as he caught sight of Caris watching.

"Now put your thumbs on top and push down until you have a little divot there. That's it." He kept his eyes on what Ari was doing. "Now, pull your thumbs out at the same speed and strength so you open up the hole."

Oz'ki gently reached forward and took hold of one of Ari's hands, pulling it away from the clay. He quickly shaped his hand so he could use the flat part of his finger between two knuckles. "Now, keep that bit against the outside, the other hand on the inside and slowly bring the clay up again. That's it, you're doing great."

Ari bit his lip as he focused, beaming as he finished. Oz'ki slowly talked him through the final step, and soon enough, Ari had a pot. It was at a slight angle and one part of the lip dipped outwards, but he loved it. "I did it, Caris!"

Caris clapped. "You did."

Now the wheel was stopped, Ari stood and threw his arms around Oz'ki's waist. "Thank you so much. I enjoyed that."

Oz'ki nodded to the pot. "What are your favorite colors?"

Ari blushed. "I like cobalt blue."

"Ah, well, how about I fire the pot for you and glaze it with a rich green and cobalt blue swirling together. You can come back tomorrow and pick it up."

"Really? I can keep it?" Ari vibrated with happiness.

"You can. You've reminded me of the joy in simply working with the clay, feeling it and letting your emotions go. Besides, look…" He gestured to a demon examining his pot.

"Not a bad attempt for your first go, young Ari." The demon ran his finger over the clay. "Not too bad at all."

Oz'ki leaned down and whispered, "That's Ir'eki, the head potter."

"Thank you, Sir. And thank you for letting Oz'ki show me what you do. It was wonderful."

Ir'eki patted Ari on the shoulder. "Young demon, Potter Oz'ki is right. It's good to see someone simply enjoy creating. If you would allow me to, I would decorate your pot for you."

Stunned gasps echoed around them.

"I would like that, Sir, thank you." Ari dipped his head.

"Come see us again, say this time tomorrow, and it shall be ready." Ir'eki gently took the pot and walked to a room towards the back of the barn.

"Ari, you're… that's… any piece by Ir'eki is highly prized. He rarely decorates much anymore as his hands get too sore. He must have taken a liking to you, to offer that." Oz'ki shook his head, completely bemused. "Thank you for brightening up our day. It's been a while since we've seen him interested in something."

"No, thank you. I had so much fun." Ari took off his apron and handed it back, smiling as Oz'ki took up his position at the wheel again.

Flagging slightly, Ari leaned his head on Caris' shoulder.

"Come on, let's get you changed and back to the palace." Caris laughed as Ari nodded, letting himself be guided back to the underwear shop to change his clothes again.

CHAPTER SEVEN

Bo's tail whipped back and forth, stirring the motes of dust underneath it. "Veris, I need to know who is involved, was involved, or even looked at Caris funny. I need to know everything you know about his kidnapping. There has to be more going on here than we know."

Bo was fighting the urge to pace. The doctors warned him too much strenuous activity for the next week would risk setting his recovery back. There was no way he would be confined to bed again. He was a man of action; sitting and doing nothing went against everything he was.

Veris groaned. "I've already told Prince Dasalin everything."

"I want to hear it again. I also want to know everything you know about what happened to Aridien."

"What do you want to know about that little—" Veris clamped his lips shut at the look of rage on Bo's face. Maybe insulting the little man was *not* the way to go.

"Wise move, Veris." Dasa drawled from the doorway. "You do not want to push Bo on this. I would suggest you choose your words carefully, but tell him what he wants to know. I would advise extreme caution over how you refer to young Aridien as well."

Veris dipped his head, closing his eyes and taking a deep breath. "I don't know if Jari had anything to do with his capture. I honestly don't. But, she didn't seem at all surprised to see him there. What's more, I would be inclined to believe she knew who he was."

"I'm sorry, what?" Bo lifted up on his hands, about to push off out of his chair before Dasa gestured for him to stay.

"You're telling us that Jari knew who Aridien was? Explain." Dasa growled.

Veris shook his head back and forth. How did he get himself into these situations? "We were supposed to be meeting a contact Jari had. I don't know who it was, or who arranged it. Jari never told me."

"I thought you were meeting the Loperis?" Dasa prompted.

"We were— we did. There were two separate meetings planned. The first was with the Loperis. We went over to their ship. Frek, it smelled disgusting." Veris swallowed back the bile rising in his throat at the memory. "Jari ordered me to sit quietly, listen and watch. She wanted to make sure we weren't being cheated. Jari never was any good at paying attention to things. She was arguing over some obscure clause in the contract she'd become convinced gave the Loperis the rights to back out of the deal at any moment without penalty. There was nothing in the clause, and there was no persuading her otherwise. Things were getting tense. I was starting to worry about how it was going to end. Suddenly, the argument was interrupted by one of the Loperis guards running in— talking about the prisoner being difficult."

Veris pinched the bridge of his nose. "Things got a little chaotic after that. They weren't prepared to let us wander about by ourselves, so we were forced to go with them. That's the first time I saw Ari." Veris winced. "Tears were flowing down his cheeks, unchecked. His eye was blackened and there were marks on his back— he was in pants, nothing else. He looked so young in that moment, I honestly thought he was a child. I was about to step in." He looked up at Bo, anguish in his eyes. "I'm many things, but even I wouldn't stand by and let what I thought was a child be hurt like that. But Jari beat me to it."

"Jari?" Bo shared a look with Dasa.

"Yes, but not for the reasons you might think. She ran over to the Loperis standing over him with a whip and hauled it out of his hands. She was screaming, 'what have you done, what have you done?' over and over at the top of her voice. No one in that room, bar her, had the faintest idea what she was going on about. When I'd managed to calm her down— she was about to take on the Loperis, you know how hot-horned she is— well, it turns out she vaguely recognized Aridien."

Dasa took a couple of steps forward, placing a calming hand on Bo's shoulder, keeping him in place. "How the frek did she recognize him? If he was never allowed out of his rooms unless necessary, how could she…" Dasa's voice trailed off as he worked through the implications.

Veris sighed deeply. "Honestly, I don't know. She refused to say how or why she knew who it was. All she would say is that the Loperis had made a huge mistake in taking him."

"Do you know when or where he was taken from?" Bo's voice was slightly hoarse with restrained emotion.

"From what I understand, just on the edge of Alliance space. Another couple of galactic hours and he would have been safe in Barin territory."

"Or not so safe," Bo growled out.

"Or not." Dasa sighed.

"Why not safe? Anything had to have been better than being held by the Loperis." Veris shifted in his seat, his injuries still bothering him slightly.

Bo and Dasa shared a look and Dasa nodded. Bo grimaced and held Veris' gaze. "Because from what he has said, Ari's mother was using him to sweeten a deal with someone in the Alliance."

Speechless, Veris could only stare in incredulity. "Are you seriously telling me Ari's own mother was basically selling him?" Veris' scales hardened the minute Dasa dipped his head in confirmation. "Oh, frek no. You'd better have guards on him. If not, let me do it. He and Caris saved my life. I owe them, and even if I didn't, I want to change. I don't want to be the Veris I was."

Bo's brow furrowed. "Did they up my pain meds and I didn't notice? Because that is the only explanation I have for what I just heard."

Dasa patted Bo on the shoulder, making sure not to hurt his back. "I don't think so, otherwise it means someone slipped me something as well."

"What are you two going on about?" Veris growled.

"You!" Dasa chuckled. "This is not the Veris we know. Since when do you care about others?"

Veris slowly let his scales soften back to skin. "I guess you're right. I never used to care. But between Ari and Caris, they've shown me that life is better, fuller when you have friends. I've not had friends, not the way Ari and Caris have both offered. Despite how I've treated Caris in the past, he extended the hand of friendship. I won't fail that gift. I've never had someone want to be friends just because. It's not something I plan on losing. Caris and Ari are, well, they're pretty damn unique. If there is ever anything I can do for them, any of you just need to say the word and I'll do it."

Dasa sank into the seat beside Bo. "You're actually serious."

Veris relaxed into his seat. "I am. I admit to being… well, you know how I was, I hardly need to explain it. I won't make excuses for it. I will say I'm ashamed. Ashamed of how I let a guild attitude change who I was as a young demon. Ashamed of the way Reds believe they are better than everyone else, some even believing they are better than you Purples as well." Veris shrugged, apologetic. "The things I saw while on board that ship were disgraceful. I'm all for increasing trading rights and opening new routes up, but what Jari suggested, what Jari has become involved in, it's too much."

Dasa reached for his ale. "We know, from what you have said, she was responsible for the death of the previous Barin Ambassador."

Veris closed his eyes briefly. "I had no idea she'd taken things so far. I may have been all for extra trading rights— I firmly believe Kenistal can get better agreements than we currently do, but I would *never* take things that far. Her actions have so far included murder, abduction, assault, bribery, corruption, and treason. I told her she was on the brink of starting a war with the Alliance, a war which, no matter how good we are, we don't have the numbers to win. I truly am sorry for my part in her actions. But, with her being friends with the princess, it was hard to believe she didn't have serious backing."

Dasa let out a long, slow exhale. "My father has spoken to my sister. She assures him she had nothing to do with what was going on. I'm not convinced. My sister always has been devious. Yet, as bad as she is, I would like to think she draws the line at what Jari was involved in. Considering my sister, Jari and even Guild Master Kinesh's involvement, I cannot fault the way you have behaved. Not many could have stood up to their combined pressure. The fact is, you stood up for what was right in the end. You helped return Caris to us, bring Ari here. The good you have done outweighs the bad."

Veris turned and looked out the window. "You know, I often wonder if we do things the wrong way."

"Meaning?" Bo prompted.

"I was never like this when I was a young demon. It all started when I was a Red. The guild made me who I am today. I don't think it's a good thing."

Bo pursed his lips. "You think the guilds should allow anyone to join?"

"I think we need to consider it. Families abandon their children when they don't make it into one of the prestigious guilds. Since when should the color of your skin really make that much of a difference? I remember how I was treated the day before my rite. The minute I was Red, people treated me better. That's not right. I want to earn someone's respect and loyalty. I don't want it because of some outward appearance."

"I think, rather than consider banishing the rite, we look at improving the way the guilds are run. It is something we need to consider." Dasa broke off as a guard coughed discreetly in the doorway.

"You asked to be informed when Masters Caris and Aridien returned."

"Thank you. We'll continue this later, Veris. In the meantime, if you hear anything, then let us know."

"I will do."

As Bo and Dasa walked back to the entrance of the palace, Caris and Ari walked in. Bo stopped, foot frozen in mid-movement. Ari had changed clothes. *Tep'rink*, Bo's mind registered. He wore green tep'rink pants, the soft sinka sliding sinuously over his muscles, highlighting the curves. As he turned to say something to Caris, Bo nearly swallowed his tongue and his horns heated, steam rising in gentle wafts. The sinka cradled Ari's ass perfectly. Bo's mind bombarded him with images of sliding his hands over the smooth material, caressing Ari through it. The tight top Ari wore was again sinka, but this time it was gold and complemented his skin tones perfectly.

Thwack.

Bo rubbed the back of his head, turning to scowl at Dasa.

"You might want to get control of yourself before we go over there, your horns are steaming." Dasa chuckled.

Bo reached a hand up, touching his horns and grinning sheepishly. "He looks so damn good."

"He does. He looks like he's had fun— judging by his smile at least." Dasa checked Bo's horns were under control. "Let's go."

As they walked over, Ari turned back around and Bo was gratified to see his face light up into a beaming smile. "Bo!"

Ari went to hug Bo, but drew back, suddenly nervous about how he would take it. He bit his bottom lip and fiddled with the pocket in his new trousers.

"Ari, you look stunning. Those tep'rink look incredible on you." Bo's eyes raked over Ari, drinking in the sight of him, committing it to memory. "The colors are perfect."

"Th-thank you," Ari stuttered.

As Bo edged closer, he frowned as he studied Ari's face. "What have you two been up to, besides shopping?" He reached out and traced a smudge along Ari's cheek. "You have something…" His voice trailed off as he peered closer. "Is that… clay?"

Ari trembled under Bo's touch, but refused to pull back. "I met the potter Oz'ki. He's Deek'in's sister's mate. He let me have a go on the wheel. I made a pot!"

Bo couldn't stop the grin at seeing how excited Ari was. He was almost vibrating with happiness. "You made a pot?" He carried on gently rubbing at Ari's skin until the clay was gone. He dropped his hand down so that it cradled Ari's neck and his thumb traced along Ari's jaw. He could feel the pulse pick up speed under his touch.

Ari swallowed. Bo's touch was both relaxing and exciting him. "I did and Master Potter Ir'eki is going to decorate it for me. He wants me to go and pick it up tomorrow."

Dasa, having been engrossed in kissing Caris, whirled around. "Wait a minute, Ir'eki is going to decorate your pot for you? Master Potter Ir'eki?"

Deek'in who waited patiently just behind his charges stepped forward. "Your Highness, Master Potter Ir'eki spoke to Ari, saying that Ari had brightened his day, the way he had simply enjoyed creating something, the simple pleasure he'd taken in it. I got the impression that he hadn't seen that in a while. He offered to decorate the pot once it was fired. A true gift, I am sure you will agree."

"Ari, you stun me. Ir'eki is normally a cantankerous demon. He's incredibly gifted, his work is highly sought after and he can command a fortune, but he is not a personable demon. The fact he's willing to decorate your pot for you shows he must have taken a great liking to you. It's a true gift and one I hope you will treasure."

"I had so much fun there. Oz'ki taught me how to throw the pot properly, use the wheel, everything. It was great, especially after the demon with the soup."

Bo's eyes narrowed to slits. "What demon, what soup." He glared at Deek'in and Yavek. "What happened? I thought you were keeping an eye on them both?"

Yavek swallowed. The last thing they wanted was their Commander angry with them. "We did look after them."

Bo looked down as a small, soft hand caressed his hardening skin.

"It was nothing, Bo. Just a disagreement about how good an Aducian soup was." Ari moved so that he was between Bo and Yavek. He stood on his tiptoes and placed his hands on Bo's chest, marveling at the way the muscles bunched underneath his palms.

Bo's tail wrapped around Ari's waist, pulling him tight into his body, protecting him. Ari sagged against Bo's body, simply enjoying the closeness.

"Explain," Bo barked out.

Dasa leaned against the wall, pulling Caris into his arms, Caris' back touching his front, as they both watched Ari try to calm Bo down, who appeared to be getting angrier with the retelling. "I don't think he can avoid admitting just how invested he is in Ari anymore." Dasa chuckled.

"Was it ever really in question? He was hooked from the first moment he laid eyes on Ari. If it wasn't then, it was the first time Ari blushed. Your commander, your friend, is most definitely off the market." Caris started to snigger. "Oh, I can't wait to see this."

"See what?" Dasa nuzzled Caris' neck.

"Ari is innocent. Very innocent. Bo is going to have to go slow. In fact, Bo is going to have to *date* Ari."

"*Date?* As in *court* him? Does Bo even have the patience for that?" Dasa pursed his lips as he thought. "Oh, this is going to be so much fun. There are going to be countless opportunities to tease him."

"That's not nice." Caris spoiled his words by smirking. "Then, again, he did give us hell."

Dasa mock-glared at his mate. "You? He barely did anything to you. It was all me."

"Aww, is my big bad demon all upset?" Caris taunted.

"You, my little dynamo, are asking for trouble."

"Oh, I definitely am." Caris waggled his brows, making Dasa pull him in tighter as he moved his hand in-between their bodies and started to caress Caris' ass.

"Fine." Bo forcibly calmed himself down. "I won't go and have words with him. But, if I hear of anything like that happening again with this demon, then I *will* be having words. In fact, Ari, I'll go with you to get your pot tomorrow. We can always stop and have a meal while we are there."

Ari frowned as Deek'in and Yavek shared a look. "What am I missing?" He looked to Bo, then Dasa and Caris.

"Just demons being demons." Caris sighed. "Want to leave them to it and go visit Mac?"

Ari looked torn.

Bo bent and buzzed the top of his head with a kiss. "Go, I'll catch up with you later."

"You promise?" Ari rested his head against Bo's chest, hearing the steady thrum of his heart.

"I promise." Bo ran his hand down Ari's back, giving him a gentle pat on the ass. "Go have fun. I shall see you later."

Ari smiled up at him before jogging after Caris, who was already walking away.

CHAPTER EIGHT

Bo itched to have Ari in his arms. There were too many demons about, looking at him, assessing him and all Bo wanted to do was pull Ari into his arms and keep him there.

Ari could see what Bo meant. Whereas with Caris yesterday people were jostling each other, fighting and laughing, with Bo there was definitely a more subdued atmosphere in the market. It was as though Bo's presence alone was enough of a reason for demons to behave. Ari, despite knowing he was safe with Bo at his side, reached out and wrapped his hand around Bo's, holding on tightly.

Bo sighed. He wanted Ari closer, but holding hands would be enough… for the moment. He lifted Ari's hand and bent to place a tender kiss on his knuckles, winking as he did so.

"Is it always like this? Wherever you go I mean?" Ari questioned.

"You mean are people on their best behavior? Most of the time. It depends on the demons. Some see me as a challenge and want to fight." Bo heard the sharply indrawn breath. "Why, Ari, are you worried about me?"

Ari peeked up from behind his lashes. "Yes," he whispered.

Bo looked around, seeing a quiet street off to one side. He quickly walked Ari over, moving till he was up against the wall. He crouched down so he was in front of him. Reaching out, he tenderly cupped Ari's face, feeling a slight tremor under his palm. "You don't need to worry about me. Surely you've noticed I'm kind of big and scary looking." Bo winked.

"Not to me," Ari whispered, barely able to look at Bo.

"Oh? What do I look like to you, then?" Bo stroked the blush rising over Ari's cheekbones.

"You look like… I…" Ari stuttered.

"Ari…" Bo's voice softened, tenderness oozing out from him. "I want to be honest with you, but I don't want to scare you. I'm attracted to you. I want to spend time with you, getting to know you better, and yes, I so badly want to kiss you."

"Y-you do?" Ari's breath quickened as he searched Bo's eyes. "B-but, I'm little and I'm shy and I've never even kissed a man before." He ducked his head, embarrassed at the admission.

Bo groaned as a primal thrill ran through him. He'd suspected Ari was totally innocent, but hearing the words sent a jolt of possessiveness through him. "Ari, that doesn't stop me wanting to do it."

"It doesn't?" Ari's head snapped up.

"No." Bo brushed his thumb along Ari's lips. "I want to taste you, these lips, hold you tight against me, protect you. I'm not going to lie to you— eventually I want to make love to you. But, I know you aren't ready for that. I didn't mean to push this far now. I know you're not r—"

Bo's words were cut off as, with a sudden burst of courage, Ari slanted his head and pressed his lips to Bo's before pulling back and, his shyness returning, trying to pull away from Bo.

"Oh no, Mek Tiko, no escaping." Bo tenderly drew Ari back towards him and gently kissed him. He kissed his eyes, his nose, his cheeks and chin before finally settling on his lips. He cupped the back of Ari's head, holding him in place, smiling against the lips as Ari sagged into his hold, giving him all his weight. He traced Ari's lips with his tongue, loving the tremble running through the man. Nipping at his lips, he pulled back, resting his forehead against Ari's.

Ari was in shock, no doubt about it. He'd had his first kiss and it was… more than he'd ever imagined it to be. His lips were tingling, his heart thumping rapidly and his skin was vibrating. He kept his eyes shut, too scared to look at Bo.

"Ari, Mek Tiko, open your eyes," Bo coaxed softly.

"What does that mean?"

Ari's voice was so quiet, Bo struggled to hear it. "Mek Tiko? It means my little warrior."

"I'm no warrior." Ari shook his head so hard his curls bounced.

"Oh, but you are. The way you helped Caris when you were both held, the way you piloted the pod, the way you have been when faced with such massive changes. You are an amazing man, Mek Tiko."

Ari's eyes snapped open. "You really think so?"

"I do." Bo tenderly brushed his lips over Ari's once again. "Now get that cute little ass of yours moving. I want to see this pot."

Ari's forehead wrinkled. "You think I'm cute?"

Bo just laughed and stood, pulling Ari with him.

To Bo, it seemed as though he glided above the ground. The sheer joy he'd experienced since Ari had taken the first tentative step and kissed him was all-consuming. Not for one minute had he believed Ari would make the first move, and so soon. He squeezed Ari's hand, smiling at him when Ari looked up, grinning. "What do you want to do, other than pick up your pot?"

Ari looked around. "It's your home, your city. Perhaps you should choose? I'm happy doing anything. I saw so much yesterday. Yet, I think I barely saw anything of what there is."

Bo looked around them. "Well, yesterday you went shopping mostly. I can take you to see the rings of Hak'ran, but I don't think there is a match on today. Unless there are warriors training, then there won't be much to see. Our options are going to see the ruins of the old palace and arena, going to the cultural center and seeing some of the crafts and artwork on display, or we could just wander around and see if anything draws your attention."

"Is it wrong to want to do all of those things?" Ari shrugged sheepishly. "I mean, I never really did anything, so I have no idea what I might like."

"How about we start with one thing today and then we can plan lots of other dates… I mean trips." Bo fumbled with his words, not wanting to spook Ari into drawing away from him.

"I like the idea of going on dates with you." Ari peeked up at Bo.

"You do?" Bo stopped in the middle of the walkway, ignoring the demons who swarmed past them. He pulled Ari into him, wrapping his tail around his waist, realizing how much that move seemed to give him comfort.

"I do. There is no one I would rather show me new things, help me learn what it is I like and what I never want to do again after trying once. I know with you there I will be brave enough to try anything."

"Ari, you are brave every single day. You don't need me here for that. You have more courage than I have seen in one person. But, if I bring you a sense of security, if I help you have courage, then I am beyond thankful for that. I want to make you happy. I want to help you settle into your new life here. Simply, I want to do anything you want, so long as I get to spend time with you."

Ari blinked back his emotions. "You know I've never had friends like Caris and Dasa. Bar my guards, I've never had *any* friends. Caris and Dasa make me feel like I have something to give, something to share, that I can be someone's friend."

Bo's harsh breath echoed between them. "Am I not your friend, Ari?" He gently caressed Ari's cheek.

Ari leaned into Bo's touch. "I…" he took a moment to steel his resolve. "I don't want to be friends with you."

"You don't?" Bo's heart sank.

Ari was shaking, but determined to say the words. "I want… more."

Barely above a whisper, Bo still heard the words loud and clear. "Oh, Mek Tiko, that's what I want too." He drew Ari into his chest, wrapping both arms around him. There in the middle of the walkway, they simply held each other for a few minutes, soaking up each other's warmth. Eventually, Bo pulled away. "Come on, let's go and wander around the ruins. We can talk peacefully at the same time. I want to learn all about you."

Ari stood stock still, staring at the ruined archway. The deep blue stone was stunning, even as worn and crumbling as it was. Engravings ran from one end of the arch to the other. He looked to Bo.

"Tep'it okri asteliki aps lekis tep'it okri keriset. It basically means 'The might of the soul is stronger than the might of blood.' It's in reference to the first rulers who were Purple. They weren't considered fighters. That has always been the Cobalts. This is over two thousand years ago. Back then, Kenistal was ruled by the Cobalts. King Uxalik was nothing short of a tyrant. He took Kenistal to the brink of destruction. Guilds waged war on each other and the population was decimated. He played guild off guild, spreading lies and rumors, to what end no one ever knew.

"It was Le'brix from the Purple guild who managed to persuade some of the Cobalts, along with a mixture of other guilds to stand against Uxalik. Demonkind was tired of the fighting, the death and destruction. Le'brix was charismatic and managed to unite the guilds. They overthrew Uxalik. The alliance of guilds declared that the wisdom of the Purples outweighed the might of the Cobalts.

From that moment on, Kenistal has been ruled by the Purple demons. The strangest part was that the Purple demons have always come from one matriarchal line. The guild selection process, the Rite of Ferik has always existed, yet the Purples never change color from the day they are born. To this day, the only Purple demons are born to Dasa's family."

"So the might of the soul refers to?" Ari questioned.

Bo ran a hand over the engraving. "The wisdom and strength of Le'brix in banding the guilds together and defeating Uxalik. At the end, the highest ranking Cobalt left, Geriok Hevalis, my ancestor, swore his allegiance to Le'brix and vowed that the Cobalts would forever protect the Purples and ensure their right to rule."

Ari traced the symbol on one end of the engraving: that of a five pointed star with a hollow center. He realized this was the symbol he'd seen on the documents he'd signed making him a citizen of Kenistal. This was the symbol for Dasa's family, for Kenistal itself. "Has it been peaceful since then?"

"Frek, no." Bo chuckled. "There have been plenty of battles and attempts to overthrow the various guilds, but it's always stopped short of outright rebellion against the Purples. The stories of what happened during that period are still passed down from generation to generation. They are considered a very cautionary tale about what can happen when greed is allowed to flourish. Yet, I can't help but feel the Reds are starting to follow the same pathway. We will be watching them closely from now on."

Ari shifted so he was in front of Bo and leaned back slightly, wanting to be close to Bo, yet scared to take the step.

Bo didn't even hesitate; he gently pulled Ari back against him and nuzzled his curls. "Want to go explore the palace?"

"Yes." Ari tilted his head back, giggling as he looked at Bo upside down. "You look strange like that."

Bo stuck his forked tongue out, gently licking Ari's nose, making him giggle. "Come on, let's go and see what we can find. Some of the rooms are fairly intact."

"Intact? Surely anything left will have been looted. I mean, doesn't that normally happen with ruins?" Ari lifted his head, scared of getting too dizzy.

"Yes, it happens with other ruins on this world, but this place is considered such an important part of our history that it's left as it is."

"But why hasn't anyone saved everything left inside?" Ari wondered.

"Frankly, no one has considered it. But, if it's survived two thousand years here, it's going to be alright. Still, it might be worth mentioning it to Dasa. I can honestly say I've never even considered that everything here could be moved and preserved. It would be tragic to lose such an important part of our past."

Bo released Ari from his arms, before grabbing one of his hands and pulling him forward. "Come on. I haven't explored this place since I was a demonling."

Ari burst out laughing at the almost child-like exuberance Bo was displaying. As they walked through the doorway to the palace, there was an immediate sense of history as though it was a palpable entity. "What is that?"

"You feel it?" Bo laid his hand over Ari's lower back, guiding him over some loose rocks. "Legend has it, that sensation is the lost souls who still wander the grounds of the palace. Those who guarded the kings back then and refused to abandon their posts, even in the face of death, still patrol the grounds now. The legend maintains if there is ever a need, they will step forth through the barrier and protect those who have need of their aid."

"Should I be scared?" Ari whispered as his gaze danced furtively around as though he was worried about spying one of the lost souls.

"No. But remember, I will always protect you." Bo led Ari off to one side, into a room that ran the entire length of the palace.

"What was this?" Ari's voice echoed around the stone walls.

"There are two opinions on that. Some believe it was a throne and meeting room, others believe it was a ballroom."

85

"A ballroom? I thought Caris told me demons don't dance?"

Bo threw back his head, howling with laughter. "Is that what Dasa told him? Oh, demons do dance, it's just Dasa who doesn't. But, that could be more to do with the fact that he can't. I've seen him try."

Ari giggled at the thought of Dasa being unable to do something. The demons always seemed so gifted at everything they did. "Do you dance?" he asked Bo shyly.

"Why, Ari, are you wanting me to hold you in my arms and sway to some music?"

Ari smiled. "I've never danced. I've never done much of anything. I couldn't risk using my compcube for music. The guards smuggled it in for me and there was no way I was going to get them into trouble for doing it. A lot of the household staff would have done anything to gain any advantage. Letting my mother know I had contraband would have given them a boost in position."

"Forgive me, but your home, your world, does not seem a very... friendly place. It seems like every Aducian is out for themselves, never caring about anyone else." Bo frowned. Kenistal had demons like that, but as a whole they all respected each other.

"Not *everyone* is like that, but Aducia is governed by trade, and everything comes down to credits. As you know with my mother, for some, there is little they won't do for credits."

"I just can't imagine that. If I am ever lucky enough to have my own demonlings, there is nothing I wouldn't do for them. They, along with my man, would be the center of my galaxy."

Ari stumbled at Bo's words. "You want your own demonlings?"

Bo took a seat on a disused bench along the wall, swiping off the dust before bringing Ari to sit in his lap. "Ari, I've always wanted my own demonlings." He relaxed as Ari got comfortable, willing his cock not to harden at the feel of Ari's sweet ass wriggling about on his lap.

86

Ari laid his head on Bo's chest as he looked around the room, wondering if Bo knew what he was. "Bo?" he asked a few minutes later, enjoying the sensation of Bo gently running his fingers through his curls.

"Yes, Tiko?" Bo's head was resting against the wall as he relished the peace for a few minutes.

"Do you know what I am?" Ari's voice quivered with nerves.

"You're a man?" Bo grinned, sensing that Ari was rolling his eyes without looking at him. He laughed when Ari gently tapped him on the stomach. "Ow, you have some power there, Tiko."

Ari giggled. "I mean, do you know about Aducians? About how we have children?"

Bo hugged Ari tighter. "I do."

"That doesn't disturb you?" Ari hid his face in Bo's shoulders.

Bo gently lifted Ari's chin up, so he could look down into his eyes. "There is nothing about you that could disturb me. But, no, men having demonlings, children, little ones, it does not upset me. There is a planet close by us. Caris has friends there. One of them, Corin, recently gave birth to a little one."

"There are other species like me where the men have children?" Ari's eyes lit up. He'd thought for sure that there were no others like him. For too long, he'd been treated like he was less than others.

"There are. Corin is mated to a clan leader on Landran. They have a son, Chance. In fact, Caris was coming back from seeing them when he was kidnapped. He can tell you more about them."

"I would like that. I've always liked children. On the few occasions I got to see them, they were always kind. They didn't judge me because of who I was, they didn't ignore me, they were kind and friendly." Ari wanted to purr, he was enjoying Bo's touch so much. He giggled at the thought.

"What are you giggling about?" Bo grinned as he nuzzled Ari's cheek.

"I was just thinking I could almost purr, I'm so content."

"I'm making you want to purr, am I?"

"Uh-huh." Ari hid his face.

"No, no hiding from me, Tiko. This is us, whatever we do, whatever we feel, we should always be honest with each other. I want to know what you are feeling. If I do something you don't like, something you are not ready for, then you need to tell me. I can't read minds, no matter how much I might want to."

Ari's heart beat so wildly, Bo could feel it through the hand resting on Ari's chest. "Oh? Is there something you don't want me to know?"

"I, um…"

"Ah, Tiko, you can tell me anything." Bo gently caressed Ari's chest.

"I want you to kiss me again."

"It would be my pleasure." Bo turned Ari so he was more comfortable and gently claimed Ari's lips. The feel of Ari surrendering to him, submitting, sent a wave of possessive heat flooding his senses. Ari was his, no doubt about it.

Ari's soul was soaring. He couldn't think, he could only feel. There was only Bo and the way they connected, the feel of Bo's lips on his, the hand caressing his neck, the one tunneled through his hair. His cock hardened painfully and he shifted about, trying to relieve the tension.

Bo pulled back. As much as he wanted to devour Ari, he needed to take it slow. "Damn, you look beautiful like that. Come on, let's go and explore some more. If we stay here, I just might ravish you." Bo grinned as he heard Ari mutter under his breath.

"I wouldn't mind being ravished."

CHAPTER NINE

Ari was trying not to make any noise. He knew Bo was indulging him. He was letting Ari hide and attempting to find him in the ruins. It was a childish thing to do, but Ari didn't care. He was loving experiencing everything he'd missed out on as a child. Trying not to make a sound, he crept through the dusty ruins, hiding behind a worn bookcase that was pulled slightly away from the wall, which was crumbled in places. He studied the hole. He could probably squeeze through there. Bo definitely wouldn't be able to follow. He smiled to himself as he eased his body through. He pushed his arm through first and eased his left shoulder through the gap. Once that was through, he knew he could get his whole body out the other side. The useless things he'd learned from the hours spent on his compcube. He watched vids of explorers in the caves of his home world, trying to find the gems that were so highly sought after.

Pushing up to standing, he looked around the new room. It appeared to be a private study. From the faded opulence, he would guess that it had belonged to a king or someone of importance. Weaves were displayed on some of the walls, and rugs were covering the floor. Being careful not to stir too much dust, he walked around the room. Judging by the lack of footprints, no one had discovered this room, or certainly hadn't for a long time.

He held his breath as he heard Bo in the first room.

"Ariiiii!" Bo's voice was almost singing. "Where are you, Mek Tiko? I want to see you, kiss you."

Ari's eyebrows narrowed. Evil demon was trying to tempt him out with kisses. Nope, not going to happen. No matter how good Bo's lips were, he wanted to win this game. Besides, he'd learned a thing or two from his time hiding out with Caris. He was going to use everything Caris taught him in his attempts to avoid Bo.

Bo looked around the room. Dust motes still danced in the air. From where he was stood, it was impossible for it to have been his movement that had stirred them. Which meant only one thing, or rather one person. Ari.

"Ari, I know you're here." He listened, hoping to detect a trace of noise. "Ari, Mek Tiko, I can see your footprints. I know you were here. I plan on finding you, you know. And when I do…. I plan on claiming your lips again."

There… was that a whimper? Bo cautiously walked further into the room. A beam of sunlight streaked across from the window to the far wall, the dust motes dancing inside it like stars glinting in the night sky. He followed the footprints to an old bookcase, many of the books still in place. A couple were lying on the floor. He knelt down, seeing a series of footprints. Ari was definitely here at some point. He frowned as he looked around the room. There was nowhere for Ari to hide, but he couldn't see any footprints leaving either. Ari was better at this game than he'd expected. He loudly walked towards the door. "I guess I'd better check another room then." He left, and moved to the side of the door, peeking in, waiting.

Ari crouched on the floor by the hole he'd climbed through. He sighed. He couldn't see anything but the bookcase. Looking around the room, he saw a loose stone at the same height as his chin. He gently eased the stone out and peeked through. He could just make out the doorway, and Bo's horns beside it. Looked like Bo was trying to trick him. Nope, he wasn't going to fall for that. He eased back from the room and quietly explored as he waited Bo out.

There was a large, carved wooden table taking a prominent position along one wall, underneath two sconces. He wondered just how old these ruins were. He ran his finger over the parchment there. Brushing the dust off, he could see delicate, scrolling handwriting. The demon language was beyond him, but the penmanship was exquisite. The pen was lying discarded to one side, a pot of ink left open, although it had long since dried up. What sort of hurry must someone have been in to leave everything like this? What's more, it looked like they had never returned. As he moved away from the desk, he stubbed his foot on something, biting his tongue to prevent crying out. Hopping about, silently cursing, he scowled down at the offending article, only to find it was a carved wooden box, the corner jutting out from underneath the desk.

Shaking off the last of the pain, he retrieved the box, lifting it up onto the desk. Feeling nervous, yet compelled to look inside, he carefully lifted the lid and gasped. There inside was a delicate… crown? It was made of what looked like braided gold, with each braid looking like a demon tail. Every so often, a braid would trail off and end in a gemstone. It was almost as if they were representing the tail of a demon. He looked closer. The uppermost part of the braid had little prongs above every tail. He grinned to himself. Horns. The crown represented the horns and tails of demons. The end of each horn glistened with a tiny crystal. The whole thing was beautiful and stunning. He gently placed it back in the box.

Looking around the room, he wondered what he should do. A sense of wrongness permeated his soul when he thought about taking it out to show Bo. Shivers wracked his spine and the air around him cooled. He carefully put the box back where he found it. He smiled softly as a sense of peace invaded him. Whatever it was, whoever it had belonged to, it needed to stay in the room. "I won't take it, I promise," he whispered into the empty room.

Taking one last look around, he checked through the smaller hole to see the coast was clear. Carefully, he returned the loose stone to its place, preventing anyone else from realizing there was a room hidden behind the bookcase. Peeking around the case, he carefully slid out from behind it. Tiptoeing to the doorway, he checked in each direction, making sure Bo wasn't visible. Laughing to himself, he ran back to the hall. He climbed up the stairs, cursing the fact demons were so tall. It was quite a stretch for his muscles, and after a couple he gave up, sitting down to wait for Bo to return.

Bo braced himself against the slightly rotten doorjamb as he watched Ari attempt to climb up the stairs. He shouldn't laugh, but the look of frustration on Ari's face was adorable. His Tiko was definitely pouting. In fact, Ari was now sitting a couple of steps up from the bottom. The stairs were tall enough for him that he was swinging his legs back and forth as he hummed to himself, the bottom of his feet just brushing over the top of the stair below him.

"Having fun there, Mek Tiko?" Bo stalked towards Ari. "I found you here. Does this mean I can claim my kiss as a reward?"

Ari narrowed his eyes. "Were you watching me climb these stairs?"

Bo opened his mouth to agree, then thought better of it. "No, why would I do that?" He aimed for his most innocent expression.

Ari raised a brow. "You were, weren't you? You watched me struggle and didn't do anything."

"The view was too good," Bo mumbled.

"What view?" Ari challenged, standing up, hands on hips.

"Uh, you heard that, then?" Bo's sheepish voice made Ari smile.

"Yes, I heard, what view?"

"I was looking at your ass." Bo looked anywhere but at Ari's face.

"You were looking at my ass." Ari stood and tried to peer over his shoulder at his own ass, making Bo laugh. "Why?"

"Because it's gorgeous." Bo waggled his eyebrows.

"It's too small," Ari whispered.

"It's perfect." Bo stepped in front of Ari, reaching around and cupping the ass in question. "It fills my hands, and has just the right amount of softness. I could feel it, look at it all day."

As Bo pulled Ari in tighter, he ghosted his lips over Ari's ear. "There's not a single part of you that doesn't drive me crazy."

"Really?" Ari whispered.

"Really." Bo risked taking another kiss, groaning as Ari surrendered to him. This time, he teased Ari's lips with his tongue until they opened, gently darting into his mouth to taste him. His cock hardened painfully when Ari tentatively countered the move with his own tongue. Knowing he needed to take things slow, he eased back before placing one last soft kiss on Ari's lips. "Come on, Tiko, I think it's time I fed you."

Ari could only nod. He slipped his hand into Bo's knowing he would happily follow Bo anywhere.

CHAPTER TEN

Bo's scales were threatening to harden. He stared Ulkrit down. He'd deliberately chosen to come to Chebrint'ki, the same restaurant Caris and Ari had gone to before. He'd promised he wasn't going to say anything, but that didn't stop him wanting to present a deliberately intimidating presence in front of the demon who had gotten angry of Ari's opinion.

"Commander Bo'saverin. It's, uh, good of you to join us today. What can I get for you?" Ulkrit's tail was tucked between his legs, the tip tucked in tight against his ankle. His skin was as soft as possible and his head was partially bowed.

Ari watched the byplay with interest. This was a totally different demon from the one he'd encountered previously. Gone was the hostility and aggression, and in its place was a mild and slightly meek demon.

"I hear you cook Aducian food." Bo deliberately baited Ulkrit. Besides, he actually wanted to try something that Ari was used to.

Ulkrit's gaze was darting back and forth between Bo and Ari. "I do."

Ari waved to Perik on the other side of the square, laughing when Perik looked between the two of them and winked. Ari grinned. He was already planning on going back to Perik's shop. The shorts they'd picked up were incredibly comfy and they made him feel sexy. As strange as it was, they had given him the confidence to kiss Bo. Not sure if his attempts at flirting were successful, he was still happy to know that Bo was responding to him. Quite why, he had no idea, they were so different, but for whatever reason Bo maintained he was attracted to him, he was going to go with it and enjoy it. Ari promised he'd give himself the freedom to experience new things, to go with the flow and be open to anything. Too many years spent cooped up and he was determined to make up for lost time. Bo's voice dragged him back to the present.

"How about you bring us a selection of both Aducian food and Kenistalian food." Bo still stared Ulkrit down. "I trust you to make a wise selection— dishes that our palates will find pleasant."

Ulkrit bowed. "It would be my honor, Commander." He turned to Ari and bowed deeply. "I apologize again for yesterday. I meant no insult. I pride myself on replicating dishes from around the universes and have never had someone question one before. I would be honored if you would let me know how I can improve on any of your native dishes."

Bo nodded at Ari to go ahead. Ulkrit seemed genuine. Of course, it wouldn't stop him keeping an eye on him for a while.

Ari's smile lit up his face. "I would be honored to help you. I thought once I left Aducia I would never get the same food again. It will be nice to know I still can."

Ulkrit breathed out a sigh of relief. "Thank you, Little Demon." He bowed again before leaving them to it.

Bo cocked his head to one side. "What's with the Little Demon?"

"Deek'in decided on the name." Ari took a sip of the teo that one of the servers brought them. The sweet, warm berry mix was perfect for him. "He told me now that I'd signed the papers to make me a Kenistalian, I was a demon. He also insisted I had the courage of a demon. From that moment, he's referred to me as the little demon."

Bo took Ari's hand across the table, gently caressing the knuckles. "He's right, you know. You have an incredible amount of courage, more than most people, whatever their race. I'm in awe of you, Tiko. I know of few demons who could have gone through what you did and still come out smiling. You are incredible. Your mother was a fool for not seeing just how special her son was. I would never want you to go through even a minute of hurt, yet I find I can't be unhappy that your life has brought you here. After all, it brought you to me. And I don't plan on letting you go any time soon."

Ari turned his hand over underneath Bo's and squeezed. "I'm glad I ended up here, with Caris, with you."

Before Bo could respond, their first dishes appeared.

Ari's eyes widened at the sheer volume of dishes crowding the octagonal table. "We can't possibly eat all this." Ari studied the vast array of different foods.

"Oh, Tiko, did no one ever explain to you? We demons have voracious appetites."

Bo's grin was so wide Ari couldn't stop laughing.

Bo selected a piece of hid'link, a small ball of meat covered in a spicy crispy crust. He held it up to Ari. "Try this."

Ari looked at Bo, then at the ball in his fingers. *Can I do this?* Rather than take the piece with his fingers, he leaned forward and gently wrapped his lips around the small ball, his tongue tracing over Bo's fingers as he did so. He did a mental fist pump when Bo's eyes flared with lust. He was starting to truly believe that Bo was interested in him. Everything the demon did demonstrated his sincerity and his attraction.

"Oh, Tiko, you're playing with fire." Bo coughed, trying to clear the hoarseness from his voice.

"Bo? Why are your horns steaming?"

Ari's innocent question brought Bo up short. His face heated.

Ari studied Bo's face. "Your cheeks are darker… Bo, are you blushing? I had no idea demons could blush."

The line of color on Bo's cheeks got deeper. "We, uh, can blush. It just doesn't happen very often."

"So why are you blushing now?" Ari whispered, somehow wary of the answer.

"Because you asked about my horns." Bo's hand instinctively went to his horns before he stopped them.

"Was it wrong to ask?" Ari ducked his head.

"No." Bo quickly ran a finger down Ari's cheek. "My, uh, horns, are steaming because I'm, umm, excited, *you* make me excited. It's taking all my willpower not to just grab you and kiss you senseless."

"I wouldn't mind that," Ari confessed.

"Oh, Tiko, you don't make things easy, do you." Bo couldn't stop the chuckle, making Ari grin. "Now be good while we eat. Then I promise I will kiss you senseless."

The dinner was full of laughter and teasing. Ari looked around at the amount of plates they'd gone through. "Demons can really eat."

Bo grinned. "I need all the strength I can get running around after Dasa. Besides, I plan on beating him at Pik'dorin."

"Do you often battle with him, then?"

"I do. There are few demons that are prepared to go head to head with him. The arena battles can be vicious. It's not like the rings of Hak'ran, where we battle for position, for rank and prestige. Pik'dorin is considered one of the ancient arts. Our ancestors practiced it and not everyone trains in it. The pole we use is sharp on one end. It helps us use it to propel our movements. The end can be driven into the ground and provide some stability. But, it can also be used as a weapon. Nowadays it's more an art form than a battle move. It's hard to describe. You get into a mental zone where all that exists is your body, the way your muscles move, the placement of your limbs. It's a hard workout, but very satisfying. It takes a lot of concentration. If you misjudge your moves by even the smallest amount, especially when you are balanced on top of the pole, it can lead to injuries."

"It sounds dangerous."

"It is, but it's also exhilarating. Will you come and watch when I battle Dasa?" Bo held his breath, worried Ari wouldn't want to.

"I would love to, as long as you aren't going to get hurt. I don't think I could watch that," Ari confessed.

"I can't promise it won't happen, but both Dasa and I are good. We rarely make mistakes. Besides, Caris and your guards will be with you the entire time. Deek'in and Yavek can tell you how things are going. I don't think Caris has watched a match before." Bo gestured to Ulkrit, handing over his credit chip.

"Did you enjoy the meal?" Ulkrit held his breath, waiting for the answer.

"It was perfect. I've missed some of the Aducian food. Thank you for making it for me. If you would like, I can come around one day and talk about spices and dishes with you," Ari offered.

Ulkrit blinked a few times. "After the way I treated you, I'm surprised you want anything to do with me, but I would gladly take you up on your offer."

"You won't be treating him like that again, will you?" Bo growled as he helped Ari stand and tucked him into his side.

"No, I won't. I've learned my lesson," Ulkrit assured them. "Please know you are both always welcome here."

Ari gestured to the plates littered behind him on their table. "With that sort of food available, I will happily come back here and often."

"Thank you." Ulkrit bowed long and deep before gesturing for servers to start clearing the table.

Ari grabbed Bo's hand and started to drag him over to the Potter's Barn.

"Excited to see your pot, are you?" Bo couldn't help teasing him.

"I had so much fun making it. I want to see how it turned out."

"I can't wait to see what Ir'eki has done for you. I don't think you realize just how special the gift he's giving you is." Bo rested his hand against the back of Ari's neck, grasping it slightly, the connection grounding him.

"I don't care that he's truly talented, or how rare a gift this is," Ari vowed. "To me, the fact that anyone would be so kind is a gift, no matter how talented they are, and I will treasure the pot no matter what."

"And that is part of the reason I have decorated it for you, Little Demon." Ir'eki spoke from just behind them, making Ari jump.

Ari turned and impulsively hugged Ir'eki, who patted him on the back as he returned the hug. "Gah, you make an old man happy, Little Demon." He ruffled Ari's curls as he pulled away. "Now, just how excited are you to see your pot?"

Bo grabbed Ari's hand. "He's been talking about it all day. Thank you for letting him work the clay. It means a lot to me that you gave him that experience."

"We didn't do it for you, but for our little demon here." Ir'eki grumbled. "His natural exuberance is hard to ignore. The joy he found in it reminded me of myself when I first started out. There is a tranquility to working the clay, the happiness in creating something from the earth. The sense of achievement you feel at your finished piece. Little Demon, you are always welcome here any time. Now, let me go and get your pot." Ir'eki slowly walked off, relying on a cane to navigate around the wheels and various tables within the barn.

Ari wandered over to one of the wheels where a potter was creating an elaborate candlestick, or at least, that's what it looked like to Ari. The way he manipulated the clay was mesmerizing. When Ir'eki returned, he was still engrossed. He jumped when he was tapped on the shoulder. He gasped when he caught sight of the pot.

"That can't be mine?" Ari studied the pot Ir'eki gave him. It looked like his shape-wise, but that was where the similarity ended. In its place was a stunning example of art. The pot was two-tone with a rich cobalt blue and a green that reminded him of his own hair. Overlaid in a delicate gold were outlines of him and Bo. At least he presumed it was the two of them. They were walking hand in hand in one scene, Bo's head dipped down to talk to Ari. In another scene, Bo was in mid-stretch reaching for a flaming ring of some kind. All around the pot there were action scenes, with one or both of them depicted. Ari's gaze flew to Ir'eki's.

"It's stunning. I… words are failing me. I have never seen something so beautiful. If I am allowed to keep it, it's something I will treasure always."

"It belongs to you, Little Demon. It was an honor to work on it for you. I know you place no monetary value on it, instead it is purely sentimental." Ir'eki's gaze collided with Bo's, clearly able to see the thanks in the Cobalt's eyes.

Bo opened his mouth to speak when there was a commotion at the entrance to the courtyard. At least five heavily armed Reds were accompanied by several Loperis. Bo's hand flew to his implant. "Emergency break-through. All Cobalts in the vicinity of Yiklin courtyard make haste. Armed Reds and Loperis here. I need help."

Even as he spoke, Bo was pulling his weapons from his belt, gaze rapidly scanning the courtyard. So many civilians and no one to help. This was not going to be pretty. As he started to shift his scales, Ari's concerned gaze collided with his.

"Bo, you can't, the doctors said you weren't healed enough."

"I don't have a choice." Bo glanced at Ir'eki. "Take Ari with you and lock down the barn. Stay until the guards get here." There was no time to wait for a response. He winced as his scales rippled into place, the damage from the beam that had fallen on him pulling at the scars still healing. All around the courtyard, demons were scrambling to get safe. Bo raised his weapons as the Reds charged.

CHAPTER ELEVEN

Bo parried a blade aimed for his throat as he pulled his arm up and slammed it into the back of the skull of a Loperis trying to sneak up on his left. He sensed a presence behind him and ducked instinctively, the sword whistling as it passed over his horns. He pushed two Reds out of the way and broke into a run as he saw the Loperis aim for the potters' barn, and Ari. His comm link was still active and he screamed for assistance.

It was Dasa's voice that replied. "Two minutes out. Hold on."

"I don't know if I can, there are—" Bo grunted as a blade slammed into his calf. The only thing stopping serious damage were his scales, but the impact still hurt, the point of the blade managing to pierce under one of his scales and slice his skin. He grabbed one of the Loperis around the neck as he reached for Ari, who was scrabbling to get away as he helped Ir'eki, who had fallen in the chaos.

"Grab the Aducian!" One of the Reds screamed over the noise of the fight. "Ignore the Commander, it's not him we're after."

Two Reds, masked to hide their identities, jumped on Bo, taking him down in a pile of twisted limbs. Two were still down, along with two of the Loperis. Yet there were still too many advancing on them. "Ari, run. RUN!"

Ari hesitated a split second, terrified to leave Bo alone, facing what looked to be certain death, before he turned to follow Bo's orders. Three Loperis advanced on him, and one of them threw a blade at Ir'eki. Ari pulled him down, the blade whizzing past their ears.

"Go, Little Demon, run," Ir'eki ground out through the pain flaring through his body.

"Ari!"

Ari focused on the shout and saw Perik gesturing wildly to him to run his way. He ran.

Perik grabbed him by the arm as soon as he was in range. "Go through the back of the shop, there's a door there." He gestured to the other shopkeepers who were standing near him. "We'll slow them down."

Ari didn't have a chance to respond as he was pushed into the shop, the demons closing ranks behind him. Some were carrying craft tools, anything they could get their hands on, prepared to defend the little demon.

Bo caught sight of Ari escaping out of the corner of his eye. He could only hope their new protectors could buy him enough time. He managed a grin as two chefs, Ulkrit one of them, raced into the fray with their knives.

The pounding of footsteps racing towards them brought relief until he saw it wasn't the guards he was hoping for— instead, it was more Reds. *What the frek were they hoping to achieve?* He managed to push his way free from the pile on the ground to find chaos all around them. The able-bodied craftsmen were doing everything they could to help him out. No doubt the dislike most guilds had for the Reds was a major part of that. More likely, it was the presence of the Loperis that had so many citizens ready to defend their Commander and the little demon. *Ari.* Bo's heart broke at the thought of him being hurt, of Bo himself being killed and never seeing him again. He ruthlessly pushed those feelings to one side. Now was not the time to become distracted. A shout snapped his head up and he caught the long pole one of the silversmiths sent flying his way. Pik'dorin. He could use his skills. He quickly jammed the pole into the ground and pushed with all his strength. The pole wobbled without the stabilizing spike driven into the ground, but it was enough to propel himself over the backs of the Loperis in front of him. He pulled the pole around, using it to sweep the Loperis off their feet. He quickly reversed the pole and slammed it into their backs. He heard a snap, hoping it was enough to take at least one of the Loperis out.

One end of the pole was suddenly grabbed and yanked. He lost his footing and stumbled to the side. The action gave two Reds enough time to grab his arms. As more Reds joined them, they started to punch into his stomach and chest, claws out, trying to do as much damage as possible.

"Where has the Aducian gone, Commander?" a deeply modulated demon voice growled out.

Bo stayed stubbornly silent. His neck snapped as his head propelled backwards by the strength of the fist slamming into his face. He spat out the blood pooling on his tongue.

"Where is he?" the demon screamed in his face.

Bo growled. "You'll never find out from me." Something slammed into the back of his legs and they buckled, driving him to his knees. His arms were forcibly extended out and back, behind him. A foot slammed into his back. Pain raced through him as some of the stitches from his surgery strained under the onslaught. With his legs out from under him, arms extended and back bowed, he was completely at their mercy. He continued to struggle, desperate to get free and race after Ari. Suddenly his horns were grabbed and yanked. His neck arched, pain slamming through him as the muscles were taxed to the limit. His defiant gaze never left the masked Red in front of him. The muted sounds of fighting permeated his mind, but he could do nothing other than focus on the demon in front of him.

"When I get the little Aducian, I plan on having my way with him before passing him on. If he's good enough, I might just pass him around my men as well."

White hot rage roared through Bo. He relaxed his body, surprising the demons holding him. Suddenly, he slammed his arms outwards, strained upwards on the tops of his feet, soles exposed, and bowed his back before immediately reversing the move, breaking free from the hold. He yanked the closest demon around, pulling him in front of him as one of the Reds slammed a blade forward. It pierced through the stomach of the Red in front of him. The blade was so sharp it went through his scales with no resistance.

He had to arch his body to avoid the tip of the blade now protruding from the back of the Red he'd used as a shield.

He freed the Red's blade from his limp hand, his own long since taken from him, and let the body drop. Out of the corner of his eye, he saw a flash of distinctive blue. Help had arrived.

Ari stumbled through the shop, knocking into displays of lacy underwear. Flinging them to one side, he could barely see as tears of worry, anger and frustration ran down his cheeks. He wanted nothing more than to turn around and help Bo. Yet what help could he be? He was no match for any demon one on one, and certainly not against that many. He simply needed to hope the other Cobalts came to Bo's aid. He'd recognized the Loperis. How could he not? They were there for him, there could be no doubt. Was this more of his mother's cronies looking for him? How had they found him?

He stumbled out of the back door of the shop, into a dark alley. All around him were doorways leading into other shops. Rather than risk bringing trouble to other people, he ran down the long alleyway and out through a slightly rundown street. With no idea where he was, he simply ran, hoping it was away from the fight. He looked around, desperately searching for any kind of landmark he could use to get his bearings. There was nothing until… *there*— in the distance, he could see the ruins Bo had taken him to earlier in the day. Trying to regulate his breathing, he put on a burst of speed. Every instinct was telling him to turn back and help Bo, but he would honor Bo's wishes and run. Away from the fight, away from the Loperis, away from the man he was falling for.

He heard the echoes of footsteps racing after him. He guessed they were still some distance away, but he didn't slow down for even a moment, racing towards the relative safety of the ruins. He dodged everything in his path, whether they were demons or objects. He slipped at one point, slamming into a wall, cursing himself. He didn't stop to check if he'd hurt himself. It wouldn't matter if they caught up with him. What he was facing was a thousand times worse than anything he could do to himself while running. The thought of what could happen spurred him on, pushing past his limits to run faster, run further.

His surroundings blurred, his focus purely on the tall, crumbling pillar of the ruins. He slowed to a jog by the time he ran past the archway he and Bo had stopped at. He ran up the steps to the entrance, thankful they weren't as steep as the stairs inside. As soon as he crossed the threshold, he turned left, running down the long corridor, straight to the previous room. He retraced his earlier steps, slipping behind the bookcase and pushing his way into the hidden room. In his desperate scramble, he forgot about a jagged rock sticking out in the middle of the crawl space and cut his arm open as he pulled himself through.

Collapsing to the floor, he fought to regulate his breathing. *Too fast, Ari, slow down, in and out, in and out.* His mental chant helped him bring not just his breathing, but the wild panic flooding his system, under control. Eventually, he managed to crawl under the desk, tucking his legs in tight, for once thankful for his small size. Even if someone managed to find the room he was hiding in, they wouldn't see him.

Tipping his head back, his eyes slid shut. *Two minutes' rest, let me get my breath back, then I'll see to my arm.* His breathing slowed as shock and exhaustion set in. Within seconds, he slipped into a deep, shock induced sleep.

Bo staggered as he deflected the blade, his knees buckling from the effort to keep going, the multiple small cuts from blades and claws, starting to take their toll when combined with the constant pain in his back. He should never have shifted; the damage to his scales had been too great. Yet, if he hadn't, he wouldn't be alive now. He swung his laser blade back around, trying to catch another weapon aimed his way, but his movements were too slow. He braced for impact.

A blade between him and his opponent sent the axe clattering to the ground. He looked up as his legs finally gave way into the concerned gaze of his prince and friend. *Dasa.*

"Frek, how badly are you injured?" Dasa dropped to the ground beside him as a ring of warriors encircled them.

"Don't know." Bo's words were soft, his strength leaving him. "Too many. Ari…"

"Where is he?" Dasa was rapidly scanning the area as more Cobalts flooded the courtyard. The Reds and Loperis were being quickly beaten and subdued in the wake of the overwhelming numbers.

"Told him to run. Went through shop. Lost sight of him. Need… to… find him." Bo's breath was coming faster now as his pain increased, the adrenaline wearing off. He tried to push up, but a hand to his chest stopped him.

"You're going nowhere. I'll send patrols out looking for him. You need to see a doctor. Frek knows what damage you've done to your back." Dasa's gaze swept over Bo, trying to assess his injuries.

"Had to buy Ari time to get away. They were after him."

"You're sure?" Dasa held Bo's gaze.

"Positive. They demanded to know where he was when they had me pinned."

"No one escaped and only one Loperis is dead. We're going to get answers to what the frek this was about one way or another. Things have just got a whole lot more complicated." Dasa scrubbed at his face.

Bo tried to look around the warriors. "Was anyone else hurt? So many demons did what they could to help both Ari and I."

Dasa tapped one of the warriors and they made a hole in the defense so they could see out. When Dasa realized the fight was over, he waved them off. "There are a couple of minor injuries, nothing major. A fair amount of damage to shops, but easily fixed."

Bo caught sight of Perik off to one side. "Help me up."

Dasa shook his head. "You need to—"

"Help. Me. Up." Bo growled out, uncaring that this was his prince.

Dasa scowled, but got Bo standing, helping him walk over to Perik, taking most of his weight as Bo struggled.

"Perik—" Bo looked around at the other shopkeepers. "All of you, thank you, for everything you did here. Neither Ari, nor I, would have made it through this without your help."

Perik's worried gaze darted between Dasa and Bo. "Is there any news on Ari?"

"We've already got guards looking for him. Every available Cobalt is patrolling the streets, both looking for any Loperis we don't know about and hunting for Ari. We will find him, make no mistake about that," Dasa vowed.

"If there is anything we can do to help, let us know." Ulkrit stepped forward. "The Little Demon has won over the hearts of everyone he's come into contact with. We'll do anything we can to find him."

All around them, other shopkeepers stepped forward, offering whatever help they could give.

"If all of you could check your shops, storerooms, anything like that, just in case he stayed close by. He doesn't know many places. I have no idea where he would have thought safe enough to run too." Bo groaned as his back spasmed.

Ulkrit nodded. "We'll check and let the guard know. You go and get looked over by a doctor. And, thank you, for protecting us, for not letting any of us get caught in the crossfire. The Cobalts don't get thanked enough, but we appreciate everything you do."

Bo tried to smile, but the pain radiating through his back was too much. He shifted to let Dasa take even more of his weight, but the spike of pain as some of his stitches tore was too much and darkness descended. As his eyes slid shut, his only thoughts were of Ari and whether he was safe. *Stay strong, Ari, we will find you.*

CHAPTER TWELVE

Ari woke with a wince of pain. His arm was caked in dried blood, but there was a fresh trickle as he shifted his arm into a better position. He ripped his top apart, lamenting ruining the cream top with blue accents. Wrapping a length around the wound, he pulled it tight, stopping the blood flow, biting his lip to prevent crying out. He blinked repeatedly, clearing the moisture gathering there. Taking a couple of deep breaths, he waited for the pain to subside.

Sudden sounds in the other room made him freeze, not daring to move even a muscle. From his position lying on the floor under the desk, he could just about see the entrance in the wall and he kept his gaze fixed firmly on the hole, wanting as much warning as possible if he was discovered. He strained to listen to what was going on.

"I'm telling you… look at the footprints. Someone has been in here."

"Frek, Tra'jin, they could have been made any time in the last thousand years."

"Don't be stupid, Ac'in. There is no dust inside the footprints, they're fresh. At most, they can be a week old. Chances are the damn Aducian was in here."

"Well, he's not in here now."

Ari listened to the two voices as they bickered. They sounded like demons, but Loperis had been in the courtyard when Bo ordered him to run. His heart stuttered at the thought of Bo. Was he safe? Injured? Alive? He quickly quashed those thoughts. No way would he even think that until he knew for sure.

"Where is he?" A new, guttural voice joined in the conversation. Definitely a Loperis.

"We can't find him," Voice One spoke.

"Then keep looking. I want off this rock!"

There was the sound of something being kicked. With mounting horror, Ari realized it was the bookcase hiding the hole. How did he always find himself in these situations? First he'd been bundled onto a ship by his mother, before he was captured by the Loperis. He and Caris had somehow managed to escape. He chuckled mentally. He either had the worst luck or the best depending on which way you looked at it. The worst because he'd been kidnapped and was now involved in another attempted kidnapping. The best because each time he'd ending up hiding in a long abandoned, unused room. Maybe there was someone smiling down on him from above. Whatever it was, he was glad for it.

Quietly shifting about, his hand grazed the box he'd replaced earlier in the day. He ran his fingers over the carvings, smiling softly as memories of being chased by Bo ran through his mind. Suddenly, a warmth enveloped him and a calmness descended on him. He looked around, trying to find the source. There was nothing.

As he traced the carvings, a gentle thrum began under his fingertips. The vibrations tickled slightly, making him smile. *What you smiling for, Ari? Boxes that have been in long hidden rooms in ruined palaces should not thrum.* Wondering why he wasn't scared, he carefully lifted the lid on the box, unsure why something compelled him. The tiny crystal on the horns of the braid shimmered and pulsed. With a slightly shaky finger, he reached out and gently touched one. Light flared from the crystal and warmth radiated up his arm, filling him with a sense of serenity, peace, and most incredibly, safety.

Whoever was in the next room, Demons and Loperis alike, were still arguing. Judging by the sounds coming from the room, both scuffles and grunts, he wondered if they were fighting. A loud crash and the bookcase started to wobble. If it fell, they would see the hole. If they saw the hole they would guess his hiding spot. His heart picked up speed and he nervously started to trace the shape of the horns and tails on the braided crown. His gaze was glued to the hole and his body started to shake. His emotions were all over the place and all he wanted was Bo's arms wrapped around him, holding him tight.

The sounds of the struggle continued. What sounded like two Loperis were arguing in their guttural language. Part of him wished he knew what they were saying, but he realized it was probably for the best that he didn't. It would only scare him. He already knew what would happen if he got caught. He would be subjected to the same treatment he'd received on the last Loperis ship. Then, he would be taken either back to his mother, or shipped straight off to Berinias and his fate with Renauld, forced to carry his children.

He peeked around the desk to the small window high up. Barely more than an arm length across, it still provided some light. What he'd presumed was the sun, was in fact the moon. How long had he slept? *How* had he slept? He shouldn't have been able to. Adrenaline, nerves, fear, they all should have kept him awake. Looking down at his arm, the blood soaked strip he'd used to bind it had fallen away. A slow and steady trickle of blood was winding its way down his arm and pooling on the floor. With a clinical detachment, he understood that if he didn't get it fixed soon, he was going to risk slipping into unconsciousness. The question was, should he risk trying to move? There was another door into the room, but, with no way of knowing if it was blocked off, or where it went. It would be dangerous to use it.

Suddenly, all sound ceased in the next room and the bookcase quivered for a moment before settling back in place. Rapid-fire guttural speech echoed around the room. A sudden commotion outside drew attention. Could he possibly hope someone was here for him?

Convinced there were people out there, Ari wasn't sure what to do. He could hear a lot of movement, more than should be possible with the Reds and Loperis chasing him. He was certain it meant there was a rescue attempt underway, but how could he be sure? How could he take the risk of climbing out of the room?

Gently easing out from underneath the desk, determined to look out the window, he pulled himself up. All of a sudden, everything seemed to tilt. His head was spinning and his vision fading, the ringing in his ears annoyingly loud. "Help me…" His whisper trailed off as everything went black.

Bo swayed on his feet. He'd given the doctors twenty minutes to patch him up and get back out there. They wanted him to stay, insisted they need to examine his back properly. Dasa had eventually intervened and overruled the doctors.

"I may have signed off on you being here—" Dasa glared at Bo— "but if you struggle any more I'm sending you back to the doctors. You're faltering and you damn well know it."

"I need to save him, Dasa, you have to understand that." Bo pleaded with his eyes to be allowed to stay.

"Look, I understand, I *do*. If it was Caris, I would be the same. But, the fact is, you *are* badly injured. Both Caris and Ari will have my tail if something happens to you. I can see it now… we rescue Ari, he sees you injured and all that feistiness we've seen flashes of will be directed my way." Dasa studied his friend— yes, pain was etched into his features, but it was Bo's eyes that drew his attention.

They were haunted in a way he'd never seen. Whatever was going on between him and Ari, it was already serious. He thought back on all the times Bo allowed him to be himself, allowed him into battle. And, most recently, had allowed him to go tearing through space on a desperate race to get the love of his life back. How could he not do the same for his friend?

Bo watched Dasa close his eyes briefly, the long, drawn-out sigh a sure sign Dasa was about to let him have his way.

"Fine. But you take the blame for this if Ari and Caris create merry hell. I can handle the doctors, I can even handle my father, but damn if I'm going to handle those two as well. Besides, I'm not about to have Caris in a bad mood."

"You just don't want him to deny you bedding rights." Bo smirked.

"Too damn right, I don't." Dasa scowled. "Now, how sure are you Ari might be here?" They both looked past the archway to the ruins.

"We were only here a couple of hours ago. We went exploring through it. Ari managed to hide from me and I still don't know how he managed that. I'd thought we'd discovered every hiding place here when we were demonlings. I can't see where else he would have known to go. When we were here, he sensed that presence. I told him about the legends. I know they are just legends, not real, but it just might be enough to make Ari feel safe. He has to be here. My men have been scouring the city and there's been no sign of him. If he isn't here, I can only imagine they have him." Steam poured from Bo's horns and he forcibly banked down his need to shift to his full scales.

"Don't think that way until we know." Dasa caught the gaze of one of the Cobalt officers, who nodded. "Come on, the teams are ready, let's go and search this place."

Ari's consciousness slowly increased. The softness underneath him was puzzling, as was the sense of safety. Keeping his eyes shut, he tried to work out where he was.

"I am aware you have awoken, young Aridien. You may as well open your eyes and see that all is well." A deep timbered voice spoke from his left.

Ari risked opening one eye just enough to peek out of. He gasped and slammed it shut. A deep chuckle echoed around the room, mingling with the sound of a crackling fire. His eyes must be playing tricks on him; there was no way what he'd seen was real, which meant he was alive, and had lost his mind, alive, but asleep and dreaming, or dead and in the afterlife. If he was honest, none were particularly appealing. But one of them must be true.

He peeked out from beneath his eyelashes again. Nope, everything was still the same. He was lying on an ornate bed. It would easily hold two demons in plenty of comfort. His head was cocooned in the softest pillow he'd ever experienced. On the wall to the right, a fire crackled in the hearth. To his left… he couldn't be sure what he saw. It sure looked like a demon, but… this demon was, not see-through exactly, but not exactly corporeal either. Whoever, whatever, it was, it was grinning at him. He blinked a couple of times before opening his eyes wide. The demon waved at him.

"I'm Drel'nic. I, along with others, keep these ruins safe. We came to your aid when you asked for help and we sensed your purity of heart and soul. Do not fear, Little Demon, you are safe. We have tended to your wound as best we can, but our state only allows us the ability to do so much."

"Am I dreaming?" Ari whispered. "Are you real?"

Drel'nic chuckled. The sound made Ari grin.

"I'm as real as I can be. Is that an answer? No, probably not. We heard your young commander, Bo'saverin, explain the legends to you. We are those legends. We are the Guardians."

Ari's mind, trying to process everything that was happening, struggled with the information. Instead, it focused on the one part of that it could comprehend. He started to giggle. The giggle became a chuckle and before long he had tears of laughter streaming down his face. The release of tension was exactly what he needed.

"Might I enquire what part of my statement was so amusing to you, young one?" Drel'nic's forehead furrowed as he studied Ari as though he was a rare specimen.

Ari managed a couple of shaky breaths, getting his laughing fit under control. "I'm sorry, it was just the way you referred to Bo as young. He doesn't seem it to me. Then all I could picture was a young Bo getting into trouble and it made me laugh."

"Ahh." Drel'nic winked. "I remember many an occasion when both Bo'saverin and Prince Dasalin were demonlings and used to explore our ruins. Those two spent many a day crawling through broken rocks, getting many a skinned knee and always ruining their clothes. I can only imagine the trouble they got themselves into when they returned home. Yet, they returned day after day. We, those like me, spent many a day simply watching over them. Those two had a unique ability to get into trouble. If you ever want to tease them, ask them what happened to the orange zubrix set."

"What's a zubrix set?" Ari went to rise but a gentle weight pressed him back down into the bed. Focusing intently, he could just about make out a blur beside the bed. He looked over to Drel'nic.

"That's Lo'jat. He struggles to become more solid than the rest of us, but he used to be a healer in his old life. It was him that stitched and rewrapped your arm."

Ari looked towards the blur. "Thank you, Lo'jat." There was a gentle pat on his arm in response.

"Zubrix is a game many demonlings play. It's a set of rings and poles. It's like a miniature version of the Rings of Hak'ran and Pik'dorin. The rings are added to stands so they can jump on, through and around. Dasalin and Bo'saverin used to bring this bright orange set into the ruins to play with. Well, it was the end of a long summer and they'd been practicing on their set all day. We could tell they were both tired, but refusing to accept it. They pushed each other, again and again to go harder, faster and longer. One of the rings was right on the edge of some unstable flooring. They were trying to be extra adventurous and were using the Pik'dorin sticks as they jumped through this ring. Only they both made the jump at the same time and crashed to the floor. The floor gave way and they tumbled down to the level below, wood, dust and rubble raining down around them. Not that they will know it, but Lo'jat here, kept them alive until help arrived. King Vict'arin yelled something fierce when he found them. I don't think their tails untucked for weeks!"

Ari had his hand over his mouth, giggling. "How old were they?"

"About nine cycles, I think. They were banned from taking their zubrix set anywhere but in one sectioned off courtyard of the palace grounds where someone could watch them."

"Did they know you helped them?" Ari shifted about warily, pleased to see a lot of his aches and pains were fading. He looked towards the depression on the end of the bed where he imagined Lo'jat sat. "Thank you."

Drel'nic shook his head. "They were both unconscious. We don't reveal ourselves often. In fact, I think over the years we've done it twice. You are one of those times."

"Why me?" Ari gestured to himself. "I'm not even a demon."

"Aren't you? Then why does everyone call you Little Demon?" Drel'nic challenged. "Besides, you picked up the braided crown, the Crown of Horns, treated it with respect and you sensed our presence. Do you know, not one demon has ever found that room?"

"What room was it? Why do I get the feeling it was so important?" Ari smiled as he watched a bandage roll itself in mid-air. At least that's what it looked like.

"He likes showing off." Drel'nic nodded towards Lo'jat.

Ari burst out laughing as the bandage sailed through the air and nailed Drel'nic right between the eyes, the trailing end fluttering about in the breeze.

Drel'nic sighed. "See what I have to put up with? Youngsters these days, hey?"

A lighter voice echoed around the room. "Young? Young! I'm almost two thousand years old, for frek's sake."

"You're still younger than me, and don't pout," Drel'nic chastised.

116

There was a long, frustrated groan before a weight settled on his legs. "Aridien, my new friend, save me."

Ari giggled. If someone had asked him if he was going to be talking to legends and ghosts, he'd have sent for the doctor for them. The fact is, he *was* talking to legends and ghosts and their banter with each other was cheering him up.

"You two remind me of Dasa and Bo." He ducked the cushion flung his way.

"No way are we like those two." Drel'nic scowled. "Don't make me rethink rescuing you." He snorted at the sudden frown on Ari's face. "Trust me, Little Demon, you're safe, I'm just teasing."

Ari stuck his tongue out. "You never told me about the room."

Drel'nic's eyes went cloudy as though he was focused elsewhere. He suddenly nodded and turned to Ari. "The room. It was a private study for one of the Cobalt commanders during the reign of King Uxalik. What few histories talk about is that this commander, Jof'ni, worked with Le'brix to bring down the king." Drel'nic studied Ari. "I know Bo'saverin told you some of the details, but are you following this?" He smiled when Ari nodded.

"Jof'ni's parents both lost their lives in a previous battle, although there isn't much information about it around now. He had no family left and was nearing the end of his time as a commander. He was getting old and Uxalik was known to want younger demons surrounding him. Jof'ni, knowing his time was drawing to a close, started to pass what information he could to the rebels, Le'brix in particular."

Ari watched as Drel'nic's gaze became unfocused. "The Dawn of the Long Blades, as that battle was known, saw Jof'ni brick up his private study, with everything still inside it. One thing he had there was the braided crown that was handed to each new king. That crown survived thousands of years before that night, in the hands of the rightful kings, and Jof'ni wanted to ensure it was safe. After bricking up his office, he and his assistant moved the bookcase to cover up what they'd done. The battle began less than an hour later."

Drel'nic's gaze became haunted. "Too many demons lost their lives that day. Both sides sure they were in the right, sure they should be the ones to hold the throne. In truth, it should never have mattered. No king of Kenistal should have been so against his people. In the final battle, it became a showdown between Uxalik and Le'brix. The two would-be kings, fighting to the death for the right to rule. At the last moment, Uxalik committed the ultimate treachery. One of his sub-commanders picked up a sword and went to drive it through Le'brix's heart. Jof'ni saw what was happening and dived in-between the two demons. He took the full impact of the blow to his chest and died instantly. He never got a chance to say a word. In the ensuing chaos, Le'brix was victorious. But the death toll was massive. Among them was not only Jof'ni, but his assistant and everyone who had known about his office. The secret died with them. The braided crown, the symbol of our rulers, of the unity of Kenistal, was lost.

"The saying on the archway— Tep'it okri asteliki aps lekis tep'it okri keriset, or, the might of the soul is stronger than the might of blood, refers not only to the strength of the souls of the demons that day, but the strength of one yet to come. That part has been lost through the generations. The full legend believes that when the braid is most needed one with a pure and strong soul will find it. That's you, Little Demon. You found it."

Ari's mind was racing at all the new information. "But, when I held it the first time, I was compelled to return it to its box. There was such a sense of wrongness. There was no way I could have taken it out, so how could it be me?"

"That was a test, to see what you would do, to see if you sensed our presence."

"Did I pass?" Ari held his breath, certain the answer was somehow important.

"That you did, Little Demon. You followed your gut, your heart, and put it back. Not even telling your Commander Bo'saverin about it."

"It just didn't feel right," Ari mumbled as he ducked his head.

"Well, you can tell both Bo and Dasa about the crown. It's time. Those of us who straddle the line between here and the afterlife have discussed it. There is strife coming Kenistal's way. The braid will help unite the guilds under a true king as only a true king can wear it."

Ari was speechless and still wondering if he was dreaming.

Drel'nic smiled. "We shall talk again, Little Demon, but for now, you need to return to the ruins proper. Your mate is waiting for you and is frantic with worry. Besides, you need to get him to see a healer. No, don't panic, he isn't that bad, but needs to learn to take it easy."

"Mate?" Ari's words echoed around his own mind as everything went black.

CHAPTER THIRTEEN

Bo suppressed the pain occupying every muscle in his body. Nothing would stop him being part of the force attempting to rescue Ari. This wasn't about being a commander of the Cobalts. This was about Ari, and his feelings for him. No way would he finally find someone who captured his attention only to lose him. No chance, no way, no how. Not on his watch.

"Stay by my side at all times." Dasa held Bo's gaze. "I mean it."

"Isn't it normally me ordering you to do that?" Bo quirked a brow.

"Maybe, but you've not normally been stupid enough to let yourself get injured," Dasa challenged.

Bo spluttered. "Did you see how many of them there were?"

"I thought the mighty Commander Bo'saverin was invincible?" Dasa looked around at several Cobalts who were nodding. "At least that's what your men think."

"I'm still here, aren't I?" Bo rolled his eyes. "Now let's get to rescuing my Little Demon."

"I see you've picked up on that name as well." Dasa tilted his neck from either side, sighing in happiness when he heard a distinctive crack.

"What can I say, it fits him." Bo's eyes softened as he thought of Ari. "He's feisty, stubborn, can be so argumentative, fiery and there is a core strength to him…" Bo's voice trailed off as his mind continued listing Ari's attributes. Sexy, kissable lips, and that ass— he wanted to sink into it and never leave.

"Oh, you are so far gone." Dasa snorted. "That Little Demon has you wrapped around his little finger, your tail all twisted and your horns steaming."

"That he has, my friend, that he has." Bo nodded to his second, Ank'tok.

With a sharp whistle, the Cobalts charged as one towards the ruins. Bo grinned at Dasa and then took up the head of the charge, bursting through the entryway with his sword drawn.

Two Reds guarding the entrance were subdued in seconds, having laid down their weapons at the overwhelming force barreling in. Ank'tok gestured to a few men to secure and guard them. The Cobalts split into groups, darting down different corridors and up the stairs.

Bo focused on getting to the room he knew Ari had been in, the one with the bookcase, having seen his footprints there earlier in the day, even if it felt like months ago. He dodged past other Cobalts racing who knew where. Dasa keeping stride by his side, both of them remained focused on the task: get to Ari and hope he was safe. As Bo ran into the room, Dasa was a beat behind him. He suddenly found himself being yanked backwards, an arm around his neck.

"Watch where you are going," Dasa hissed in his ear. Both of them jerked slightly as a knife went sailing through the space Bo had been in and wedged into the wall behind them.

"Frek," Bo cursed, annoyed at his own lack of attention. He clapped Dasa on the shoulder. "Thank you."

Dasa just shrugged and lifted his laser sword. "Ready?" At Bo's nod, they both charged into the room.

Bo registered the chaos around him. The room was trashed. The window was smashed to pieces, jagged glass littering the floor. Books lay in heaps everywhere around the bookcase, and a painting lay ripped to shreds on the floor. Two Reds were battling with a Loperis in the middle of the room. Another Loperis lay clutching his stomach to one side of the fight. Two other Reds stood guard over him. All the Reds were still masked. There was no doubt they were working against Ari, against Kenistal.

Bo muttered to Dasa, "I'll take the Loperis."

"No. I want that bastard." He whistled to two Cobalts racing along the corridor. They came running in. "Take the Reds. The Loperis is mine. You…" He pointed to Bo. "Stand there and watch the others. No arguments."

Bo, of course, was going to argue, but the glare from Dasa soon shut him up. He knew when to push his friend and when to stand back. Now was the time to stand down and be quiet.

Dasa slammed into the Loperis, knocking him free from the two Reds, confident the Cobalts with him would keep them away as he fought the Loperis. Pushing the Loperis back, he swung his sword around, cutting into its thigh. An angry snarl came from the orange beast-like man before rapid-fire Loperian sprung from his lips. Dasa refused to let himself be distracted; instead he swung his blade again, this time from the opposite direction, slicing into the other thigh.

Bo pointed his sword tip against the throat of the Loperis on the ground, who'd made as if to go and defend his teammate. "Stay down." Anger dripped from him. "If Ari is hurt, so much as a scratch, you will regret landing on Kenistal. You'll probably regret it anyway. But, trust me, King Vict'arin will have nothing on me if you have harmed Ari in any way. Now sit down and shut up before you give me reason to ignore my training and run you through."

Bo, keeping most of his gaze on Dasa, flicked his gaze briefly to the two Reds. "Why? Why would you do this? What has Ari ever done to you? I can guess who you are working for. It's not exactly difficult. The one thing I don't understand is why you would risk taking Kenistal to war over trade rights."

The Red on the left spat at Bo's feet. "Have you ever thought the Reds know we should rule? You Cobalts are worth nothing, you never have been. You're nothing better than glorified fodder for wars. Losing all of you will do us no harm. As for the Purples …" The Red spat again. "They don't deserve the crown. What have they done to advance Kenistal? All they do is hamper us with politics and trade deals that keep us from making the credits we truly deserve."

"Oh, you mean the trade agreements that allow our ships safe passage through areas? Yes, we give some of our profits over to other worlds for that safe passage. A necessary and profitable exchange."

"We don't need any protection. We. Are. Demons," the other Red interrupted.

"Demons who can still die, demons who have died trying to trade in sectors with superior races," Bo retorted.

"There are no superior races to demons. We are the best. It is us who should rule, not only the sector, or galaxy, but the entire universe," the second Red vowed.

Bo shook his head. There was no point engaging zealots like this. Nothing would ever change their mind and it would just increase his anger to argue further. He turned his back on them, the ultimate sign of disrespect and totally confident in his Cobalts' ability to protect them all.

Dasa was almost toying with the Loperis. Assessing his prince, he was pleased to see there wasn't so much as a scratch on him, whereas the Loperis was littered with them. "Finish it, Dasa."

Dasa growled, but sliced through the neck of the Loperis, watching as the head unceremoniously rolled along the floor. Bo walked over. "If Ari was here…" He let his words trail off, unable to give voice to his concern.

Dasa grabbed Bo's bicep and pulled him to one side, away from any listening ears. "Stop thinking like that. He's a resourceful man. I can just picture him hiding out, ready to pop up the minute he sees someone he knows he's safe with."

Bo dipped his head, acknowledging Dasa's words. "I hope you're right. May the stars favor us this night."

Ari groaned as he sat up. He was lying back on the floor of the room he'd originally been in. The box containing the crown was in front of him. As his memory returned, his hand went to his arm. It was wrapped up and he could feel a series of stitches underneath. He smiled as he thought of Lo'jat and Drel'nic. They'd helped him, kept him safe, and they were legends. He was still struggling to come to terms with exactly what had happened, but the fact his arm was bandaged meant he definitely hadn't been dreaming.

Sounds of battle reached his ears. He bolted upright, rushing to the window, yet unable to see anything going on. It was then a deeply recognizable voice filtered into his mind. *Bo... Bo is close.*

Ari moved into the hole between the rooms, but couldn't see anything. The sound of both Bo and Dasa's voices became louder. He was safe; they'd found him. He pushed out of the hole, steadying himself briefly as he stood, letting his balance settle.

He smiled when he heard Dasa's words. "I can just picture him hiding out, ready to pop up the minute he sees someone he knows he's safe with."

He grinned to himself, wondering if this would make them jump. He started to step out from behind the bookcase as Bo spoke. "I hope you're right. May the stars favor us this night."

"Well, Dasa is right. I know I'm safe now that you are here." Ari stopped a couple of paces away from Bo and smiled up at him.

Stunned silence met his entry. He scanned the room, seeing the dead and prisoners dotted about the now destroyed room. "What, no hello?" he asked.

Bo broke from his stupor. "Ari!" His cry echoed around the room, and in two quick strides, he reached Ari, pulling him up into an embrace and wrapping both his arms and tail around him, determined to keep his little demon safe from those left in the room.

He ignored the snarls from the Reds behind him as he bent his head and took possession of Ari's lips in a searing kiss.

Ari relaxed into Bo's hold, his arms winding up and around Bo's neck, holding on tight, his hands still clasping the wooden box. As Bo lifted him, he wrapped his legs around Bo's waist. When Bo winced, he let his legs drop and tapped him on the shoulder, pulling back from the kiss. "Let me down, you're hurt."

"I'm hurt? I'm hurt! Damn it, Ari, you've been missing and…" As Bo scanned Ari from head to toe, he took in his disheveled state, the steam coming from his horns getting thicker and thicker, his tail twitching back and forth, scales rippling.

"Stay calm, Bo," Dasa cautioned.

"Stay calm? How the frek do you expect me to stay calm? Look at him, Dasa! He's injured, he's not wearing a tunic, his body is covered in scratches, there's dried blood, he's got a bandage on—"

"And he's safe, here, in your arms, so calm the frek down before you make your own injuries worse," Dasa chastised him.

Bo fought to get his anger under control. He grabbed Ari's hand and refused to let go. As Ank'tok walked into the room, he whistled. "Was this all your doing?" He stared at Bo.

"No. Now see to the traitors over there." Bo pointed at the Reds and single Loperis left alive.

"Will do. Go and get him to safety." Ank'tok smiled at Ari. "It's good to see you safe."

Bo went to pick up Ari, but his hands were smacked away.

"Oh, no you don't." Ari jabbed a finger into Bo's chest. "Not a chance you are risking doing yourself more damage. I didn't just run away when you asked, which nearly destroyed me, by the way, escape my would-be kidnappers and hide, only to find you and have you collapse." Ari kept jabbing a finger into Bo's chest.

Bo stood there, mouth open in stunned surprise. Dasa looked back and forth between them, chuckling away. Bo growled at Dasa before grabbing Ari and hauling him in for another toe-curling kiss.

Ari melted. There was no other word for it. The way Bo dominated him, made him feel safe and treasured, sent thrills through him, blasting away his anger at Bo for trying to be reckless. Someone clapped him on the shoulder, but Bo refused to let go until he was ready. Finally, as they came up for air, he turned to see Dasa smiling at him.

"Damn, Ari, I haven't seen someone dish it out to our Commander here like that in a long time. None of his Cobalts are brave enough to go up against the legendary anger of the mighty Commander Bo'saverin." Dasa continued to chuckle away.

Ari peeked around Bo. The few Cobalts in the room, including Bo's second, were all nodding furiously. Looking back at Bo, he smiled at the massive grin on his face. "Are you going to be alright? Just how badly injured are you?"

"I'll be fine, Tiko." Bo smoothed down Ari's curls which were even wilder than normal.

"Huh. Tiko is a good name for you, Ari." Dasa once again clapped Ari on the back, unintentionally making him stagger forward a step, laughing when Ari scowled. "Yes, Tiko is definitely the right name for you, along with Little Demon. I can see your natural feistiness start to shine through. Oh, Bo, you are in for a universe of trouble."

"Shut up." Bo advanced on Dasa.

Ari took the moment of distraction to walk up to the Reds, the Cobalts on guard trying to keep him back.

"You." Ari jabbed his finger at the nearest Red. "I know who you're working with."

The Red stared at Ari. "People like you should know their place."

"People like me? You mean because I'm lenis?" Ari demanded.

"We heard all about the likes of you from the Loperis here. An abomination of nature, that's what you are. Besides, you're a no-horn." The Red spat at him, leaving a grotty trail running down his bare chest.

Ari never had time to respond. Bo crossed the room in two strides. The Red was pinned to the wall by Bo's hand. His claws dug into the Red's throat, blood oozing in a trail down the wall. "You want to risk repeating that again." Bo barely got the words out through his anger. His scales were at maximum.

This was the most demonic Ari had ever seen Bo, yet not once did he shy away from him. Not for a minute was he repulsed. He placed the box down on a table by Dasa, surprisingly still standing. He gently laid a hand on Bo's arm.

"Careful, Little Demon." One of the guards went to move Ari away and Dasa waved him off.

"Bo won't hurt me." Ari focused all his attention on Bo. "Bo… my warrior, please. Put the Red demon down."

Bo's head whipped around. Steam was pouring from his horns. His face creased, mouth open in a snarl. His eyes, full of anger, focused on Ari. Slowly, the anger receded, replaced with a warmth that made Ari's heart soar.

"Put the demon down, Bo." Ari gently ran his hand along Bo's arm and up to his face, cupping the scaled cheek. "Please? For me?"

Every other demon, and even the Loperis in the room, held their breath. No one dared move a muscle. This far into anger, demons were notoriously hard to reason with. Many a demon had lost their heads trying to reason with one this far gone.

Ari merely stood his ground, holding Bo's gaze and gently stroking his cheek, ignoring the Red gasping for breath still pinned against the wall.

A minute passed. Bo's body rippled and his scales pulled back slightly. The Red was unceremoniously dropped to the floor as Bo's scales relaxed back into a slightly less defensive position. He wrapped his arms around Ari and pulled him over to the other side of the room, away from prying eyes.

Every time Ari tried to talk, Bo shut him up with a look. Instead, Bo examined every inch of Ari, checking on his previous injuries, making sure he hadn't been hurt when he stood up to him. "Are you out of your frekking mind?" Bo grabbed Ari around the upper arms, lifting him off the floor to eye height.

Ari stayed relaxed and just smiled softly.

"I could have hurt you! Never, ever interrupt a demon when he's like that. Frek, Tiko, I could have really hurt you." Anguish radiated out from Bo.

"No." Ari shook his head. "There is just no way you would ever hurt me. I know that. I don't know a lot, but one thing I do know is you, my warrior, would never hurt me."

"You don't know that!" Bo's breath stuttered, the panic at seeing Ari in such a position still riding him hard.

"Yes, I do. I know you, Bo. You would never, could never, hurt me. Now, let's go and get you seen by a healer, hey?"

Bo closed his eyes and leaned his forehead against Ari's for a moment, breathing in his unique scent. With one last, shuddering breath, he lowered him back to the ground, taking his hand in his.

Ari picked the wooden box back up from the table beside Dasa and nodded he was ready. "Come on, I need to see Vict and you need to see a healer."

"Why do you need to see my father?" Dasa held Ank'tok's gaze for a moment before walking out the door.

"I'll explain when I see him. Not here, not now," Ari spoke softly, hoping Dasa would understand the need for discretion.

"We better get to it then." Dasa led them out the door and back to safety.

CHAPTER FOURTEEN

Ari, standing with his arms crossed over his chest, glared at Bo as he stood guard by the door, refusing to let him leave. "You will sit there and be quiet until this kind doctor has finished with you."

Bo's gaze looked murderous, but he sat still, his gaze settling into a pout when he realized Ari would not be budged. "At least let them check your arm out," Bo sullenly complained.

"Fine." Ari rolled his eyes. "But I'm telling you, it's already been treated. I don't need it looked at."

"And you've failed to tell me who treated you," Bo snapped, annoyed at feeling like he'd failed Ari all over again.

"I've told you, I'll explain when we go and see Vict. Now sit there and let the doctor work." Ari blew a curl out of his eyes.

"Fine," Bo snarled before looking contrite. "I'm sorry, I just don't do well with having to sit still and be tended to."

Ari walked over to Bo and kissed him softly on the cheek. "I know, but do it for me, please? I need to know you're going to be okay. You got injured defending me, after all."

Bo pulled Ari into his lap, much to the annoyance of the doctor, but he relaxed enough for the doctor to carry on treating him.

Ari held his arm out to another smiling doctor, who quickly unwrapped the bandages.

Elik, the doctor, whistled. "Whoever stitched you up did an incredible job. This won't leave a scar, or if it does, it will be minimal. I haven't seen stitching this good in a long time." He turned to Bo. "I assure you, everything is fine. There will be no issues for him." He quickly rewrapped the wound. "He has a lot of bruising and minor scratches, but everything will heal in a few days."

Relief swamped Bo and he kissed the top of Ari's face. He smiled when he realized Ari was snuggling in deeper, his eyes slowly drifting closed.

Caris, sat with Dasa to one side, leaned in close. "I have to wonder what happened on their date. Before the Reds and the attack, I mean. Ari seems to be very comfortable around Bo. More so than he was before."

Dasa waggled his eyebrows. "Well, judging by the couple of scorching kisses I saw them share, I would say things are progressing nicely for them."

Caris' eyebrows shot up. "Really? Good on them." He studied Bo as he spoke. "How bad was it?"

"Bad. Another minute and he wouldn't be with us. He was vastly outnumbered and even with many of those shopkeepers helping, he couldn't have taken everyone out. His injuries are fairly extensive, but normally, he would have been able to keep fighting."

"But he was still recovering." Caris pursed his lips.

"Exactly."

"Will this set his recovery back?"

"I don't know. I hope not. He won't want Ari unguarded at all now. Not that I'm going to let either of you go anywhere without guards."

"We already have Deek'in and Yavek."

"I'm not sure that's enough," Dasa muttered.

Caris hummed, but kept quiet. When both demons were in full protection mode like this, there would be no point in arguing.

The doctor finally rolled his stool back from Bo. "You're lucky. Somehow despite tearing a few stitches and a little break in the wound site, which I've repaired, you didn't do any further damage to your scales. How, I have no idea. As for your other injuries, they should heal in a couple of days. But… I'm going to insist you take it easy for a while, Commander. You were lucky, luckier than I think you realize. You could have done some serious damage."

"I nearly died, doctor. I would have died if it hadn't been for the prince. I would also have done it happily to keep this one safe." Bo's voice trailed off as he took in the sleeping form in his arms.

"Yes, well, I'm glad we have young Master Aridien back safe and sound, but please be careful. We do only have one Commander like you, after all," the doctor chastised.

"I promise to try and be more careful."

The doctor shook his head. "I guess that's all I can ask. Now, as long as you take it easy, there is no need to be banished back to your former bed beside Mac'likrit. Although, I'm quite sure he wouldn't have minded the company."

Caris piped up from his seat. "Tell him I'll pop in and see him later."

"That will make him happy, and maybe he might annoy my medics a bit less." The doctor chuckled as he left the room.

"Let him sleep for a few more minutes?" Bo shared a look with Dasa. "I want to know what happened to him, but he needs sleep. He has to be exhausted."

"We'll leave you two here. Come join us when you're ready. I want to know exactly what happened." Dasa and Caris swept from the room.

Bo tightened his grip on Ari, his tail wrapping around his waist, anchoring Ari to him, and closed his eyes.

Ari was still slightly groggy, but the berry slush he was drinking was perking him up fairly quickly. He still sipped as he walked into Vict's study. He stopped in the doorway as he took in the faces. Vict, Dasa, Caris, Alenska, Meklin, Dasa's mother and Ubrix, one of Vict's advisors.

"Aridien, come sit down and you, Commander." Vict gestured to the two seats left. "Now, Commander, I want to hear everything that happened."

Ari struggled to stay calm as Bo recounted his version of events. His heart stuttered at the matter-of-fact way Bo described the fight and his near death at the hands of the Reds and Loperis. At one point, Bo had tightened his grip on his hand, Caris grabbing his other hand, both of them holding tight as the panic rose in him at the thought of Bo dying.

"It's alright," Caris whispered, his mouth almost touching Ari's ear. "You can see he's safe. Keep that in your mind. This is something you will have to get used to if you want to be with him. You need to allow him to be who he is, to command the warriors, without worrying about how you are dealing with it. I promise it will ease in time, but until then, you have to fake being strong about it until you are. It's what he needs."

Ari calmed himself down and held Caris' gaze. "I can do that. I want to be what he needs. I want to be with him."

"I know, and he wants you as well. You only need to watch the way he looks at you to know that. Now, let's get this meeting over with and you can spend some quality time with him, showing him you're okay."

Ari smiled sadly. "This meeting will go on longer than you realize, once I tell everyone what happened."

"Oh?" Caris cocked his head to one side, but was smart enough not to push Ari.

Vict made an angry rumbling sound in his throat, making Ari's head snap up. "So we know there were Reds and Loperis involved. The Reds in particular are being questioned as we speak. We will find out just who is involved. Make no mistake about that. I will rip the Reds apart until I get to the bottom of this. There will not be a single stone left unturned until I know everything. Know everyone involved in this treason. I will not let such arrogance and behavior become part of life on Kenistal."

All around Ari there were solemn faces, bar Alenska, who looked both bored and frustrated. He would have to ask Bo exactly what was going on with her. He didn't like her. She reminded him too much of his mother.

Bo sent him a quizzical look, but Ari just shook his head. Until he had a reason not to trust Alenska, he would keep his thoughts to himself. After all, if Dasa and Bo both trusted her, then he should too.

Vict, seeing Ari had finished his drink, waved an assistant forward. "Please get some refreshments for everyone before we ask Aridien to go through his ordeal."

Ari dipped his head. "Thank you."

Vict shook his head. "No, thank you, I know this won't be easy. I have to say, this nickname I've been hearing for you, Little Demon, seems most apt. You've managed to evade kidnap and come through it relatively unscathed. I'm impressed. Added into what you achieved bringing Caris home to us and you, my young Aridien, are fast becoming indispensable to us."

Ari blushed under the praise. When one of the assistants handed him a fresh berry crush, he smiled widely. "Thank you, Dof'vik."

Vict looked up from his davroc, an incredulous stare on his face. "You know his name?" He gestured to the bronze demon.

"Of course." Ari's nose wrinkled. "Why wouldn't I? He's the one that makes these amazing berry crushes."

Vict's smile was beaming. "Not many demons bother to learn the names of those who serve them."

"I don't see why not, they have a job to do, same as everyone else. They are just as important as anyone else, even the commander here." Ari winked at Bo.

Alenska gasped. "That's outrageous. How you can possibly think a servant is better than a Cobalt is beyond me. Next thing you know, you'll be saying everyone is as important as us Purples."

Ari looked at Alenska as he scratched at his cheek, his eyebrows drawn together. "Well, they are. Sure, Vict runs the world, but without demons like Dof'vik, his life would not run smoothly and he would no doubt be swamped by the mundane aspects of life. He would not have enough time to devote to the important things. Demons like Dof'vik give him the time to focus his energy and attention where they are needed most."

Vict, sipping his davroc, nodded as Ari spoke. "He's right. If I didn't have the likes of Dof'vik and Helic here…" He gestured to another assistant setting out food "Keeping me fed and the palace running smoothly, I would never get anything done. Frankly, Alenska, I'm beginning to believe I have no choice but to put you on a tour of the guilds. You need to learn some humility. Your attitude and the company you keep is becoming quite concerning. I suggest you smarten up before I take a long look at the way you are leading your life."

Alenska kept her posture ramrod straight as she curtly nodded at her father's words, her expression bordering on mutinous.

"Now, Ari, are you comfortable telling us what happened to you?" Vict prompted.

Ari looked around the room, seeing all the faces he didn't know. A sense of trepidation slid over him and a shiver wracked his body. "I… uh…." He clutched the wooden box tight, willing the strength of the Guardians he'd met to infuse him. He looked up at Vict and held his gaze, hoping to convey without words how serious he was in his request. "If it's alright with you, I would like to do this with as few people here as possible. There are things I would rather not talk about with so many people listening."

Vict searched Ari's eyes, finding both pleading and desperation in his gaze. After a long, considering look, he dipped his head. "Very well, everyone please leave."

The guards and assistants quickly left, leaving the family and Ubrix. Ari trembled, but held his ground as he kept his gaze locked with Vict's. His was imploring, almost begging Vict to understand.

Vict broke the gaze, turning to Ubrix. "I shall be fine here. Please check on how things are going with the prisoners."

Ubrix waited a moment, then slowly rose, leaving the room without so much as a word spoken.

Vict turned to his queen, Meklin, and Alenska. "If you demonesses would be so kind as to retire, it would be much appreciated."

Meklin rose gracefully, her pale green skin showing a purple overlay, a characteristic trait of anyone mated into the royal family. She turned to both Ari and Caris. "It was lovely to meet you. I am sorry it wasn't under better circumstances. I hope to get to know you both soon."

Alenska, on the other hand, remained sitting, arms folded resolutely across her chest. "I'm staying. I need to know what he has to say." She stared Ari down, making him grip Bo's hand tighter.

"You don't need to hear anything," Vict chastised. "You want to hear it, but that is something entirely different."

"I'm not leaving." Steam rose out from the bottom of her horns. "I have every right to be here. I *am* Princess Alenska, after all."

"And I *am* King Vict'arin, ruler of Kenistal and your father. Leave, now, or I will have the guards remove you. Aridien has asked for as few demons as possible and I fully intend to honor that request. You are *not* needed here."

Father and daughter engaged in a silent stare-off. Dasa, perfectly relaxed in his seat, watched with mild disinterest. When Ari grabbed his attention and went to suggest staying, Dasa merely shook his head.

"I can stay this way all evening. You will leave before Aridien says a word. I can make good on my threat to send you to the guilds. Frankly, I'm considering it anyway. You seem to have become unduly interested in certain aspects of political life. What's more, your 'friends' leave a lot to be desired. Leave, now, or prepare for the guilds." Vict sat comfortably in his chair, completely at ease as he waited his daughter out.

Eventually, Alenska growled and kicking her chair back as she rose and stormed from the room, slamming the door.

Ari looked to the floor. "I'm sorry."

"Don't be," Vict assured him. "She was always a willful demonling, and her attitude hasn't improved over the years. I have no doubt a big confrontation is coming. Now, are you okay with the four of us being here?"

Ari smiled at Vict, Dasa, Caris and finally Bo. "Yes." He took a deep breath and began his story. It wasn't until he got to the ruins that he had their rapt attention. By the time he'd finished recounting everything, up to finding the braided crown, he had their rapt attention.

"Are you seriously trying to tell me, you found the Crown of Horns?" Vict's lips were pressed into a fine line. "The braided crown that Uxalik and Le'brix fought over? The one that's been missing for thousands of years?" Vict scoffed, his disbelief evident.

"That's the one. It was taken by one of Uxalik's Commanders. A Cobalt by the name of Jof'ni. He hid it from Uxalik and defected to Le'brix's side."

"That's not possible. It would have been found by now." Dasa frowned. "Those ruins have been explored by demons for thousands of years."

"As I said, I was told it was bricked up and hidden. When Jof'ni gave his life to spare Le'brix, the secret died with him."

"How can you know all this?" Dasa studied Ari. "And if you've seen the Crown of Horns, where is it?"

Ari carefully, and with a healthy dose of trepidation, gently placed the wooden box on the table they were sitting around and opened the lid. Stunned silence reigned in the room as they all focused on the now open box.

Vict reached out with a trembling hand. His finger gently traced the horns circling the braid. His gaze went to Ari. "How?"

"It's like I told you, I found it in the room."

"But how did you know what happened to it? Even if you found it in a room, there would be no way for you to know those details. You said someone told you— who? And who fixed up your arm, because there is no way you could do that yourself." Vict stared Ari down, wondering, assessing, needing to know everything.

Ari looked to Bo for strength, relaxing slightly when he smiled at him. "When we went to the ruins earlier today, yesterday, whenever it was, Bo mentioned a legend. One where there is a sensation which can be experienced in the ruins. One where the lost souls still wander the grounds of the palace. Bo told me those who guarded the kings back then and refused to abandon their posts even in death still patrol the grounds now. He explained the legend maintains if there is ever a need, they will step forth through the barrier and protect those who have need of their aid. That's what happened to me."

Ari closed his eyes, his memories taking over. He recited the events, watching them play out behind his eyes. "I'd cut my arm crawling through the hole behind the bookcase to the relative safety of the room I'd discovered. I knew I was fairly safe there. I barely made it through— there was no way a demon or Loperis would make it. Not without making the hole larger. I know I passed out. I don't entirely know why, but when I came to, I heard a commotion outside. I got up to see, but my arm was still bleeding. I was weak and I collapsed. I remember begging somebody, anybody to help me as everything went black. I woke up in a different room. The bed was a little slice of tranquility. That room surrounded me in peace and protection instantly. I wasn't scared. I should have been, not knowing where I was, but I knew I was as safe there as I am when

I'm with Bo." Ari stroked the back of Bo's hand, still clasped in his, with a finger from his other hand.

"I remember wondering if I was dreaming, hallucinating or dead. There was a demon there, but not quite. It's hard to explain, but while he was everything I know a demon to be, he was also sort of see-through. There was this almost ghostly appearance to him. That was Drel'nic."

Bo gasped.

Ari's eyes flew open. "What?"

"Drel'nic? I… one of my ancestors was called Drel'nic. He was a legendary commander of the Cobalts. He died in an assassination attempt, giving his life for a young prince." Bo's eyes held a wealth of emotion, too much to pinpoint even one.

"He never said he was related to you. He told me he, along with other Guardians, kept the ruins safe. They heard my pleas for help and came to my aid. Apparently I have a pure heart and soul." Ari blushed at that. "Drel'nic kept referring to you as young Bo'saverin. He made me laugh with that. He told me you and Dasa used to get in trouble as demonlings in the ruins. Anyway, one of the others was called Lo'jat. I only heard him and saw a shimmer. Apparently he wasn't as gifted at becoming corporeal as Drel'nic. He treated my arm. It's his stitches that are there now."

Dasa looked to his father. "Wasn't Lo'jat one of King Adrik's doctors and also his lover?"

"I think so. I'm not as good on my histories as I should be." Vict frowned at Ari. "In fact, I'm wondering how Ari could possibly know any of this."

Ari ignored the comment and carried on with his retelling. "The two of them kept arguing. Drel'nic insisting that Lo'jat was just a young demon. They bickered. It reminded me of you two." He grinned as both Caris and Vict laughed, Dasa and Bo scowling instead. "Drel'nic spoke about the Dawn of the Long Blades. What happened, the final battle between Uxalik and Le'brix. He spoke about Uxalik committing the ultimate treachery. On his orders, one of his sub-commanders picked up a sword and went to drive it through Le'brix's heart. Jof'ni intervened and dived in-between the two demons. He took the full impact of the blow to his chest and died instantly. It was apparently enough to turn more Cobalts to Le'brix's side. Jof'ni was well-loved. That was the night Le'brix won."

Vict rapidly shook his head. "This isn't possible. There is no way. You must have read this in our histories. You must have been dreaming."

Ari shrugged. "I thought I was at first, but then how do you explain my arm being treated?"

Vict looked puzzled and slightly unsure. "I don't know."

"What would it take for you to believe me?" Ari refused to back down. The conviction in him of what happened to him being true was absolute. He would not back down from this.

"I don't know." Vict's tail was twitching rapidly, his agitation clear.

Ari sat quietly for a moment as Dasa, Vict and Bo went back and forth over what he'd told them. He didn't take it personally they were trying to work out if it was true. He would have a hard time believing what he was saying in their situation. Suddenly, another memory came to him and he burst out laughing, startling everyone. "I know how I can convince you."

Wary expressions pinned him in place.

Ari grinned away. "Tell me something... whatever happened to your orange zubrix set?"

Vict got it first. "I haven't thought about that day in years. How could you possibly know that?"

"What, that it's a miniature version of the ring of Hak'ran and Pik'dorin? How at the end of a long summer these two had been practicing with their zubrix set all day? I heard how one of the rings was set up on the edge of some loose flooring. Dasa and Bo were being adventurous—using the Pik'dorin sticks as they jumped through the ring. Apparently they both made the jump at the same time and crashed to the floor. The floor gave way and they tumbled down to the level below, wood, dust and rubble raining down around them."

Bo's mouth dropped. "How can you *know* that?"

Dasa shook his head. "I'd forgotten about that day."

"One thing you don't know about that day is Lo'jat kept you alive until help arrived. Apparently, you were yelling something fierce when you found them, Vict. Drel'nic told me your tails didn't untuck for weeks! You were nine cycles at the time and banned from taking your zubrix set anywhere but the palace courtyard with a guard in place to watch over you. They didn't reveal themselves to you. You were too young. In fact, they've only revealed themselves twice. Once was me."

"There is no way you could have known that." Vict picked up the Crown of Horns and ran his fingers over it. "Everything you're saying is true, isn't it? It's not just a legend. The ruins really are protected."

"They are." Ari sighed. "That's not everything."

At three slightly impatient glares, he carried on. "I asked why me. Why did they reveal themselves to me? Apparently it was the fact I picked up the braided crown, treated it with respect and sensed their presence. Do you know, they told me not one demon has ever found that room?"

"What room was it?" Vict leaned forward, beginning to truly believe Ari's story, wanting to know everything.

"Like I said, it was Jof'ni's room."

"Ah yes, I understand. Sorry, with all this new information, my mind feels on overload." Vict rubbed at his forehead. "This is just incredible. What else is in that room?"

"I don't know, a lot of books, scrolls, a set of armor. I didn't explore it too much."

Caris' eyes lit up. "Can you imagine the information in those books? Histories and so on, long since believed lost? Vict, you need to arrange for someone to gather everything together and bring it back."

Vict dipped his head in agreement. "Why now?" Vict's troubled gaze pierced into Ari's. "Did they say why the crown has been found now? Why they revealed themselves to you?"

"When Jof'ni and those who knew where the crown was died, the secret died with them. The braided crown, the symbol of the right to rule, of the unity of Kenistal, became lost. Drel'nic spoke about the saying on the archway— Tep'it okri asteliki aps lekis tep'it okri keriset, or, the might of the soul is stronger than the might of blood. He told me the saying refers not only to the strength of the souls of the men that day, but the strength of one yet to come. That part has apparently been lost through the generations. The full legend states that when the braid is most needed one with a pure and strong soul will find it." Ari held Vict's gaze. "Drel'nic told me that's me. He asked me to tell both you, well, Bo and Dasa, but I knew he meant you as well, about the braid. He told me those who know how to straddle the line between here and the afterlife discussed it. They believe there is strife coming Kenistal's way. They told me the braid will help unite the guilds under a true king as only a true king can wear it."

Ari took a long drink of his berry crush. "That's it. That's all they told me. Other than to say they would speak to me again. The next thing I knew I was back in Jof'ni's room and heard Bo and Dasa's voices."

The room stayed silent, everyone trying to come to terms with what had happened. Vict finally blew out a long breath. "Thank you for asking everyone to leave. This is not information I would want to become common knowledge. I have a feeling there will come a time when having the Crown of Horns will be the only thing that allows me to keep the throne. The Reds are pushing incessantly forward with their desire for trade rights and power. I doubt it will be long before we see an outright power play for the crown. I will not reveal its existence until that point. I do not begin to know why they chose you, Ari. But, I find no fault in it. You have shown yourself to be courageous, wise and open to such a thing. I'm not sure I would have reacted the same way in the circumstances."

Dasa eased his posture, finally relaxing slightly. "For the moment, all we can do is watch and wait. Keep an eye on the most likely of suspects to move against us." He hesitated, long enough that Vict picked up on it.

"Go ahead and say it."

"I don't like that I've even considered this, but… I want you to keep an eye on Alenska. Her attitude lately has been wrong. And she's getting worse. I don't know who she is keeping as friends, but we know Jari was mixed up in everything. I hate the thought that my sister, no matter how much we don't get on, could potentially be working against us, against our family."

Vict's head bowed for a long moment. When he lifted his head, Ari could see the hurt, betrayal and resignation written all over his face. "I don't like to consider this, but you are right. She bears watching, and closely. I will see it done. In the meantime, we carry on as normal. Heal and live. Just be on guard, whatever you do."

He looked at the timepiece in the corner of the room. "It's… actually early morning and none of us have slept. Why don't you retire and we can discuss this again tomorrow?"

As one, they stood.

"Son, stay for a bit?" Vict asked.

Dasa nodded, kissing Caris swiftly. "I'll see you shortly."

Ari was almost dead on his feet as he and Bo walked back to Bo's suite.

CHAPTER FIFTEEN

THREE WEEKS LATER

Ari, lounging on a recliner in Bo's bedroom, laughed as Bo grumbled about the final examination the doctors were giving him. It had taken him longer to heal than anyone expected. The doctors had explained, a week after the attempted kidnap, and the first time Bo had tried to reactivate his scales, that one had reset badly. When Bo had shifted, the damage was done. A clutch of scales were ripped free and Bo underwent emergency surgery. Thankfully, during that period things had been quiet. Vict and Dasa still met daily. From what Caris had told him, Ari knew it was about the unrest in the guilds, as well as the Crown of Horns. He'd not heard from Drel'nic, but, if he was honest, that in itself was a relief. He couldn't help but think the next time he heard from him, things would be a lot more serious.

Historians, under the watchful eye of both Vict and Dasa, had removed everything from the room Ari had found. Vict had been stunned when he'd seen it. The damage was minimal, as though something, or someone, had been keeping a close eye on the room.

Having spent the last few weeks starting to learn the demonic language, he and Caris were slowly getting out and about. Neither of them strayed too far, both still keeping Bo and Mac company. They'd both been released with much fanfare two nights previously. Ari was nervous. Now Bo was healed, what would happen between them? They'd shared plenty of kisses, much to the amusement of the medics, who'd insisted that Ari was the only one who could stop the Cobalt Commander from driving them crazy.

Now though, he worried if Bo would still want him, and if he did, what would happen. He'd decided to talk to Caris. They arranged to go out, sneaking past Dasa and Bo, with the help of Deek'in and Yavek, the guards who they now counted among their friends.

They were sat in a tavern, The Mighty Krenk, drinking an ale that literally smoked in the goblet. Ari found himself mesmerized by the swirling mix of greens and yellows as they rose up above the lip.

"You look like you're trying to find the answers to life in that smoke." Deek'in clapped him gently on the back with one hand as he downed another of the ales. "I promise it won't bite you. Although it does have quite a punch to it."

Yavek snorted at Deek's words. They shortened both names now, Deek and Yav happily accepting their new names.

"Has it occurred to you that's what I'm worried about?" Ari drawled, finally comfortable around them and able to be himself. Ari, braver than he had been when he first landed on Kenistal, took a small sip. Flavors exploded on his tongue and his head jerked in surprise. On one hand part of the drink was sweet and warm, yet at the same time, the other half was ice cold and woodsy. When he swallowed, his mouth gaped. "How is that possible?"

Yav shrugged. "It's a family recipe from one of the brewers. It's one of our favorites though."

Caris, already on his second, tilted his head to one side and pulled a face. "I can see why."

"So, Little Demon, now our Commander is out of his med bed, when are you going to wrap your tail around him and claim him?"

Caris snorted. "I think Bo's tail is twisted enough for both of them. Have you seen the longing looks he casts in Ari's direction whenever he thinks no one is looking?"

Deek let his eyes widen, his forehead wrinkle and a pout appear. "Kind of like this, you mean?"

Caris spluttered. "That is so wrong, funny, but wrong."

Ari blushed. He was trying to curb the habit, but it still sometimes got the better of him. "He doesn't actually look like that... does he?"

Three stupefied faces looked at him. Deek turned to Caris. "Is he actually serious?"

"Sadly, I think he is." Caris turned to study Ari. "Are you seriously telling me you don't know how Bo feels about you?"

Ari looked around at his friends. "Well, I know he likes me as a man. But, beyond that... I guess we've shared kisses, but... I don't know. I want him too. I mean, you must know I want to be with him."

Caris smiled softly. "Trust me, we know, both that you want to be with him and he wants to be with you. I think the only reason he hasn't done anything is because he's been healing. Plus, he's been giving you time to get used to being here on Kenistal, gaining your freedom and learning more about yourself."

Deek nodded along to Caris' words. "He's been holding back. I'm pretty sure he's spent the weeks since you arrived with his tail permanently twisted. There's one thing you should know about demons, Ari. We don't date. We fuck. There are no feelings unless it's with your mate. It's all casual— we just aren't built that way. But with you, our commander is trying everything he can to date you, to take it slow. I've never seen him like this. None of us have."

Yav draped his arm over Ari's shoulder. "Our commander has fallen for you, make no mistake about that. If you had seen him back when you were missing and there was the possibility you'd been taken... I have never seen someone fight like that. We were part of the first ones on the scene. He was being held in place by several demons. No one should have even been able to move even the tiniest bit, yet he got himself out of it, taking some of them out in the process. He was... words fail me in describing what it was like watching him, fighting alongside him that day. We all knew he was impressive, but that, the display he put on, it was all for you, Ari. He fought like that, never gave up, for you. Most of us would be dead— we would have been dead inside a minute. But he held out longer than any of us believed possible. In fact, he didn't just hold out, he was the victor in it. He was fueled by anger, over you. Never ever question how he feels about you. We all see it. That demon would do anything for you."

Deek tapped his goblet against Yav's. "Here's to the Commander."

"Commander Bo'saverin!" Yav shouted.

All around the tavern, the cry echoed, lots of Cobalts relaxing there on their evening off.

"He really is well liked, isn't he?" Caris looked around the room at the number of goblets raised in the air.

Dev chuckled. "He is, and everyone knows about his Little Demon here. Ari, you have more eyes watching out for you than you could possibly know. You know, there was one morning we all knew you'd kissed him."

Ari's blush rose fast and furious.

Deek knocked back the remaining ale in his goblet, waving it at one of the servers for a refill. "I'm not saying this to embarrass you, but his horns were still steaming slightly and the smile on his face was unnerving. At first, us Cobalts at training worried that he was smiling because he planned to make our life hell. But no, he was simply in a good mood. You'd done that, Ari. It was the first day of training that the Commander has led that half the company didn't end up visiting the medics. He is a notorious taskmaster. He went easy on us that day. We know it was because of you. So you see, every Cobalt knows about you. We all hope you and he become mates. It would make our lives so much better. We're cheering you on, hoping you two get together. Is it selfish? Yes! But hey, we want a slightly easier life. So we decided with Caris here that we were going to talk to you. Find out what's holding you back from claiming your demon."

Ari looked around the table. These were his friends, and they truly cared about him. He took a deep breath, mentally preparing himself. "I'm scared."

146

"Of what?" Yav squeezed his neck.

"Of him rejecting me, of not being good enough, of not knowing what I'm doing, of being so innocent, of not being a demon, of not being sexy enough. Basically I'm scared of everything." Ari hid his eyes behind his curls, refusing to look at anyone.

"Oh, Ari. I thought you'd found more confidence." Caris' soft voice reached him.

"I have, just… not where Bo is concerned."

Ari's trembling voice tore at Caris. "Then let's work out a plan to show you just how much you are perfect for him."

"I like that idea." Deek grinned. "This is going to be a lot of fun, but can I suggest we get out of here. There are too many ears listening and as much as the Cobalts are rooting for these two to get together, I doubt the commander would appreciate everyone knowing all of his business."

"You know what this situation needs?" Yav laughed. "Pie."

"Pie?" Ari looked at Yav, his nose wrinkled.

"Pie fixes everything. Especially if it's a Kerin pie." Deek's voice was almost reverent.

"What's so special about Kerin pie?" Caris shared a bemused look with Ari.

"It's beauty and happiness in a pie. I could describe it, but you have to taste it to believe it." Deek slammed back his freshly delivered ale and jumped up. "Come on then. We can sneak into the kitchens. I know there is always a secret stash there and as long as we don't get discovered, we'll be fine."

Caris jumped up, extending a hand to Ari. "I'm game. Come on, we have to try this."

"Shh, we don't want to get caught." Deek hissed at the giggling pair of non-demons. "I don't want to have to bribe tonight's guards with extra shifts because you two can't hold your ale." He snorted. "Lightweights."

Ari put a finger to his lips and solemnly nodded, the action spoiled by his body shaking with laughter.

Yav led them into a little used room next to the main banquet room. Traditionally, it was used by the servers who waited on the king and queen. Ari and Caris waited not so patiently for Deek to return. When he came in, Ari's eyes widened at the bright green crust. He didn't know why, when food was so different on this planet, but he expected the pie to be, well, pie colored.

Ari blinked rapidly, watching at Deek cut into the pie. Gentle puffs of silver clouds were released as the knife sank in. As he dished up a slice, a gold mousse filling appeared. Ari studied it, bemused. "How are the little puffs silver, and the crust green, but the filling is gold?"

"That, Little Demon, is the magic of Kerin pie." Deek handed Ari the plate and spoon.

Taking his first tentative bite, Ari soon moaned and scooped a large spoonful. His eyes slid shut and a long throaty moan escaped. "This tastes like edible sunshine and happiness. I don't care what it is, I love it."

Caris was just taking his first bite and Ari mumbled around his own mouthful as Caris groaned in delight. They both demolished their slices, staring forlornly at the now empty dish.

Yav sat back, rubbing his belly. "So, I think you need to take Bo out on a date tomorrow night. Choose the extra special underwear and tease him with it. Maybe by wearing the slightly sheer pants you got the other day when you dragged us shopping again." Yav rolled his eyes, but everyone knew he much preferred trailing after them than any other duties. "It's going to drive him crazy to see that ass of yours on display and he'll go into 'mine' mode. Not only will he not let you out of his sight, I'd bet five of the worst shifts imaginable that he won't let you out of the palace. He'll insist on keeping you in his quarters."

Caris swayed slightly in his seat. *Damn, that pie is good.* "I like his idea. It'll work."

Ari went to talk, but all that came out was a long, loud burp. He slapped his hand over his mouth. "Sorry." His words came out muffled.

"That better not be who I think it is hiding in there!" A voice boomed down the long corridor to the kitchens. "If I find out you've been sneaking my pies again, young demon, I will take my pastry beater to that backside of yours."

Deek groaned. "That's my mate's mother." He tucked the dishes on a chair and pushed it in under the table. He motioned to Ari to wipe the gold smudge of his cheek. They were all sitting, goblets of berry rush in hand, as the door burst open, an irate demoness hurtling in.

"I knew it was you, Deek'in. Why are you…" Her voice trailed off as she caught sight of Caris and Ari. "Oh, I'm sorry." She glared at Deek. "I didn't know you were in here, sirs."

Caris, ever the diplomat, stood and took her hand between his. "It is I who is sorry. I didn't mean to disturb you, but I needed someplace quiet to talk without anyone overhearing. Particularly Prince Dasa or Commander Bo'saverin."

"Oh no, Master Caris, I thought it was this one sneaking in to get my pies. I can't leave them out for two minutes when he's around." The demoness whacked him on the back of the head with a piece of kitchen equipment.

"Mamki." Deek groaned, rubbing his head. "Why have you got to embarrass me all the time?"

"Pfft, you think I'm bad, wait until I tell your mother."

Deek went as pale as a Cobalt possibly could. Yav was snickering away.

"Yavek, don't forget I know your mother as well. I'm sure she would love to know what a pie thief you are."

Both warriors sat with pouts on their lips. She cast an evil eye at both of them, before her expression softened as she looked at Ari. "You need feeding up, Little Demon, get some padding on you for Commander Bo'saverin to grab onto." She cackled as Ari blushed profusely. "I be teasing you. In case you haven't worked it out, I'm the mami of this reprobate's mate. I'm Jiska."

"It's lovely to meet you." Caris took over for a still mortified Ari. He kissed her hand, laughing as she waved him away.

"Get on with you. Now, I'll leave you to your secret meeting. But, mark my words. Get that Commander, grab him and don't let go. That man adores you." With that Jiska flounced out of the room, cuffing Deek on the head one last time.

There were a couple of beats of silence before the entire room burst into laughter. "Man, I bet your home life is never dull if your mate is anything like her mother." Caris smirked at Deek's groan.

Deek looked at the timepiece on the wall and winced. "Now if you two are in for the night, I'd better get going before I get in even more trouble than I'm in already."

When Caris insisted they were in for the night, both guards quickly jumped up. Yav peeked around the door, checking the coast was clear. "Quick, grab the dishes before she comes back."

Deek pulled back the chair, wincing when it squeaked, grabbed them and darted to the door. Both guards looked over their shoulders, impish grins on their faces. "See you in the morning." Deek bumped Yav with his shoulder and they both ran.

Caris and Ari sat there stunned for a moment. "I want more pie." Caris' eyes lit with a wicked light. "Want to go see if there's more?"

"Definitely." Ari pushed his chair back, giggling as he stumbled slightly. "Damn, that must be the ale we drank." They hooked arms and tiptoed to the kitchen. Finding the store cupboard, they shared a triumphant look, Ari bumping his hips into Caris. There on a shelf were six perfectly baked Kerin pies.

Caris peeked back out the large store cupboard. Seeing no one there, he grabbed two spoons and darted back in. Soon they both had a pie dish balanced on their laps as they leaned against a set of shelves. Spoons worked methodically from dish to mouth.

Ari let out another burp, dropping his spoon into the almost empty dish. "That is just so good."

"It's close to sex."

Caris' awestruck voice made Ari giggle. "I wouldn't know."

"Tomorrow we have to arrange for you and Bo to have a night out. Yav was right. Let Bo get one peek of you in the sexiest underwear we got and he'll be begging you to take him to bed."

Ari swayed slightly. "Is it me or is the room spinning."

Caris sat up, groaned and flopped back down. "The room's spinning."

"I think I'm just going to close my eyes for a moment until it stops." Ari muttered as his head flopped onto Caris' shoulder.

"Good idea." Caris slumped down. Within seconds, they were both snoring.

CHAPTER SIXTEEN

Bo and Dasa were talking quietly to Vict. So far, things with the Reds had been quiet. They'd broken the demons captured in the attack, but none of them knew anything. It looked like all comms had been encrypted and encoded. The techs were working on a back trace, but weren't optimistic. Another trail gone cold.

"Whoever it is, they will make a move soon. They've already shown they're desperate to get their hands on Ari, and I don't see them stopping in their attempts any time soon." Vict paced the length of his room, his tail brushing the floor in agitated sweeps.

"They won't stop. I'm sure of it." Bo's skin rippled slightly before he got it under control. "A request came across my desk this morning."

"Oh?" Dasa knew Bo never bothered them with the more mundane aspects of being the Commander of the Cobalts. The fact he was mentioning something now meant he thought there was more to whatever was going on than it seemed on face value.

"The Reds are requesting permission for a trade delegation from Trevon to visit in two days' time."

Vict's tail smacked into a chair, sending it toppling as he whirled around. "Unless I'm mistaken, Trevon is one of Aducia's neighbors."

"They are," Bo confirmed. "I take it I'm not the only one who finds that suspicious. Especially as we have never traded with them before now."

"I would be inclined to believe that it is a cover and they plan on bringing either more Loperis or…" Dasa's words trailed off with a hesitant look at Bo.

"Or, it's Ari's mother coming under another planet's banner," Bo finished Dasa's sentence.

"Exactly." Dasa snarled, his horns steaming, although it was nothing in comparison to Bo's.

"Is there a political reason I can turn them down?" Bo's tone was almost pleading. Some inner instinct demanded caution, insisting it was wrong to let the delegation land on Kenistal.

"We can refuse…" Vict looked off into the distance. "But…"

"If their request is genuine, we risk alienating a potentially wealthy trading partner," Dasa finished his father's sentence.

Vict grabbed a goblet close by and crushed it. Bo coughed to cover his laugh.

"Something funny, Commander?" Vict stood over Bo, who calmly stayed seated.

"I see that's a trait Dasa must have inherited from you. Although, I have to admit, he's calmed down on the number of goblets he's crushed recently. I imagine the silver guild is not particularly happy. The housekeepers have reduced their weekly order."

Vict raised a brow at Dasa. "Maybe you should buy a trinket or ten from them for Caris. In one move, you appease them and gain bonus credits with your mate."

Dasa looked to be seriously considering the idea when there was a cough in the doorway.

"Commander, Prince Dasalin, there is an, uh… incident in the kitchens that requires your attention." The guard on duty refused to meet anyone's gaze.

"An incident?" Bo stood, strapping his sword belt back on.

"Uh, yes, both of you are needed." The guard stepped back.

Dasa and Bo shared a look and ran, Vict following them at a more stately pace.

As Bo rounded the corner into the kitchen, he saw a collection of guards around one of the storerooms trying to suppress their laughter. He pushed his way through and stood there, jaw slack, stunned.

"What's going on?" Dasa' voice asked slightly frantic until he stopped next to Bo.

There in front of them, slumped on the floor, snoring away were Caris and Ari, both obviously inebriated.

"Is that Kerin pie?" Dasa bent down and swiped his finger through the remnants in the dish still sitting in Caris' lap. He groaned. "It is. Krexjins, the pair of them. Did no one tell these idiots that Kerin pie is like alcohol to anyone not of demon blood?"

Vict, now stood behind his son, was openly laughing. "I'm guessing by the state of them, no one did. There are going to be some sore heads in the morning."

"And sore asses once I get done smacking it," Dasa muttered under his breath.

With a weary sigh, both demons handed the empty dishes off to the demons behind them and scooped the drunken duo up and into their arms. Caris didn't even twitch.

Ari, as if he sensed Bo's proximity, burrowed in as close as possible to his chest, laying his head so his ear was right over Bo's heart.

"Take them to their quarters." Vict gently ruffled both heads. "We'll finish our discussion first thing in the morning."

"Yes, Your Majesty." Bo dipped his head, unable to bow with his arms full. He turned, his demons parting to make way for him, and swiftly walked through the palace. Halfway up the second flight of stairs, Ari stirred.

"Mmm, just where I've always dreamed of being. Safe in Bo's arms."

Bo grinned. Ari was completely unaware he was talking out loud, and wasn't he pleased to hear that little tidbit of information?

"You know, I've always wanted to touch those horns." Ari reached up and circled one of Bo's now steaming horns before he gently started to stroke it.

Bo cursed as his cock sprang to life.

Ari gently stroked the horns that kept grabbing his attention. "They're smoother than I thought they would be, and hot. I didn't expect them to be hot. Or is that because of the steam? Huh, I could swear more steam is appearing. Why is that?"

Bo looked into Ari's glassy eyes and chuckled. Ari was sozzled. "How much pie did you eat?"

Ari absentmindedly stroked Bo's horns as he thought, totally unaware of the effect he was having on the demon. "I don't know, why? I remember going to the tavern and the weird hot and cold ale. Then we came back here. We all shared the first pie. Then Caris and I went to find more. It was so good I couldn't resist."

"And that's where we found you, in the stock room eating pie."

"I didn't want to move," Ari protested, "it was comfy there. Not as comfy as being in your arms is. That's the best feeling ever. Especially when you wrap your tail around me. I love that. It makes me feel safe and secure, even if the tip does tickle."

Bo's already hardening cock was suddenly as hard as his horns. "You like being in my arms, then?" He knew it was mean, but a drunk Ari talked more freely than he normally did and Bo was desperate to know how he truly felt about him.

Ari gently traced a pattern on Bo's chest. "You know, you have a really impressive chest. I like looking at it. I like it even more when I can touch it. It's strong and the scales protect you, just like you protect me and everyone else when you're in commander mode. I like that you protect me. You're the only one I feel truly safe with. I have since the moment I first saw you. Even though you were all scaled up, and this hulking big horned man from a race I'd never seen, I knew you wouldn't hurt me."

Bo's heart stuttered in his chest as he listened to Ari ramble. He wasn't sure if Ari was actually talking to him, or talking to himself.

155

"Then, when you protected me from the beam, I was so stunned. No one has ever done something like that for me. I wanted to kiss you then. Even when everything was going crazy and I was so scared, I still knew I was safe with you. But I couldn't wake you. That's when I got truly scared, not for me, but for you."

"But you did wake me, Ari. *You* kept *me* safe." Bo gently kissed the top of Ari's head.

"Huh, maybe I did, does that make me a badass Cobalt?" Ari pretended to flex his muscles, groaning when he got dizzy.

"Maybe less of the moving, hey?" Bo chuckled as Ari tilted his head back, a streak of pie smeared on his cheek. *Oh, I want to lick that off.*

"I'm spinning, but bouncing. Why am I bouncing? Bo, are you making me bounce?"

Bo closed his eyes, praying for strength as visions of Ari bouncing on his cock blasted his mind. "Frek, Ari, the things you say…"

"What did I say? And you didn't answer my question. Why am I bouncing?"

Bo couldn't help the laugh at Ari's wrinkled up face.

"You're bouncing because I've just carried you up the stairs. We're now walking back to our suite and I shall put you to bed."

"Oh. Are you coming with me? You know, it's a good thing you're carrying me."

"Why's that?" Bo ignored the comment about going to bed with Ari.

"Because I don't think my legs are working properly."

"Probably not, you're drunk."

"I am not!" Ari scowled, indignant.

"You are. The pie you ate? That's like alcohol to any non-demon. One slice will leave you feeling the effects."

"But I ate more than a pie!" Ari burped. "Oops, sorry."

Bo muttered under his breath. "How can he be adorable when he burps, for frek's sake."

"What did you say?" Ari asked.

"Doesn't matter." Bo passed the guards outside his suite, the warning glare more than enough for them to be quiet, but he didn't miss the smiles they tried to hide.

Bo strode to Ari's room and whipped back the soft, silver covers. As he went to lay Ari down, he noticed the streaks of pie on Ari's tunic and the crumbs stuck to his tep'rink trousers. He gently leaned Ari against the wall beside his bed and started to tug up his tunic top.

"Oh, are we going to have some fun? I want to have some fun with you. I want to feel this chest against mine. I dream of falling asleep wrapped in your arms."

Bo's horns were in full-on steam mode. Damn, but Ari had a mouth on him when he stopped worrying about what he was saying. His tail wrapped around one of Ari's wrists and pinned it to the wall. He wrestled with Ari as he tugged his arm through the sleeve of his tunic.

"But I want to feel your chest." Ari pouted.

"I need to get you into bed. If you still want to feel my chest tomorrow, then just ask. Right now, you need to sleep that pie off."

Finally wrestling the top free, Bo stood speechless for a moment. His forked tongue flicked over his lips. He'd forgotten about this… Ari's nipples were green and looked perfect to bite and tease with his tongue. He'd seen them when Ari was injured back in the ruins, but his mind was purely focused on keeping Ari safe and checking for injuries. They were pebbled, whether from the air or something else, Bo had no idea. Fighting Ari's wandering hands, he gave up and pinned both Ari's hands against the wall by his hip, using his tail.

Dropping to his knees, he undid the tep'rink and pulled them down, his hands freezing in mid-movement. His stunned gaze flew up to Ari's face. "A—" He coughed to clear his throat. "Ari... what are these?"

"My underwear. I like them, do you?" Ari asked innocently.

Bo's gaze dropped back down. Ari was wearing little shorts. Cobalt blue shorts. Only they had vertical stripes. One set of stripes were solid material, but the other... they were mesh and see-through. He could see Ari's cock. Ari's hard cock. When Ari did a little shimmy, he groaned, his own cock leaking.

"They make me feel sexy."

Bo cleared his throat again. His words still came out as a growl. "They *are* sexy. *You* are sexy." His hands were itching to touch, and his tongue wanted to trace the cock on display, just for him. His horns were so hot he'd have to stop Ari touching them in case they burned him. He would never do anything to put his Ari at risk. Oh, how he wanted Ari to be his, but not like this. With a restraint he never knew he possessed, he finished pulling down Ari's tep'rink, picked him up, placed him gently in the bed and pulled the covers up, breathing a sigh of relief that he wouldn't be able to see his tempting body anymore.

"Are you getting in with me?" Ari grabbed a pillow and cuddled it to him, wishing it was Bo.

"Not tonight, Tiko. You need to sleep off that pie. If you still feel that way in the morning, then I will happily sleep with you any night you ask."

"Hmm, okay..." Ari mumbled as his eyes slowly closed. "Bo?"

"Yes, Tiko?" Bo gently pushed Ari's curls off his face.

"I really like you." Ari smiled softly.

"I really like you too." Bo bent down and gently pressed a kiss to Ari's forehead. "Sleep well." He chuckled as he realized Ari was already out for the count. Trailing his fingers down Ari's cheek, he watched him sleep for a few minutes, enjoying the freedom to simply look. Hearing his comm link chirp, he got up, turned the lights down low and left, closing the door softly behind him.

"Bo'saverin here," he barked into the link.

"How's Ari doing?" Dasa's amused voice came through the link.

"I've just put him to bed." Bo groaned as he poured himself a large ronix, a clear, sharp, berry based alcohol. Knocking back half the glass, he topped it up before flinging himself into his usual seat, a double sized padded chair.

"That groan doesn't sound good." Dasa was still chuckling away.

"Yeah, it wasn't. Caris alright?"

"Out cold, but fine. Enough of him, I want to know about Ari. In fact, hold your thoughts, I'm on my way."

Bo went to say no, but Dasa had already terminated the link. He didn't bother trying to reconnect; Dasa wouldn't answer anyway. He simply poured another drink and set it on the table next to his. Less than two minutes later, Dasa strode through the door, going straight to the drink and knocking it back without saying a word. He brought the bottle over, putting it on the table.

"It's going to be one of those nights, then?" Bo raised a brow.

"I have the distinct impression we are both going to need it."

Bo groaned. "You're not wrong there."

Dasa chuckled. "So… what happened? Ari seemed particularly… vocal as you walked up the stairs."

"Frek, the mouth on him when he's not worrying about what he's saying."

"That bad?" Dasa frowned.

"No, that good. He was stroking my horns…"

"Oh, frek." Dasa burst out laughing. "He has no idea what that does to a demon, does he?"

"No, not in the slightest. Then of course there was—" Bo shut up.

"Oh, come on," Dasa protested. "You can't leave it there."

159

Bo shook his head. At least he knew Dasa was discrete and wouldn't say anything. "He was covered in that damn pie. I had to strip him. He was wearing these… shorts that were… Well, they were something else. They have to have been the sexiest thing I have ever seen anyone wear."

"Really? Considering all the demons, both male and female, who have flung themselves at you in various stages of undress, that's saying something." Dasa sighed as the ronix started to seep into his system.

"It wasn't that they were overtly sexy. It was… they were understated teasing. It's hard to explain. They steamed my horns more than anything ever has before. They were simply him. Shy but adventurous, practical but sexy, innocent but daring."

"Damn, all that in some underwear."

"I would say you have to see them to believe them, but yeah, that's not going to happen. Ever." Bo growled out.

Dasa smirked, his eyes dancing. "Is that right?"

Bo stood, his whole body vibrating, scales flickering back and forth as he tried to get himself under control. "That. Is. Right!" His roar echoed around the room.

"Frek, Bo, you have to know I was just teasing you." Dasa held up his hands, palms out trying to placate his friend.

Bo slumped back into his chair, burying his face into his hands. "Frek, I'm sorry."

"No need. But you need to do something about this. It's obvious you have a lot of feelings for Ari. You need to tell him. As far as I know, all you two have done is kiss."

"Because I've been healing and he's innocent." Bo's face was a mask of frustration when he looked up at his closest friend.

"He may be innocent, but you're a fool if you can't see how much he feels for you. Look, I get why you want to go slow, but honestly? I think you're running out of time."

Bo's head snapped up at Dasa's words. "Why do you say that?"

"You know my father considers him one of us, but if we're right and the Trevon ship does have Aducians on board, and I suspect it will be his mother, she will do everything in her power to get him back. Now my father will do everything he can to keep him here, but, if you've mated him, if he's considered yours in the eyes of our world, it will make it easier if she lodges any complaints with the Interplanetary Judiciary."

Bo groaned at the mention of the independent group who oversaw complaints between worlds. They were an arbitrary panel who assessed any disputes.

"Exactly." Dasa sighed at Bo's groan. "We get them involved and it's going to drag on and they might want Ari held elsewhere for his safety. Then you won't be able to protect him. Is that what you want?"

"Frek, no. I'm not letting him leave. Unless he wants to."

"But here's the thing… what if she gets to him and tells him the only way to keep you safe, to keep Kenistal safe, is to go with her? You have to know he would go in a heartbeat to keep everyone safe. That's who he is."

Bo's scales transformed straight to their toughest setting. "She can't have him!"

"Then do something about it," Dasa challenged. "Stop waiting, start doing. I know you've been giving him time, that you couldn't do much while injured. But you have to consider he's too shy to make the move. It needs to be you."

"But, what if—"

Dasa interrupted with a scowl. "Don't you dare say what if he doesn't have feelings for you. Frek, Bo, we all see it. If he isn't in love with you, he's pretty frekking near it."

Bo took a deep breath. "I'm never this unsure."

"Welcome to being in love, it freks with your mind." Dasa flat-out laughed. "Now you know what I went through with Caris."

Bo downed the rest of his glass. "Frek it. While they're recovering in the morning and before we have to meet your father, want to go shopping with me?"

The look of horror and distaste on Dasa's face made Bo snort.

"Do we have to?"

"Trust me, you want Caris in what I saw Ari in."

"Fine. You better pass over the ronix. I think I need fortification."

Bo snorted but passed it over. The rest of the evening was spent doing what they normally did, discussing the warriors' training and who was going to beat who at their upcoming Pik'dorin match.

CHAPTER SEVENTEEN

Dasa frowned as they walked through the market the next morning. "It was you two, wasn't it?" He looked pointedly at Deek'in and Yavek.

Deek'in tried not to fidget at the fierce look on his prince's face. "We didn't know. That it was alcohol to them, I mean. We just know it's really good pie."

Yavek's gaze went from Bo to Dasa. "You have to know we would never do anything to hurt either one of them. They may be our charges, but they've become friends as well."

Bo sighed. "I know. Why are you here anyway? It's not as if we need the protection. I'm Commander of the Cobalts, for frek's sake, and this is Prince Dasalin we're talking about. I would hardly call him useless at defending himself."

"We are here under King Vict'arin's orders and begging your forgiveness, Prince Dasalin, but his order trumps both yours and the Commander's." Deek kept his head dipped.

Bo rolled his eyes. "The one person we can't overrule. Fine. Come on then, but be warned, we're going shopping."

Yavek groaned, leaning in to Deek to whisper, "I thought it was bad enough having to go shopping with Caris and Ari, but really, our Commander and Prince are going shopping?"

Bo overheard the comment and his grin was wicked. "I guess you'll have to show us where they went then."

Deek pretended to cry. "Oh, the things I end up doing as a Cobalt."

"You love it really." Bo stared Deek down.

"You know I do, all of us Cobalts do. Just say the word and we'll take you to the shop where they went shopping for new…" Deek gestured to the lower half of his body.

Bo and Dasa shared a grin. This was going to be a good trip.

"This is so not a good trip." Bo groaned a little while later. They were standing outside 'Cherished Soul,' the underwear shop. He looked at Dasa whose face was wrinkled. "Come on, let's get this over with."

"The things I do for that man." Dasa mumbled as he followed Bo into the shop. "It's a good thing he's my friend."

They both stood in the doorway, stunned at what they were seeing. The walls and tables were covered in all kinds of undergarments. Some of them were… Dasa's mind couldn't even think of the words to describe what some were.

Perik bowed deeply to Dasa. "Welcome, Your Highness, Commander. To what do I owe this unexpected visit? Although, it's good to see you back to normal again, Commander."

Bo stunned Perik by bowing slightly to him. "I have to thank you for everything you did for Ari. He escaped because you helped him. You showed him a way to safety and I will never be able to repay that. If you ever have need of something, ask. I will do everything in my power to make it yours."

Perik bowed back. "Thank you, but I didn't do it to incur a debt from you. I did it for Ari." Perik noticed how uncomfortable they were in his shop. "If I may be so bold… I'm guessing you are both here to purchase presents for Aridien and Caris?"

Dasa, still looking around wild-eyed, grunted.

"May I be so bold as to offer my services? We discussed what their likes were and what they had no interest in. I can point you in the direction of items that would be suitable for them?"

Bo sagged with relief. "Thank you, I have no idea where to even begin."

Perik gestured to a large table off to one side of the room. "If you want to wait there, I will bring things over."

"Good idea, I'm too big to be charging around a shop like this. Everything looks so flimsy." Bo picked up a scrap of lace from the table. It looked barely more than pieces of thread bound together in his large hands. "I mean, how do you even put this on? Surely it would snap?"

Dasa took the garment from Bo and held it up. It was so fine he could almost feel it catch on the calluses on his hands. Behind them, Deek and Yav were trying not to laugh. Deek was eyeing up a full body number which would look amazing on his mate. "Uh, Commander?"

Bo turned, raising an eyebrow.

"Would you object if I take five minutes to get something for my mate? I rarely get any time in the day free to get here. It's her naming day coming up soon."

"And you want to get in the good books." Bo grinned. "Of course. I'm guessing we may be here for a while."

Deek looked abashed, but beckoned Bo closer. "If it helps, Commander, Ari was drawn to anything cobalt blue. Although he did like some of the rich browns and greens, the blue was definitely his favorite."

"For that, find something your mate would like and I'll add it to my pile to pay for. Yavek, you too. I'm in a great mood and you two have been incredibly helpful to Ari."

Both men grinned and went off looking.

Bo closed his eyes, warmth radiating through him. A hand cuffed him on the back of the head. "What was that for?" He playfully shoved Dasa.

"Maybe now you know he's deliberately choosing cobalt underwear, you will realize he doesn't stop thinking about you. He's just too shy to admit it."

Bo snorted. "You should have heard him last night. He was definitely not shy."

"Then be thankful for the pie. Deek'in and Yavek did you a favor when they gave those two the pie." Dasa caught Deek's sheepish expression as he tried to hide behind a rack of decidedly racy two-piece sets. "What made you give them the pie?"

Deek slumped. "We took them to the Krenk, then they wanted to gossip without anyone hearing so we went back for pie. We honestly didn't know it would do that to them. We wouldn't have—"

Dasa waved his hand for Deek to shut up. "Don't apologize. You didn't put them in danger. You took them to the one tavern they would be totally safe in and kept an eye on them at all times. It's good Ari is getting to explore new things. There is so much he hasn't tried."

"We were supposed to take them out again today, but when we checked in with Caris, he told us in no uncertain terms to frek off." Yav looked beyond contrite.

"He was not happy this morning. I was cursed quite a bit when I cheerfully told him good morning." Dasa snickered.

"Better than Ari." Bo laughed. "All I got was a grunt and a pillow thrown at me."

"I'm sure they'll be causing merry havoc tomorrow, mark my words." Dasa scrubbed his face, knowing those two would always get into trouble. It seemed drawn to them like a poko to a flame.

"Here we go." Perik came back with an armful of items. "Now, I've selected the colors and styles I know they liked when they were here, so anything on this table will put you in the good books, I promise."

Bo tentatively walked towards the table seeing a mountain of colors and fabrics. The first pair he picked up he dismissed— they were bold red and longer than the rest— they seemed boring to him. He would never admit it to anyone, but seeing Ari last night in the stripes had fired his blood more than he'd thought was possible. He'd looked so sensual lying on the bed, even drunk, that he couldn't wait to experience it again. Only this time, Ari would be sober and Bo would be in bed with him.

He picked up a pair of green striped ones. This time though, the solid stripes were thin, while the mesh ones were thick. He put them to one side. He spied a couple of pairs like them in different colors and added them to his pile. Next he picked up a rich brown, lace pair. They were so delicate he could rip them with his teeth... *Oh frek me, I'm getting these.* He didn't pay any attention to what Dasa was doing with his pile, he was enjoying this too much. Imagining Ari in these, now he'd seen him in almost all his glory, made him more determined to get his man.

Dasa peeked at Bo out of the corner of his eye. Seeing him smiling away as he built up a pile made him snort. Then he looked at his own pile. Who knew shopping could be such fun? The red mesh ones got added to his pile of purples. Yeah, he wanted to see Caris wearing his color; it was another way to put his mark on his man.

Bo nearly choked when he picked up the next pair. He held them up as he cocked his head to one side. He held a pair which were fully mesh and see-through. He ran his fingers over the thick ribbon around the top. He frowned at the ribbon in the middle, with a bit of mesh sticking out of it. "What the frek is that?"

Perik laughed. He stuck his fingers in the middle of the mesh and waggled it about. "That's exactly what Ari asked me. This is where—"

Bo's incredulous gaze collided with Dasa's. "Frek me, they're a bit..."

Dasa coughed. "Yeah, they are." He promptly dug through his own pile looking for some.

Bo grabbed the pair from Perik and added them to his rapidly expanding pile.

"How about something like this?" Perik held up a pair of sheer tep'rink trousers. "These are great for getting into the mood of things. If you're wondering what they look like on—" he coughed at the wild-eyed look of the four demons in his shop— "I'm not offering to model them! I was going to say look at that shop model there." He pointed to the carved demonic form posed by one of the tables in the center of the shop floor.

Bo walked over, moving around the model, trailing his fingers over the backside. They were not only completely see-through, but incredibly soft and silky to the touch. His mind went into overdrive imagining Ari wearing it with nothing underneath, or just a pair of the lace shorts. "What colors does it come in?"

Perik grinned. "The same colors as the underwear."

"I'll take cobalt blue, the rich green and the rich brown." Bo was sure those colors would look perfect against Ari's skin. Besides, it was *his* color. What could be better than that?

By the time they got around to pay, they had huge piles. Even Yav and Deek had got some extras on top of what Dasa and Bo had offered to get for them.

"What about you demons? Can I interest you in wearing some of those?"

Perik's voice was slightly challenging and Bo was about to say no, but… "You know what. I'll take a mix of them in green. If I want Ari to wear them, I might as well wear them myself. Not for everyday, mind."

"We have some great ones for everyday warrior use." Perik perked up. He grabbed a pair of demis, laying them out on the counter. "These are designed with a warrior's muscles and scales in mind. They help the muscles stay warm so they don't lock up, as well as helping the oxygen flow through the body properly. As you can see they are very tight. All the better for appreciating a package. If anything, they enhance the package. If you look here—" he turned one pair inside out— "They have a special pouch to hold everything in place. The added bonus of that is they frankly make everything appear bigger. In case you are worried, they are designed to adjust as you activate your scales. If you then go back to just your skin they to return to their original state."

Bo picked up a pair, testing them on his arm. "Huh, seeing as I'm here you may as well add in some pairs for all of us. Even those two there." Bo gestured to the two guards behind him. "They've been good to endure this twice."

As Perik started to ring Dasa's purchases up first, he was a prince after all, Dasa looked around the store.

"Are you the owner here?"

"I am. It's just me. There normally aren't many demons interested in this sort of underwear."

"Well, if these have the effect we expect them to, then we will be regular customers. Hopefully it will bring more of the warriors in, whether for themselves or their mates." Dasa winked at Perik. "Besides, if they know we're here, and judging by the crowd outside trying to watch without being seen to be watching, we've definitely been discovered, then they won't feel so embarrassed. You might as well ring everything up under my bill."

Bo's head whipped around to look at his friend. "Are you serious? That's a small fortune there."

"It is, but it's going to be worth it. Besides, what else do we really spend money on?" Dasa nodded to the two guards behind him. "I mean theirs as well, even the bits they planned on paying for themselves."

"Your Highness," Deek protested, "we couldn't possibly ask that of you. We fully intended to pay for that ourselves."

"I know you did, but what you've done for Caris and Ari is huge."

"We didn't do anything," Deek insisted. "King Vict'arin ordered us to guard them."

"Yes, my father did. But, he didn't order you to befriend them, to have fun with them, to take them drinking with the warriors and treat them like they were demons. You've helped both fully settle here. You've helped Ari grow more comfortable in his own skin. Don't think we haven't noticed how much you've helped him." Dasa crossed his arms, legs planted wide, and stared them down.

"I would give in gracefully if I were you." Bo gestured to Dasa's pose. "When he's like this, there is no changing his mind."

Perik was watching the back and forth with interest.

Yav and Deek shared a look before they bowed deeply in front of Dasa.

"Get up, you krexjins." He turned to Perik who was trying not to snigger too loudly. "And as for you…"

Perik gulped.

"I suggest you take some commission on this as well. You've been helpful here with us, helpful with those two before, and you went above and beyond when the Commander here needed the help."

Perik shook his head. "You're doing more than enough simply shopping here."

Bo patted Perik on the shoulder, laughing when he took a stumbling step forward. "He won't stop harassing you. You might as well just agree. You really don't want him to pull the prince card. When he does that, he becomes totally insufferable."

Perik's gaze darted between them all.

Deek dropped his arm over Perik's shoulders. "If we had to give in, you might as well. I have a feeling we're going to be stuck here until you do."

Perik nervously held Dasa's gaze. "If you insist, but *only* if you do."

170

"I do. Now get to it."

CHAPTER EIGHTEEN

"**G**o away." Ari whimpered.

"Ariiiii." A far too perky voice sing-songed beside his bed.

"What?" Ari grumbled.

"I have coffee," the voice continued.

Now that got Ari's attention. "Real coffee? None of that stupid demon stuff?"

"Real Terran coffee, the good stuff as well."

Ari peeked out from underneath his pillow to see Caris. Only he looked the most disheveled Ari had ever seen him. "What happened?" He grabbed the coffee, cradling it like it was his most treasured possession. With shaky hands, he brought the goblet to his lips. Perfect.

Ari's sigh of pure pleasure made Caris smile. "We apparently ate too much."

"I don't understand. Isn't it drink too much? Besides, we only had two drinks, didn't we?"

"We did. But apparently kerin pie has the same effects as alcohol to any non-demon."

"But we ate a full pie each!" Ari's head whipped around to stare at his friend, swiftly followed by a stream of curses as a full scale battle seemed to be reenacted inside his head.

"Yeah." Caris crawled up into bed beside Ari, leaning his head on Ari's shoulder. "Trust me, I heard all about it from Dasa before he left for who knows where this morning. I must admit, Deek was looking especially contrite when he asked if we wanted to go out. Seems those two didn't know the effect it would have on us."

Ari simply grunted, not wanting to stop sipping his coffee for long enough to answer.

"I let you sleep. It's past lunch time."

Ari's eyes shot open. He scowled at the pain radiating out from then. "Really?"

"Yup, Bo must have checked on you and left you sleeping." Caris shrugged.

Ari went to take another sip of coffee, but his goblet froze midway to his lips. He lifted the covers and peered down at himself. He handed his goblet to Caris and flopped back on the bed, arm covering his eyes.

Caris carefully placed the goblet on the stand by the bed and lifted Ari's arms. "What is it?"

Ari gestured to himself. "Look."

"At what?" Caris asked.

Ari pulled back the covers.

Caris shrugged. "I don't get it?"

"I didn't undress myself," Ari whispered.

"Ahh. And you're wearing the sexy underwear. Well, if that didn't get Bo's horns steaming, nothing will."

Ari cringed.

"What now?" Caris raised a brow.

"I think, I mean, I sort of remember stroking Bo's horns last night," Ari confessed.

Caris went bug-eyed. "You do know what effect that has on them, right?"

"Umm, not really. I mean you mentioned something before, but I just remember you saying they steamed."

"Ari, I hate to be the one to tell you this, but stroking a demon's horns is basically the same as stroking their cock."

Ari yanked up the covers and hid. "I'm never coming out," he mumbled.

Caris wiggled his way under the covers and pulled the smaller man into his arms. "Hey, don't be embarrassed. I'm betting it took everything in him to hold back last night. I'm also betting you will see a change in him today. If I was you I'd be ready."

"For what?" Ari peeked through a curtain of curls.

"For Bo to claim you. I don't think, after seeing you in those, he will have any patience left."

"I hope so," Ari whispered.

Caris smacked Ari's butt as he rolled over trying to reach his coffee. "Right, come on. I think we should get out of here while we can. If I'm right, he's going to come looking for you as soon as he's finished working on whatever it is he's doing. You want to make him work for it?"

Ari shyly nodded.

"Then let's get to it." Caris whipped back the covers. "I dismissed Deek and Yav for the day, so we'll have to stay in the palace."

Ari suddenly got a wicked gleam in his eyes.

"What?" Caris asked suspiciously.

"Well, you know I said I could hack things. What about if I hack their comm implants."

"To do what?"

"I could make them blare an alarm, play a tune, just about anything," Ari admitted.

"We do this, you know you'll push him over the edge. You'll have to hide."

"He won't hurt me." Ari shook his head.

"Only in the best possible way." Caris threw clothes at Ari. "Come on, before they get back."

Ari raced for the bathroom, his headache long forgotten.

"Shh," Ari whispered as Caris tried to muffle his laughter. They'd managed to sneak into one of the tech centers. There was one tech demon on duty across the room, but by the sounds of it, he was listening to music as he worked and wouldn't hear them until it was too late.

"Do we do this to all Cobalt implants, or just theirs?" Caris watched Ari pull out a toolset and start stripping off a panel from the comm tower.

"You choose." Ari pulled out the set Bo had gotten him, smiling to himself that Bo had given him the means to do this.

Caris pursed his lips. "As much as I want to do it to everyone, I don't want to cause too many problems. I know Deek and Yav went with Dasa and Bo, so how about just the four of them? Can you do that?"

Ari hummed as he typed rapidly onto his data entry pad. Within minutes, he'd bypassed the security programs. "You know, they really should have more in place than this. Someone needs to upgrade their systems. That was far too easy."

"I trust your judgment. I have absolutely no idea what you are doing." Caris leaned against one of the comms towers as he sat on the floor next to Ari, keeping a watch on the tech demon and the door.

"I'm going to have to say something to Bo. I don't want to get anyone in trouble…"

"But if it's that easy, someone needs to know so it can be fixed," Caris finished.

"Exactly." Ari pulled up the comm list. It detailed the wavelength and vibrations of all Cobalt implants. He made a note of the four he wanted and backed out of the system, making sure to leave no trace he was there. Working quickly, he lost himself in the coding sequences. He swiftly set up a sliva beast, a special type of comp program that would work its way through the security protocols before it would lodge itself in the emergency breakthrough controls. Right where he needed to work.

Satisfied that one was working, he grinned to himself. Time for a bit more fun while he was here. He accessed the door controls for all the Cobalt only areas. Surprisingly, there was very little for him to do other than tweak the voice command. He changed it from 'welcome warrior' to 'enter at your own risk.' Once that was done, he went back to the comms control. The sliva beast he'd set up was finished and 'access granted' flashed on the screen. He quickly changed the coding so a breakthrough to the four demons in question would set a roll of drums echoing through the link. He carefully pulled out of the system and recalled the sliva. He covered up his tracks and shut everything down. Quickly replacing the panel, he then tucked everything away in the bag he'd carried with him.

"All done," he mouthed.

"Already?" Caris whispered.

"I'm good at this." Ari kept a little device with him that, at a push of a button, would set the breakthrough going. "Come on, let's get out of here and hide."

Once they were in a safe part of the palace, away from the tech center, they both finally gave into the laughter riding them.

"We have to watch what happens." Caris led Ari down a corridor, looking around for the perfect spot. "Here." He pulled him into a room and eased the door until it was just ajar. "That's one of the Cobalt doors just there. We can wait for one of them to appear."

"And just who are we waiting on appearing?" A voice boomed out behind them.

Both men froze. The only things that moved were their eyes as they looked at each other as best they could in their positions. "That's Vict," Ari hissed to Caris.

"Why yes, yes, it is." Vict moved to stand behind them and placed a hand on each of their shoulders, gently pulling on their tops until they stood. He turned them round to face him. He called on all his royal bearing to keep a straight face. These two looked worse than when he'd caught Dasa and Bo sneaking out for food in the middle of the night as demonlings.

"So… who are we waiting on?" Vict moved so that he stood with his arms crossed over his chest, looking down as he towered above them.

Ari slumped, took a deep breath and looked up. "We're waiting on one of the Cobalts appearing."

"And why is that so interesting? If I'm not mistaken, that's one of the rooms they post shift details in. Hardly the most exciting room in the palace."

Ari looked around, groaning when he spied what looked to be a reading room. "I'm sorry if we disturbed your peace, Your Majesty." Ari went to bow, but Vict waggled his finger.

"Nope, I thought we agreed it was Vict for you two."

Both men nodded in unison.

"And yes, this is one of my private reading rooms. I have an agreement with Bo'saverin that I can be on my own in here as it's in the heart of Cobalt space. No one knows about it, well, apart from you now. The door over there connects to my office in the State Wing."

Vict moved around them and peered out in the corridor. "So, what, or who are we waiting for. I want the truth now." He used the same tone he'd used on Dasa as a demonling.

Ari hid behind his hair, not wanting to answer, but then he decided... no, he'd done this, he should accept whatever happened because of it. "I hacked into the tech center. I reprogrammed Bo, Dasa, Deek and Yav's comm implants to play a drumbeat when I press a button. Then I reprogrammed all the Cobalt only access doors to say 'enter at your own risk' when they open them."

There was a beat of silence before Vict threw back his head and laughed, long and loud. His tail was twirling in circles, his whole body vibrating with the force of his laughter. When he'd calmed down enough, he crouched down in front of the door, leaving space for both of them and beckoned them over. "Now this I have got to see."

Ari shared a surprised look with Caris and joined Vict. They watched as two Cobalts walked down the corridor chatting. One of them pressed his palm to the input panel and the door slid open.

"Enter at your own risk!" the mechanical voice boomed out.

One of the Cobalts dropped the stack of comm devices he was carrying. The other jumped back a couple of feet, screaming. Vict clamped a hand over both Caris and Ari's mouths as they threatened to laugh too loudly. He'd sucked his own cheeks in to dampen down his own laughter.

"What the frek!" one of the guards yelled as he looked up and down the corridor. "Regik, what the frek happened to the doors?"

Another Cobalt ran up and joined them. "What do you mean, what happened to the doors? Nothing happened to them."

"Oh, really? Then you frekking use it."

The Cobalt used the panel... "Enter at your own risk!" the voice boomed once again.

"What the frek!" the demon yelled. He tapped his comm implant. "Tech, we have a situation in corridor B5j4."

"Uh oh." Vict looked sheepish.

"What?" Caris turned.

"That's going to set all sorts of alarms going. And it's going to alert Bo and Dasa because this room is here." Vict looked around the room quickly. He jumped up and raced over to a set of double doors. "In here!" He beckoned them over.

Ari raced after him, tugging Caris' hand behind him.

"Commander, we have a situation."

Bo groaned at the security officer's words. "Report."

"Reports of a situation in B5j4." The officer's voice came through steady, but with a hint of nerves.

Bo did a double take and tapped Dasa on the shoulder. "I'm sorry, did you just say there is a situation in B5j4?"

Dasa jerked to a stop and stared at Bo, searching his gaze.

"I did," the officer confirmed.

"We're on our way." Bo shut the link down.

Yav and Deek were already grabbing their bags from them. Less than ten seconds later, Bo and Dasa, in full scale defensive mode, were sprinting back to the palace.

"Do we know what?" Dasa's voice was steady, even though they ran at their maximum pace.

"No idea, just that it was a situation."

"Frek." Dasa looked at Bo and they both dug down deep to find an extra burst of speed.

As soon as they hit the palace proper, their faces must have said it all as demons flattened themselves against walls, giving them room to get by. Far more demons than usual were clustered in the hallways and around doors, which were being held open for them so nothing would slow them down. Bo ignored everyone and everything. Little registered until they made it to B5j4. As soon as the group of demons were in sight, Bo was yelling. "Report!"

"Commander, something is wrong with the door." One of the demons scowled.

There was a beat of silence. "What?" Bo demanded as he pulled to a stop.

"The door. There's something wrong," the demon repeated.

"Are you seriously telling me this alert is about a frekking door?" Bo's voice echoed off the walls around them.

"Well, yes. What else would it be about? I'm thinking someone tampered with it."

That comment pulled both Bo and Dasa up short. They'd both been in mid-reach about to throttle the closest demon.

"What do you mean?" Dasa growled.

It finally dawned on the Cobalts in the corridor something was going on. Both their prince and commander were dangerously on edge. One of them went up to the input panel and repeated the process to enter.

"Enter at your own risk," the mechanical voice droned out.

Bo pulled up short.

"That should not be happening." Bo narrowed his gaze. "Who discovered this?"

"I did." A Cobalt stepped forward. "We were just going in to register some new training shifts. We haven't gone in. I don't know what's going on, but we contacted the security center as soon as it happened."

Bo shared a look with Dasa and they drew their swords together. This was one of the most protected corridors in the wing considering what room lay opposite. He could only hope Vict wasn't hiding out there. He keyed his implant to link to Vict's personal guards. "Is the King safe?"

"He's in his office, working," came the reply.

With a relieved breath, both he and Dasa walked into the shift room, swords drawn. There was nothing, absolutely nothing wrong. Not an item was out of place as far as Bo could tell and there was no one in there. He turned back around to look at Dasa. "What the frek was this about?"

"It looks all clear." His voice rang out down the corridor. "Everyone return to your stations." He touched his implant. "Security, stand down to level 3 alert. I have this under control. Will notify for more assistance."

"Confirmed, Commander."

Once the corridor was clear, both Bo and Dasa drew their swords again and pushed against the door to Vict's private reading room. Looking around, nothing seemed to be out of place. Bo relaxed his stance. "What the frek is all this about?"

Vict struggled not to laugh. Caris and Ari were sniggering away. Ari gestured to the little pad he carried with him and Caris nodded. Vict narrowed his eyes at the pair of them.

Ari took a deep breath and pressed the button. He struggled to contain his reaction as he watched.

Bo grabbed his ear as his comm started sounding out a heavy drumbeat. "What the frek!" His voice rattled the windows.

Dasa attempted to slam his link closed. The drums kept going, the beat getting faster and faster. "Bo, what the frek?"

"I don't know." Bo tried to switch it off, but nothing happened. "Try yours."

Dasa fiddled with his implant. "Nothing."

Bo moved towards the door as though he was going to call for help.

Ari, watching from the doorway, switched the drumbeat off. Vict tapped him on the shoulder and gave a gimmie sign to him. Ari pouted, but handed it over.

Vict pointed at the button, his eye's flaring with evil glee when Ari nodded.

"Something is going on. I just wish I knew what." Bo growled out, frustration riding him. Pressing the implant, he connected to the security center. "Report."

"Commander, we are getting reports that all doorways within the Cobalt area of the palace are reacting the same as the one in your location. Instinct tells me there's been an electronic intrusion of some kind."

"I thought our system was completely isolated and secure? That no one would be able to access it from the outside." Bo's anger was riding him. His tail was whipping back and forth, slamming into anything in its path.

"Commander, it *is* a closed system."

"Find out what the frek is going on."

"Yes, Commander." The security officer closed the link down.

"Wh—" Dasa groaned as his link chirped. "Report." He rolled his eyes at Bo.

"My Liege, it's Cobalt Deek'in here. Commander Bo'saverin's link is busy. Yavek and I have just had a strange breakthrough on our implants. It was an odd drumbeat. I just wanted to make sure it was nothing serious and that both Caris and Aridien are alright."

Dasa went to respond they were fine, but he paused. "I'll get back to you. Get to the palace anyway."

"We're already on our way, Sir. We shall be with you shortly."

Vict grinned wickedly and pressed the button. Both Dasa and Bo started to fiddle with their comms. Ten seconds later, Vict switched it off.

"What the frek is going on?" Dasa scowled.

Bo was keying his implant. "Report." He barked out to the two guards outside his and Ari's suite.

"Everything is quiet here, Commander. Aridien left with Caris a little while ago," Bekrit, the warrior on duty, said.

"Do you know where they went?"

"No, Commander, but they did look excited. Begging your pardon, Commander, but they seemed especially eager to be getting somewhere. Too eager, considering they should be suffering the effects from the pie last night."

"Hmm. Very well. Thank you, Bekrit." Bo pursed his lips as he looked at Dasa.

"What is it," Dasa demanded.

"By the looks of things, Ari and Caris left our suite earlier today, excited about something."

"They wouldn't leave the palace, not without their guards." Dasa was positive about that.

"No, they wouldn't. But those two would get up to mischief." Bo quirked up a brow.

"Yes, they would, but what are you suggesting? That they somehow had a hand in the things going on around us?" Dasa scoffed.

"That's exactly what I'm suggesting." Bo paced back and forth. "Think about it. While on board the Loperis ship, getting them back here, the tech shop in the market. All the signs point to Ari being exceptionally gifted with any tech device."

Dasa pinched the bridge of his nose. "You're right."

"Besides, this is Caris and Ari we're talking about. They always seem to be around when there's trouble."

"So we need to find them." Dasa walked over to the window, his palm resting flat against the pane. "When I get my hands on him…"

"Oh, have no worries, Ari is going to be in a whole heap of trouble. As well as anyone who has had a hand in this. I don't care who it is they're going to get a piece of my mind. I can't believe anyone could have been so stupid as to encourage them. With everything going on, doing this is just…" Bo let his words trail off, so angry he struggled to even find the words.

"I doubt they realized what they were doing was that bad," Dasa intervened.

Bo found a chair nearby and dropped into it. "You're right. They wouldn't have realized. But, if it was Ari, he shouldn't have been able to get into our systems. No one should. I'm going to have to get someone to go over everything. But who? It's obvious the tech we have missed something."

"By accident or on purpose?" Dasa clarified.

Bo's head snapped up. "Frek. I hadn't thought of that. You think…"

"I don't know what to think. One way or the other we need to get to the bottom of this, starting with where those men of ours are."

In the bathroom, Vict, Caris and Ari shared a look. Vict winked and motioned for them to wait where they were. He stepped out of the bathroom.

"Son, Bo'saverin. Might I ask what you're doing in my reading room?"

"Why aren't you in your office? You should be there?" Dasa whirled around to face his father.

"Nice to see you too, son." Vict stared pointedly at Dasa.

Dasa grumbled, but walked over and embraced his father. "Sorry. I was just worried about you. There's been a couple of issues today and we're trying to figure out what they mean. I spoke to your guards and they said you were in your office."

"According to them, I am." Vict shrugged like it was no big deal.

"Father, do I need to remind you—"

"Son, you don't need to remind me about anything, especially safety. I am well aware of the risks. I take what precautions I can, but I will not be held prisoner in my own palace. There is too much for me to do to be forced to stay behind a wall of warriors. If I do that, you have to know what will be said, especially by the Reds."

Dasa slumped into the seat next to Bo. "Frek!" It was his turn to rattle the windows.

"Now about your two young men. They aren't really in trouble are they?" Vict stared them both down.

"No, but I'd like to know how they mana—" Bo stopped as his implant started to beat with drums.

Dasa ignored his own. Instead, he focused on his father, who had his hand behind his back, a determinedly neutral expression on his face. "What are you doing?"

"What?" Vict's gaze flicked to Dasa before darting away again.

"I said… what are you doing?"

"Nothing." Vict went to walk to his desk.

"No, wait. You're up to something. You look fidgety and determinedly blank. You never use that look when we're on our own. You, father, are most definitely up to something."

Bo sighed when the drums stopped.

"There! You did something, I know it." Dasa stalked towards his father.

"Now, son, I don't know what you think I did, but…"

185

"I don't think, I know. Hand it over." Dasa held out his hand.

"Hand what over?" Vict shifted.

Dasa waggled his fingertips. "Come on."

Bo stood, walking over to them, trying to work out what Dasa knew that he didn't. His mouth dropped as Vict scowled and dropped something into his son's hand.

Dasa groaned and passed it over to Bo.

Bo looked it over and pressed the button on the small device. The drum beats started. Pressing it again, he was relieved when they stopped. Looking back and forth between the device and Vict, he was stunned. This was… it was…

"Who made it?" Dasa crossed his arms over his chest and stared his father down.

"No one." Vict looked as defensive as any demonling getting in trouble.

"Come on, you'll be in less trouble if you admit the truth." Dasa's tail tapped against his leg as he waited.

"I *am* the king, you know. I don't think you have the right to get me in trouble, besides that, I'm *your* father." Vict stared his son down.

"Well, right now, you're not acting like either, so come on, spill. I want to know."

In the closet, Ari turned to Caris. "I'm going out there. I made the device. It's unfair to let Vict get in trouble from it."

Caris hugged him tight. "Come on, let's go and face the music."

Ari held Caris' hand tight for support and slowly opened the door, taking a step into the room.

Vict saw his two co-conspirators out of the corner of his eyes. He shook his head, silently trying to tell them to go back in and he'd handle it.

Bo caught the move and followed Vict's gaze. He coughed trying to hide his laugh. Ari and Caris were stood in the doorway looking both sheepish and decidedly hungover. "I knew it. You'd better get in here."

Ari let go of Caris' hand as Dasa tugged his mate into his arms and climbed up onto the chair. Damn stupid things really were too tall for him. He felt like a child with his legs swinging back and forth. Fairly apt, considering he was about to get told off.

"You should have stayed hidden," Vict protested.

Ari shook his head. "I made them. If anyone is getting in trouble, it should be me. I'm the one who hacked the systems."

"Twice." Bo stared Ari down. It wasn't a question.

Ari shrugged. "Yes, twice." He took a long, deep breath, found his courage and stared Bo down. "You know, it wasn't that hard, even feeling rough after pie… It shouldn't have been that easy. Not just for me to make the changes, but to sneak into the room in the first place."

Bo watched as fire sparked behind Ari's eyes. Pleased to see Ari getting his courage and standing up for himself, it was just typical it was when he did something Bo should really tell him off for.

"He's right, Bo'saverin." Vict passed Ari a freshly poured concoction. "Drink this. Trust me, it will help with the after-effects of all that pie."

Ari looked at the drink. There were layers of a bright orange liquid, followed by such a vibrant pink, it almost hurt his head to look at the damn thing. With a grimace, he went to hand it back to Vict.

Vict gently pushed the glass back to him. "Trust me. You too, Caris." He handed him his own glass.

Ari held Caris' gaze as he took a tentative sip. The orange part tasted like mint and the pink soothed his throat, bringing a surprising amount of energy into his system. "I don't know how you demons make the food and drink you do, but I thank you for it. Even the…

187

pie." He grimaced slightly at the memory. "Everything is so strange, but delicious. Thank you."

Hearing Ari's words, Caris quickly took a sip, groaning at the relief that flooded through him.

Ari took another fortifying sip and looked up at Bo through his lashes. "I'm sorry." His throat tightened, and he couldn't bear to look at Bo. "We were just having fun. I didn't mean to cause any problems or to anger you. I would never want to do that." Ari's voice trailed off as he fought back the wave of emotions threatening to engulf him.

Bo squatted down in front of Ari, reaching out a hand to cup his face. "Tiko, don't be sad. I was worried more than anything. I didn't want anyone I care about in this palace to not be safe. I'm not angry with you. Angry at the situation, but not at you. I'll need to look at the vids of the Cobalts you caught off guard. I can only imagine their reactions. Did you watch?"

Ari nodded, still refusing to look at Bo.

"What happened?" Bo asked gently.

"One of them jumped a span and screamed, and the other dropped what he was carrying. They both looked so surprised," Ari whispered.

"Looks like I need to toughen my Cobalts up then. Bunch of krexjins." Bo's thumb continued to sweep back and forth over Ari's cheekbone. "Tiko, I promise I'm not mad at you. I could never be mad at you."

"You promise?" Ari finally looked up at Bo, his eyes haunted.

"Oh, Tiko, I promise." Bo moved his other hand and carefully cradled Ari's face, leaning in to softly kiss him. When Ari immediately submitted to him, he groaned and deepened the kiss.

Vict turned his back on the two, giving them some privacy. Dasa and Caris following suit. "We need to look into just how bad our security is. This shouldn't have been able to happen. The question is,

I don't see how we can trust our techs, seeing as they are the ones who let this happen in the first place."

Dasa and Vict wracked their brains trying to think of a way around it.

Caris suddenly perked up. "Get Ari to do it. I mean, I have no idea what he actually did, but he did it fast and, as you know, it worked."

Vict rocked back on his heels, leaning against the desk behind him. "You know, that's the perfect idea. Besides, that should force the tech demons to shape up. They won't like being shown up by a non-demon, even though Ari is now a demon, you know what I mean."

Dasa reached back and tapped Bo on the shoulder, not wanting to embarrass Ari by calling them out, but wanting them in on the conversation.

Bo slowly pulled back from the kiss, trailing a last couple along Ari's jaw, before standing up and turning to face everyone. "What's up?"

Rather than answer him, Vict turned to Ari. "Would you do something for me?"

"Anything." Ari looked up at the demon who'd been so kind to him, so welcoming and who'd been more of a father figure than anyone else in his life.

"We know you're gifted from the way you pulled both these things off at the same time. I'm deeply concerned at how easy it was."

Tech was the one thing Ari was comfortable with, and his voice was confident and steady. "Frankly, you should be. It was far too easy to bypass the security protocols in place. There was so little there as a defense, most mid-level techers could bypass it."

"That's what concerns me. Would you be able to work on the system and identify where we need to make changes?" Vict couldn't stop his smile as Ari's face lit up with joy.

"I would love to. It would make me feel useful and not like I'm just living off your kindness."

"You're doing nothing of the sort. It's a pleasure to have you here, especially since it's obvious you bring joy to Bo'saverin here."

Ari looked at Bo, blushing.

"He's right, Tiko." Bo winked at Ari.

"When do you want me to start?" Ari looked at the three demons in turn.

"I would suggest taking it easy for the rest of the day after that pie." Vict laughed at Ari's groan.

"How did you hear about that?" Ari blushed deeply.

"Nothing stays quiet in the palace for long. Besides, I was there last night."

"You were? I don't remember that."

"With due respect, you were pretty out of it." Vict laughed. "I imagine Bo'saverin here had his hands full getting you safely back to your bed."

Ari's face drained of color before the green flush spread over his cheeks. He couldn't look anyone in the eye.

Vict, taking pity on him, pushed up from the table he was leaning against. "I'd better get back to work. Take the rest of the day to recover and you can look into it tomorrow. Besides, if you try and work on the security now, I imagine the techs will be on guard."

"They'd better be." Bo growled out. "Tempted to demote the lot of them."

Ari closed his eyes briefly, working up the courage for his next comment. "I hate to say this…"

"Go on." Bo grasped his hand.

"I don't think they are incompetent." Ari held Bo's gaze. "I think someone, maybe more than one, is corrupt. There is no way

190

anyone with decent tech knowledge should have left such an easy pathway for access."

"What do you mean?" Vict asked.

"I mean it was deliberate. I got into the comms system easily, far too easily. I found the identifiers for each implant. Then I got into the system to hijack that. When you add in the fact that bypassing the commands on the doors in what should be one of the most secure areas of the palace and it's too coincidental."

Dasa whistled. "When you put it like that."

"It means we have a security nightmare." Bo scrubbed his face. "Will our systems hold for today?"

"They will, partly because what I did has an automatic defensive mechanism. It's the way I designed it. That will actually plug the gap in your system until I can work on it properly. I can set up an alert remotely so if someone attempts to gain access, I'll know."

Bo blew out a relieved breath. "You're amazing, do you know that?" He kissed Ari's forehead.

"Well, if everything will hold till tomorrow, go and have a relaxing afternoon. I have a feeling we're all going to need it over the coming days." Vict held both Dasa's and Bo's gaze.

There was something going on there, Ari could tell, but he would leave it for the moment. There was only so much his mind could process, especially with this hangover. He was never eating that pie again…. Who was he kidding? It was so delicious he'd have more in a heartbeat. Just not right then.

CHAPTER NINETEEN

Ari moved to the bed, nervously sitting and playing with a thread from his tunic. He was too embarrassed to look at Bo. Throughout the day his memories of the night before had returned. Being honest with himself, he was absolutely mortified. The things he'd said and done. They weren't him. Well they were, he'd meant them, he still did, but he wished he hadn't said them. What would Bo think of him now?

Bo gently took a seat next to Ari and grasped his hand with his, threading their fingers together. "I think it's time we talked, don't you?" Bo held Ari's gaze, saddened to see the worry in his eyes. "No, don't be scared, this is nothing bad. I just think it's time I was fully honest with you. Ari… From the moment I first saw you I wanted to draw you into my arms and protect you. When I carried you from the pod, having you in my arms was right. It was as though that's where you were always meant to be. When the ceiling came down, the only thought in my head was about protecting you, making sure you were safe. It wasn't about being a Cobalt. It was all about you. I wanted to kiss you so badly that day."

Bo grinned sheepishly before continuing. "But, I found out you were innocent and I promised myself I would take time and not rush you. I wanted to be sure if anything happened between us it was on your terms and because you wanted it to happen. Waiting has been torture. Then, last night happened. I loved seeing the carefree, talkative Ari last night."

"You did?" Ari whispered.

"I truly did. You've been discovering who you are and getting stronger, braver, more confident and definitely feistier. I have loved every minute of watching you become comfortable in your own skin, in finding what you truly like."

"I want to be brave. I don't want to hide who or what I am."

The sadness on Ari's face nearly undid Bo. "Oh, Tiko, you are brave, so incredibly brave. You helped Caris escape, you piloted the pod back here, you've faced massive changes to your life and done so with a grace and dignity few can match. You've refused to worry about conventions and taken the time to learn what you like to do, what you like to wear…" Bo took a moment, holding Ari's gaze. "I am in awe of you, Ari. I don't want to rush you. It's the last thing I want to do. But last night… it made me realize I can't hide the truth from you either. You have to know, or at least you shouldn't be surprised to know I've fallen for you."

Burgeoning hope flooded Ari. Did this mean he hadn't made a total fool of himself the night before? He hadn't destroyed any chance of happiness with Bo? Stars, he hoped so. "You have?"

"I have, Ari, more than you could probably understand or I could easily express." Bo wrapped his hand around Ari's neck drawing him close. "When you said what you did last night—"

"I'm sorry!" Ari cried.

"No! Frek, no. Don't you dare say sorry, Tiko. I loved every bit of what you said."

"You did?" Ari's startled gaze searched Bo's.

"I did. It gave me the courage to talk to you." Bo did a half-hearted grin. "I know, right? The Cobalt Commander who has been scared to admit he's falling in love."

Ari squeaked. "Did you just say…"

"That I was falling in love with you? Yes, although, I'm pretty much there already. But I wasn't sure you felt the same. I know we've shared kisses, but love is something else entirely."

Ari sat stock still, completely stunned. His heart was racing a span a minute and his throat closed up. Unable to say anything, he simply stared at Bo. Was it possible the man he'd fallen in love with truly felt the same? Could he be that lucky?

Bo pulled back, letting his arms drop as he took in Ari's reaction. "You don't feel the same, do you? It's okay, you know, I understand. I'll leave you in peace." Bo pushed himself off the bed only to be yanked back down by Ari. Not expecting the move, he flopped onto his back.

Ari, still unable to find his voice, quickly climbed on top of Bo and grabbed his face in his hands and kissed him with everything he had in him. He hoped his action could portray his feelings the way his lack of words could not.

Bo lay there, completely stunned for a moment before instinct kicked in and he wrapped his arms around Ari, deepening and controlling the kiss. He sighed into Ari's mouth as his man, and that was how he thought of Ari, relaxed against him, spreading out so he was laying fully on top of Bo.

Ari lost all track of time. He lost himself to the kiss, the feel of Bo's body hardening beneath him, the gentle caress along his back, the tail wrapped around his waist, just like he'd told Bo he loved the night before in his drunken state. Suddenly something clicked in his head. Bo really was serious. He really did want him. *Him*. Little old Ari who didn't get a chance to grow up properly, who was innocent in most ways— him. Emboldened by that thought, he slid his hands under Bo's tunic and pushed up.

Bo broke away to stare at Ari. "What does this mean?" He stilled Ari's hands, not wanting to get in any deeper, to lose his heart any further, when it would all end in mere moments.

"It means I've fallen for you too. I think from the first moment I set eyes on you. I could just never believe that you might want me too. People said you did, but I couldn't see it."

"People have been talking about us?" Bo groaned at himself as he couldn't resist trailing a path of kisses over Ari's face, across his jaw and down his neck. That damn blush was just too tempting.

"Caris, Deek, Yav… yeah… them." Ari tilted his head back to give Bo more access. When the move pushed his groin into Bo's, he whimpered and thrust his hips forward.

"I didn't mean to start this." Bo grabbed Ari by the hips and kept him in place as he thrust up against him.

"You didn't. I did." Ari wanted to touch his cock, it was aching, but that meant moving and the feelings coursing through him at Bo's touch were obliterating his ability to do anything. "I want to touch you," he pleaded.

Bo let go, only for as long as it took to yank his tunic over his head. After a second of hesitation, he pulled off Ari's too. "Frek, Tiko. Those nipples of yours haunted my dreams last night."

Ari moved his hands onto Bo's chest, groaning at the warmth radiating out from him. "You've seen them before."

"When you were injured." Bo growled. "All I wanted then was to make sure you were safe. But seeing them last night, seeing what you were wearing. Frek, it took every drop of strength I possessed, and then some, to resist touching you."

Ari blushed at the memory of what he'd been wearing. "You stripped me. You saw…"

Bo's cock pulsed against Ari's. "I did. I've never been so damn turned on in my life. Frek, Tiko, you looked stunning in them."

"I did? They weren't too rude, or demoness-like?"

"I wouldn't care even if they were. They are you, Ari. It's only ever about what you like, what you want, what makes you feel sexy and comfortable. But, frek, did they turn me on."

"I like them. They make me feel sexy."

"They don't just make you feel sexy, Tiko, you looked so damn hot in them. You made my horns steam more than they ever have before."

"Ah, umm, sorry for stroking them last night. Caris told me it was like I was stroking your… cock." Ari bit his lip, trying to stop his moan escaping as Bo pinched one of his nipples.

"Oh, frek me, that's hot."

"What is?" Ari was convinced he was losing track of this conversation.

"Your nipples get brighter as you get more excited." Bo leaned forward and flicked his tongue over one, making Ari cry out.

"But seriously, I loved you touching my horns, even if it frustrated me that I couldn't do anything about it. You, Tiko, can touch my horns any time you want. You can touch me anytime you want." There was so much Bo wanted to do to Ari, but they needed to go at Ari's pace. "I want to touch you everywhere, do everything to you and with you. But we need to go slow."

"Frek going slow, I've waited long enough." Ari cried out as Bo pinched his nipple. "I want whatever you are prepared to give me."

Bo's cock was dripping with precum as he wrapped his arms around Ari and held him tight for a moment before flipping them over so Ari was lying back on the bed. With a wicked grin, he held himself over Ari and slowly started to kiss down Ari's chest. As he reached Ari's hips, he flicked his tongue over the sensitive join of his leg. Hooking his fingers into the waistband of Ari's pants, he pulled them down and stopped, stunned at the vision before him. Ari was wearing another pair of shorts, this time a rich brown. They were mainly mesh, but with a gentle swirling pattern of thicker material. They did absolutely nothing to hide Ari's erection. The sight was too tempting and Bo leaned down, taking the tip of Ari's cock into his mouth, fabric and all.

Words failed Ari. The things Bo was doing to him blasted his ability to do anything other than enjoy the moment. Bo was sucking the tip of his cock as his tongue seemed to be everywhere at once. It was snaking around the top as the forked tip teased the head. He couldn't stop leaking, or moaning. Bo's hands moved to cup his ass, holding him against his mouth. Suddenly, a growl of frustration echoed around the room and there was a resounding rip. Cool air danced over his over-heated groin for a moment before Bo swallowed him whole. "Bo!"

Bo hummed around Ari. He refused to give up his prize. Ari tasted divine. There was a sweetness to him Bo knew he would never get enough of. As his mouth and tongue worked Ari, his hands kneaded his ass cheeks, slowly starting to spread Ari wider. He pulled off briefly. "If I do anything, anything at all you don't like, say stop and I'll stop. This is all about giving you pleasure. Do you understand, Tiko?"

Ari, still at a loss for words, could only nod.

Bo took that as a go and went back to teasing Ari's cock. Yet, it wasn't enough. He wanted more, everything, with Ari. He pulled off Ari with a loud pop and ignored the cry from him. He tipped Ari's hips and lowered his head, this time teasing Ari's balls with his tongue. Needing his hands to keep Ari in position, he ran his tail up Ari's legs until it wrapped around his cock and started to stroke, the slightly furry end tickling Ari, making him writhe against the bed. Letting go of Ari's balls with a soft pop, his tongue slowly worked towards his hole.

"Bo…" Ari's shaky voice stopped Bo in mid movement.

"Are you okay? Want me to stop?" Bo held his position, waiting. Despite how much he wanted to carry on, he'd meant what he'd said. If Ari said stop, he stopped.

"No! I just, you can't be about to… you know…"

"Taste your ass?" Bo grinned as Ari's blush ran down from his cheeks and across his chest.

All Ari could do was nod, too embarrassed to say the words.

"I can and I will. What's more, you are going to love every minute of it, I promise you." To prove his point Bo flicked his tongue against Ari's hole. The only thing that kept Ari in position was his superior strength. Ari bucked wildly against him.

"What… that's… I… you…"

"Relax, love, just enjoy." Bo swiped his tongue against Ari again, this time prepared for the involuntary thrust of Ari's hips. With teasing circles, he slowly got Ari used to him being there. He gently started to probe Ari with his tongue. The first time he slipped inside, Ari reflexively tightened around him. Frek, he was going to be so tight if Bo was ever lucky enough to experience being inside of him. His cock pulsed where it was trapped inside his pants, but he refused to spare even a second to adjust it. All he wanted was to make Ari's first time memorable.

Ari forced himself to relax. Bo's tongue teased him, tasted him and drove him wild. If this was what Bo wanted to do to him, he would let him. He was loving every minute of it, even if he was embarrassed for Bo to be *there...*

Bo sensed the moment Ari relaxed around him and gave in to what he was experiencing. He circled his tongue, slowly teasing Ari open as much as possible. He probed forward with his tongue, humming when Ari cried out. He hadn't been sure if Ari would have something similar to the bundle of nerves the demons had, as his anatomy was so different. As he caressed it with his tongue, sometimes pushing harder, other times soft, Ari went wild underneath him.

"Don't stop. Oh, please, I don't know what... just don't... I need..." Ari's mind was gone, lost in sensation overdrive. Thoughts, words, everything was beyond him bar the ability to feel.

Bo pulled back briefly. "I've got you, I know what you need, let go and feel." He went back to winding his tongue around Ari's balls and gently eased a finger into his mouth wetting it, before sliding it into Ari and gently rubbing the bundle of nerves he discovered there. Deciding he wanted to see Ari in the throes of passion, he moved his tail and wrapped it around Ari's balls, teasing them as he swallowed Ari's cock once again. He didn't stop until Ari hit the back of his throat, his nose nuzzling along the hair at his base. He nearly choked when Ari grabbed his horns, stroking them with everything he had.

Ari, determined to not be a silent partner, or an inactive one, teased Bo's horns. After what Bo had said, he wanted to see what sort of a reaction he could get and he knew it wouldn't be long before he lost control. He tightened the grip on one horn before keeping a steady up and down movement. With his fingertips he teased the other one, drawing tiny circles around the tip, before radiating them down. When he got to the bottom, where the horn joined Bo's head, he massaged around the join. The bone-deep shudder that ran through Bo had him stunned. He went to pull away, worried he'd hurt Bo, when a hand shot up and pinned his wrist in place.

"For the love of all things celestial, don't stop, that's incredible." Bo started working Ari's cock with renewed vigor. Both of them were moving in sync now. Faster and faster, their movements on counterpoint to one another.

Ari let go and simply gave in to the sensations. Loving the feel of being partially pinned to the bed by Bo. The feel of Bo being in control of his pleasure, of pleasing Bo, of being so in tune with each other they almost didn't need words. The base of his spine started to sizzle, and he tried to fight it, didn't want this experience to ever end, but the pleasure was relentless. When Bo tightened the suction even more and slowly pulled along his length before using his hands to thrust him forward and into Bo's throat, it was all it took. His grip on Bo's horns tightened as his back bowed off the bed. His eyes opened wide, yet were unseeing as sensations consumed him. He could have sworn shooting stars darted across his line of vision. They were the only bursts of color visible as the rest of his vision faded.

Bo's gaze was trained on Ari's face as he came apart. The look of ecstasy took Bo's breath away. The lines of Ari's slender body as he arched into his release were a vision he could watch forever. Ari's taste exploded on his tongue and he swallowed every drop greedily, twirling his tongue around, determined to get every last drop. The taste, the experience overwhelmed him and he thrust his hips against the bed. The pressure was enough to tip him over the edge and he cried out around Ari's cock, his own release spilling from him.

They lay there, both struggling to get their breath back. Once Bo's shaky legs were stable enough to support his weight, he went to the bathroom, quickly washing himself and wetting a cloth with warm water. Staggering back, he cleaned Ari up before dropping the cloth next to the bed. Settling into the middle of the bed, he pulled Ari into his arms. Keeping one arm and his tail wrapped securely around him, the other hand gently trailed through Ari's hair, massaging his curls. He smiled at the soft snore coming from Ari less than a minute later. The sound, Ari's heat, the release all combined to drag him under a few minutes after Ari.

CHAPTER TWENTY

Bo woke groggy, unsure where he was. He cocked his head to one side, looking at the cream ceiling with a crack to one side. Shifting slightly, feeling the warm body in his arms brought a smile to his face. Ari. His Tiko. Memories flooded his mind— everything they'd done earlier in the day. How he'd finally been honest with Ari about his feelings. The nerves had been overwhelming. The fear of Ari refusing him terrified him; it still did. But those were worries for another day. He gently ran one hand through Ari's hair, deliberately curling a strand around his fingers. His tail snaked up and traced lazy patterns on Ari's back, making him shiver. He couldn't resist grabbing a quick, gentle kiss, Ari's lips far too tempting.

Ari refused to wake up any more than he was. If this was a dream, he didn't want it to end. He was in Bo's arms, they'd talked some, kissed— he fought the rising blush— and done so much more. He'd loved every minute of it. The feeling when Bo attempted to walk away from him almost consumed him and he'd reacted. He smiled at the memory. Yeah, taking that leap of faith, grabbing and kissing Bo had been worth it.

"What are you smiling about?"

The sound of Bo's voice brought Ari out of his introspection. "You." He blushed profusely. "Us. What we did."

"Do you regret it?" Bo asked hesitantly.

Ari looked up at Bo's face, almost pouting at having to leave the warmth of Bo's chest. "No, not even slightly. I want..." Ari steadied his nerves. If there was ever a time to be courageous, it was now. "I want everything with you. Everything you're prepared to offer me, I'll gratefully accept."

"And if I want everything with you?" Bo challenged. "If I want you in my bed, in my arms every night? If I want the right to kiss you whenever I want, the right to pull you into my arms in front of anyone, the right to run my hand over your ass? The right to help keep you safe, help you make decisions, the right to talk about things in our lives? The right to come to you for comfort, to be where you go when you need comfort? What if I want everything with you forever?" Bo searched Ari's gaze. It was a scary thing, putting his feelings, his heart, on the line, but like most things, the scarier they are, the greater the reward. Having Ari in his life was all the reward he would ever need.

Ari studied Bo's face, searched his eyes, seeking out the truth behind his words. The desire for what he wanted was clearly reflected in Bo's steady gaze. "That's what I want with you. I want all those things. I want to be that person for you, the one who gives you strength, the one who is there for you when you need to just be yourself, rather than the Cobalt Commander. The one where you don't need to put up a front. The one who will hold you in his arms at the end of a bad day. The one who will care for you, the same way you will care for me."

"Even though I'm the only demon, the only person you have ever been with? You don't want to explore what is out there now you have your freedom?" It was one of the things Bo worried about. "You don't want to see if there are other people out there who are better for you than I am? I'm big and gruff. I'm a warrior. I don't get to sit around with a steady life. It's fast and frantic at times, dangerous. You don't want to see if you can find someone who is better for you than I am?"

Ari took Bo's face in his hands. "There could be no one better for me than you. You are everything I could ever *want*, everything I could ever *need*. I love your protective streak, how much you care about those you are charged with protecting. I love the fact you worry about me. I love the fact that you are big and gruff. It makes me feel safe and protected. Your arms are the only place I have ever been free to truly be me. You give me strength. You give me courage. Hope for the future, power to face my fears and my enemies head on. Freedom to find myself and the feeling of being… loved, I guess. You let me know through everything that you do that you will always be at my side, no matter what. I know there will be times I'll annoy you, times I do things you don't like. Tampering with your tech, for example…"

Ari looked contrite as Bo rolled his eyes. "But I know you will support me as I find myself. Many people talk about freedom, but I don't think they understand it. Not really. I was kept under lock and key for so long, unable to make even the simplest of decisions myself, that to have the ability now is huge. To have the freedom to make my own mistakes is something I will forever cherish. You giving me that freedom, supporting me completely, no matter what, means everything to me."

"I worry that learning what you love, finding yourself, will take you away from me," Bo confessed, giving voice to his darkest fear.

Ari shook his head. "What I'm trying to explain is… I can be me, the real me, because I have *you* by my side. *You* give me the strength to move forward with my life. *You* give me the courage to explore who I am. *You* give me freedom to make mistakes and learn from them. *You* give me the ability to experiment with who I am safely. *You*, Bo, it's all *you*. It's been *you* since the moment I first laid eyes on you. It simply took me a while to be able to admit it. Yet, through all that time, you have stood unwavering at my side. You never pushed me to do something, and you never tried to stop me doing things. You trust me and want to see me become the man I always wanted to be, Bo. There is no one in the universe who could ever replace you in my heart. *You*, Bo, it always has been you. It always will be you. *Only you. Forever you.*"

The smile spread slowly across Bo's face. "From the moment I first saw you, you captivated me. The bravery inside you was magnificent to behold. Your steely determination, you hunger for freedom, your ability to love and live, to fight for what you want… It's all I've seen since the moment I first laid eyes on you. You are one of the strongest people I have ever met. I feel privileged that you have chosen me to walk beside you as you embark on your new life. Privileged that it's me who gets to hold you in my arms and kiss you. Me who gets to keep you safe and protect you from the world around you. Me who gets to see you grow into the man you should be."

Bo pulled Ari so he was lying fully over him. He spread his legs wide, letting Ari's nestle comfortably between them. With one hand still threaded through Ari's hair, his tail still stroking Ari's back, his other hand found its new favorite resting place. Ari's ass. He squeezed, loving the groan that fell from Ari's lips.

Ari gave himself up to Bo's kiss. There was nothing better than having Bo love on him. When Bo's hand started to drift between his cheeks, his breath hitched and he tried to spread himself wider. Bo teased at his hole, but didn't push inside. Instead, he broke the kiss and held his gaze.

"There's a couple of things I want, and we need, to talk about."

Bo looked concerned, worrying Ari, who tried to pull away, but was held firm in Bo's grasp.

"I want you to know I want you, more than anything I want to take you, be inside you, taking you to the heights of passion…"

"There's a but in there. I know there is." Ari searched Bo's face for clues.

"There is. Firstly, you're innocent— you're much smaller than me and, well, I'm not exactly small in that department." Bo gestured vaguely to his groin. "So I want us to go slow and build you up to that, if it's something you want. I also want you to know, if that's not what you want, if you would rather be inside me, I can do that. I've never done it, but for you… there is nothing I wouldn't do for you, Tiko."

Ari melted against Bo, relaxing at the conversation. "Maybe someday in the future, but all I can think about is you inside of me. There was something else though?"

"It's…" Bo trailed off, unsure how to word what he wanted to say.

"Just say it, you're not going to upset me." *I hope.*

Bo pushed down the fear of upsetting Ari. "I know you're lenis. I can't say I fully understand all the biology of it, and I don't know how our biology is compatible, but we would need to be careful, I'm guessing, or you would end up…"

"With child," Ari finished off.

"Exactly. And while it may be something we would want to think about in the future, that you may want in the future, I want you to know there would never be any pressure from me about it. But that doesn't resolve how we stop it from happening in the meantime."

Ari wracked his brains, trying to think. Haunted eyes looked up at Bo. "I honestly don't know how to stop it. I was never allowed to know. Those weren't my decisions to make. I was told it would always be up to the man I married. That *he* would make the decisions about when I would carry a babe."

"Oh, Tiko." Bo tightened his grip on Ari. "I guess we have some research to do, see if there is a way to prevent it from happening. I would always want you to be the one to make the decision, not me. If and when you do, we will need to research our compatibility. I would never, not for one moment, want to risk you or your health. Obviously, I know the way we prevent our demonesses getting pregnant, but who knows if it would work on you? I wouldn't want to say let's use that, put our trust in that, and it doesn't work, would never have worked."

Ari captured Bo's lips. His demon, and he was finally beginning to believe that Bo really was his, cared so much about him and would do anything for him. Pulling back, he grinned wickedly and kissed the base of each horn, making Bo shiver. "I'll see what I can find out. I don't know how long it will take though."

"We have plenty of time," Bo vowed. "I'm not going anywhere. You're stuck with me until you decide otherwise."

"I might just kick you to the grass if you keep ripping my underwear. I liked that pair." Ari deliberately pouted.

Bo's eyes lit with fire. "Don't remind me, or I'll want to do it all over again."

"No way, you are not ruining my other pairs. I like them too much."

"Maybe…" Bo released Ari and sprang from the bed, rushing out of Ari's room and into his own.

Ari took the moment to study Bo's naked retreating form. Damn, the demon was a work of art. The way his muscles flexed, the grace and sinuosity he presented, were a study in beauty. He couldn't help but lick his lips.

Bo smirked when he returned; seeing Ari watch him had his cock plumping rapidly. "If you keep looking at me like that, we'll never get out of bed."

"I doubt I'd complain at that." As soon as Bo was close enough, Ari ran his hands over his chest, marveling at the way the muscles flexed under his palm. He noticed Bo was carrying a bag. In fact, two large bags with a very familiar logo on them. These were from Cherished Soul, the shop where he got his shorts from.

"After I saw them last night, which stunned me stupid by the way… well, I persuaded Deek'in and Yavek to take Dasa and I there. I went shopping and I, umm, got you some things." Bo thrust the bags into Ari's hands and climbed back into bed, suddenly nervous. Damn, he should have taken a comp device with him. The only thing he could do was watch Ari nervously.

Ari opened the first bag and peered in. Stunned, his gaze snapped up to Bo's. "How many did you buy?" He turned the bag upside down and a rainbow of colors and array of materials tumbled to the bed. He ran his hands through, picking up pair after pair and examining them. The collection was full of his favorite styles and colors. They ranged from the everyday ones, to the really sexy ones.

Bo grunted as his arms were suddenly full of Ari. He knew Ari only had two arms, but they were suddenly everywhere. As were Ari's lips. They were trailing teasing nips and kisses all over his skin. His cock was hardening and his horns were steaming. Only Ari had provoked this sort of response from him. So quickly, so completely, any moment with Ari in his arms was exquisite.

"Ari," he managed to speak before his brain short-circuited. "There's another bag. It's got other things in it." As suddenly as Ari was in his arms, he was gone again. Bo blinked his eyes open to see Ari peering into the second bag.

Ari pulled out the sheerest pair of tep'rink imaginable. They were a rich cobalt blue and he grinned at that. It looked like Bo loved him in his colors as much as he loved wearing them. They were softer than he imagined such sheer fabric could be. Around the waistband and cuffs, there was a curling motif that reminded him of the Crown of Horns. They were stunning. He lifted his eyes to Bo's. "I love them. Thank you."

"There's several pairs, all fairly similar. I, uh, thought you might like wearing them around our suite."

"I would love too." Ari grinned, wickedness shining from his eyes. "You know, this makes me think. There is so much going on at the moment. With the crown, the kidnapping attempt, the problems to start with. Do you have any idea who is behind it all?"

"We do—" Bo broke off as his implant chirped. "Bo'saverin."

"I'm sorry, Bo, but we need you here. We need to give an answer over the trade delegation." Dasa sounded resigned.

"I'll be there in ten." Bo cut the link and grabbed Ari's face in his hands. "I'm sorry. I have to go. Know I would do anything to stay with you."

Ari kissed Bo swiftly. "Go, you wouldn't be the man I'm falling for if you stayed." Bo's look curled Ari's toes and he was still grinning when Bo left. Only two minutes late, those two minutes filled with an all-consuming kiss that left his lips swollen and tingling. It was a promise. For more, so much more.

CHAPTER TWENTY ONE

Bo stalked towards the command center, the scowl on his face sending more than one demon scurrying away with their tail tucked between their legs. The only thing to make him smile was when he placed his hand on the command door input console and the mechanical door informed him to enter at his own risk. He would need to get Ari to fix that when he checked out the systems.

Dasa studied him as he strode to the long table he and several officers were sitting around. "I can't decide what's more disturbing, the fact you're still scowling after some peace, or that you're managing to pull off both a smile and a scowl at the same time."

Bo grinned wickedly. "I think I freaked out a couple of demons back there."

"Sounds about right." Dasa laughed.

The door opened again and Vict breezed in, smiling.

"Frek, now that is disturbing. Both of you smiling at once. You wait, we'll see demons flocking to the temples," Dasa drawled. "Seeing you two smiling as you walk around will have them thinking the end of the world is nigh."

Vict cuffed Dasa on the back of the head as he walked by. "So the Reds want the Trevon delegation to land. Do we have a passenger manifest yet?"

"We do." One of the officers passed a list around.

Bo scanned it, looking for one name in particular— Agota Kelotian, Ari's mother. He breathed a sigh of relief when it wasn't there. "I don't recognize any of these names. Not that it means anything, other than she isn't on it."

Dasa and Vict both nodded, they'd been looking for the same name.

"Have these names been run through the databanks?" Bo looked around at his officers.

"They have," Wol'ir answered. "Nothing has been flagged up, no wanted criminals or alerts."

"So there is logically no reason we could deny them entry. It is possible this is just a trade envoy." Dasa pursed his lips.

"Come on, you can't believe that any more than I do." Bo stared at Dasa.

"I don't believe it, but without proof, we have no reason to deny them access. If we do, not only do we risk alienating the Trevons, but relations between the palace and the Reds could deteriorate even further."

Vict frowned. "They gave us the manifest when asked. They've been polite, I take it?" He looked to Wol'ir, who nodded. "So... if we refuse them now, it will look petty and spiteful. There really isn't any choice but to allow them down."

"They're approaching preliminary orbit. Once they've entered a stationary orbit, they've requested a flightpath for a cruiser to come in. They'll be here tomorrow afternoon."

"What, too good for a normal shuttle?" Bo smirked at the use of the more luxurious cruiser for such a short journey, rather than a simple transport vessel.

Vict looked around the room, taking in his advisors and the highest ranking Cobalts. "Allow them to land. But I want a full complement of Cobalts and advisors with them. Not one of them is to be allowed to wander about by themselves. Escort them everywhere. I don't care how much the Reds complain about that. I want extra guards posted around the spaceport, monitoring the cruiser at all times. I won't think everyone has left, only to discover there were Loperis hiding aboard. We still don't know how the last set got here."

"Actually…" Officer Rog'vec handed out some data pads. "We found evidence of a craft landing in Sector 73."

Bo's eyes widened. "Sector 73 is solid mountains."

"It is. When I say landed, technically they didn't land from what we can tell. They hovered just above the land. Evidence shows multiple bodies landed heavily. I'm guessing they rappelled down."

"So there is no way to know who aided them, other than the Reds we caught," Vict stated.

Bo shook his head. "They have been less than forthcoming in their answers. We've been through everything we have, without resorting to our more extreme measure of information retrieval."

Vict closed his eyes for a moment, shuttering his reaction. When they opened, all that was visible was a steely determination. "Do it."

"Yes, Your Majesty." Bo bowed his head.

"I want Aridien kept away from them as much as possible. I have no plans to court any interaction. It would be best if they left without ever knowing he was here." Vict looked around at the gathered demons.

Deek'in grinned at Bo. "Your Majesty, we've all come to respect Aridien. He *is* a Little Demon. The Cobalts see him as one of ours. He's our Commander's mate, whether the two of them have accepted it yet or not."

Vict snorted at the scowl on Bo's face. "Well, the quicker he claims him, the better. Mates have more rights than adopted citizens." He stared Bo down. "Well, Bo'saverin? You going to untwist your tail and get to it?"

Bo glared at his king. "Does a demon get no peace to choose his own mate?"

All around him demons, especially Vict and Dasa, were shaking their heads.
"Frek, I can't believe I'm actually about to admit this in front of you lot, but I'm making progress. There, happy now?" Bo groaned at the sea of grinning faces.

"About damn time," Vict muttered. "Have I taught you demonlings nothing?"

"Hey!" Dasa scowled. "I'll have you know I claimed—"

Dasa's words were cut off when Vict hit him around the shoulders with his tail. "Hey! What was that for?"

"Krexjin, I don't want to know about what my son and his mate get up to."

Bo sniggered away, glad the focus was off him for the time being. He was too private a man to have such interference in his love life, but everyone was looking out for Ari so he shouldn't complain *too* much. He just didn't have to like it.

"I'll get everything in place for tomorrow. Frek, I feel the need to blow off some of this steam." Bo gestured to his horns, which were happily pumping out small tufts of hot air.

"You know there are several ways to do that." Dasa waggled his eyebrows, groaning when Vict hit him again. "You've been given the all clear to train fully, yes?"

Bo tipped his head to one side, wondering where this was going. "Yes…"

"You and me, Pik'dorin in the morning before they get here. It might make us both more amenable to coping with this envoy."

Bo cracked his knuckles. "Now this sounds like a perfect plan. I plan on beating your sorry ass. We need to decide who is better after the Rings came back as a dead heat."

"Oh, Bo, you're deluded if you think you're going to beat me." Dasa flexed his muscles. "Besides, my mate will be there to cheer me on."

"So will mine." Bo growled out, eyes going wide when he realized what he'd said.

Dasa sat back with a self-righteous smile on his face.

"You did that on purpose." Bo's horns were steaming even more now.

Dasa made a 'who me' face full of innocence.

"Yes, you." Bo grabbed a kisshin fruit and threw it at Dasa.

Dasa caught it, shrugged and bit into it.

Bo dropped his head into his hands. "I'm doomed I tell you, doomed."

Vict simply chuckled away looking smug as he strolled out the room and left them to the security discussions. He had more important places to be.

"How did I guess? I knew you two would be hiding out and gossiping." Vict's voice carried from the doorway to the sofas Caris and Ari were relaxing on.

Caris waved him over. "Want a drink?"

Vict was about to say no, but changed his mind. "Why not. What you two are drinking looks interesting enough."

Caris hid a smile. They were drinking an old earth concoction. Made from frozen cream and carbonated berry juice. He passed a glass over, watching Vict's reaction. He didn't disappoint.

Vict tentatively took a sip, his eyes lighting up, before he downed the glass as quickly as possible. He suddenly grasped his head. "Ahh, what is that?"

"You drank it too fast. When that happens, your brain gets frozen."

"What?" Vict's voice rang with alarm, bringing his guards running in. He waved them off. "I'm fine." He managed to get out while blowing the freezing air out of his mouth. His face was pinched together.

"Next time, drink slower." Caris smirked.

"But it was tasty." Vict whined, happily taking another one when Ari passed it over. Taking his seat, leaning back diagonally against the end of the sofa, he flipped his tail over the top. "So, because my son is evil, he forced it out of Bo that there has been progress between you two."

Ari squeaked and ducked his head. "I can't believe he told you that."

"I think it was more a case of Dasa pulled it out of him. Now, I know you have no family here, so I'm going to slip into father mode for a few minutes. I know demons. They can be pretty forceful when they want to be. I just want to make sure this is who you want, what you want. You staying here on Kenistal is not dependent on any relationship with Bo'saverin or anyone else for that matter."

A strange warmth radiated through Ari. Both his heart and soul soared at Vict's words. Since he'd been here, it was as though he'd been adopted into a slightly crazy family and he loved every minute of it. "I want Bo. He's who I want. He's who I…" Ari took a deep breath, wanting to try out the words before he said them to Bo. "I love him. Not that I've told him that. It's probably too soon for me to say it. I mean he told me he was falling in love with me, but…"

Vict's expression softened and he patted Ari on the hand. "There are many types of love. It isn't one size fits all. There are loves that are instantaneous. You look across the room and see the demoness you are destined to spend the rest of your life with. That's what happened to me. There are loves like Caris and my son. They fell for each other straight away, even if Dasa didn't realize it. But once they got together, that was explosive. I almost wish I'd been around to see Dasa suffer." He winked at them both. "Then there is love borne from friendship. My mother and father were like that. Theirs was an arranged mating. They didn't meet each other until the day of the official mating ceremony."

Vict smiled at the memory of his mother telling him how much she'd cursed her new mate out that day. "But they started out as friends and their love grew from there. There is no right or wrong way to love, or how soon it hits you. What you feel is right, don't ever let anyone ever tell you any differently. If *you* know you love Bo'saverin and he knows he loves you, that is *all* that matters. Don't wait to tell him. I'll tell you one thing. That demonling is the most insecure I have ever seen him. He worries he isn't good enough for you."

Ari looked up in surprise, spluttering as he took a sip of his drink. "That's not true! He's too good for me."

"Not the way he sees it. You are *everything* to him, whether he has admitted it yet or not. You could really hurt him, Aridien. He adores you. If you have any reservations about him, I ask you not to say those words of love to him yet. I think it would destroy him to have you say them and walk away."

Ari was shaking his head. "I'm not walking away. Bo is everything I want. *He. Is. Mine.* No one else gets to love him. No one else gets to look after him. *Only* me."

Caris grinned at Ari's sudden feistiness and Vict's look of smug satisfaction.

"What just happened?" Ari looked back and forth between them, wondering why they were smiling.

"You've just proved you're the perfect mate for him, and he for you. You have a feisty streak in you, young Aridien, and will defend what you consider yours. That is exactly what Bo needs. He needs someone who will let him protect them, but will also stand up for themselves when they need to. He needs someone who will go up against him, but also let him have his way when he really needs it. You two complement each other perfectly. Neither of you ever needed it, but you have my blessing anyway. I see you both as extra sons and I couldn't be happier with your choice of mate."

Relief brought a shudder to Ari. "You all keep saying mate. On Aducia, we have marriage. When two people join their love and households together, they get married. Is that what a mating is?"

Vict looked across at Caris. "You may be better at explaining this as you are more aware of what a… marriage is."

214

Caris took over. "A mating is very similar to a marriage, but there are many variations across planets and sectors. For demons, a mating is joining your lives together, entwining them, just like a marriage, but there are some differences. When you mate on Kenistal, one demon renounces his ties to the family guilds."

Ari wrinkled his nose as he looked back and forth between them.

Caris thought for a moment. "Alright, let me use Mac as an example. When Kery'alin was born she would have been given membership of two guilds. These aren't normal memberships— they are family ones. She wouldn't hold full rights, but she would always be able to call on both guilds for support should she have lost her parents at a young age. When demons go through their Rite of Ferik, they change color and join that guild. The Rite of Ferik always happens on the day of maturity, their twentieth naming day. Understand so far?"

Ari nodded. "So when they have their twentieth birth day, or naming day, they actually have three guilds?"

Caris nodded. "Yes, their skin changes color to display what guild they are in once they have gone through the rite. That is their lifetime guild. They will hold full rights within that guild. Until the day the mate, they are still covered by their parent's guilds as well. From what I've read in the history books, it was a practice adopted when there was a lot of guild warfare. Many demonlings were left without parents, and when they went through their rites, their family guilds tried to cut all ties so they didn't have to support them. The new guild refused to support them as it was their adult guild and they should be able to support themselves by that point. Many new demons were left starving and destitute by these rules."

Vict snarled, his scales rippling. "It was my grandfather who changed the rules."

"I'm glad they've changed." Caris smiled. "It's one of many changes I've read about that show why this family is suited to ruling."

"Okay, I understand all that, but what changes when you mate someone?" Ari tucked his feet up underneath him.

"So to carry on with Kery and Mac as an example, when Kery mated with Mac, she gave up all family rights with her parents' guilds. She had the full rights of her own guild and she received family rights from Mac's guild – the Cobalts. If anything were to happen to Mac, and from what I understand the family rights for Cobalts are slightly different than others, she would receive a stipend to live off, with extra as they have demonlings."

Vict joined in. "The Cobalts have an extra layer of protection in place for family members as there is a greater chance of something happening since it's the warrior guild."

"So what happens when I... if I mate with Bo?"

Both Vict and Caris struggled to suppress their grins at Ari's slip.

Caris smiled. "You will receive the full family rights from the Cobalts."

Ari nodded. "Does that mean officially that I have no more ties with my own family back on Aducia?"

"Following Kenistalian tradition, yes," Caris confirmed.

Ari jumped up, surprising them both and did a shimmy around the room.

"I take it you're happy then?" Vict chuckled as Ari grabbed Caris' hand and dragged him up to dance with him.

"Incredibly happy. It's not a reason I'd mate with Bo. But it's a great bonus." Ari twirled around, his curls flying around his head.

Bo walked into his suite and stopped dead in the doorway. Ari was dancing. His jaw dropped and cock hardened at the vision before him.

"Tiko, you look beautiful." Finally, having regained his voice he stalked forward and grabbed Ari, holding him tight and spinning him round, his legs flying out as he grasped him around his waist. "What's got you so happy?"

Ari smiled up at Bo, not wanting Bo to think he wanted to mate with him purely to cut all ties with his birth family. "Nothing. I'm just happy."

"Well, whatever put you in this mood, I'm glad." As Bo spun Ari around, he finally noticed Vict and Caris. He tucked his face into Ari's hair and tried to hide. "I'm not really here. Save me."

Vict chuckled. "Too late, I see you, Bo'saverin."

"Are you here to annoy me some more?" Bo scowled.

Vict's tail shifted so it tapped rhythmically against his leg. "Now, is that any way to talk to your king?"

"Are you being my king right now, or are you just being an annoying father-figure?"

"Can't I be both?"

"Urgh." Bo walked over to one of the sofas, dragging Ari with him. As soon as he sat, he pulled Ari into his lap, wrapping his tail around his waist and nuzzling into his neck.

"I was about to tell these two about tomorrow's match." Vict smirked at Bo and Dasa who joined Caris on his sofa with a swift kiss.

"Match?" Caris batted Dasa away, too interested in what Vict was talking about.

Dasa's eyes were shooting daggers at his father.

Vict's grin was wicked. "Bo announced he needed to blow off some steam. So these two have finally decided to have the Pik'dorin match they've been threatening to have for weeks."

Caris turned to Dasa. "Were you going to tell me?"

Dasa shiftily looked everywhere but at Caris. "Umm, yes?"

Caris narrowed his eyes. "You'd better have. I will be there. Ari, you're coming with me. In fact… We'll make a trip of it."

Vict stretched lazily. "I'll sit with you. I fancy seeing if my son has gone soft lately now that he's mated."

Dasa spluttered. "If you weren't my king as well as my father, I'd challenge you as well and then we'll see who has gone soft."

Vict shook his head, making a soft tsking sound. "Dasalin, when will you learn? You will never beat me."

Dasa scoffed. "One day, old demon, one day, I will get you in the rings and then we'll see."

Vict's gaze never left his son. "One day I'm going to surprise you and take you up on that challenge. Then we'll see just how fast you try and back out of it."

Ari shifted so he could whisper in Bo's ear. "Are they always like this?"

"Not usually. But since Caris and Dasa mated, they've both softened a bit and got closer. There was a time when they couldn't seem to strike the right balance in their relationship. It's good to see, if I'm honest. It's made them both happy. You and Caris really are changing plenty of Kenistal for the better."

"I don't care about Kenistal in that sense. All I care about is making *you* happy."

Bo caressed Ari's back. "Oh, Tiko, you make me so damn happy my warriors are wondering what the frek is wrong with me. They keep running away thinking I'm out to make life hell for them."

Ari giggled at the idea of all these big bad warriors running away like scared demonlings.

Vict suddenly got a wicked grin on his face. "Here, son, Bo'saverin, you need to try this drink Caris made. It's incredible." Vict winked at Ari, putting his fingers to his lips when Ari struggled not to laugh.

Ari looked at Caris and they both shrugged as if to say. "What are you going to do?"

CHAPTER TWENTY TWO

Ari finished his shower. He's taken the time to spread some cream over his body, making sure every part of him was super soft. *Except a certain bit that is always hard for Bo.*

He carefully pulled up the gold lace shorts, swiftly followed by the blue sheer tep'rink. Taking a deep breath, strengthening his resolve, he opened the door and walked into the reception room of their suite, thankful Bo had gotten rid of their guests earlier so his plan would work.

Hearing Ari behind him, Bo called out. "You want a drink?"

"I'm good." Ari slowly walked towards Bo, his nerves getting the better of him, making him tremble.

"You sure?" Bo turned around. The goblet slipped from his fingers. The berry juice splashed up his legs, not that he noticed. His cock reacted instantly to the sight of Ari walking towards him. His knees wanted to buckle and he grabbed blindly for the table behind him. His eyes devoured Ari. "Frek, Tiko, you're… simply…" He shook his head trying to clear some of the fog that descended on him. "Stunning."

Ari stood there as Bo stalked towards him, the lust blazing from Bo's eyes boosting his confidence.

Bo reached out and ran a gentle hand over Ari's chest, pinching Ari's nipples gently. "Tiko, if you want to take things slow between us, this is not the way to ensure that happens."

"I don't remember anything about saying I want to go slow. I want you, Bo, I always have." Ari traced a pattern over Bo's hip, working his way underneath his tunic, pushing it up until Bo got the hint and stripped it off.

Bo's movements were sluggish, his mind distracted by the vision before him. It took a moment to realize Ari had dropped to his knees and was tugging at his workout trousers. "Ari?"

Ari let his gaze meander up Bo's body before it connected with Bo's hooded gaze. "I want to taste you."

Bo's knees finally buckled and he aimed for the sofa, grabbing on. "Not here." He regained his balance. "I won't risk anyone walking in and seeing you."

"Always my protector," Ari soothed as he took Bo's hand, walking towards his bedroom.

Bo resisted. "Can we go to mine? I want you in my bed. I've dreamed of you in my bed for so long."

Ari leaned up and pecked Bo on the lips. Walking towards Bo's bedroom with an extra sway to his hips, he smiled to himself when he heard Bo stumble behind him. He led Bo to the bed and pushed him down. "Now, where was I?" He gestured for Bo to scoot back a bit and straddled his waist. "This will be easier." He went back to pulling Bo's pants down, gasping when he saw the demis he was wearing. These were the same ones he's seen in Perik's shop. "Did you buy these for me?"

Bo couldn't look Ari in the eye. He simply nodded.

"The fact you got them, wore them for me, means a lot." Ari trailed kisses over the skin at the edge of the waistband.

"They're comfy as well. I might have to get more," Bo admitted.

"Hmm, now that is hot. I wonder what else you would wear for me?"

"Anything," Bo assured Ari. "I would wear anything, *do* anything for you."

Ari tugged down the long shorts, gasping when Bo's cock sprang free. This was his first look at it and he licked his lips. With a long, heated look up Bo's body, he bent his head and took Bo in his mouth. His heart was hammering, worried about doing this wrong.

There would be no way he could take all of Bo into his mouth. He looked up when Bo caressed his cheek.

"Take what you can. Whatever you do will be good, I promise." Bo fought with all the strength of will he possessed against the overwhelming desire to thrust into the tightness of Ari's mouth. The fact Ari was willing to try this with him, and was so enthusiastic in his approach, drove him wild. Slowly, Ari started to take more of him, sucking his cock like it was the best snack he'd tasted. When Ari hummed, his hips bucked involuntarily.

Ari pulled off. "Sorry. You did that to me. I thought you might like it."

"Oh, I do, I couldn't help that. I wanted nothing more than to drive my cock into your willing mouth, again and again, but I know you aren't ready for that. You simply took me by surprise."

With a smile, Ari went back to enjoying sucking on Bo's length. Feeling emboldened by how he was affecting this big strong warrior, he reached his hand down and grasped one of Bo's balls, giving it a gentle squeeze. He smiled as Bo's legs trembled with the force he exerted trying to hold still. He alternated between the two. He would tug, then stroke, caress then tap. Trying everything, trying to keep Bo on edge.

"Tiko, if you keep this up, I'm going to come." Bo tried to push Ari away. He didn't want to come, but having Ari do this, when it was the last thing he'd expected and when it was the first time Ari had done this, was too much. When Ari tapped slightly harder, it sent a jolt of pleasure spiking through him. "Frek, Ari, pull off, I'm going to come."

Ari refused to move. He wanted to try everything with Bo and that included tasting his release. He doubled his efforts, thrilled when Bo stiffened. There was a moment where Bo seemed to be suspended, back arched high off the bed. Suddenly, he was coming. Wave after wave flooded into Ari's mouth and he tried to swallow it all, but there was too much and a little dribbled back out.

Bo collapsed back onto the bed, trying to regain his breath. He looked down at Ari and beckoned him closer. Ari scrambled up his body, slightly shy. "Ari, you take my breath away in more ways than one. That was incredible." He traced Ari's swollen lips with his tongue, cleaning up the last of his release, pushing into Ari's mouth and dueling with his tongue. Slowly, he pulled back and patted his chest. "Head here."

Ari wriggled about, getting comfy, sighing as he heard Bo's heart beat beneath his head. "Was I okay?" He nervously traced patterns on Bo's chest with the tip of one finger.

"You were amazing. But you have to know I would have been okay if you'd never done that. I was happy being able to please you. I never want you to think you have to do anything you don't want to do."

Ari smacked the other side of Bo's chest. "I wanted to do it. I want to do it again."

Bo's groan vibrated his chest, making Ari's head bounce a little. "Give me a few minutes to recover. I'm not that young anymore."

Ari laughed. "You're not old, you know."

"I feel it right now." Bo groaned as his muscles refused to work properly. "Damn, Tiko, what did you do to me? Now, get up here so I can return the favor."

Ari's blush was so instantaneous it shocked Bo. "What's up?"

"I got so excited by doing that to you, that I, umm…"

"You what?"

"I came when you did." Ari kept his gaze focused straight ahead.

"That is so hot."

"It is?" Ari whispered.

Bo turned Ari's face so he could see the sincerity in his eyes. "The fact doing that to me turned you on so much? Frek yes."

Ari's yawn took him by surprise. "Why do I feel so sleepy again?"

"Coming can make you do that. Want to nap with me?" Bo stroked a hand over Ari's curls.

"Uh huh," Ari mumbled.

Bo smiled and used his tail to drag the covers up and over them.

CHAPTER TWENTY THREE

Ari followed Vict into the royal box. He had no idea what to expect, but it wasn't the view in front of him. The arena was fully teched out. Large screens were dotted about so that everyone had the opportunity to see the action. There must have been seating for several thousand demons.

The royal box currently only held Vict, Caris and Ari, although their guards were all stationed around them. There were empty seats, but Vict had insisted he wanted to watch the friendly match with no distractions from Guild Masters trying to curry favor.

Ari, both excited and nervous, struggled to sit in his seat without fidgeting. "Are we supposed to sit on either side of Vict?"

Caris looked at him confused.

"Well, aren't we going to be cheering against each other?" Ari gestured towards the arena floor where both Dasa and Bo would fight.

"Huh, I guess so, but then again, it should be two against one. Isn't that right, Vict?"

"Ahh, you forget, as the king I have to be neutral. I shall not be cheering either of them on. It is unbecoming for a king to show that much enthusiasm." Vict kept his regal face on, despite a stray, concealed cough from behind him. He turned glaring at the guards. "Stocks. I should put the lot of you in stocks." He scowled when they all kept their gazes firmly forward.

"So Pik'dorin is basically fighting with sticks?" Ari looked to Vict for an answer.

"It's a bit more complicated than that, but at its most basic level, yes."

"What are the sticks made out of?"

"Depending on what they have agreed on, they can be made out of wood, metals, alloys or even bamklin, a special type of grass."

"Grass?" Ari's nose wrinkled.

"Bamklin is incredibly strong and able to withstand forces much greater than its own weight. The tubes grow with hollow cores. They can be flexible or completely rigid, depending on the age of the plant they are taken from. This being Bo and Dasa though, I imagine they will go all out and use the metal poles. Even then they are still referred to as sticks, it's just the way things are."

Vict gestured to a far archway where Bo and Dasa strolled through, the demons in the arena jumping to their feet and cheering.

Suddenly, a heavy beat of drums echoed around the arena.

"Now you see why the fact you changed their implants to drums made me smile so much. The drums play throughout the entire match. It helps some warriors keep track of movements, especially when they are practicing."

"How long will the battle go on for?" Ari's eyes stayed locked on Bo, tracking his movements.

"Until one is defeated or submits. I've seen battles last two minutes, I've seen them last two hours. With those two, I would bet on it being a longer match. Especially as young Bo'saverin is going to be determined to prove himself to you." Vict nodded to a couple of Guild Masters as they walked past the royal box, eyeing the occupants with envy.

Ari adamantly shook his head. "Bo doesn't need to prove himself to me or to anyone."

Vict kept watching the two demons limber up. "Sadly, he will feel like that— he does feel like that. He lost his parents when he was fifteen, obviously five years before his rite. His parents were from the Silver and Cobalt guilds and died in an explosion. A faulty piece of equipment at the restaurant they were dining at. Nothing nefarious, but just as devastating. It was his mother that was a

Cobalt. The Cobalts wanted to take him in, there were plenty of families willing, but Dasa and Bo'saverin have always been close. I broke with tradition and took him into the royal wing. There was a lot of opposition about it. It wasn't the done thing. Many saw it as favoring one guild. Yet how could it when he had yet to go through his rite. The Cobalts were happy they were not going to bear the burden. Oh, they would have done, but…"

Both Caris and Ari were listening intently.

"He's never mentioned family beyond his brother, Dea." Ari remembered meeting the enigmatic Space Commander. He was on duty at the space dock, overseeing the repair to his ship, the KS Hek'rajin. He was due back in a couple of days and while Ari had already met Dea, it was brief and before he and Bo were… whatever they were.

"Those two fight like anything, but there is a core of love between them. Dea was twenty, and just past his rite when their parents died. He was still an apprentice and barely able to support himself, let alone a younger brother. He was thrilled when I took Bo'saverin in. It was one less thing for him to be overwhelmed by."

Vict chuckled fondly at the memories. "Bo resisted his brother having any say over his life. It worked out for the best, though. I knew he and Dasa would always be friends and I wasn't in the least bit surprised when Bo'saverin became a Cobalt. You know, he rose through the ranks just about the fastest anyone ever has. I held no sway on that decision either."

Vict tapped a finger against his lips. "I don't know if he was compelled to prove himself to us. But he worked harder, trained longer, studied more intensively than any other trainee the Cobalts have had. His instructors were stunned. He was quickly assigned to Dasa's guard duty, but within a couple of years, he was running all the protection details. When the last Commander retired, Bo was put forward by the men under his command."

"I don't understand?" Ari thought for a moment. "Wouldn't it be the Guild Master who made the decision?"

"Ultimately, yes. But, they long ago realized that it was better if the average warrior had a say in it. They put forward at least fifty percent of the names to go to a review panel. The review panel is made up of a selection of officers and guild leaders. They chose Bo'saverin."

Caris' eyebrows shot up. "I've never heard of it being done that way, but I can see how well it works. No matter how good an officer may be, if he doesn't have the respect of those under his command, it will never work. This way you ensure you have someone who is qualified and holds the ability to lead, but is also well-respected by the demons under his control."

"Bo has never once let them down. He's a hard taskmaster, and won't suffer fools, but he is fair and honest. His door is always open, even for the trainees. The demons respect him for that. He is probably one of the best Cobalt Commanders Kenistal has had in a long time." Vict's face bore the evidence of remembered pain.

"Watching him go through what he did at such a young age… many expected him to go off balance and act out. All he did was buckle down and work hard. I know it was tough on him, but he has become a fine young man, and one I am proud to have as our Cobalt Commander and a part of my extended family. I couldn't ask for a better friend for my son. It has never been about political advantage or what he can get out of it, it's a genuine friendship and I couldn't be more thankful for them both to have that."

Caris waved as Dasa looked up at them. "You know, Bo does Dasa the world of good. He won't let him get too big for his horns, he teases him, fights with him, everything friends do."

Vict grinned. "Bo'saverin has never cared that Dasa is a Prince, not in that respect anyway. He has only ever cared that Dasa is his friend."

Suddenly, the drums started to crescendo before ending in a resounding crash.

"It's time," Vict declared.

Bo turned to Dasa and bowed long and deep. Dasa, always respectful, returned the bow, although as per protocol, his was a smaller bow than Bo's. Both turned to the royal box and bowed, holding it until Vict bellowed out to rise.

Dasa stared Bo down, his face a mask of neutrality that was spoiled by the twinkle in his eyes. "I'm going to enjoy beating you in front of Ari."

"Not a chance. Your tail is going to be so twisted by the end of today, Caris will have to spend hours on it."

"He can spend hours doing something, that's for sure."

Bo groaned at Dasa's words. "I seriously do not want to be hearing about what you and Caris get up to in the bedroom."

"Who said anything about the bedroom. I'll have you know…"

"Frek, enough already." Bo held his pole at the ready. "Prepare to lose."

"Never." Dasa got into the starting position and they locked gazes.

Bo quickly flexed in his suit, making sure it was comfortable. The suits were designed with the metal poles in mind. They were made of a special alloy of metals that were incredibly flexible with a large tensile strength. They easily adapted to whatever form the demon was in, whether that was just their skin or in full-on scales mode. The suits would cushion about ninety-five percent of the impacts. Of course it meant any fighter still needed to be careful. The blows still had the ability to wind them and the points of the poles were sharp. Bo's stick was solid silver that seemed to glow in the light shining into the arena. Dasa's was more golden in color.

As they waited for the drumbeat to start up again, Bo ran his hands down the stick to check the joint was secure. With a flick of a button, the pole could be extended, and with another press, it could be split in two. It kept the battles interesting as you never knew what move your opponent would pull off.

There was a massive drum roll. It was time. The battle was on.

Neither demon moved as the drums built. They held each other's gazes and neither so much as twitched their tails. Suddenly, Bo slammed the pointed end of the stick into the ground and propelled himself up and over Dasa's head, pulling the stick up and out behind him. Landing gracefully in a crouch, he swept the stick low and wide, bringing it round towards Dasa's ankles.

Dasa jumped, easily avoiding the strike. "You need to be quicker than that," he taunted, before cursing as Bo swept his stick back around at waist height, fighting the momentum. Dasa thrust his ass backwards watching as the point scraped across his suit, leaving a tiny scuff. "Feisty today, or just showing off for your man?"

"He isn't just my man, he's my mate!" Bo fought to get his emotions under control, aware of Dasa's attempts to deliberately bait him.

"Really? Does he know that?" Dasa watched as Bo slowly pulled up from the crouch. He jammed his stick into the ground, grabbed the middle and jumped, swinging his body out and around. Pulling his leg back, he aimed a kick in Bo's direction.

Bo dropped to the floor, bringing his pole straight up, trying to hit Dasa between the legs in the middle of his move.

"Playing dirty, are we?" Dasa sprung out of the way.

"You should know by now… I will never go easy on you." Bo took off at a run, aiming for the series of stones lining one of the walls in the arena. Jumping onto the first, he bounded up them, his feet easily finding the tiny grooves to keep him stable. He'd run this course so many times, he didn't even need to look, knowing just how much pressure to use to push off for the next jump and land cleanly. Looking around, he tracked Dasa's movements. As much as Bo had gone high, Dasa had gone low, his back braced against one of the pillars in the center of the arena. Both of them stared each other down. Bo backed up a few steps until he was balanced on the edge of the rock. Rocking back on his feet, he suddenly tipped his body forward and launched into a full on sprint across the stone. With the press of a button, he flattened the end of his stick, slammed it into the rock and used it to propel himself through the air, somersaulting high above Dasa before landing on one foot on the top of Dasa's pillar. He leaned over the edge and smirked.

"You getting tired down there?"

"Just bored waiting for you to finish showing off, that's all." Dasa tipped his head back and grinned. "You know you just want to look good for Ari."

"True, not that it's hard. I *always* look good."

"Arrogant much?" Dasa shook his head.

"No, just realistic. I mean— I work out constantly, running about after those damn Cobalts, not sitting in an office all day like some we know." Bo looked pointedly as his friend.

Dasa scowled. "Get your tail down here so I can kick it. I'm growing old over here."

"You're the one who said it, not me!" Bo yelled down as he did a quick one-armed handstand while still holding onto his pole with his other hand.

Dasa twirled his stick so it spun rapidly in the palm of his hand, the light glinting off the natural prisms, sending shards of golden light dancing about the arena floor.

All of a sudden, there was a thump beside him. "Want to say you're going to kick my ass to my face? I grew bored of waiting up there."

Dasa slowly got to his feet, smirking as Bo tapped his foot. "Impatient for a kicking?"

"Only if it involves me winning." Bo didn't wait. He charged. Pressing the button to lengthen the pole, he rammed it into the ground and clambered up it, hand over hand, racing upwards until he was balanced on the top of the pole, still swaying with his efforts. Out of the sea of faces, his gaze connected briefly with Ari's. His man looked stunned and slightly pale. He was worrying a curl of hair between his lips. Bo winked, then flipped so his body weight was braced on one hand on the top of the pole. Looking at Dasa from up high, he maneuvered his body so he grasped the end with one hand.

"I could just hit your stick and take you out, you know." Dasa carefully circled around the base of Bo's pole, ever watchful, ever wary.

"You could try." Bo loosely grasped the pole before opening his grip and sliding downwards, his body flush to the metal, his descent speeding up. As he passed the break in the metal, he flicked the switch, separating it into two. Wrapping his legs around the pole, he squeezed his thighs together, slowing his descent as he spun his arms out, the half pole extended out and held in front of him, protecting from Dasa's flat out charge.

Ari tightened his grip on Vict's arm. He kept ducking his head and hiding it against Vict's skin. The battle was too hard to watch. He was trying to be strong for Bo, but the moves the demon pulled off made his heart race like a rocket. When Dasa split his own pole in two, Ari knew they were done playing about. The real fighting was about to begin.

Ari watched as Dasa and Bo seemed to dance about each other. Their sticks were twirling at such speed it was difficult to track. Even over the drum beats, Ari could hear the steady thwack of the poles hitting each other. Occasionally, it was accompanied by a pained grunt, no doubt as a defense failed and someone was hit.

"You doing alright there, Aridien?" Vict patted his head when it was burrowed into his arm.

Ari winced as another hit sounded. "How can you watch this?"

"You forget— we are brought up like this. For us, it is normal. I don't know if Bo'saverin told you, but those suits they are wearing—"

"The skintight ones, you mean?" A shiver ran through Ari at the memory of Bo with all his muscles on display. He didn't know whether to map every curve and arc with his eyes, or run down there and cover him up so others wouldn't see.

"Yes, those. Well, they absorb a lot of the power. They are getting at most ten percent of the force. So while they are grunting from the impact, they aren't really getting hurt."

Ari blew out a relieved breath. "It would have been nice if someone had told me that earlier." He grouched, scowling when Vict simply patted him on the head.

Suddenly, Dasa had Bo pinned in a move so fast, Ari missed it.

"You giving in?" Dasa straddled Bo's body, his stick held against Bo's throat. Bo stayed completely still, refusing to respond. Ever so slowly, he eased one of his sticks free from its position trapped underneath him. Sliding his arm slowly out to the side, he tightened his grip on the pole. Refusing to look away from Dasa, he suddenly swung his arm back towards his body, slamming it across Dasa's back.

As Dasa lost his ability to breathe from the force of the impact, Bo pushed him off and rolled out, going to his hands and knees, one hand rubbing at his throat. He coughed a couple of times as he forced his breathing too slow, steadily refilling his lungs. He looked over to Dasa who was flat out on the floor. He wasn't stupid enough to think he'd really taken him out. He took the time Dasa was giving him to get his breath back. It was almost as if Dasa was deliberately trying to wear him out. The question was why?

Dasa lay as still as possible. If Bo ran true to form, he would attack in a minute, sure Dasa was out cold or close to it. At that point, the fight would be back on for real. No way was he going to let Bo win. Not with Caris and his father in the stands.

Bo pushed himself to his feet, using one of his pole pieces for balance. While he was waiting for whatever Dasa had planned, he swiftly locked the two pieces together. He slowly circled around Dasa, refusing to give in and attack. He'd learned that lesson long ago. He started to twirl his stick, spinning it between his arms, across his chest and around his neck. Not once did his gaze stray from his prince on the ground. "You might as well get up. I'm not coming over there to get you. I know what you're up to."

Dasa grunted, spitting out the sand that had somehow got into his mouth. "I was sure you were going to fall for that again." He jumped up, his stick still in two pieces, and faced Bo.

"I'm nothing if I'm not adaptable." Bo held the pole in one arm and beckoned to Dasa. "Let's do this. No mucking about, no fancy moves, just an honest workout. I have a feeling we're both going to need it." He pitched his voice low enough so no one could overhear them, especially not all the cameras trained on them and broadcasting their every move.

"Why?" Dasa narrowed his eyes.

"The Trevon ship was maneuvering into a stationary orbit as I walked over here. It won't be long before they land."

"Whatever happens I want both Caris and Ari hidden from view as much as possible."

"Trust me, I'm not letting the Trevon anywhere close to them if I can help it. I still think they're up to something."

"Come on, let's do this. Work out our aggression, then we can go and protect the men we love." Dasa quickly looked at the royal box, checking Caris was alright.

"Who said anything about love?" Bo shook his head.

"Are you trying to deny it to me or yourself? Admit it, not only are you in love with Ari, he's your mate. You admitted that earlier."

Bo shook his head at Dasa. "I'm not saying a word about this. If and when I'm ready to say anything, the first person to hear it will be Ari. Now stop talking and start fighting." Bo charged.

Ari forced himself to watch the rest of the battle. He would be no good to Bo as a partner if he couldn't face the prospect of him getting injured again. Sooner or later, it was going to happen. He stiffened his spine, let go of Vict and sat up straight.

"Good. I wondered how long it was going to take you."

Ari shot Vict a questioning glance.

"To come to the conclusion that you needed to be strong and to support Bo whatever he does. Which means watching even though it hurts to see. You'll get used to it. You never know, one day you and Caris could always try it out. I'm sure that would freak them both out. I would enjoy watching that happen."

Caris turned to Vict. "Are you serious?"

"I don't see why not. I would make sure you wore the suits and used the softest of weapons, but I think it would be fun for the two of you."

"Ari, what do you think?" Caris turned hopeful eyes his way.

"I like the sound of that. Besides, you know I'm happy to try anything once. But, will Dasa and Bo agree?"

"Who says you have to tell them?" Vict looked decidedly regal in that moment. "I am the king, after all. I have ways to work around the both of them without them knowing. As much as they like to believe otherwise, they do not know everything that goes on within the palace. I have my people in places they really wouldn't believe. Isn't that right, Deek'in and Yavek?"

"Yes, Your Majesty." Both guards bowed deeply. Deek winked at Ari as he rose.

"As you've probably guessed, I know exactly what you have been up to. For example, I happen to know you are fans of Cherished Soul, how much you've made friends with the potters, your time going over all that tech. Let's just say I know a lot."

Ari blushed furiously at the thought of Vict knowing what he'd been buying. Vict nudged him to look at Caris. "If you think you're embarrassed, then take a look at Caris there."

Ari looked. Caris' cheeks were such a vibrant red, he would almost have expected them to be burning to the touch. "Caris?"

"I can't believe my mate's father knows what underwear I've been buying. Because that's not mortifying at all, is it?"

Vict couldn't stop chuckling. "Would it help if I told you I shopped there?"

Both Caris and Ari spat their drinks out in a rainbow of juice. They stared in unison at Vict. A choking sound caught Ari's attention. Looking over his shoulder, he saw Deek bending over Yav who was collapsed on the floor. He sprang up. "What happened?"

"He was eating a meat treat when Vict spoke. It's stuck." Deek was trying to help him, but had no idea how.

Ari dropped down beside them. All the methods he knew to help someone choking might not work— who knew what demon anatomy was like? Taking a risk, he bent Yav's head back, using his horns for leverage. "Tip his chin up as much as possible," he ordered Deek.

Vict was already on his implant, trying to summon help.

"I need someone to tilt his body up, so I can tilt his head right back."

Deek helped him into position.

"Caris, come here and hold his horns so his head stays back."

Caris ran and took over.

Ari stood up mumbling to himself. "I can't believe I'm about to do this." He positioned himself so he was straddling Yav's body. He linked his hands together and pointed the joined fists just below where he guessed his chest area was. Taking a deep breath, he slammed himself down so his fists rammed into Yav's body.

"What are you doing?" Deek asked.

Ari ignored him, stood up and dropped down again. They all watched as a piece of meat flew out of Yav's mouth. There was a cry of warning from one of the other guards and Ari looked up just in time to see a blur of purple slam into him.

He went flying, skidding along the floor of the royal box, knocking over chairs as he crashed into the wall, head first.

Chaos broke out. Caris leapt up, trying to get to Ari, and was backhanded across the face by a Red demon. The guards' hands were fluttering about by their swords, unsure what to do.

Vict slammed his implant. "Dasa, Bo'saverin, here. Now!" he bellowed.

Bo, about to take Dasa out, jerked at the blast in his ear. With a puzzled look at Dasa, they both turned to the royal box. There was a fight going on there. Sparing no time, he started to run, pole in hand. There was no time to race out of the combat area and up the stairs. He thanked the designers of the arena for putting the royal box low enough he could pull this move off. He ran, holding his pole out in front of him at waist height, the pole flexing slightly. As he got close to the wall of the arena, he could hear the crowd muttering, but pushed it out of his mind. He dropped the pole, bracing it between the wall and ground. The momentum he'd achieved made the pole bend before straightening as he held on to the top. He pushed his legs upwards, forcing his body to arc, holding onto the tip. He cleared the wall of the royal box and let go of his pole. Twisting in the air, he righted his body and landed with a thud, the impact sending reverberations through his body. Barely two seconds later, another thud sounded beside him. Dasa.

In those precious seconds, he'd assessed the situation. He ran at the Red demon who'd just lifted a dazed Ari from the floor. Swiping his legs out, he sent the demon careening, grabbing Ari from him as he relaxed his grip in an attempt to steady himself.

"Here!" Vict gestured to Bo.

Bo carefully placed Ari into the king's arms and turned back around, grabbing the Red who'd charged him and pinning him to the wall, his scaled hand locked around the demon's throat. The demon's own blade, liberated as the demon clawed at Bo's hand, was now pressed up against his chest.

Bo looked to his right and saw Dasa had pinned his own sister to the wall. Alenska was snarling at Dasa.

"Enough," Vict roared. All movement ceased. "You will *all* stand down."

Deek helped Yav to his feet as he still struggled to regulate his breathing. When Vict gestured to a chair, Deek righted it and helped Yav into it.

Both Dasa and Bo refused to let their targets go.

Vict gently passed Ari over to Caris before he stormed up to his daughter and gestured for Dasa to let go. When Dasa didn't move, Vict snarled.

Dasa fought for control and slowly pulled back his anger. He released his sister and let her drop unceremoniously to the floor.

Vict grabbed Alenska by the tunic and hauled her back up, slamming her back into the wall himself. "What the frek are you doing?"

Alenska's scales were rippling, her control slipping. "The no horn was attacking a demon." She spat towards Ari who was now being cradled by Caris and guarded by Deek.

"He was doing no such thing." Vict shook his head. "Did you even bother to wait a second to assess the situation before charging in like you're a savior?"

"I know what I saw." Her roar echoed around the arena.

Vict turned to one of the guards. "See the arena cleared."

237

"Yes, Your Majesty." The guard ran.

Bo was fighting the need to check on Ari, but he reassured himself he was safe in Caris' arms. As soon as the threat was neutralized, he would be there in a heartbeat.

"What you saw was wrong. Aridien was saving Yavek. He was choking. How do you expect someone that small to help someone as big as a demon? He was the only one who reacted quickly enough. He saved Yavek's *life*. You ran in without thought and attacked him. Someone I have given shelter to, someone I consider part of the *family*. Why you did that, I'm not entirely sure. If the guards weren't reacting, why you believed you needed too, I have no idea. What were you *thinking*!" Vict's voice rose with each sentence until he was bellowing at his daughter.

"I was thinking that I would protect a demon, one of my own, against them." She gestured to Ari and Caris, her hand subtly performing a rude gesture.

Dasa caught the move and stepped forward, only to be blocked by his father's arm. "I don't know where your attitude is coming from Alenska, but I've had enough. It's time. You are to do a tour of the guilds. I think you'd better start with the Bronze. Some time serving other people may, I hope, give you a lesson in humility."

"Father!" She turned her incredulous gaze Vict's way. "You can't possibly mean that? I'm a Purple. I don't serve others."

"That's where you're *wrong*. Purples serve everyone. We serve each member of our race, serve them by leading them. I have no idea where you have learned this attitude from. I can only believe it's the Reds, seeing as that is who you occupy your time with. I think it's time we limit that as well. You are to have no contact with them until I believe you are changing for the better."

When Alenska went to protest, Vict simply held his hand up. "Enough. If you want to behave like a demonling in a full fit, I will treat you that way and keep you secluded in the palace. Don't push me, demonling."

Vict turned to the Cobalt sub-commander, Jeek'sin. "See her back to the castle and double her detail. I don't want her going anywhere without an escort. I want nightly reports as to her activities. Nothing is to be left out or there will be punishments metered out. Do I make myself clear?"

"Yes, Your Majesty." Jeek'sin bowed before turning to Alenska and directing her to the door. "I'll leave Fre'dint here to help with the Red."

Vict turned his attention to the Red in question. "Anything to say?"

The Red shook his head.

"Nothing? Why does that not surprise me in the slightest. Fine. A couple of days in the cells for a willful attack on another citizen of Kenistal."

"That is not a citizen of Kenistal." The Red stared at Ari with a look of utter contempt.

Vict turned to Fre'dint. "Make that four days in the cells. I will not tolerate this sort of attitude."

"Yes, Your Majesty." Fre'dint gestured to two Cobalts who stepped forward and hauled the Red away.

Immediately everyone moved to Ari and Caris' sides, now they were safe.

"Ari, Tiko, can you hear me?" Bo picked up Ari before sitting down on the floor of the royal box, Ari safe in his arms.

"Bo?" Ari blinked groggily.

Bo blew out a relieved breath. "It's me."

"Ow." Ari stared at his wrist. "I think it's broken."

Caris peered over from his own place in Dasa's arms. "There's no think about it, it's definitely broken." There was a bone jutting out, although it hadn't broken the skin.

Deek checked on the progress of the med team. "They should be here in two minutes."

"Why so long?" Vict paced back and forth. "There should be a team here at the arena any time there is a match."

"Apparently there was a training accident and one of the warriors took a pole to the chest. He's being transported to the med center now," Deek relayed.

Vict squatted in front of Ari and took his good hand. "What were you doing?"

Ari cocked his head to one side. "Um, I would have thought it was obvious." He blushed at talking back to a king.

Vict simply smiled.

Ari tried to ignore the throbbing agony of his wrist. "I know the moves for Aducians, but I had no idea if they would work on a demon. I wasn't sure if a demon's anatomy is in the same place as mine. Besides, he's too damn tall, I wouldn't have been able to do it. I couldn't think of anything else, so I did what I could to copy the move as best as possible."

"By slamming into his chest?" Deek asked incredulously.

Ari glared. "It worked, didn't it? Besides, I was aiming for the bit just below his chest."

Yav still fought for breath, his skin incredibly pale for a Cobalt as he leaned back on Deek, letting his friend and fellow guard support his weight. "Ari, I can't thank you enough. You saved my life. I was so stunned by what was said—" Deek and Yav both blushed at the memory— "I forgot what I was doing and forgot to swallow properly."

"That's what started all this?" Vict looked around as Deek, Yav, Caris and Ari all nodded. He fought the rising smile on his face, but quickly gave up and laughed long and loud.

Bo looked at Ari, then at Vict. "What did I miss?"

Ari, despite the pain he was in, smirked. "Trust me, you probably don't want to know and I know Dasa definitely won't want to."

"Now I have to know." Bo gestured for Ari to go ahead.

Ari tilted his head so he could reach Bo's ear and whispered what had happened.

Bo blinked a couple of times, staring wide-eyed at Vict, who just smirked at him. "I could have gone a thousand lifetimes without ever knowing that."

Dasa opened his mouth to ask.

Bo resolutely shook his head. "You don't want to know, *trust me*, like you never trusted me before, you do *not* want to know."

"I do."

Caris snickered at the pout on Dasa's face.

"My Little Dynamo, you know you can never keep anything from me…" Dasa attempted to flutter his eyelashes at Caris.

"That looks so wrong on a demon's face." Caris looked at Vict.

Vict shrugged. "I'm not embarrassed about it."

Bo groaned and hid his face in his hands. "Don't blame me when you can't get the images out of your head. It'll be your own damn fault."

Dasa turned to Caris, all eager for answers.

Knowing everyone else was aware of what happened, Caris didn't bother whispering. "We were discussing how Vict has been keeping an eye on us from afar. How he knows about the tech and the potters barn. He mentioned that he knew we'd been shopping in Cherished Soul. I happened to say 'I can't believe my mate's father knows what underwear I've been buying. Because that's not mortifying at all, is it?' To which your father replied… 'Would it help if I told you I shopped there?'"

Dasa's eyes went wide, his jaw dropped and he spluttered. After a stunned minute, he shook his head and his face contorted. "Eww, that's… the images… help me… they burn…"

Vict rolled his eyes. "A bit melodramatic there, son."

241

Dasa adamantly shook his head. "There can be nothing too dramatic for that. It's…" He whirled on Bo. "Why the frek didn't you stop me asking!"

Bo huffed out a laugh. "I did warn you. You only have yourself to blame for this."

Dasa's face was still contorted as though he'd eaten something disgusting. "I need to scrub out my mind."

"Oh, son, so your parents still have an active sex life. Get over it."

Dasa jammed his fingers in his ears, and sang to himself. "Nope, don't want to hear it, think it or talk about it. Thank you very much."

They were all still laughing as the medics finally arrived.

Ari batted Bo's hands away. "Seriously, I'm okay."

"No, you're not. You hit your head, your wrist is broken. She hurt you." Bo's horns were starting to steam again.

"Bo, stop. You were there, you saved me. I don't want to spend any more time thinking about what happened. The medics fixed my wrist, it doesn't hurt, and I can still move my fingers. Look." Ari waggled them where they peeked out of the golden brace wrapped around his wrist.

"You're not supposed to get hurt, again." Bo's arm around Ari's shoulder tightened reflexively.

Ari stopped in the middle of the street, the guards waiting patiently, Caris and Dasa walking ahead. "Bo, please, I'm alright. Now, shut up with the worrying and kiss me. I've wanted to kiss you since I saw what you were wearing when you stepped out into the arena."

"Is that right?" Bo grinned down at Ari.

Ari scowled when Bo didn't move fast enough for his liking. He jumped, confident in the knowledge that Bo would catch him.

Bo groaned as his arms were suddenly full of a squirming Ari, his hands naturally moving to cup Ari's ass as he wrapped his legs around his waist. "What are you—"

His words were cut off as Ari's lips claimed his. He took control of the kiss and kneaded the globes of Ari's delectable ass. Forcing himself to calm down, he pulled away. "We need to stop. At least wait until we get back to our suite."

Ari groaned and laid his head against Bo's shoulder. "Fine." He suddenly pulled back. "But you're carrying me."

"Happily." Bo smiled.

"Not like this." Ari rolled his eyes as Bo started walking. Instead, he shifted around so he was on Bo's back, his legs still wrapped around his waist, arms draped over Bo's shoulders. He kicked Bo's hips with his foot. "Come on, I want to go fast."

The guards were smiling away. "Fancy a race?" Deek challenged.

"Yes!" Ari grabbed hold off Bo's horns before dropping them like they were fire. "Oops, sorry," he whispered into Bo's ear, giving it a quick kiss. "Come on, let's race."

"I'm a Commander, we don't race…" Ari scowled against his neck. "We win!" He took off down the street, his arms holding Ari securely to him as he bounced on his back.

Ari let out a massive whoop of joy. This was fun. He hadn't been sure if Bo would do it, but he loved him for the fact he did. In fact, he was pretty sure he loved Bo, nothing more, nothing less. The question was when to say the words. Pushing that to the back of his mind, he enjoyed the ride, waving to Perik and Oz'ki as they darted past the entrance to the courtyard. A couple of younger demonlings raced beside them and Ari waved down at them. "Come on, you want to beat those slow Cobalts back there, don't you?" He cackled at the glare Deek shot him.

Bo's implant started to buzz. "Ari. press the implant for me."

"Which bit do I press?" Ari started to fumble behind Bo's ear. "Damn, where is it?" He pressed random bits. "Ah ha."

"Bo'saverin here." As he spoke, they turned the corner and ran up the walkway.

"Do not come back." Dasa bellowed in his ear. "The Trevon are here."

"Too damn late." Bo drawled as the group on the stairs turned to study them. Dasa and Caris were off to one side, both looking angry. "Frek." Bo cursed, slowing his pace, but refusing to lower Ari to the ground.

"Bo…" Ari's voice trembled. "Why is my mother here?"

Bo nearly dropped Ari as he jerked to a stop.

CHAPTER TWENTY FOUR

"**I**'m sorry, did you just say your mother?" Bo stopped at the bottom of the stairs, ignoring everyone and gently lowered Ari down, keeping him safe in his arms, hating how violently Ari trembled.

"Yes. Why is she here, Bo? Why would any of you let her come here?" Ari's gaze held Bo's the look of horror and fear tore at Bo.

"There's supposed to be a delegation of Trevons here. That's it. We wondered if they were up to something, we even checked the passenger manifest, but your mother's name wasn't there. They weren't due till later. I was going to keep you occupied in our suite so you didn't have to see any of them. I didn't even want you to know they were here. I didn't want you upset. I am so sorry I failed you."

Ari gripped Bo tight. "You didn't fail me, not even slightly. You tried to keep them away from me. Can I ask one thing?"

"Anything," Bo vowed.

"Stay with me? Don't leave me with her."

"Never." Bo kept his arm around Ari as they turned to face the group.

"I'm sorry," Dasa mouthed.

Ari shook his head. It wasn't their fault. He took a deep breath and walked up the stairs. "Mother. I wasn't aware you were coming here. After all, you weren't on the passenger list. Then again, nothing you do surprises me anymore. You always have been able to make things go your way."

"How dare you talk to me that way. You always were a willful, tempestuous child." Agota Kelotian glared at her son. "You are to come here right now. I will see my guards escort you back to our cruiser. You will board and wait for me there. We will return to Aducia and Xerves as soon as I have conducted my business."

Bo squeezed Ari's hand, letting him know he was there, supporting him, but trying to give him the chance to face his mother head on, stand up to her and prove to himself how much he'd grown.

Ari drew strength from Bo beside him. "I will not be returning with you to Aducia or to see Father. You no longer hold any rights over me. You have no power to tell me what to do."

"Oh course I have the power over you. You are my son. I can do as I want." Agota sneered at her son. "Aducian law allows me complete control over my lenis son."

Ari locked his knees, refusing to let her see how affected he was by her demands.

Vict joined the group on the stairs. He was in full regal attire. Agota held her hand out to him. "Your Majesty."

Vict stopped, looked down at her hand, then back up. The look of disgust on his face made the guards around him force their faces into neutral expressions. "If you think I am going to shake the hand of someone who gives away their son for trading rights, you are woefully mistaken." He brushed past her and went to stand behind Ari, resting his hands on Ari's shoulders.

"Aridien is no longer your son. He is no longer Aducian. He is Kenistalian. He. Is. Demon. The documents have been signed, notarized and filed. You have no further claim to him. What is more… he is an adult and can make his own decisions."

Agota spluttered for a moment. "How dare you think you can take my property from me."

Vict drew himself up to his full height, anger making his tail restless. "Your property?" His voice was eerily calm. The guards around them taking an involuntary step back, fully aware of how dangerous their king was in this sort of mood. "No man is property.

Slavery was abolished across the universes long ago. Your son has made us fully aware of how you treat your supposed property."

"He is lenis. He isn't a man. He isn't worthy of rights." Agota narrowed her eyes at Ari. "I suggest you come here, or there will be consequences."

Vict went to speak, but Ari lifted his hand, resting it over Vict's on his shoulder. "I won't be coming there, or going anywhere with you, *Agota*." Never again would he call her his mother. The minute he'd cut ties with Aducia, it was over.

"You lost the right to tell me what to do. It was bad enough that you kept me locked up from an early age, forced me to train to be some consort to whoever you deemed could help you the most. But, no, you then shipped me off in a rusty ship with virtually no guards. Being on such a ship let the Loperis take me captive easily. Do you have any idea what they planned? Did you even try to rescue me? If you considered it, no doubt you weighed up the pros and cons of how expensive it would be."

Agota looked stunned. Never before had he spoken like this to her. "You know, I don't think you or Xerves ever cared for me. Did you celebrate when I was born? I bet you did, but not because you were happy I was healthy. No, I bet you celebrated because I was lenis and you could sell me, trade me." Ari angrily swiped at the lone tear that fell down his face. What else could he say? It wouldn't change the past. Nothing would.

"Whatever relationship we had, in whatever capacity we had— it is *done*. I'm done. No, I won't come with you. I am Kenistalian. *I am demon*. I live here now. Surrounded by people who care for me, who I care for, who I—" Ari paused for a moment, fully aware of everyone watching him, from the guards to his friends, Agota to Bo, and even the Trevon who were expressionless. He leaned back so he could look into Bo's eyes. "Who I *do* love. Because I *do* love you, Bo. You, Bo'saverin Hevalis, are it for me. I don't want anyone else. I am yours for as long as you want me to be."

Bo, still stunned with pride at the way Ari had stood up to his mother, spun him round. He tenderly cradled Ari's face in his hands. "Say it *again*."

Ari took a deep breath. "I said… I love you."

Bo searched Ari's eyes, seeing the love shining back at him. "Tiko, I love you too. I think I loved you from the time you tried to help me as the ceiling came down around us. No matter how scared you were, you got me the best help you could. I didn't know it then, it took me a while to see it, but you mean everything to me. You are it for me. This is not the place I ever imagined saying these words, but we are surrounded by the people who are important to us, and I don't mean her." Bo gestured to Agota on the stairs.

He dropped down onto his knees and held Ari's hands in his. "Aridien, I love you with all that I am. I would be honored if you would agree to be my mate."

Ari gasped. "Really?"

"Yes, really." Bo chuckled.

"Yes!" Ari flung himself into Bo's arms, simply breathing in his scent.

The Cobalts, who had gathered around to see what was going on, closed ranks around their Commander, shielding him and his new mate from view and drumming their feet onto the ground to drown out the sounds of the abuse and vitriol Agota hurled at them both.

Vict's lips were twitching. Caris, completely forgetting every ounce of diplomatic training, let out a whoop of joy. Dasa's fist, clenched at his side, shook gently as he squeezed.

"No!" Agota's voice screeched. "I forbid it. You are to remain pure, and you will marry who I insist you marry. You do not get to choose! I do. I am your mother, you will—"

"You will shut up!" Vict roared. With a last, lingering smile over his shoulder at Bo and Ari, he stalked up the stairs, his expression morphing into his normal regal bearing. "What rights you had to your son have long since expired. How any parent could treat a child of theirs the way you have treated young Aridien is beyond me. Many worlds maintain we demons are barbaric, purely based on our appearance. You are far more barbaric then we could ever be. I would be ashamed if you were a demon. I thank the stars you are not. Make no mistake, you have lost young Aridien. He will never come to you, never go with you. He will no longer have anything to do with you."

Vict's snarl was so intense, Agota took a fearful step back before her eyes hardened and she stood her ground.

Vict ignored her reaction. "He is welcome here. He has been welcomed with open arms since the first moment we met him. He is loved and well respected. He contributes to all of our lives. They are richer for having him in it. I wonder, do you even know anything about your own son? I doubt you do. More fool you, your loss is our gain."

Agota tried to see past the wall of Cobalts, her anger rising when she couldn't. "This is a betrayal, Aridien. Do you hear me? You have betrayed me, betrayed your father, betrayed your world. You are lenis, you have no rights, you should be at home, doing as I tell you to do. You have disgraced me. Me! I am one of the most powerful traders—"

Dasa stepped up to join his father. He turned to the closest Cobalt officer. "Escort the delegation to the meeting room. I want them out of sight of your commander and his new mate."

The officer nodded and beckoned to the nearby guards who were not ringed around Bo and Ari. They herded the delegation back into the palace and away from the steps. Once they were gone, Vict let out a heavy breath. "How the frek did this happen? They weren't due here for hours."

Dasa looked his father in the eye. "They lied. They got the preapproved flight plan, but came ahead of schedule. We have to be pleased there were no scheduled take offs. If there had been…"

"It could have been disastrous." Vict paused mid-step to think. "Why would they take the risk? They would know it would only anger us further. On top of the manifest being a fabrication… there is more going on here. Caris, would you object to sitting in on this trade meeting? You have dealt with so many races, you will probably see some of the nuances far better than we would."

"Oh, I'll be there." Caris gestured to the retreating group. "There is no way I'm letting them get the better end of a deal, if you even choose to trade with them. Who organized this anyway?"

"Guild Master Kinesh." Dasa sighed. "No real surprises there, I guess. But, it makes me wonder if they knew this was about more than the Trevon."

"Have the Trevon actually said anything or did they let her say everything?" Vict wondered.

"They were all talking. We had no way of knowing it was her. They didn't introduce everyone, just Traders Trinke and Gevero."

"So a lie by omission in many ways, but still a lie." Vict stared after the group. "I want them watched at all times. Make sure the guards are on full patrol. No one gets to walk around unaccompanied. I don't trust any of this. She is definitely up to something. I don't for one minute believe she doesn't have a back-up plan for if and when Ari refused to go with her."

"You think she expected him to refuse?" Dasa smiled as he looked towards Bo and Ari who were still in a loving embrace.

Vict patted Caris on the shoulder, trying to instill calm. "I don't know. You have to admit Ari has come a long way since he got here. Can any of us honestly say he wouldn't have gone if she'd been here soon after he arrived? It's taken time for him to gain the confidence he has now. There is one thing for sure, he isn't going anywhere, unless he truly wants to."

"Somehow, I don't see him leaving Bo, do you?" Caris couldn't stop the smile. He was thrilled for them both. "Did you expect any of that?"

Dasa frowned at his mate. "Don't you think I would have mentioned something to you if I had?"

"Good, I was gearing up to be annoyed at you for keeping secrets from me." Caris crossed his arms.

"Aww, you're cute when you pout."

Dasa grimaced when Caris whacked him in the stomach. He looked to his father. "Did you see that? Are you going to stand for your son and heir being treated that way?"

Vict grinned. "Yes, especially if you deserve it."

"It's so nice to be loved," Dasa drawled, bending to kiss Caris on the forehead.

"Aww, I love you, even if you do pout better than me," Caris teased.

Vict bit his lip as Dasa spluttered. "Come on, I want to congratulate those two before we go and deal with everything."

CHAPTER TWENTY FIVE

Bo gently eased back from Ari's lips, smiling as Ari blinked a couple of times, the fog in his eyes slowly lifting. "I love you, Ari, never doubt that, but are you sure this is what you want. Don't do this just to escape from your mother. I will protect you no matter what."

Ari narrowed his eyes. "Of course I meant it." His hands went to his hips as he tilted his head back to look Bo in the eyes. "There is no way I'm going anywhere with her. I wouldn't have gone even if you hadn't asked me to mate with you." His nose wrinkled for a moment. "Umm, one quick question. What does mating actually involve? I haven't just signed on to be your consort, have I? Like some pampered trophy?"

Bo stroked a finger over Ari's eyebrows and down his nose, wanting to always remember this moment. "No, Tiko, being mated is much like being married. I promise you won't be a trophy anything. I want you by my side, helping me, supporting me as I support you. I want to come home at the end of a long day and lay with you in my arms. I would love to see you interact with our society more, maybe spend time with the other Cobalt families. I want you to explore anything you might want to do, pottery, more tech, whatever it is. I don't want you to feel you have to, I simply want you to know you can."

Ari grinned. "I can do that."

A warning cough sounded, accompanied by a muttered, "incoming."

Bo grabbed hold of Ari's hand. "Ready to face Caris, Dasa and Vict?"

"No." Ari paled as the memory of who else had witnessed their moment slammed into him.

"No, don't think of her, not yet. Let's just enjoy our moment before the rest of the universe intrudes." Bo squeezed his hand tightly.

There was no more time for words. The Cobalts around them parted and Caris came running at Ari full tilt. Within seconds, Caris hugged him tight. "I am so damn happy for you."

Ari was about to reply before he was pulled out of Caris' arms and into Vict's.

Vict hugged Ari firmly, yet gently. "Welcome to the family, son."

Ari caught Bo's gaze over Vict's shoulder as Dasa congratulated his closest friend with what looked like a play fight.

Vict made a noise in the back of his throat. "They're doing that fighting thing again, aren't they?"

Caris giggled and nodded.

"There was enough of that when they were demonlings. Things never change." He wrapped one arm around Ari's shoulders as he pulled back, the other around Caris'. He gently steered them towards their mates.

Bo grinned at how proud Vict looked. "I have four sons now."

Dasa frowned. "You mean I need to think of Bo as my brother? Eww." He ran as Bo lunged for him.

They chased each other around the courtyard.

"Was the arena not enough for you two?" Vict called out.

Dasa jogged back over. "We didn't get to find out who won, you called us before it ended."

Vict rolled his eyes. "I swear you are as bad now as you were as a demonling. Come on, we'd better get inside and deal with this."

The happy atmosphere disappeared. Ari stiffened his spine. "We'd better go in."

Vict stopped him with a gentle hand to his shoulder. "You don't have to. We were planning on keeping the Trevon delegation away from you anyway."

Ari shook his head. "No, Agota will expect me to hide. She's almost counting on it. I want to show her she hasn't made me as scared as she thinks she has." He turned to Bo. "Promise me—"

"I won't leave your side for anything."

A throat clearing made them all jump. "Am I hearing the rumors correctly?"

"Mac!" Ari raced across and hugged him, Caris not far behind him.

"How are you, Mac'likrit?" Vict looked him over.

"Getting there, Your Majesty. Out and about in the chair now. I actually walked the other day. It was three stumbling steps but…"

"It's a start." Bo grinned. "And what rumors are you hearing?"

"That you and Ari are going to be mated." Mac's smile was wide. "Congratulations and about damn time."

Bo whistled. "I knew gossip spread quickly, but frek, that was fast. It was ten minutes ago."

Mac scoffed. "This is Kenistal, and the palace in particular. Nothing stays quiet for long."

Dasa watched Caris hug Mac tight now that Ari had let go. "Does this mean you're ready to come back and be a companion and helper to these two?"

Mac held Dasa's gaze. "Did you mean that?"

"Yes. If you want, you can start now. There is a delegation here…"

Mac took in the expressions on the faces around him. "What are you not telling me?"

As they made their way into the palace, Dasa and Bo filled Mac in. Anger was too tame a word for it. "Ari, she won't get near you. If I have to give my life to stop it, I will."

Ari reached around Caris and tapped Mac on the head. "Stop talking like that." He scowled.

Mac's eyebrows shot up.

Bo smirked at the shocked look. "He's getting feisty now, Mac, you'd better watch out."

"No, Commander, *you'd* better watch out."

"Ain't that the truth," Bo muttered under his breath.

Ari banked down his nerves and walked into the meeting room to face Agota and the Trevons. She immediately stood up. "You should leave, this meeting is for me, not lenis."

Vict slammed his hand down on the table, the goblets rattling against each other. "Enough. If you can't keep a civil tongue, you will be escorted back to your ship under armed guard. You will be kept there until it is time for the rest of your party to leave. You are on dangerous ground, Agota Kelotian. I would not push me. This is *my* planet, *my* kingdom. You would do well to respect that."

She sat sullenly with her arms crossed.

Just then, the door burst open and Guild Master Kinesh, leader of the Red guild, came bustling in. He pulled up short when he saw who was sat around the table. "Vict'arin, what are you doing here?"

Vict focused his gaze on Kinesh until he dropped his head forward in a small approximation of a bow. "That's King Vict'arin to you. Why wouldn't I be here? These are negotiations for trade agreements between two planets. I think I am the one demon who

255

should be here, don't you? You think I would leave something so important to someone else?"

"I can handle this." Kinesh puffed his chest out.

"I'm sure you *think* you can. It doesn't mean you will. Besides, I will make sure all of Kenistal will benefit, not just a select few." Vict pointed to a chair at the end of the table. "Sit."

Kinesh looked mutinous but sat. The three Reds with him took seats behind him, but watched everything.

Ari shivered as the feeling of someone watching him intently slid over him. It wasn't Agota; she was staring between Vict and Kinesh at that point. He almost didn't want to look and see. Bo's hand found his under the table and Bo's thumb took up a reassuring stroking across it.

Vict looked at the Trevons. They were a slightly strange race. Their ears were long, thin oblongs, running down the entire side of their faces. They had three nostrils and two eyes, with no eyebrows. They were all shades of silver and gold, but dull and matte rather than vibrant like the demons. Their language was soft and lyrical, at odds with their often aggressive behavior. They were sly and manipulative.

Vict focused on Traders Trinke and Gevero, the two whose names he knew. "I am aware you have dealt with Guild Master Kinesh up until now. However, if you plan on negotiating large scale trading rights, trading corridors in our space territories, rather than smaller, single item trades, you can understand why this needs to be dealt with on a higher level."

Trader Trinke laid his head sideways on his large shoulder, a move common among Trevons. "We can understand this. Trade is key, not for lesser apprentices."

Kinesh's face mottled. "I am not some lesser Demon or apprentice." He spat the word out like it was dirty. "I am leader of the most important guild on Kenistal."

Bo coughed and pointedly looked from Kinesh to Vict. "I believe you may have that wrong, don't you? The most important guild are the Purples, our rulers. Or had you temporarily forgotten about them?"

Caris, closest to Kinesh, was the only one who heard Kinesh's muttered comment.

"Not for long."

Caris stiffened. Just what were the Reds up to? Thankful for his years of diplomatic work, he didn't react to the comment. He turned to Trader Trinke. "I am Caris Dealyn."

"The Ambassador?" Trinke's nostrils flared.

"I was, but I left the post when I moved here. I'm going to be blunt, Trader Trinke, what is it you want with a trade deal? We, that is, Kenistalians, are not natural trading partners for you. The distance between the two planets is fairly prohibitive to trading most things and still be financially viable. Or are there other reasons you wished your delegation access?"

Trinke's eyes took on a calculating hue. He blinked a couple of times, his eyelids moving vertically across his eyes, rather than downwards like most races. "The universe is becoming overpopulated. Too many trades. We wish something different. Going to new sectors means new trade. New trade means exclusive. Why would there be other needs to be here."

Caris, used to the way some races battled with galactic standard, easily interpreted Trinke's words. "I understand the trade, but let me get to the point. Why did you bring an Aducian with you?"

"I'm not just any Aducian." Agota geared up for another rant, but Vict sent her a quelling look and she shut up, her expression murderous.

"It was requested by others." Gevero joined in the discussion. "Paid handsomely for it. We saw opportunity for trade and credits from escort. Credits make worthwhile."

All eyes turned to Agota.

Bo was fuming. Ari squeezed his leg as best he could, his turn to reassure his new mate. As Bo opened his mouth to speak, Ari beat him to it. "You paid them to bring you over here, to come in quietly so we didn't know you were coming."

The smug look on Agota's face said more than words ever could.

Ari narrowed his eyes, staring down Agota. "There's something I don't get…"

"Really? Why does that not surprise me. You never were an intelligent boy." Agota's lips kicked up at the side. She kept her gaze on Bo, and Ari knew she was trying to bait him into attacking.

"And you were never a decent mother. But, see, here's the thing. You paid the Trevon to fly you over here. Even if you consider the trade money they could make, you must be paying handsomely. Why? Just who were you going to trade me to? I mean, I'm guessing Renauld would refuse me now that you can't guarantee I'm pure. What does anyone have on you..." Ari's eyes widened with realization. "If the Loperis were defeated, how did you even know I was *here*? How did you know it was the demons who rescued me?"

Bo wrapped his hand around the back of Ari's neck. "You rescued yourself and you know it. All we did was be here for your landing."

Ari tipped his head giving Bo greater access. He shivered under Bo's caress and straightened up. "Someone told you."

"What?" A chorus of echoes blasted the room.

Ari held Agota's gaze firmly with his own "It's the only logical explanation. There is no other way Agota could have known. Think about it, Bo."

Bo's gaze collided with Dasa's, even as his mind went over everything. "We have a spy."

"It's the only way she could know." Ari's gaze stayed fixed on Agota as chaos broke out. "You won't win. You won't get me back. Whatever your plans are, they are done."

A scuffle broke out between the two Aducians there with Agota and the Cobalt Guards stationed in the room. The Trevon tried to protect the Aducians and it wasn't long before the room was swarming with guards, some surrounding an angry Vict, others trying to pull Dasa and Bo away.

In the melee, no one noticed Agota rise from her seat and storm over to Ari. She wrapped her hand around his throat, bending to whisper in his ear. "Make no mistake, *lenis*, I will succeed. You will be on my cruiser when I leave and you *will* be marrying Renauld. I have more friends than you could possibly realize and they will help any way needed. I will not see my plans thwarted because of you. You are nothing more than a pawn, a piece in a large assembly. You will go where I need you to be. I have no care what happens to you when you get there, but I will fulfill my bargain."

"What did I ever do to you?" The huskiness in Ari's voice betrayed his struggle. Tears streamed down his face, not from hurt, but partly from anger and partly as he struggled to breathe.

"There is nothing you could do to me. You were born, that is all that mattered. Born lenis, giving me the chance to close in on the deal of a lifetime. Make no mistake, you will rue the day you crossed me, whether it's sooner or later. I will get my revenge on you. But know this. You will be coming back with me." Agota squeezed harder and Ari fought against her hold, but he was still weakened after the attack at the arena, and with only one hand working there was little he could do. His vision was fading. He did the only thing left he could— he used up the last of his breathe to scream one word at the top of his voice. "Bo!"

Mac was the first to notice Ari was in trouble as two guards moved towards the Trevons and away from Vict. "Ari!" He wheeled himself over, cursing his useless legs. He got there just as Agota let him drop to the floor. He surged out of the wheelchair, barely mindful of his foot, took a few haltingly painful steps forward and scooped Ari into his arms. His foot started to buckle under the weight and he grabbed for the table, holding Ari to him with one arm. Nudging a chair out with his hip, he dropped down into the chair and cradled Ari against his chest, extending his neck, trying to open his airway.

Bo watched the scene play out as he pushed through the throng of fighters. His heart had skipped a beat at the sight of Agota attempting to crush Ari's throat. When Mac beat him to it, his heart began to beat fully again. "Is he breathing?" Bo shouted over the din.

Mac, bracing against his own pain, yelled back, "Yes, go, get her, I have him."

Bo nodded and chased after the escaping Agota. Within seconds, other Cobalts joined him as more swarmed into the area. Seeing a couple of city guards walking up the steps of the palace, he yelled out, "Grab her!"

The guards took too long to react and she managed to slip underneath their outstretched arms. Bo shot them a withering look as he ran past. *Damn woman is fast.* His feet pounded the walkways as he chased after her. Where she thought she could go, he had no idea. She ran down side streets, ducking around wandering demons, many seeing another race and attempting to grab her. Crafty iglink kept evading them. Huh, another word he would have to teach Ari— it basically meant bitch.

Bo caught a flash of metal as sunshine beamed into the courtyard entrance. He narrowed his eyes as he raced on, only to see Ulkrit slam a massive pot into her stomach as she ran by. She dropped to the ground like a stone. Ulkrit stood over her, his makeshift weapon in both hands. "I figured you wanted her stopped, Commander."

Bo had no chance of suppressing his chuckle at the prim Agota sprawled in the dirt like some gutter dweller. "Thank you. Despite the somewhat disastrous early beginning, you are certainly proving yourself to be quite the demon."

Ulkrit looked pained. "I will forever be in young Aridien's debt over the way I treated him at first, yet he's treated me with nothing but kindness."

"Just treat him how you are now and all will be good. He wants nothing more than friends here," Bo assured him.

"That, I can assure you, Commander, he will have plenty of. He has a knack for finding his way into people's hearts."

"That he does."

"Yours especially, I'm thinking." Ulkrit scowled down at the woman as she started to stir. "Who is this anyway. She almost looks familiar." As she turned over, Ulkrit did a double take. "She's Aducian… is she…"

"Sadly, yes, that's Ari's mother. I use the term loosely as she in nothing short of an evil iglink who treated him… let's simply say it was bad."

Perik, who had joined them, scowled at her. "Can I kick her?"

Bo somehow managed to keep a professional façade. "Feeling a little bloodthirsty there, Perik?"

"When it comes to anyone hurting the Little Demon, then yes." Perik started to pull back his leg, but Bo shook his head.

"Spoil my fun, why don't you." Perik pouted. "Fine. But you better make sure she suffers."

"She will." Bo gestured towards some guards. "I want her escorted back to her ship and a ring of guards surrounding it. No one is allowed off."

Dasa, having joined the group, snarled at Agota, who was slowly coming to. "If I had my way, you would face charges and imprisonment here, but I will not drag Kenistal into a diplomatic incident over you. Under order of my father, King Vict'arin of Kenistal, you are hereby banned from visiting any and all demonic territories. Any attempts to return will be met with the full might of the Cobalts. Rest assured, Commander Bo'saverin here, Aridien's *mate*, will be more than happy to deal with you should you attempt to breach this order."

Dasa turned to the Cobalts. "Get her out of here." Dasa dipped his head slightly in Ulkrit's direction. "Thank you for your assistance today. It is most appreciated and won't be forgotten. Caris and I will drop by soon for a meal."

Ulkrit's smile was massive. "Thank you, Your Highness. I look forward to serving you personally." The prestige of having the prince at his business would be huge.

Dasa gestured to Bo. "We best get back, things were calming as I left, but we need medics to look over both Ari and Mac."

Bo groaned. "I really am going to have my work cut out with him, aren't I?"

Dasa smirked. "Yes, but you wouldn't have him any other way."

Bo's eyes reflected his love for Ari. "You're right, I wouldn't."

CHAPTER TWENTY SIX

Ari woke coughing. What was up with his throat? It hurt like it'd been doused in fire.

"Shh, you're okay, take slow breaths, then you can have some water."

That was Bo's voice. If Bo was there, everything would be fine. "W-what…" Trying to talk ripped Ari's throat.

"Don't try to talk, it's going to hurt for a little while. The doctor will be back in a minute with a spray that will help. If you're asking what happened… I'm sorry, Tiko, your mother was trying to strangle you. Mac got to you first and once I knew you were going to be alright, I gave chase."

Bo laid a gentle hand over Ari's mouth. "Let me talk, okay? If you still have questions after, you can write them down." He waited until Ari nodded.

"We caught up with her near the market. She was taken out by Ulkrit and a pan." Bo's eyes sparkled as Ari gaped. "Yeah, he smacked her with it, allowed us to catch up with her. She's been escorted to her cruiser. You never need to see her again. Vict'arin has banished her from all demon territory. The Trevons and Aducians are currently being spoken to. Dasa wants to see if he can find out anything else about the potential spy we have."

Ari went to talk but froze, not needing Bo to remind him about his throat. "Mac?" He mouthed.

Bo scowled. "Foolish demon got out of his chair to rescue you. Don't get me wrong, I'm glad someone got there quicker than I could, but with his foot, what he did was stupid. He's a krexjin!" Bo's voice rose.

"I did what needed doing!" Mac shouted back.

Ari looked around questioningly. Bo rolled his eyes, but pulled back the divider separating the two beds.

Ari's expression dropped. He stared at Mac with mounting horror, before he focused on Mac's foot suspended in the air with some sort of metal contraption.

"Ari, no. Don't get upset. I'm fine, honestly. This is just a precaution." He gestured to his leg. "It's a little swollen and they just want to give it some time to rest, that's all. I'll be out of here tomorrow."

"I'm sorry!" Ari mouthed as he blinked to clear the moisture trying to form in his eyes.

"Stop. It wasn't your fault, and honestly, I'll be just fine. I was more worried about you." Mac gestured to his throat. "We all were."

Ari held Mac's gaze before nodding. He motioned to Bo that he wanted a comp pad. Bo's eyebrows drew together. "I don't know what you want."

Ari scowled and mimed like he was writing something.

"Oh." Bo raced off to grab something.

Mac grinned like a fool. "You have his tail all in a twist."

Ari chuckled silently.

"Seriously, Ari, that demon adores you. You have made him so happy. I've known him for years. He's always had this gruff exterior with everyone, except maybe the prince. There has to be a slight distance between him and the Cobalts, it's the way it needs to be with him as commander. But that has come at a cost. To him personally, I mean. Losing his parents as well… I've often wondered if he's lonely. Not anymore. You are perfect for him, Ari. His life, our lives, are richer for you being in them. I wish you hadn't gone through what you did when Caris found you, but I'm glad it led you here."

Ari sniffed back the tears, desperately wanting to speak, but unable to. Instead he climbed out of bed, ignoring Mac's protests, and walked unsteadily to Mac's side before flinging his arms around him.

Mac gently hugged Ari, slowly stroking his hair, much the same way he would to calm his demonlings. "It's okay if you need to let it out, you know. You've been through so much lately. No one will think less of you."

Mac's words, his simple kindness seemed to break down Ari's last wall and the tears came. His capture and subsequent escape, the second attempted kidnapping, his mother, the fights. The stress and emotions came pouring out, like a dam had finally burst under the pressure of what it held back.

Mac looked up as Bo walked through the door and stopped dead, taking in Ari's quaking body in his arms. Bo dropped the comp pad on a table and rushed over. Mac gently eased his hold on Ari, smiling slightly as Ari clung to him until he realized Bo was there, turning to fling his arms around his new mate.

Bo gathered Ari into his arms and took him back to his bed, sitting with his back propped against the headboard, holding Ari tight and letting him cry it out. He didn't bother saying platitudes. There was little he could say. Ari had been through so much in a relatively short period of time. With the altercations with his mother, the final death knell to everything he'd known before had been sounded. Bo simply sat there, sharing a long, pained look with Mac as Ari broke apart in his arms.

Ari slowly became aware of comfort. Heat radiated around him and the sense of security, peace and rightness could only ever mean one thing— Bo. He snuggled deeper into the warm chest beneath him, ignoring the chuckles all around. That was more than Bo, he was pretty sure it was more than Bo and Mac, but right now all he wanted was to luxuriate in the peacefulness he'd found. He let his mind drift, vaguely aware of conversations going on around him.

"How's he doing?" Vict studied Ari, wrapped up in Bo's loving arms.

"He finally broke down. I'm not surprised." Bo gently kissed the top of Ari's head.

"Honestly, the only thing I'm surprised about is it's taken this long." Vict took a seat beside Ari's bed, running a gentle hand over Ari's curls, marveling at how tiny he seemed beneath his own large hand.

"I think, with the amount of… incidents we've had, he's not really had a moment to sit and let things fully settle. It was always going to hit him at some point. Everything with his mother finally brought it all to a head. I wanted to kill her, you know?" Bo held Vict's gaze. "That's not me, I use killing as a last resort, you know that. Oh, don't get me wrong, I'll take lives if I need to but…"

Vict took a goblet of davroc from a guard, smiling wide as he took his first sip. "You'd rather not need to. That's what makes you a good commander. But those feelings, wanting to end this for Ari once and for all are not unusual. He's hurting, and that makes you hurt. You just want to fix everything for him. All you long for is to see him happy. The things she did to him… We don't know how much physical abuse there was, but what she did was definitely mental abuse, cruel and, frankly, evil."

Vict peered into his davroc as though it held the answers to life itself. "I have no idea what life is really like on Aducia, if the way she treated him is normal for lenis to be treated. But if it is, it really isn't the sort of society I would want to trade with. To alienate, mistreat and vilify an entire section of their population for an accident of birth, for genetics, is disgraceful. I know Kenistal isn't perfect, the guild system far from it, but we would never treat one section of people like she has treated Ari and I imagine all lenis."

"There is little we can do for them." Bo wanted to though. The thought of thousands of young ones going through what Ari went through tore at his heart.

"We can't though. Even if we were part of the Barin Alliance and in a position to protest it, they are not. We can only hope someone on Aducia has the courage to stand up for what is right. In the meantime, we focus on what we can change— Ari's life."

Bo looked out the window and off into the distance to where he knew the cruiser was being heavily guarded. "What is going to happen to them?"

"The cruiser will be escorted back to their ship and then the ship will be escorted out of our space. Commander Urias is coming in with the KS Zerkin." Vict looked over his shoulder at Deek'in. "Get your commander a davroc?"

Bo smiled his thanks once his massive yawn had finished. "I'm not sure Dea will appreciate Commander Urias coming to help."

Vict pursed his lips. "The last time I saw them in a room together, it looked like they wanted to rip each other's horns out."

Bo's eyebrows darted up briefly. "I did wonder. I haven't seen them together. But when I mentioned Urias, Dea seemed… I'm not sure, something was off though."

Vict rolled his eyes. "Your brother always did keep his tail tucked close."

Bo laughed, jostling Ari slightly, soothing him when he moaned. "You're not wrong there. He's the best secret keeper I have ever known. Seriously, I doubt anyone could ever torture anything out of him. I do worry about him though. He took on so much when our parents died."

Vict nodded. "He was at the age where he wanted to prove he could do it all. He wanted so badly to look after you. He considered it his failing that he couldn't."

Bo's gaze snapped up from where he's been watching his fingers twine in Ari's hair. "He never said anything."

"He wouldn't have. He fought to help you for as long as he could. He nearly exhausted himself doing it. That's when I stepped in. He hated that, but knew it was for the best. I often wonder if he fully let himself grieve their loss. He closed up his heart. I've never seen or heard of him having a companion."

Bo frowned. "I didn't know you kept that close an eye on him."

Vict looked incredulous. "Considering what you are to Dasa, considering what your mother was to me, how could I not? I miss her, you know? Your mother, I mean. She would have been so proud of you— they both would. She was an exceptional Captain of my guard. She would have made a brilliant commander."

"She refused to leave your guard, didn't she?"

"She did, and as much as I would have liked her wisdom as a commander, I didn't push. It meant she got to spend more time with you." Vict's face softened at the memories running rampant through his mind. "She was a good demon. She would have been so incredibly proud of you both. She would have loved Aridien. They both would have."

Both demons turned contemplative for a few minutes. Vict looked towards Mac. "He's foolish, but I can't help but be thankful that he was there. I know you were fighting through, but another minute with her hands around his neck…"

"And I could have lost him." Bo heart skipped a beat at the mere idea.

"But, you didn't. Hold on to that. I know he's a trouble magnet, much like Caris is… but, try not to restrict him too much. He needs the freedom to make his own mistakes, to explore who he really is, who he wants to be. It will be hard…"

"But I need to let him live." Bo rubbed a weary hand over his face. "It will be hard."

"Isn't everything in life worth having like that though?" Vict lifted his brows.

Bo scowled. "It doesn't make it any easier."

"I never said it did."

"We'll need to talk to Aridien soon. See if she said anything." Vict's eyes once again rested on Ari.

Bo grinned at a curl he was trying to flatten. Every time he pushed it behind Ari's ear, it sprung back up. "I imagine she said quite a bit, most of it upsetting. I hate to put him through it, but we need to."

"I'm okay to talk. Sort of." Ari's voice was deep and husky, the effects on his throat from her attack obvious.

Bo lifted Ari's chin. "Tiko…" he scanned Ari's eyes, "I'm sorry I failed you, again."

Ari lifted a hand and slapped Bo on the chest, his eyes blazing with fire. His voice was husky and raw, but he managed to speak. "You didn't fail me. You, along with everyone else there, saved me. Again. And if you don't stop with this failed talk, I'll tweak your tail."

"Nice to have you back, Aridien." Vict couldn't stop his quiet chuckle at the look of astonishment on Bo's face. "Maybe you shouldn't talk too much, Little Demon. I know that the doctors gave you spray for your throat, but you do not need to overtax it."

Ari was about to respond when a cool breeze washed over him. He scanned the room, seeing a slight depression on the edge of the bed. "Lo'jat? How are you here?"

"Who are you talking to?" Bo could see no one else in the room.

"Lo'jat." Ari smiled widely.

"He wishes you to tip your head back, Little Demon." Drel'nic appeared in his ghostly form beside Lo'jat's depression on the bed.

Bo froze as the ghostly apparition appeared. He couldn't tear his gaze away. "Am I seeing things?"

"If you are, then I am as well." Vict reached out a tentative hand, as though to touch Drel'nic, before thinking better of it.

Ari watched as Drel'nic dropped to one knee in front of Vict before bowing his head forward, so low it almost touched the ground. "My King."

"Rise." Vict's voice shook slightly, stunned at what was transpiring. "You are the ones who helped young Aridien in the ruins?"

"We are." Drel'nic's deep voice rumbled.

"You told him to bring the Crown of Horns to me?" Vict asked.

"We did. It is time." Drel'nic held Vict's gaze.

"Time for what?" Vict cast a quick look to Bo.

Drel'nic refused to let Vict break his gaze. "A challenge is coming. They mean to take Kenistal, be warned. Death with come easily to those ill prepared. The Guardians have little wish to see the Purple guild fall. The consequences will be severe. You will need the crown to stave off the challenge. Be wise, King Vict'arin. Trust only those you know you can. Believe in them to help see you through and you will be victorious."

Satisfied Vict had heeded his words, Drel'nic turned to Bo. "Bo'saverin, your mate is blessed. Trust in him, have faith in his abilities. Even when every instinct cries out to keep him with you, you *must* let him go. He has his own path to follow and follow it he will. Events are unfolding as they should. Do not fear, you will not lose what is most precious, but *only* if you have faith. Do you understand, young demon?"

Bo bowed as best he could with Ari still in his arms. "I do. I do not like the thought of it, but I do understand and will heed your words."

Ari's throat was tipped backwards as gentle hands moved with precision over his skin. With each icy touch, the rawness in his throat diminished and the pain ebbed. He let out a sigh of relief, laughing as Lo'jat tickled underneath his chin. A ghostly chuckle echoed his own.

Bo gazed in wonder at Ari's throat. Only a tinge of redness remained. He looked to where he imagined the second guardian stood. "Thank you. Those words cannot fully convey the gratitude I feel, but I feel it none-the-less. I felt useless, being unable to help him."

"Such is the way. It is done. Our Little Demon is good now, Commander." Lo'jat's voice was like a whisper on the wind, soft and delicate. He moved over to Mac. Unable to fully heal him— he could bend the rules, not break them— he never-the-less healed as much as he was allowed to. It would mean Mac would properly walk again, and without a limp.

"Ah, Aridien, you got yourself into bother again. You are most definitely a troublemaker, are you not?" Drel'nic stared him down.

"I don't mean to be." Ari pouted.

"That does not make it less so, though." Drel'nic chuckled. "I am sorry your mother is as she is. If I could take the pain from you, I would. But know this, you are loved. You are cherished and you are respected. Make your home here, Aridien. Embrace your new life and any gifts that come along."

"Gifts?" Ari questioned.

"When the time is right, you will know. It is not my place to say, I fear I have already said too much. We have our own rules we are bound by and we already skirt the edges." Drel'nic leaned down and whispered in Ari's ear, and not even Bo, as close as he was, could hear. "When the time comes, do not fight being taken. It will play out as it must. We will be with you, watching over you. It is time for the enemy to reveal themselves in this manner. It is only then that Vict'arin can work on ridding the rot once and for all."

Ari's heart rate doubled. He was going to be kidnapped again. That was how he understood Drel'nic's words. How could he let himself be taken, he had no idea. But, if it was what needed to happen… He trusted Drel'nic and Lo'jat before and he needed to trust them again now. He gulped. "Okay."

Drel'nic ruffled his hair and stood. "We must take our leave. It is taxing being away from the ruins for too long. May wisdom guide you all."

With a quick pat on the cheek from Lo'jat, both Guardians vanished.

Vict slumped back in his chair. "I believed you, okay, not at first, but after your full story, I believed you… I just… seeing them…"

Ari grinned. "I understand."

Vict looked around the room, seeing the guards come to life as if they had been in a daze. "Osk'it, could you find my son for me please?"

The warrior bowed and immediately left the room.

"It looks like we have a lot to discuss." Vict studied Ari's throat. "It's good to see you looking better."

"Thank you. It means I can do what I need to do." Ari looked up at Bo as he was squeezed gently.

"You have nothing you need to do." Bo shook his head.

"Agota…" Ari closed his eyes briefly, gathering the strength. "When she attacked… she told me that I will be leaving on her cruiser, that I will be marrying Renauld. I will never do that, but that isn't what concerns me. Her next words do. She told me she has more friends than I could ever possibly realize. That I am nothing more than a pawn, a piece in a large assembly. She spoke about a bargain being fulfilled. I can't help but think she meant she has friends here. If you add that to what we already know…"

"We definitely have spies or traitors in our midst," Bo surmised.

"There is little doubt now." Vict fought to stop his tail twitching, one of the easiest ways to see just how angry or stressed a demon was.

"It means—" Ari looked back and forth between the two demons, not wanting to be the one to say it— "It means they are demons. Traitors, rather than spies. Spies would find it too hard on Kenistal. Agota has a lot of contacts, but none that could be easily concealed amongst demons. It's both an advantage for Kenistal and a disadvantage. Because it means if her contacts are here…" He let his words trail off.

"They are almost certainly demons. Three guesses as to which guild." Vict shook his head. "The Red guild is pushing more and more. This is what Drel'nic was talking about, isn't it?"

"I fear it is." Bo cocked his head. "Tiko, what were you talking about? You said you can do what you need to now."

Ari kept one part of what he would need to do quiet, as Drel'nic had requested. "The tech center. I need to repair what I did, but also look it over. I have a feeling you have breaches there. It was too easy to do what I did."

Bo went to disagree, but stopped. Drel'nic had only just said to let him go, to trust him when his instincts wanted Ari by his side at all times. He forced the fear over Ari's safety to the depths of his mind. "Okay. But… can I ask you take tonight to recover from today. I'm not stopping you, but think the night of rest will help."

Ari nodded, happy Bo wasn't going to argue.

Just then, Dasa and Caris walked in. Both smiled as the saw Ari awake and in Bo's arms. Caris jogged over to the bed, looking Ari over, checking he really was alright. "Uh, your throat, it almost looks like nothing happened, how is that possible? Aducians don't heal that fast, do they?"

Vict gestured to the guards who pulled over some new seats. "Stay outside for a bit, please." They nodded and left. "Someone wake up Mac. I have no idea how he slept through that."

"I didn't." Mac's sheepish voice made Ari jump. "There was no way I could have missed either the chill or the visit. I just thought I should stay quiet and keep it to myself. I figured if you wanted me to know you would say something."

"Thank you for your discretion, Mac'likrit." Vict dipped his head. "You really are an exceptional warrior and friend to my two new sons. Caris made the right choice when he took you with him that day at the arena."

"I will be forever grateful it was me he spoke to. My life has changed for the better since that day." Mac smiled over at his friends.

"Even though you have been injured because of these two?" Dasa asked.

"Yes, because I would do it all again in a tail twitch. I consider them my friends." Mac winked at Ari.

"What, not us?" Dasa frowned at Mac.

Mac gulped. "Uh, well, that is... you're my prince, he's my commander..."

"True, but when it's just us, use our names rather than titles. I like to think we're friends too now." Bo smiled.

Mac, slightly speechless, just nodded.

"So you summoned me, father, what's happened?" Dasa sprawled in the chair, smirking at Caris' 'eep' as he pulled him into his lap rather than let him take his own chair.

"What, I can't just want to see you, son? Check you're alright after the fight?" Vict kicked Dasa's foot a little.

Dasa sighed. "Oh, you're on fine form today. Yes, you can, but that's not what this is, is it? You knew we were dealing with questioning the Trevons, who unsurprisingly have little to say. I don't want to use more drastic methods and start an intergalactic incident, so we may never know what their motives in all this were."

Vict let out a weary moan. "Basically what I expected. It was worth a shot anyway. The reason Ari's throat looks so much better is not because he's healed quickly, it's because he had help, from an unexpected source."

"Who?" Dasa narrowed his eyes.

"Drel'nic and Lo'jat." Vict watched his son's reaction.

"The... Guardians? Are you serious? Did you see them?" Dasa looked from his father to Mac to Bo.

"We all did. Let me fill you in…"

CHAPTER TWENTY SEVEN

"**I** feel like I've been in this position before." Ari looked up at Bo's smiling face.

"You have." Bo chuckled. "You just probably don't remember it."

"The pie." Ari groaned.

"Yes, the pie, when you couldn't keep your hands off my horns." Bo groaned at the memory.

"What like this?" Ari reached up and stroked both of Bo's horns.

Bo stopped halfway up the stairs and shifted Ari so he was pinned against the wall, chuckling when Ari immediately wrapped his legs around his waist. He lifted Ari's chin and claimed his mouth, the kiss turning carnal in seconds. Using his greater weight, he thrust his rapidly rising cock against Ari, groaning as it slid along the smooth, glossy finish of the tep'rink Ari wore. He loved the fact Ari had taken to the traditional demonic clothes, but damn if they didn't tease him constantly.

Ari surrendered to the kiss. This was what he'd wanted ever since he'd woken up in the med bed in Bo's arms. He wanted it all and he wanted it right then. He thrust back into Bo, loving every minute of it.

"Ari, if you don't stop…" Bo leaned his head against the wall beside Ari's head.

"I don't want you to stop."

Bo's head jerked up and he searched Ari's eyes. "What do you mean?"

Ari rolled his eyes. "And here I thought you were smart." He squeaked when Bo tapped him on the ass gently. "I mean… I want you to take me."

"But what about…" Bo let his eyes drift to Ari's stomach.

"We don't even know if we're compatible in that way. I know I can get pregnant, but we have no idea if I can get pregnant by you."

"It's still a risk. I can always contact Corin on Landran. He may know of a way to prevent it."

Ari blushed at the thought of people knowing about his sex life. "Tomorrow. But I still want tonight."

"But if we… tonight, you still might get…" Bo gulped as a riot of thoughts and feelings rolled through him. A sudden burning desire to see Ari pregnant with his demonling, a desire to wait until they were settled, a hunger to simply be buried deep in his mate. They all tangled up into a confusing mess.

"I might, but right now, I don't care. I want you. Now." Ari was desperately thrusting his hips against Bo, the rub of material against his cock driving him crazy.

Bo's control broke seeing the passion consuming Ari. "Damn it." He tightened his grip on his mate and ran up the rest of the stairs, smiling as Ari laughed. Bo shot a look at the guards on duty in the corridor as he raced past. They would keep quiet, but it didn't hurt to remind them. He kicked the suite door closed behind him, not stopping until he was in his bedroom, and dropped Ari onto the bed, stripping as he watched Ari bounce about for a moment.

Ari slipped his hands into the waistband of his tep'rink, stopping as Bo pushed his pants down. The vision of Bo completely naked was stunning. The expanse of muscles, the way they moved, all he could do was watch and let his hand drift towards his cock as it begged for attention.

"What are you doing there, Tiko?" Bo kicked away his pants as he stalked towards the bed.

"I need…" Ari thrust his hips, his cock sliding easily through his hands, his precum easing the way.

"Want me to take over?" Bo straddled Ari's legs and slowly moved up the bed, trailing a hand along the inside of Ari's leg.

"Yes." Ari begged. "I don't know what to do, other than what we've already done." Ari hid his face from Bo's penetrating gaze.

"Ah, Tiko, that is not a bad thing. It merely means I have the fun in showing you the ways of it."

"I don't disappoint you in my lack of knowing what to do?"

"If anything, it fires my blood to know you have no experience. I'm honored to share your firsts. Just remember, if you want to stop at any time…"

Ari grabbed one of Bo's horns and pulled him down, taking his lips in a kiss. When he pulled back, he growled. "Don't you dare stop."

Bo winked. "Yes, Sir." He grabbed Ari around the back of the neck and pulled him upwards, demanding his surrender. Ari gave it willingly. As Bo kissed him, he eased his hand downwards, teasing Ari's nipples, swallowing his cries. Every move Ari made, every sound, stirred him like nothing before. He wasn't some demon intent on furthering their position, intent on trying to entice Bo into something he didn't want. This was Ari, part feisty, part shy and downright horny. Bo loved every part of it.

Ari surrendered to the sensations. He wanted to please Bo, tease him, but the sensations were so overwhelming he couldn't focus. When Bo eased his grip, lowering him back to the bed, he went willingly, blushing as his legs seemed to spread wide of their own volition.

Bo's hooded gaze travelled the length of Ari's body, taking in the delicate green flush, the perky nipples and hard, weeping length. As Bo moved to take Ari in his mouth, he was surprised when he shook his head.

"Please. If you do that, I won't last. I don't want to… before you… before we…" Ari turned his face into the covers beside him.

Bo let him hide for a moment, then he grabbed the oil beside his bed and quickly slicked his fingers. He took the time to gently tease Ari, slowly preparing him, no matter how much Ari begged otherwise.

"Bo! I'm going crazy, I won't survive."

"You will survive."

"No! I'm going to break apart, it's too intense."

Bo slipped a finger inside, brushing past that spot in Ari that made him buck wildly. As he slid his finger in higher, he jerked in surprise to find another bundle of nerves. This was something demons didn't have. He tentatively brushed over it and watched Ari's eyes roll to the back of his head. With a wicked grin, he started rubbing it gently, loving the way Ari was coming undone beneath him. Adding in a second finger, he increased the pressure against that extra spot. All of a sudden, Ari screamed, his body locked down and his hips bucked wildly. All signs pointed to Ari having an intense orgasm, yet no cum blasted from his cock, which remained hard throughout.

"Ari?" he whispered, stunned, yet not wanting to break the mood.

"What was that?" Ari struggled to breathe properly.

"You tell me."

"I came." Ari wrinkled his nose. "That was intense and…"

"Ari, you didn't come, you're still hard." Bo looked pointedly at Ari's hard and still leaking length.

"But, I just…"

Bo eyes went carnal and his fingers started to brush that spot again, wanting to see if he could repeat it.

Ari was lost. He could do nothing but succumb to the sensations Bo pulled from him. The same incessant heat radiated out from where Bo's fingers were, and when Bo pressed forward, the pleasure spiked, stealing his breath. When Bo slid in a third finger, the reaction was instant. He screamed, the pressure against that spot too much. His body arched hard and high, freezing in that position as every cell in his body seemed to stop for a brief moment in time. Then, just as suddenly, everything exploded. He couldn't have said where he was or even who he was, all he knew was the blinding pleasure streaking through his body in wave after wave. How long it lasted he could not say— it simply did.

Bo watched Ari writhe on his fingers. His orgasms were seemingly endless, yet his cock stayed hard throughout. Ari's internal muscles were rippling against his fingers and the second bundle of nerves seemed to swell and press harder against the intrusion. Was this some kind of special Aducian anatomy? He longed to experience Ari orgasming around his cock. Although, judging by the vise grip on his fingers, he would lose it as soon as Ari did.

Bo slowly eased back the pressure on Ari's nerves, gentling him with a delicate hand over his chest until Ari finally opened heavy-lidded eyes.

"Welcome back." Bo grinned at the relaxed look on Ari's features.

"I…" Ari's voice was hoarse, from crying out Bo's name.

"Good?" Bo teased, laughing when all Ari did was nod. "You're ready for me. We can stop now if you want."

"Don't you dare." Ari attempted to hit Bo, but his arm flopped by his side. "I think you might need to do all the work. I'm not sure I can feel my arms or legs."

"Happy to do that." Bo winked, positioning himself at Ari's entrance. "If this hurts, tell me."

"Uhhuh, just get to it." Ari blushed, but tipped his hips upward.

Bo took that for the invitation it was and slid slowly inside. He heard Ari's breath hitch briefly as he passed the first bundle of nerves, but on the second, there was an all over quiver, causing Ari to lock down around his cock. He fought the urge to come, and slowly pushed his way forward until at last he bottomed out. Holding Ari's gaze, he waited until he could move.

"What are you waiting for?" Ari whispered.

"To make sure you're not hurting."

"Move then!" Ari demanded, trying to thrust his own hips and force Bo into action. The pain had been brief, and nothing compared to the pleasure of having Bo inside him. It felt right, like this was what was meant to be. His biology accepting its purpose.

"Feisty tonight, Tiko. If you can still talk, maybe I'm not doing this right. How about…" Bo pulled back and thrust forward. "This."

Ari clung onto Bo, words escaping him. He let Bo own him, his body. He gave up every shred of control happily, confident in the knowledge Bo would make it good for them both.

Bo forced his eyes to stay open, to watch every reaction Ari had. He refused to hurt his mate for even a second. He lost all track of time; only the movement of their bodies told him time still marched forward. He wrapped his tail around Ari's cock, pulling it tight, squeezing him with each glide. Ari, almost incoherent with pleasure, grabbed his horns, making a fist around them and stroking at the same pace he moved. Their bodies, now slick with sweat, glided against each other. "Ah, Mek Tiko, I love you so." Bo picked up the pace, his need for release driving him ever faster.

"I love you too." Ari forced his lips to work.

"I need to come, Tiko, I can't stop it." Bo was holding back as much as possible, his thrusts picking up speed with each pass.

"Then don't!" Ari cried. Both his cock and the bundle of nerves inside him felt like they were on fire.

Bo shifted slightly, altering the position, and slammed forward, hitting both spots in Ari on the same stroke. It was all it took. His movements stopped instantly as Ari came hard. Cum shot between their bodies, the sights and smell of Ari's release, coupled with his grip on Bo's cock, pushed Bo over the edge. His body froze as jet after jet of cum spilled deep inside Ari's body. His orgasm seemed to trigger one last, smaller orgasm in Ari and he shook through the force of holding his position, refusing to relax before Ari finished.

Ari's hands dropped from Bo's horns, all ability to move gone. He hissed slightly as Bo slowly pulled out, not even able to move as Bo tenderly kissed him as his heart rate slowed. When Bo got up, he didn't even have the strength to open his eyes. Unable to do anything else, he let sleep claim him.

Washcloth in hand, Bo cleaned Ari and dropped the cloth at the side of the bed. Climbing under the covers, he pulled an exhausted Ari into his arms. "I love you, Tiko. I'll keep you safe and never let you go, I promise." Seconds later, his eyes slid shut and he followed Ari into a deep sleep.

CHAPTER TWENTY EIGHT

Ari stretched, wincing slightly, but smiling at the reminder of his night before with Bo. He remembered little after Bo had taken him so thoroughly; he must have passed out. He giggled softly.

"And what is so amusing so early in the day?" Bo's smiling face appeared above him.

"I passed out last night, didn't I?"

"You did. Then again, after the amount and way you came, I'm not surprised." Bo traced over Ari's naked chest slowly. "I'm actually a little jealous."

Ari blinked. "You are?"

"Mmm, you looked like you had a lot of fun." Bo bent and captured one of Ari's nipples in his mouth.

"Again?" Ari stroked Bo's horns, loving the way he shivered in his arms.

"As much as I would like to, you'll be sore. Besides, I thought you wanted to look at the tech center today?"

Ari pouted. "I do, but I want to stay with you."

"I would love nothing more than spending the day relaxing in bed with you. We'll just have to wait until tonight. I guess the quicker we get everything done, the better." Bo placed one last delicate kiss on Ari's nipple and pulled up, pulling back the covers as he did so. "Come on, lazy, up we get."

Ari continued to pout, even as he got out of bed and staggered to the washroom.

"Do you know you look sexy when you stomp?" Bo called after Ari, chuckling when the door slammed.

Bo whistled as he got ready, laying out some clothes for Ari as he went. He was just about to join Ari in the bathing pool when the door opened again to Ari. He was as white as a sheet. Bo ran to him, scooping him up in his arms. "Tiko? What's the matter?"

Ari pushed his curls back from where they lay against his forehead. All around the hairline, markings had appeared. They were a mix of blue and green, Bo's and his colors. It was an intricate design of looping scrolls entwined together with orbs dotted about the design.

Bo traced the markings, stunned. They were beautiful, there was no doubt, but *what* they were was another thing entirely. "What are they?"

Ari jerked back. "What do you mean, what are they? You're the one who's meant to know!"

"How the frek should I know? They're on you." Bo frowned as he studied them. "You honestly don't know what they are?"

"No, I don't. I thought they were to do with mating you?"

Bo shook his head slowly. "Unless it's just one of those combined genetics things. It's the only explanation I have if you don't know what they are."

Ari's face scrunched up as he thought. "I can't see how it would be anything else considering what we did last night." And there went his blush again.

"Come on, let's get some breakfast and then I'll escort you to the tech center." When Ari went to protest, Bo stopped him. "I won't hover, but I am going to walk you over there. Besides, my office is just down from there, or had you forgotten that when you were sneaking about and hiding out in Vict's reading room? While you're busy in the tech center, I'm going to spend my time seeing if I can't find out what those markings mean. I'll try to get a message to Corin on Landran, but we can never be sure if messages are going to make it through their nebula. So as a back-up, I'll be scouring what medical texts I can find."

"Thank you. I don't want to be worried about them, but…" Ari's voice trailed off.

"Let's just see what I find out. We can worry when we have cause too." What Bo didn't tell Ari was that he would worry until they got an answer anyway.

Suddenly, Ari tried to bite back his laugh, but failed completely. "I was just thinking… at least my escapades give me a reason to look through your tech systems."

They both sobered at the implication.

"Part of me hopes you don't find anything, yet… there is nothing I want more than to find the traitor, or traitors— who knows how many there are. There must be at least one of them who is ranked fairly high."

"Kinesh?" Ari asked. "I mean, he *is* the Red Guild Master."

"It could be, but it still doesn't explain the tech. If it's been tampered with, that is."

"Only one way to find out." Ari gestured to the door and they walked out hand in hand, much to the amusement of the guards on duty.

Somehow, they managed to avoid everyone at breakfast. Good as his word, Bo walked Ari to the tech center, leaving him with a scorching kiss before retreating to his own office to research.

Ari could tell Deek was desperate to ask about his new markings, but they weren't alone so it would need to wait.

Ari took a deep breath and walked in, ignoring the scowls from the techs around him. Most of the demons were the Lime Green of the tech guild, but dotted about were the odd Cobalts and occasionally a Grey tinker. He looked for the highest ranking demon, only he had no idea who that was. Deek came to his rescue.

"Vac'lin!" Deek's voice boomed around the room. "Get your tail over here."

A tall, lanky Lime Green demon strode over, muttering to himself. "Damn it, Deek, I nearly soldered my hand to the control board there. What the frek do you want. You destroy another piece of tech? I should ban you from using anything."

"Vac, meet Aridien, Ari meet Vac'lin, head of tech for the Cobalts." Deek waved back and forth between them.

Vac'lin studied Ari, looking down his snub nose. "You're the little bit that the Commander is fooling around with. The one who hijacked our systems."

Ari, fed up with being treated like dirt, stared the demon down. "And you're an arrogant ass. But I'm not holding it against you."

There was a beat of silence before Vac'lin burst out laughing. "Oh, feisty, I like that. Not what I heard about you, but hey, not all rumors are right. So, you're here to fix what you… let's be polite and say changed then?"

Deek and Ari shared a look. "I am."

"If I leave you in peace, will you behave?" Vac'lin challenged.

"I promise," Ari vowed.

"Very well. Call if you need help. Oh, and here, you might as well have this." Vac'lin thrust a portable comm unit at him.

"Thank you." Ari smiled widely. He quickly took up position at a terminal away from the other techs. He couldn't be bothered to get into arguments with them, nor did he have the desire to prove how good he was. It took him no longer than a few minutes to fix the voice commands on the door and neutralize the device stored in his bag that had changed the emergency breakthrough to drum beats.

Vaguely aware Deek had left him to work in peace, he studied the mainframe. Everything seemed to be working as it should, but Ari of all people knew appearances could be deceptive. He peeled back the layers of code one at a time until he got to the base programming. His mind whirled as he noticed an odd recurring line of code that appeared in almost every system. Tracing it through the computer pathways, he expected to end up in Bo or Dasa's comp terminals. It made sense that there would be a way for them to monitor everything. Once he'd isolated the terminal all the information was being routed to, he backed slowly out of the system. Some inner instinct urged him caution. Making sure he left no trace, he blew out a relieved breath and looked around, seeing no one spared him more than the odd cursory glance.

He shifted to a different system. This one logged who each terminal belonged to. The one where everything was being routed to didn't belong to Dasa or Bo, or even Vict; it instead belonged to Kinesh, Master of the Red guild. Fighting his instinctive reaction, he pulled out quickly and brought up the implant codes.

Sensing a presence behind him, he turned around to be greeted to a stunning Lime demon. "Hello." He kept his expression deliberately neutral.

"What are you doing?" The demon growled. "Who gave you access to the implant codes?"

"Commander Bo'saverin gave me the right to access everything I need."

"You shouldn't be in there. Frek, you shouldn't even be on the planet, let alone in this room. No-horn's like you don't belong on Kenistal."

"Is that right?" Ari really didn't need to be dealing with this at the moment. He desperately needed to talk to Bo. "If you don't mind, I have a call to make."

The demon leaned back against the terminal behind him. "Go ahead, I'm not stopping you."

Ari shrugged. "Fine." He activated his link. Now how was he going to talk to Bo with not only someone listening up close, but every comm link being monitored? Every vid throughout the palace was accessible from Kinesh's console.

"Bo'saverin."

"Hello, Hevalis, you sexy demon you."

"Ari?"

Ari could hear the confusion in Bo's voice. *Come on, Bo, pick up on what I'm doing.* "I'm missing you." Ari held the demon's gaze as he spoke to Bo. "Want to come and have some kinky fun with me? We could meet in our secret room where you caught me the other day. I loved the trouble I was in that day. I've been so bad. I'm wearing another pair of those sexy undies you like."

Ari heard startled coughs and sniggers as he realized more than one demon was listening in on his call. As much as he was embarrassed using language like that, he needed to do it. Now it was up to Bo to figure it out.

"Ari, I'm on my way."

Ari could hear the urgency in Bo's voice. Good, he understood.

"Perfect." Ari purred, "I'll see you there." He cut the link and stood. "Excuse me." He smiled sweetly to the Lime demon stood in his way. "I have places to be."

"We heard." The demon sneered. "You fix your prank?"

"I did." Ari stared at him. "Now, anything else? I need to go."

The demon spat at him. "Disgusting no-horn slut. Get out of here and don't come back. You aren't welcome."

Ari steeled his heart against the insult and sauntered out of the room casually. He waved Deek off. As much as he could do with both the company and the protection, it would destroy the illusion he'd created if he took Deek with him.

Deek narrowed his eyes before frowning.

Ari could tell Deek knew something was up. He tried to send him a look to let him know to stay and watch.

Eventually, Deek nodded. "I'll wait for you here. Don't be too long. Neither of us want me to have to come looking for you."

Ari chuckled good-naturedly as he walked away. As soon as he was around the corner, he broke into a sprint, aiming for Vict's private reading room. Bursting in, he was only partly relieved it was empty. It might have been easier if Vict himself was there. He paced as he waited, gaze trained on the door.

Bo sprinted along the corridor, cursing the fact he hadn't been in his office. He'd been called to the training complex to referee a dispute between two Cobalt officers. Damn gossip had to be spreading from the techs already. He could see the knowing smirks of the demons he raced past. He didn't care. Something was definitely wrong. Ari would never say those things, never behave like that. It simply wasn't in his nature. It meant he'd found something and couldn't say what. There was a traitor and judging by Ari's behavior, at least one of them was a tech.

"Move or face extra duties!" He bellowed down the corridor to a group of demons blocking the way.

They took one look at his face and shrank back.

His desperate sprint across the palace grounds did not go unnoticed, but few dared even contemplate trying to find out what was wrong. They simply left him to it.

As he reached the Cobalt wing, he growled at each locked door, slamming his hand onto the input screen. The few Cobalts around soon realized something had upset him and quickly scanned their own hands, holding the doors open for him. He did little more than nod as he raced past.

Soon enough, he passed the tech center, alarmed to see Deek outside with a worried expression. He held his gaze for a split second and raced on, ignoring the ribald comments coming from the techs gathered behind Deek.

He careened into the door of Vict's reading room and slammed it shut, relieved to see Ari there and looking unharmed. He strode over and pulled Ari up and into his arms, guiding Ari's legs to wrap around his waist. He kissed Ari almost savagely, all his pent up fear and apprehension playing out in the kiss.

As soon as Ari could ease his lips from Bo's, he moved his mouth to Bo's ear. "Does this room have any type of monitoring device? Comms, visual, anything?"

Bo startled slightly. *Just what the frek is going on?* "No. Nothing. Officially, this room has no purpose. Only Vict's guards, Dasa and I know of it. What the frek is going on, Tiko?"

"I fixed everything in the tech center, but I also took a look around like we planned. Every single system there is being monitored."

"It's supposed to be. There are techs monitoring it. Each sector also has its own security station with monitors for that sector."

"I know that. But on top of that, every single system is being routed through to one terminal. That terminal has access to absolutely everything."

Bo narrowed his eyes. "Who's terminal?"

"Kinesh." Ari held Bo's gaze.

"You're sure?"

"Positive. And at least some of the techs know about it. There are markers there to say which ones, I just don't know who the markers belong to. I was being watched or I could have checked. I just couldn't risk going into that system."

"That's why you said what you did." Bo grinned. "I knew the second you called me Hevalis that there was something wrong. Besides, you just don't talk that way."

"I knew you would catch on." Ari's face fell at the memories of the comments.

"What?" Bo studied the crestfallen look on his mate's face. "Someone said something to you."

"It doesn't matter." Ari dipped his head, hiding his eyes.

Bo lifted his chin gently. "It does, Tiko, tell me."

Ari never could refuse Bo anything. "One of the demons called me a disgusting no-horn slut."

Bo's scales went instantly to full attack mode. "Who."

Ari shook his head.

"Who, Ari?"

Uh oh, Bo was calling him Ari. "Bo, please, if you say something, it will just make it worse. Besides, he could have been one of the ones working with the Reds, especially as we know there have to be techs working with them."

Bo fought for control. "I need to protect you."

Ari caressed Bo's face. "You do, but you can't fight everyone who says something bad about me or to me."

"Why not?" Bo scowled.

"You know you can't. Come on, let's focus on what to do now." Ari simply waited him out.

Bo calmed enough to think rationally, although if he ever found out which tech, there would be a de-horning going on. He grabbed Ari's hand and led him towards the drinks cabinet in the corner of the room. Opening up the chest from the middle, he smirked at Ari's stunned look.

Ari ran his hand over a console, a console with a lot of tech on it.

"You didn't honestly think we left Vict in here all alone without protection? There are panic alarms and countermeasures all over the room. And here." Bo flicked a switch. One of the wall panels glided up silently revealing a reinforced metal corridor.

Ari gaped in disbelief, walking forward when Bo beckoned him on. When he came to another door, he stopped and turned around, seeing Bo shutting the door at the end.

"You can't have both doors open at the same time."

"Smart." Ari bit his lip as Bo strode towards him.

Bo watched Ari, the flash of desire in his eyes, the way he nibbled on his lip, and he deliberately put an extra swagger in his step.

As soon as Bo was in range, Ari jumped, sure in the knowledge Bo would catch him.

Bo would have chuckled at Ari's jump, but his hands were full of a wriggling mate, who was kissing him like his life depended on it. "Ari, we can't, not here."

"Are there cameras?"

"No."

"Then we can." Ari claimed Bo's lips again, reaching up and rubbing Bo's horns.

Bo growled into Ari's mouth, spinning them round and pinning Ari to the wall. He jostled Ari until he could free one hand and plunged it into his tep'rink, encountering the softest shorts Ari had worn yet. He pushed then down, making a mental note to look at them later, and grasped Ari's cock, starting a long, slow glide along his length. The pre-cum lubricating his way nicely, he picked up the pace.

Neither of them heard the door closest to them open.

"When you two have quite finished converting my passageway into a second bedroom, you might want to come in and get a davroc." Vict's voice echoed all around them.

Bo groaned as the door slid shut again, smiling when Ari not only wilted in his hand but buried his face in Bo's shoulder.

"I'm so embarrassed," Ari whispered.

"Come on, let's get you straightened up and we'll brave him together."

"Will he be mad?"

"No, but be prepared for the teasing." Bo pushed back Ari's hair. "I love you, Tiko, never forget that. I don't care who knows it."

"I love you too, Bo, more than anything."

CHAPTER TWENTY NINE

Vict laughed as Ari hid behind Bo, peeking out, no doubt checking to see if he was mad. He wasn't. He'd heard them, and simply couldn't resist teasing them. "Come on, take a seat and tell me why you're hiding in my passageway, other than the obvious reason, that is."

Ari took a seat, keeping his head down, not wanting to look at Vict in case he was angry.

Vict was about to ask what was going on, when he looked at how Ari was hiding. "Little Demon, won't you look at me? I'm not mad, I promise. I couldn't resist teasing you, that's all."

Ari cautiously looked up at Vict. "I'm sorry, I didn't mean to—" He waved at the corridor— "You know."

Vict leaned forward, studying Ari intently. Getting up, he walked around his desk and squatted in front of Ari, reaching forward and brushing his hair away from his face. "I'm not imagining this, am I? Ari, you have… are they markings?" Vict looked between Bo and Ari.

"We aren't totally sure what they are. We, uh, wondered if they were part of the mating process." Bo managed to stop his cheeks heating, but only just. "I was going to do some research and call Corin on Landran first thing, but then I got distracted by issues at the training complex. Then Ari called."

"Yes, I can imagine that was distracting," Vict drawled.

Bo snorted. "It was, but not in the way you think. Is Dasa about? I think he needs to hear this as well."

"He should be. He was on his way over before I found you two… Let's simply say before I found you two." Vict put a finger to his implant. "Son, are you on your way?"

"I'm just coming into the royal wing now. Be there in a moment."

Vict cut the connection, getting up to pour Bo a davroc and Ari a berry juice. With a fresh davroc himself, he leaned back in his chair, propping his feet up on the stool in front of him and stretching back. "I take it you two want to make the mating official? Are you wanting a full ceremony?"

"I haven't spoken to Ari about it yet." Bo winked at Ari. "Once everything is settled, we'll talk about it then. I don't want him to feel like he needs to go through with it just to be able to stay here on Kenistal."

Vict nodded. "Not a bad reason, but don't leave it too long. I plan to see the two of you mated, not just pledged to each other. So while we wait—" Vict traced the markings around Ari's hairline. "They are impressive. Is this part of Aducian mating?"

Ari shook his head, loose curls ticking the back of Vict's hands. "Not that I know, although she kept me sheltered, so it's possible, but I have never seen them on another Aducian. Mind you, I never really saw a lot of them, Agota made sure of that."

Vict traced a delicate swirl. "The colors are both of yours. It would be logical to think it had something to do with your mating. I cannot see what else it is. They are beautiful though."

"You think so?" Ari shifted about self-consciously.

Vict patted Ari's cheek. "There is no part of you that isn't, Little Demon."

As Vict stood up, Dasa walked in grinning. Quickly followed by Caris, he smiled sheepishly when Vict caught him staring at Dasa's ass as it flexed while he walked.

Retaking his seat, Vict gestured to Ari. "Before we start talking over what I'm guessing is quite serious, you two better take a good look at Aridien."

Caris raised a brow, but moved in front of Ari and did a double take. "Uh, Ari, what happened?" He whacked Dasa in the stomach to grab his attention, pointing at Ari's hairline.

Ari looked at everyone. "We don't know."

Bo stepped in, sensing Ari's discomfort. "They were there when we woke up this morning. I'll be calling Corin later. If anyone knows, he will."

"Good idea." Caris smiled in thanks as Dasa handed him a sweet teo. "So it sounded like you have news, Vict."

"Not me." Vict gestured to Bo. "These two do."

Bo looked to Ari. "Why don't you explain. You know everything."

Ari grasped Bo's hand, needing his strength as he hastily filled everyone in.

Caris grabbed Ari's hand as they ran out the room. Both of them slumped against the wall outside of Vict's office. The two guards drew their weapons, about to run in when Caris held out a hand, stopping them. "There's nothing wrong. He's angry, that's all."

One of the guards eased the door open and peeked inside, quickly pulling back as a crushed goblet came flying through the slim gap in the doorway. He hastily shut the door with a wary look. "What the frek happened? I've not seen him that angry in a long time."

When Caris went to refuse to answer, the guard held up his hand. "Don't answer, it wasn't a real question. It's not my right to know, and frankly, I think we'll be happier not knowing." The other guard nodded his agreement.

Caris and Ari sniggered. "Wise choice." Caris moved to Vict's assistant's desk. "Any current problems with the Barin Alliance?"

Fred'ikel shook his head. "We've heard nothing since we sent the last communiqué."

Caris narrowed his eyes. "Nothing?"

"No, why?" Fred'ikel finished prepping some documents for Vict to sign.

"They are bureaucratic to the extreme. If they are still wanting Kenistal to join, which I'm sure they are, I'm surprised they haven't sent another Ambassador."

A slightly calmer voice sounded behind him. "Considering the first was murdered and the second resigned and is mated to a demon… then I can only imagine their reluctance to send any more here."

Caris turned to see a completely unruffled Vict. If he hadn't been in the room and seen Vict's anger for himself, there would have been no way he'd believed it had happened. Vict beckoned them both back into the room.

As they took their seats again, Ari looked around. The room looked like it had hastily been put back to rights, but there were still odd books scattered on the floor.

"I'm sorry if I scared you." Vict held his gaze.

"I'm fine." Ari smiled. "I was used to her shouting at me over the years. It doesn't scare me."

Relief swamped Vict; the last thing he wanted to do was scare the young man. "So you're sure about what you found?"

"Completely. All monitoring streams are being routed to Kinesh's terminal. From what I can tell, he's got access to every system there is. There is at least one tech demon helping him. I can see their signature, but to go looking for who it belonged to would have drawn too much attention."

"Smart way of avoiding anyone finding out what you were up to, by the way." Dasa grinned at Ari's rising blush. "Bo told us what was said to you. I'm sorry. You have to know there aren't many demons who believe as he did. But, should anyone treat you like that again, let us know. I'll be joining Bo in de-horning them."

"Is that actually a thing?" Ari asked

"De-horning?" Vict clarified. "It is. It's one of the most severe punishments we can give out without killing someone. It is only ever used when a demon has either brought shame to Kenistal, or in cases of treason. Which, in this demon's case, sounds very much like it could be both. I am sorry you had to hear what he said, to be subjected to his cruelty. Even if he is not part of this conspiracy, he will be reprimanded." Vict held up a hand to stall any comment from Ari. "I know you're going to say it isn't that important. But, it is. You see, you are a demon now, but if you weren't you would be Aducian. It is a poor king that lets a visitor to our world be treated with such disdain. He will be punished for bringing Kenistal into disrepute, and not just because you are the Commander's mate."

"Thank you, I was more angry than anything else. Besides, he shouldn't have been listening in on a private conversation." Ari crossed his arms. If he ever got a chance, that demon was going to get quite the verbal lashing from him. "I guess that's what all this boils down to in the end."

"It is." Vict tapped his tail against the edge of his desk. "If you had full access, could you get me the proof?"

"Yes." Ari's answer was swift and sure.

"Good. The question remains how we resolve this. It's obvious Kinesh and the Reds are making a play for the throne. I would imagine not only has Kinesh been monitoring our communications for a long time, but he's been manipulating some of the other guilds against us as well. That doesn't even begin to discuss what he must be doing on other planets. He, his guild, have always had a fair amount of freedom to conduct the minor trade deals. I have to wonder just how long he has been working against the crown."

"A long time it would seem." Dasa growled.

Caris squeezed Dasa's hand. "I'm going to reach out to some contacts, see what I can find out. These are people I trust implicitly. They will not betray my confidence in asking. They will do everything they can to help. My first port of call will be Havernia."

"Why do I recognize the name?" Vict's tail twitched lazily in its resting place.

"Hunter, one of the Avanti, is Havernian. I was a guardian for his siblings. You no doubt have heard me talk of them." Caris grinned at the mention of Hunter's kids. He missed them something fierce and they hadn't been gone that long. He hoped they were settling well on Landran. "They are honest, hardworking people, and they will not stand to hear of what is happening here. That is, if you allow me to brief one or two of them. What I cannot find out myself, they may have the contacts."

"Agreed. This rot is spreading too far." Vict frowned. "Why now? What has changed in the last galactic year or so to make Kinesh strive for the crown?"

Everyone lapsed into a contemplative silence.

Ari, used to having to sit on some of the trade deals discussed at dinners where he was on show, had a greater grasp of the intricacies of deals than most people, even Agota, realized. "Caris, you spoke about the Avanti and what happened to their ship— the Delphini, was it?"

"I did." Caris cocked his head to one side, wondering where Ari was going with this.

"I have to wonder… Agota has always wanted more. More power, more wealth, more prestige. Her trade deals are designed to maximize those. She was going to gift, trade, whatever me to Renauld, a founder within the Barin Alliance. I have no idea why, or just what trade she was aiming for. The Red guild here are striving for more trade. You have already spoken about the previous ambassador here. There were also rumors on Aducia that the Toclin are embroiled in a bloody feud between the two ruling continents. The rumors mention weapons on both sides that the Toclin are not known for. You've spoken about Landran having issues of its own. Landran, Toclin, Aducia, Kenistal, the ambassador and the Delphini, and you can add in the Barin Alliance to that list. There seem to be a lot of worlds who are going through… I don't know what you could call it, flux? I have to wonder how many more planets out there are undergoing change."

"Add in the Loperis. Yevtabrin, one of the biggest Alliance supporters, are undergoing protests from their citizens over food shortages." Caris shared a wide-eyed look with Ari. "There are several planets going through a period of immense change. You're suggesting they may be linked, aren't you?"

Ari frowned. "I don't know, but it's possible. The Toclin used to be one of the most peaceful planets around. For them to feud in this way, something big has to be going on."

Vict stood up, walking over to the window, watching the bustle of demons going about their business. "This keeps stemming back to the Alliance. We had no problems until the first Ambassador showed up, three years ago now. We sent him packing, but slowly more and more guilds agreed to listen to what they had to say. Then Tremont appeared. He seemed to find friends amongst the Reds. I now have to wonder just what he was promising them."

"So we now believe Kinesh is working with the Aducians? What, and the Alliance?" Dasa frowned.

"Or maybe just one sector of the Alliance." Bo drummed his fingers on the edge of his seat. "What if this has more to do with the state of the Alliance than any individual world? What if this is one group within the power dealers at Barin headquarters who wish to take control? What if this is nothing more than two opposing factions drawing in as many pawns as they can to fight their battles for them?"

Caris leaned over, grabbing the warmed pot of teo and pouring another cup for himself. "If that is the case, this is being kept quiet on Barin and throughout the Alliance. I never heard anything to suggest this was the case. Which could mean several things, but one of the most likely answers is that the game is being played very carefully."

"As selfish as it may be, right now I care little for what is happening within the Alliance. What I do care about is Kinesh." Vict crushed the goblet in his hand.

"I see the silversmiths will be happy." Caris tried to lighten the mood slightly, smiling when Vict looked over his shoulder and quirked a brow. "I annoyed Dasa so much in those early days he had a standing order for new goblets each week. Since I succumbed to his charms, he's stopped crushing them. I'm sure the silversmiths rued the day. But looking at the evidence around me, I see you have taken up his habit." Caris gestured pointedly to several crushed goblets around the room.

"Better a goblet than someone's head." Vict's haughty voice was tempered by the twitch to his lips.

"What do you want me to do about the tech center?" Ari looked to the three demons. "I can fix it, but the minute I go into those systems, alarms are going to ring. The head tech guy—" Ari scowled at the memory of being called a little bit— "Vac'lin, seems like a decent guy. Arrogant, but decent. Deek seemed to know him."

Vict gestured to Bo who clicked his implant, contacting Deek. "Deek'in, could you come to the King's office please."

"Yes, Commander, on my way." Bo smirked at the audible gulp from Deek. No one liked being summoned by their boss, but being summoned to the King's office? He could imagine the dread Deek was feeling.

A cautious knock on the door a few minutes later heralded Deek's arrival. He bowed long and deep to Vict before standing straight, gaze focused on the wall waiting for his Commander.

"Relax, Cobalt, you aren't in trouble." Bo beckoned Ari into his lap, smiling when Ari happily complied. "Take a seat, Cobalt."

Sitting, Deek looked warily around.

"Deek'in, our Little Demon here tells me you know Vac'lin from the tech center." Vict handed a fresh goblet to Dasa.

Dasa frowned, but got up and poured more davroc for his father.

"I do." Deek's gaze found Ari's, relaxing slightly at his reassuring smile.

Vict savored his drink for a moment. "How well do you know him?"

"He's mated to Gil'per, an Amber and my cousin. Gil'per is a professor in the astromechanics department, and a decent, hard-working demon." Deek considered whether he could risk asking what he wanted to. "Is he in trouble? I've never known him do anything wrong. Ari, the way he was with you, that's—"

Ari rested his hand on Deek's arm. "It's not about that, he was fine with me." Ari shook his head at Bo's questioning look.

Bo, Dasa and Vict seemed to have a silent conversation before Vict briefly dipped his head. Bo turned to Deek. "Cobalt, what we are about to discuss is both deadly serious and completely confidential. We're talking de-horning should this ever become public."

Deek's eyes widened momentarily. "I promise, I take my job, my role within our society, very seriously. I would never do anything to hurt Kenistal, the royal family, or my charges here."

Bo filled Deek in on some of what was happening. Not everything, but enough.

Another knock at the door and Fred'ikel poked his head around. "There's a comp call for Aridien."

"For me?" Ari asked, confused.

"It's Op'ik, the tinkerer."

Ari grinned and clambered off Bo's lap. "Back in two."

Out in Fred'ikel's office, Ari picked up the link. "Op'ik, how are you?"

"Good. Mostly anyway. I've ordered the parts I need to create those devices for you, but some of them are going to take a couple of months. Add in the build time and we could be looking at a year before I can get them all made. I'm sorry."

"No, that's fine. I realized it might take a while."

"I wondered as well if you might come and take a look at a project I'm working on. The coding and style reminds me of a comp cube, so I think your expertise will help a lot."

Ari's face lit up with excitement. The chance to work on more tech? No way was he going to pass that up. "I'd love to. I'll be there shortly."

"See you then and thanks, Ari."

"Anytime." Ari closed the link with a smile on his face. It was great to feel needed and welcome by at least some demons.

Returning to the king's office, he sat back down on Bo's lap as he curled his arms around him.

"What are you so happy about?" Bo nuzzled Ari's neck, breathing in his unique scent.

"That was Op'ik. He needs some help with a tech issue. I said I'd go."

Bo's arms stiffened and his tail instinctively wrapped around Ari keeping him close. "I don't want—" He was about to say he didn't want Ari to go, but then Drel'nic's words came back to him. How, no matter how much he wanted to keep Ari with him at all times, he must have faith in Ari and let him go. How he had his own path he must walk. Bo couldn't help but feel if he let Ari go now, something bad was going to happen. He couldn't risk losing Ari, yet didn't Drel'nic insist that he wouldn't lose him? That he simply needed to have faith?

Bo fought against the instinct to keep Ari at his side. "Alright, but you'll take Deek'in and Yavek with you." It wasn't a question.

"I will. I'll be in Op'ik's shop, nowhere else. I promise." Ari snuggled up tight to Bo. For some reason he was wary about leaving the comfort of his arms. Drel'nic's whispered words came back to him. *'When the time comes, do not fight being taken. It will play out as it must. We will be with you, watching over you. It is time for the enemy to reveal themselves in this manner. It is only then that Vict'arin can work on ridding the rot once and for all.'* Was this that time? Probably. Was he ready to be taken again? Not really. But, for the sake of Bo, Vict and Kenistal? He would do whatever was asked of him, no matter how much it had him quaking in his tep'rink.

Bo lifted Ari from his lap, gently setting him on the floor. Taking him by the hand, he led him to a small closet just off to the side of the room.

"A closet? Really, Bo?" Dasa drawled.

Bo gave him a rude gesture over the shoulder and shut the door. He pulled Ari into his arms and kissed him until Ari whimpered and sagged against him. Slowly, he eased back from the kiss, keeping Ari pinned to his chest. "Promise me, whatever happens, you will keep yourself safe. No matter what happens today, or any other day, make sure you come back to me."

"I promise you, Bo. You are everything I want in my life. You and Kenistal. I will never walk away from you. You're stuck with me."

"Good. Just the way I want it." Bo kept Ari in his arms for a few minutes, simply holding him tight, before logic returned and he let him go. He stole one last, lingering kiss before he released his hold on Ari and gently led him back into the room. Surprisingly, Dasa wasn't teasing him. Instead, his face bore sympathy. He had to wonder just how much of his emotions were written across his face for all to see.

He walked up to Deek'in, who'd been joined by Yavek. "Promise me you'll keep him safe."

"Commander, you know we will protect him with our lives if it comes to it," Yavek assured Bo.

"Just watch. Agota may be under guard in her cruiser, but something tells me we haven't heard the last from her. I don't see her stopping until she gets what she wants."

"She won't." Ari wrapped his arms around Bo's waist. Or rather he attempted to, but the demon was too damn big.

Bo grasped the back of Ari's neck, tilting his face upwards as he stole a kiss, uncaring who was watching. The dazed look from Ari afterwards filled him with a primal satisfaction. Smacking Ari's ass gently he pushed him towards the door.

"We shall see you soon, Little Demon. Stay safe." Vict repressed his chuckle as Ari nodded still in a slight daze. As soon as Ari was out of the room, Vict turned to everyone. "Now, let's start talking about how we can take that iglink down."

CHAPTER THIRTY

Ari waved to some of the little demonlings darting about playing some game that was obviously highly competitive judging by the argument over the score going on. Demons all around them stood watching with a fond exasperation while they talked, no doubt to the other parents.

A sudden gust of wind made the disc they were playing with spin right past Ari and into an alleyway.

"Tobrix!" a chorus of angry voices shouted.

Ari loved seeing this aspect of life on Kenistal, the little demonlings free to be themselves. With the way their guild system worked, there was little pressure on them at such a young age to spend hours training for some adult role. Instead, they were free to be children, something few on Aducia experienced. Jogging into the alleyway to retrieve the disc for them, he was still mulling over the differences between the two planets as he bent to collect the disc, surprised to find it ice cold to the touch. The shiver from the disc turned into dread as something was pressed into his lower back, the sharp point breaking the skin, even though his clothes.

"Straighten up slowly, or feel my blade run you through," the heavily masked voice demanded.

Fear raced through his system, his heart picked up speed, the beats sending the blood pumping around his body so fast he could hear it in his ears. He carefully stood.

"Turn around. Slowly."

He did as he was told, coming face to mask with a demon. A Red, by the color on the demon's neck.

"You have two options. Come quietly and no one will be hurt. Or… make life difficult for us and the demonlings out there will be the ones to suffer."

"I'll come quietly." Again, Drel'nic's words came to him. *'When the time comes, do not fight being taken. It will play out as it must. We will be with you, watching over you.* Ari steeled his resolve. This is what was meant to happen. In truth, he'd known he wouldn't escape another confrontation with Agota. It wasn't her style to let things go so easily. He was more convinced than ever that the Red guild had turned full traitors. Maybe not all of them, but certainly a large portion. A gentle weight settled on his shoulder and with a casual, careful glance, he confirmed what he'd suspected. A vague shimmer, an impression of something was there. Drel'nic or Lo'jat. It had to be. They'd promised they would be here with him and they were. He straightened up, found some inner strength he wasn't sure he possessed and nodded to the demon in front of him. "I'm ready, I'll go with you, but don't hurt the demonlings."

The demon moved to stand behind him. That's when he saw four other demons emerge from the shadows. A blade was pressed against his throat. "Walk forward."

Ari carefully took his first step, keeping half an eye on where he was going. The last thing he wanted to do was trip and impale himself on that blade. As he reached the end of the alleyway, he saw Deek start to enter, no doubt wondering what was taking him so long.

Deek went to draw his blade, alerting Yavek, who spun around.

"I wouldn't." The demon beside them growled. "You wouldn't want his hand to slip now, would you?"

Deek and Yavek let their hands drop.

"Don't even think about going for your implants either. We'll be leaving here with this no-horn. If we don't, you know what will happen." The leader pointed towards the demonlings who were still arguing.

To Ari's relief, no one had noticed the confrontation. *Yet.* He didn't want to think about what would happen if someone did and went for their implant.

"Are you okay?" Deek asked him quietly.

"I am. Don't fight this. It was always going to happen. She won't let me go without a fight. I won't see them hurt." He looked pointedly at the demonlings.

"Enough talking." The demon holding him growled in his ear.

Ari shut up. The blade tip had already pierced his skin slightly. A cool trickle of blood was oozing down his neck.

The lead demon carefully walked past Deek and Yav, keeping his body between them and Ari. Both Cobalts vibrated with rage. A sudden scream pierced the air. Someone had finally noticed.

"Keep calm and stay quiet," Deek shouted to the gathered demons. "Let them go. Do not do anything. Let them take him and this will be over shortly." Deek grimaced as more masked Red demons swarmed the area. Ari would likely walk away from this safely; after all, his mother wanted him alive. Whether he and Yav would be so lucky was another matter entirely.

A sense of calm invaded Ari as he worried about what would happen to his two Cobalt friends. A gentle ice cold breeze passed over his ear. "They will live. I promise you." Drel'nic's words reassured him, but didn't stop the worry completely. With a last lingering look at Deek and Yav, he made himself watch where he was going. *Stay strong, Ari, think of Bo, of the strength he gives you. Get through this and you'll see him again. Have faith.* He kept up the stay strong mantra as he trekked through the back alleys, the Reds keeping them out of sight. The sounds of fighting in the distance could still be heard. He could only hope someone had been able to call for back-up and all the demonlings were safe.

"You couldn't have just let them go?" His bravado was false, but he needed to get into the mindset before doing battle with Agota.

"You think we want the Commander and half the damn Cobalts chasing after us? You'll get what's coming to you, and soon enough,

Kenistal will belong to the Reds." The demon had eased his knife away from Ari's throat, but it once again rested at the base of his back. The implication was clear. One false move and they'd cut him, Agota or not.

"You really believe Vict will let you take Kenistal? You're a fool if you believe that."

"He'll have no choice if he wants to avoid the mass slaughter of demons. Within two days the most powerful guild on Kenistal will be the Reds. We will hold the throne. You can count on that."

The demon beside Ari sneered. "Besides, Agota has assured us of victory. She will do what needs to be done to see us take the throne."

Ari couldn't help it. He laughed. A deep bellied laugh. "You're fools if you truly believe Agota will do anything for you. She doesn't care what happens to you or to Kenistal. She's used you to get to me. Once you've served her purpose, she'll walk away without a second glance or a thought in her mind. The only reason she would continue to offer any support is if there is something in it for her."

A wary look passed between two of the demons. "What, you don't believe me? I'm her son. If she can do this to me, what makes you think for even a second that she would hesitate in betraying you? The only person Agota cares about is Agota. She's using you. The sooner you see that the better."

"Shut up!"

Ari couldn't have said which demon roared. It didn't matter; seconds later, he cried out as something slammed into the back of his head. As his vision swirled and his grip on consciousness faded, he heard an angry hiss.

"What did you do that for, you krexjin. Now one of us is going to have to carry him."

It was the last thing he heard for a while.

"Bo'saverin." Bo groaned as his implant chimed. Could he get one damn minute's peace to drink his davroc? He'd only just left Vict and wanted to catch up on warrior rotations. He wanted to make sure there were enough guards throughout the city. Things were definitely coming to a head.

"Commander, this is Op'ik. I was wondering when Ari might arrive."

Bo froze. His scales rapidly flicked between maximum hardness and his skin. "He left over an hour ago. He should be with you."

"He never arrived." Op'ik's voice was soft, as though he was scared of angering him.

"Hold the line." Bo rapidly tried to raise the two Cobalt guards from the comm device on his desk. No answer. Cobalts were trained to flick the answer switch no matter what the situation. They were trained to always call for back-up if needed. The fact there had been nothing from either of them was a worry. He strapped on his laser sword as he linked to Dasa. "Meet me at the front steps now. I think Ari's been taken."

"On it." Dasa cut the link.

Switching back to his implant, he left his office at a sprint. "We're on our way. If you see anything, contact me." He shut the link, not waiting for a reply. "Cobalts to me." His roar vibrated the pane of glass in the window beside him. Cobalts streamed all around him as he patched through to the security center. "Cobalts Deek'in and Yavek are unresponsive while on protection duties with Aridien. Engage all Cobalts and city guards. Spread out and look for him."

"Yes, Sir." The Cobalt officer on duty shut the link, and seconds later, there was a cobalt-wide broadcast sounding in his ears. Hitting the top step, Dasa fell into stride with him. "What do we know?"

"He never turned up at Op'ik's. His guards aren't responding. I've deployed the Cobalts. I'm headed to the cruiser. The iglink has got to him. I know it."

Dasa bellowed for people to move out of the way. He caught the odd smug look on Red faces as he sprinted by. There was little doubt in his mind now. The Reds were not only helping Agota, they were making their play for the throne. He hit his implant connecting to his father on his personal link. "Father…"

"I heard. They're making moves now. Stay safe, son. I've got a full contingent of guards around me. I won't leave the office, but if they come here, and I believe Kinesh will, I will fight."

"Stay safe, father. Make sure mother…"

"She's already left to be with family in the mountains— she left last night. I have no idea where Alenska is. She isn't answering her link."

"She's a gifted warrior in her own right," Dasa tempered. He may not like Alenska, but she was still his sister.

"Keep me updated."

"I will do." Dasa cut the link and Bo picked up the pace, determined to rescue his mate.

CHAPTER THIRTY ONE

A cramp in his leg finally raised Ari to full consciousness. Yet, despite the pain, he didn't move a muscle. He took stock of his surroundings. He lay face down on what could only be grass. All around him, angry voices where arguing back and forth. A sword was once again pressed into his back.

"You so much as make a move towards your implant and I'll drive this blade into his spine," a demonic voice yelled out over the din, no doubt towards the Cobalt Guards surrounding Agota's cruiser. Silence descended so suddenly the absence of sound almost hurt. "Good. Now lower your weapons to the ground slowly."

Ari was trying to have faith. He really was, but this was hard. He understood why the Cobalts weren't risking attacking— they didn't want to see him hurt, but the thought of being taken off Kenistal hurt more than he ever believed possible.

A ghostly voice drifted on the wind. *"Faith, young one, have faith."*

He couldn't puzzle the voice out. It possessed the same sound as Drel'nic and Lo'jat, but it didn't belong to them.

The swish of metal doors broke the silence amongst the demons gathered. "What are you doing! Pull him up immediately. If you've harmed him, you'll be dead inside a minute."

Ah, the screeching sounds of Agota's voice. He wondered when she would appear. He let himself be lifted, the movement jarring his leg enough to break the grip of pain. Letting his head fall forward, shielding his eyes, he continued to pretend to be unconscious.

"What have you done to him?"

Oh, Agota was pissed.

"He wouldn't shut up, so I made him," one of the demons responded, a lift to the voice telling Ari he was at least smiling.

"Bring him here." Agota snarled, her worlds barely discernable.

"I suggest you drop your weapons and gently lower Aridien to the ground." That was a new voice. One Ari vaguely recognized. But who? He chanced opening his eyes to slits. He caught a flash of forest green. Space-faring demons? What were they doing there? Not that he was complaining.

"Who are you to tell me what to do?" Agota's shrill voice demanded.

"I am Dea'saverin Hevalis, Commander of the KS Hek'rajin. I believe you've met my brother... Bo'saverin." Bo's brother! Ari thrilled at the news. Maybe there was still hope.

"Attack!" The command came out of nowhere and Ari was unceremoniously flung towards Agota.

He had no choice but to brace himself or he'd have smacked face first into the hull of the crusier. He couldn't miss the triumphant gleam in her face as she grabbed his arm and spun him around to face her.

"What have you done!" Agota screamed at him.

"What?" Ari tried to back away, but one of the Trevon blocked his path. All around him the battle raged as Dea's men and the guard keeping Agota from leaving battled the Trevons, Aducians and demons from the Red guild.

Agota grabbed his hair and pulled his head back, brushing his curls away from his face. She stared at him, momentarily speechless.

She knew, whatever the markings were, she knew.

She slapped him hard across the face, one of her rings cutting into the corner of his lip. He spat out blood at her feet. "How could you do this. You've ruined my plans. Renauld won't take you spoiled like this. You're a disgrace, an insult to all that is Aducian. An insult to me!"

313

Even the Trevon started to back away at the hate burning in her eyes.

"I have no idea what you are going on about, Agota." Ari looked around, trying to find a weapon, anything.

"You always were stupid." She went to slap him again, but he ducked out of the way. "You really don't know what that means, do you?" She cackled as she gestured to his head.

"The markings?" He touched them briefly. What was she so upset about?

Agota looked to the Trevon. "I need a witness. Come here."

The Trevon stepped forward warily.

"Aridien Gerosa Kelotian, I hereby renounce you as my son. You have brought shame to the Kelotian name, shame to Aducia, shame to your family, shame to me. You no longer have the right to use that name, you no longer have the right to call any Kelotian family. I will petition the Grand Council to have you stricken from the annuals of births."

Even the Trevon were staring in wide-eyed astonishment. For someone so starsbent on getting her hands on him, she had changed her mind pretty quickly. Was he dying? Was he infected with some terrible curse? Oh stars, had he infected Bo? His heart broke at the thought he'd cause Bo any pain.

"I don't care about any of that! What's wrong with me?" he screamed at her, finally losing his patience.

"Wrong? Nothing is wrong. Except the shame you bring on letting some demon make you pregnant." Agota snarled.

Ari stopped reaching for the weapon. "I'm what?"

Agota scoffed. "Those marks are pregnancy marks, you idiot. It means you're with child. You're no use to me now. All that time and money spent on you for nothing. I should have you run through." She yanked a sword out of the closest Red demon's hands, the shock of this tiny woman stealing it allowing it to slip from his fingers.

Ari backed up, hands extended. "You can't kill me. You'll be killing your grandchild."

"You think I care about some half demon brat? It will probably be lenis like you. I'm not waiting another twenty years for my plans to come to pass!" She lunged with the blade.

Ari tried to move back and dodge, but his movements were halted by a Red demon. He had a brief moment to think of Bo as he closed his eyes and waited for the killing blow. Instead, all he heard was the clash of metal on metal. His eyes sprang open, staring at the Forest Green demon who had deflected her blow.

She screamed in disbelief. "I will come for you, Aridien. Mark my words, you and that spawn of yours will die. Sooner rather than later." She turned and sprinted for the cruiser door, the Trevons and Aducians following her.

Ari went to stop her, but a gentle voice stopped him. "Let her go, we need to get you to safety. The battle still rages around us. There are far more Reds than Cobalts and us space demons put together."

Ari let out a shaky breath, his hand drifting to his abdomen. He nodded meekly, too shocked to do anything but follow the gentle voice.

CHAPTER THIRTY TWO

Bo ran for the speeder a Cobalt had ready for him, Dasa's speeder next to his. Clambering on, he pulled out of the courtyard at breakneck speed, Dasa right behind him. Zipping through the streets, a grim satisfaction radiated through him as demons plastered themselves to walls and doors to stay out of their way. Turning a corner, he cursed at sight before him. Deek'in and Yavek were in the fight of their lives. Both faced off with at least four Red demons. A group of city guards, not nearly as well trained as the Cobalts, battled with a contingent of Reds. He scanned for Ari, seeing nothing, even as he dismounted from his speeder and ran to Deek.

"Where is Ari," he cried, even as he struck a deathblow to one of the Reds.

"Taken at knifepoint. They went to Agota. Go, we'll be okay here." Deek deflected a strike aimed to take both their heads.

"I can't leave you like this, no matter how much I want to race after Ari." Bo wanted to rescue his mate, but he would be a poor commander, leaving his demons to die.

"You aren't leaving me alone." Deek tipped his head back the way Bo had come, as if he could read his Commander's thoughts.

Bo chanced a glance behind him. Two of the troop transports had come to a halt and as soon as the doors opened, Cobalts poured from within, immediately engaging the Reds.

"Go, save him," Yavek shouted.

Bo nodded, mortally wounding another demon as he turned on his tail back to the speeder.

Dasa, having dispatched his own Red, quickly joined him. They took off, zipping through the streets.

Bo kicked his speeder into high gear. "His mother has him."

"We should have gone straight there." Dasa grimaced.

"Considering the cruiser is guarded by a full contingent, there should be no way for anything to happen. But…"

"The Reds have chosen now to attack. If they're attacking here, I wouldn't put it past them to attack there," Dasa finished Bo's sentence. "This has been planned, that much is obvious. The one thing I have to question is how they knew Ari would be out and about with only two guards."

"You aren't the only one wondering that." One part of Bo's mind had been focused on that from the second he'd heard Ari was taken.

"You think it was Op'ik?" Dasa turned his implant up so he could hear over the roar of the engines.

Bo didn't hesitate with his answer. "No, I don't. It was Op'ik who contacted me wondering where Ari was. I heard his voice, not only did he not know anything, he was deeply concerned. No, our traitor isn't him."

"But we do have one. There is little doubt now. The only thing we don't know is who." Dasa pushed his speeder faster, matching Bo, ignoring the heat from the engine as they both taxed the machines to the limit. It was a good job their scales were at maximum; if they hadn't been, they may have suffered burns.

Bo wondered if the speeders were going to last until they got to the cruiser. The engines were whining, smoke pouring from the mechanics beneath him. He coughed, pleased the wind was at least working with them. At least he could still see.

They turned the corner towards the space dock. The cruiser had been isolated off to one side and Bo's eyes widened at the scene of utter chaos around it. His Cobalts, some Forest Greens, and Reds, were all battling each other. There were no Trevons, Aducians or Loperis in sight. He frantically scanned the battlefield looking for Ari. As they got closer, one demon stood out from all the others. Dea.

"Dea!" Bo shut the engine off, even as it spluttered and vaulted over to his brother, his laser sword already in hand.

Dea'saverin Hevalis may have been a commander in Kenistal's space fleet, but he was still a gifted warrior in his own right and more than capable of holding his own against untrained Reds. "Little brother, good of you to finally delight us with your presence," he drawled.

Bo huffed. "Good to see you too. Surprised you left your oblish."

"Would you stop referring to my ship as my honey?" Dea scowled as he slammed the butt of his laser-sword down onto the head of the Red he was fighting, who paused briefly, staring at them both in astonishment. "Krexjin. Some of us can do two things at once."

"You know you love her," Bo taunted, spinning around and taking the legs out from a Red sneaking up behind them.

"True, the only female I will ever love." Dea grinned.

Having scanned the area while fighting, Bo could find no trace of Ari. "That iglink better not have him."

"She doesn't, if you mean the woman arguing with him. She ran back inside after…"

"What?" Bo narrowed his eyes.

"After her attempt to kill him failed. One of my officers got there just in time." Dea grimaced at the look of abject rage on Bo's face.

"Where is he?" Bo spun around again, desperately searching for his mate.

"Over by the wall to the left." Dea gestured to where there was a group of his crew standing guard. Presumably over Ari.

Bo started to run, but called out over his shoulder. "Thank you, brother. Now, don't get yourself killed."

"I won't!" Dea called after him.

Bo heard the distinctive whir of troop transports racing to join the battle. A good thing too, as more Reds were pouring in from all sides. There was no mistaking they'd planned to fight, whether here or elsewhere. They'd been ready. As he ran on, a new thrum drew his attention. He spun his head from side to side, trying to find the source of the sound.

"Frek!" His bellow barely drew any attention amongst the noises of battle. He slammed a button on his implant. "I need an emergency breakthrough on all frequencies at my location. Not just Cobalt, all," he demanded.

The comms officer on the end gulped. "Sir, there are—"

"All of them and now!" Bo heard the distinctive bleeping sound.

"Done, Sir."

Bo didn't reply, he simply started broadcasting. "All demons in the vicinity of the Trevon cruiser, back the frek up, she's powering her engines."

When only a handful of demons made any attempt to move, Bo screamed into his implant. "Move or die! The cruiser is going up. You'll be vaporized if you're in the ignition zone."

That got demons moving. For some reason, the demons around Ari weren't moving. Whether they figured they were out of blast range, or simply couldn't hear him, Bo didn't know. He picked up his pace. As soon as he was in verbal range, he started to scream at them to move.

Ari could have sworn he could hear Bo, but how was that possible? Bo was spans away in the palace, and he was simply here hiding out behind a wall of green, unable to take his mind off the fact his mother had just tried to kill him, had disowned him, called him a traitor, and oh yes… that little bomb she dropped that his new markings meant he was pregnant. He didn't even know how to start feeling about that little revelation. Voices swirled all around him, but the words didn't register. He hugged his knees tighter, unable to look around, listen, or worry about the battle raging around him. He rested his head on his knees and closed his eyes. It was all getting too much.

"Go! Go!" Bo yelled. The guards around Ari finally perked up at his voice. Their frantic glances around meant they finally understood what he was yelling. His only focus now was on Ari. As worried as he was at the listless appearance of Ari, he didn't stop to talk, he scooped Ari up in his arms, turned on his heel and ran.

All around him Demons were running, the battle forgotten in an effort to save themselves from the backblast of Agota's ship taking off. A quick glance ahead and relief swamped him. Dasa was safe and out of range. He shouldn't have been so focused on Ari, he forgot his prince. He would chastise himself for that later, right now he needed to get to safety.

A loud cry made him whip his head around. Dea! He'd been tackled by a Red who didn't seem to care about the ship, taking a blade to the stomach as he fell. Bo made to run towards him, even with Ari in his arms, when a Forest Green demon streaked past him.

"Go! I'll get him." Bo didn't even register who it was, he simply ran on with Ari in his arms.

As he neared safety, he chanced a glance over his shoulder, finally recognizing who carried his brother. That was Commander Urias and his brother was slung over his shoulder. How the frek was Urias there? He was supposed to be in space. He saw Dasa running towards him and frantically waved him back.

Dasa ignored him, running up and grabbing Ari from his arms. "Go help him!"

Bo nodded and ran back just as Urias nearly stumbled. "I'll take him. Go." Urias went to argue with him, but stopped and quickly handed him over. They both knew Bo was the better demon to carry him. His constant training and innate strength as a Cobalt would see to that. Urias ran on ahead of him and Bo picked up speed, the first whine of engines telling him the cruiser was lifting off. He heard Dasa screaming at him to run. Drawing on what little reserves he had left, he pushed himself harder, every muscle straining.

Heat slammed into his back and he adjusted Dea to being carried in his arms, rather than over his shoulder. Dea, unconscious as he was, didn't have his scales activated. If he got hit by any of the blast, he wouldn't survive. Bo at least stood a chance.

All the demons, including Dasa, and Ari, still in his arms, had retreated behind the safety wall. A few Cobalts stood ready at the doors to slam them shut, two others were beckoning him to run faster, their eyes wide at what was happening behind him. Bo didn't dare look. The heat licking at his back was becoming intolerable and Bo knew he had seconds left to get them through the door. He would not lose his brother, and he would not die, not when he just found Ari.

The rumble of the cruiser taking off sounded as Bo hit the doors. He was yanked unceremoniously to the side, tripping and nearly losing his balance. Multiple sets of hands steadied him as the doors were slammed shut by the Cobalts waiting. Seconds later, the roar of flames could be heard, and seen, as the cruiser blasted its way through the Kenistalian atmosphere.

Bo let the arms holding him guide him to the ground. He was about to refuse, thinking only of the Reds who'd attacked, but looking around, he saw they too were resting on the ground stunned.

Dasa gently sat next to Bo, Ari in his arms. He kept looking at Ari, but so far he was still unresponsive.

"Let me take him." Bo's voice croaked, a combination of his mad dash and the smoke from the launch.

"Not until someone checks out your back." Dasa stubbornly held onto Ari before Bo slumped forward.

"Fine, get it done quickly."

Dasa beckoned over a medic, a full contingent of Cobalts now swarming the area. Many of the Reds had beat a hasty retreat as they ran from the cruiser. Not one of them had helped anyone else in the frantic dash for safety, even after Bo had made sure to warn everyone, allies and enemies alike.

A medic squatted down, quickly examining Bo. Shortly after, a cooling gel spray was applied to his back and Bo sighed in relief. The concoction, a mix of anesthetic, antiseptic and localized pain killer soon worked its magic.

"You're extraordinarily lucky." The medic, now in front of him checking for any other injuries, was scowling. "How you didn't do any permanent damage is beyond me. You should be healed within a day."

"Good. Now could you please check out my mate." Bo's voice was gritty as he attempted to hold back his anger. "And is someone checking on my damn brother!"

Dasa pointed over his shoulder. Bo turned, seeing his brother being tended to by two medics, Urias at his side. "I thought they hated each other?" he muttered as he focused back on his mate.

"Dislike, I would guess so… but nowhere near enough to abandon him to that fate." Dasa gestured vaguely to the dock behind the wall.

"Frek, the iglink could have taken out a massive section of our society. Do we even know what happened yet?" Bo looked around for anyone to report to him.

A Forest Green stepped forward. "Begging your pardon, Your Highness, Commander…"

Both demons looked up. "Yes…" Dasa prompted.

"I'm Navigator Broc'tak. I was there when everything happened." He gestured to the space between them, sitting when Dasa nodded to go ahead.

"I'm the navigator on the Hek'rajin. We were just coming back from checking on the repairs. Commander Dea saw Ari being carried into the dock and knew something was up, especially as it was Reds carrying him. He asked if we would go with him, but refused to order us as we aren't fully trained." Broc'tak snorted. "As if us not going was ever going to happen. There was fighting all around, Reds on Cobalts. We engaged them as much as we could, the Reds, I mean. I was close to your mate. I couldn't hear exactly what was being said, but the woman, she was… frek, she screamed at him, ranted and raved. Some of what she spoke about was him being a traitor to her and to his world. She disowned him."

Bo's head snapped up from where he'd been studying Ari. "She did what?"

"She disowned him. Then she, she drew a sword on him and tried to kill him. I was already running towards him at that point. I managed to deflect the blade, and several Cobalts joined me. I pulled him to safety. Her last words to him…" Broc'tak stopped, the fact he'd overheard that the commander's mate was pregnant was not his place to share. "They were 'I will come for you, Aridien. Mark my words, you will die. Sooner rather than later.' He seemed to go into shock. I retreated with him and a group of Cobalts raced over to protect him, refusing to give up their post to join the battle."

Bo was thrilled to hear how protective his Cobalts were. Yet, if Ari hadn't been injured, why was he like this? As Dasa carried on talking to Broc'tak, Bo tenderly swept Ari's hair back, tracing his new markings. "What can you tell me?" His voice was soft as he spoke to the medics.

Medic Vec'as was the one to answer. "He's in shock, no doubt about that. Otherwise, there doesn't appear to be any injuries other than minor scratches and bruising. For the shock, keep talking to him, let him know he is safe and cared for. His body temperature has dropped, so he will need keeping warm. I've given him an electrolyte boost which should help stabilize him, otherwise this is an emotional response to a traumatic situation. His mind simply needs time to come to terms to what has happened to him. The med transports are coming in now. You can go with them to the med center, or you can take him back to your suite. I can check on him over the next few hours and you can always call me personally if you are worried. It's up to you what you want to do."

"I'll take him home." Bo grasped the medic's hand. "Thank you for everything."

"You're welcome, Commander. I'll go and see who else needs help. There are far too many injuries here, and even though some are the Reds who attacked, I can't not help them." With a self-deprecating smile, Vec'as left.

Bo beckoned a group of his officers over. Thankfully uninjured, they freely took over securing the scene and taking witness statements. Having a good group of officers, ones he'd handpicked over the years, was one of the greatest things about being a Commander. When he needed to step away, for whatever reason, he knew the Cobalts were in safe hands.

CHAPTER THIRTY THREE

Bo grudgingly stood, brushing a kiss across Ari's head, before leaving him wrapped up in bed. Finally stripping out of his bloodied, dirty clothes, he took a quick shower, not even relishing the soothing effect on his muscles. His mind wouldn't calm for even a minute. All he could focus on was the attack and Ari.

When he finally walked out into his reception room, it was to grim faces all around. "How bad?"

Vict's face rippled with a mix of anger and sorrow. "Seventy-five dead across the clans, one hundred and eighty-six injured, thirty-eight are critical."

Bo dropped into a chair, knocking back the ale Dasa handed to him. "My officers reported in. The city is officially on lockdown, but there are still Reds trying to sneak about. Right now, families are returning to their homes from work and locking up tight. I've ordered patrols and recalled all those Cobalts on any type of leave. They are all battle-armed, rather than standard patrol armed. I don't like the thought of using weapons on our own people, so I've asked they all be equipped with neutralizing batons. Once night hits, we need to be prepared here as well as on the streets. I can't help but think they will try an all-out attack on the palace."

Dasa sipped at his own ale. "I don't see what else could happen now. Kinesh has already set this plan in motion. He must know he needs to see this to the bitter end now. If he were to just give up, he would face ridicule amongst the other guilds. His pride is too great. No, the only thing Kinesh can do now is go on an all-out attack."

"Are you so sure, young demon?" A deep timbered voice spoke directly in Dasa's ear, making him jump up from his seat. He whirled around, already reaching for his weapon.

"What the frek!" Dasa stared in outright astonishment at the apparition before him.

Drel'nic stood chuckling as Vict shook his head.

"You just had to freak out my son, didn't you, Drel'nic." Vict chuckled at the wide grin on the Guardian's face. "Son, this is Drel'nic one of the Guardians of the ruins we told you about. Seeing as we never see you alone, can I presume Lo'jat is about somewhere?"

"He is currently with our Little Demon." Drel'nic held up a hand stopping Bo from standing. "Leave them be, Lo'jat is helping him. I know you fear for him, but, as I promised you, everything will be alright."

Bo gritted his teeth, but wisely stayed silent.

Drel'nic perched on the side of Dasa's seat, grinning at him occasionally. Every so often, he would peer closely at him.

"Could you possibly stop testing my son and let us know what is happening?" Vict asked.

"Such impatience, even in kings." Drel'nic shook his head. "But, I ask again, now this one has calmed slightly, are you sure that is Kinesh's only option? Think carefully."

Lo'jat rested his hands just over Ari's belly, a slightly ghostly glow radiating from them. His face was a mask of concentration as he scanned for the tiny presence deep within Ari's abdomen. A soft smile gradually grew as he detected everything was as it should be.

Moving on, he scanned every part of Ari's body, checking for hidden injuries or traumas. Thankfully, what damage he found was minor. With a slight tremble to his hand, he reached towards Ari's head and scanned. Unknown to Ari, they'd shielded him as much as possible throughout the fight. But, there was only so much even they could do without fully revealing themselves.

He worked quickly on Ari's mind, searching out the emotional trauma and using what power he had to take away some of the impact. He wouldn't take it all, Ari would need to heal emotionally from this, to process it and grow from it, but he would take enough to help him wake and face the world. Finally finished, he sat on the bed and stroked Ari's hair back from his forehead, smiling at the tell-tale markings. He and the other Guardians had discussed telling Ari before he saw his mother, but it wouldn't have changed what happened and they were limited to the amount of times and ways they could interfere. Far better to save it for when they really needed to.

"Little Demon." Lo'jat sing-songed. "It's time to wake up now."

Ari fought against the darkness consuming him. A soft hum drew his attention, the sound comforting him more than he could believe possible.

"That's it, open those eyes for me. I want to show you something."

"L-lo'jat," Ari stuttered out the word.

"It is I. Now, open your eyes for me. You want to see this."

Ari grumbled, but fought to do as Lo'jat wanted. The moment they were open, he stared. "Lo'jat? I can see you!"

"I've been practicing." Lo'jat beamed with pride, making Ari smile.

Ari reached up to hug Lo'jat, unsure if it were possible, or if his hands would go straight through. He watched as Lo'jat scrunched up his face concentrating, nodded and drew him into his arms, hugging him tight. Eventually, Lo'jat started to lose solidity. Ari sadly pulled away.

"Ah, Little Demon, it's not that bad."

"She... the things she said." Ari's haunted eyes begged Lo'jat to tell him he was wrong and it hadn't happened.

"I know, but there is something you need to think on. You have family here. King Vict'arin has taken you under his wing, and he will always be like a father to you. Prince Dasalin, Caris, they will always be brothers to you, as well as friends. Deek'in, Yavek, Op'ik, Perik…. The list goes on. You have friends and family here. Then there is young Bo'saverin. He is your mate, the father of your babe, and he loves you with everything he is. He has a brother still. Then there are the Guardians. I would be honored to call you family, Little Demon."

Ari's chin trembled as he held back his tears. "Thank you, Lo'jat, I would be honored to call you family as well."

"Good, now how about we go and see the rest of them? I know your Bo is incredibly worried about you. He was letting you sleep while he talks security with the king."

"It's bad, isn't it? The amount of Reds who attacked… my mother has stirred all this up. Not that she is anymore, my mother, I mean."

Lo'jat traced Ari's cheek with barely-there fingers. "It's bad, yes, but this is about more than just your mother. She has probably brought the timetable forward, but that's it. This was going to happen anyway. The Red guild have been building towards this for a long time. Things are in place." Lo'jat held Ari's gaze trying to say things without saying them. "All will work as it should."

Ari cocked his head to one side. He wasn't sure what Lo'jat was trying to say. Raised voices came through the doorway and Ari stopped to listen.

Vict studied Drel'nic. "You ask if Kinesh's only option is to attack. It must be, there are no other avenues open to him."

"Are you so sure?" Drel'nic prompted.

"Of course he's sure!" Dasa bellowed.

"Now, young demon, do not get too upset, that will simply cloud your mind." Drel'nic stood at ease, now leaning against the wall by the drinks, eyeing them with a certain amount of longing.

"There are no other options!" Dasa insisted, still angry, but slightly calmer.

"There is." Ari's quiet voice from the doorway made them all jump, the contrast from Dasa's anger stunning.

"Tiko." Bo jumped from his seat, grimacing at the bite of pain, and pulled Ari into his arms. "Oh, Love, I was so worried about you." He smiled up at Lo'jat. "Thank you. Thank you for bringing him back."

"The little demon is special. How could I not?" Lo'jat winked.

"Are you..." Bo didn't know quite how to ask how Ari was doing, almost scared to know the truth.

"I'm not great, there is a lot I have to work through, but I *will* work through it. Enough of that for now though. Dasa, you said there are no other options, but there is."

"Aridien, I know you want to help, but if we can't see any other option..." Vict's words trailed off as Ari glared.

"I have three words for you." Ari crossed his arms and stared them all down. "Crown of Horns."

Several sharply indrawn breaths echoed around the room.

"Well, frek, he's right." Vict looked stunned. "I hadn't even thought about it."

Bo walked back to his seat, pulling Ari with him, arranging him in his lap and sighing as Ari snuggled in.

"I take it the legend of the Crown of Horns is well known?" Ari looked around at all the nods. "Well, if you met him in any battle or confrontation wearing the crown, then I can't see how any demons could imply anything other than you are Kenistal's rightful king." He shrugged and happily carried on snuggling into Bo.

Vict's mouth opened and shut repeatedly. "Frek me, he's right. The Crown of Horns is the symbol, the ancient symbol of Kings. If I'm wearing it, after it has long been thought lost, it will pull any demons who are considering siding with the Reds to our side. I doubt it will sway any Reds, but if they have no other guild support… it might be enough. We just have to stop the fighting long enough for everyone to see it."

"The question is how," Dasa mused.

"Sorry, can't help with that." Ari smothered a yawn.

"You tired?" Bo smoothed back his curls.

"No, just trying to fully come to. Lo'jat was incredible at helping me wake up." Ari sent a grin towards Lo'jat who still had a look of concentration on his face as though he was completely focused on staying visible. Ari let out a gentle snicker at the ghostly tongue peeking out of his mouth. When Lo'jat caught him looking, he stuck it out further, making Ari giggle.

Bo warmed at the sound of Ari laughing. After what happened at the cruiser, he worried he'd never hear it again. He gently burrowed his hand into Ari's hair, gently massaging his head. The groan Ari let loose went straight to his cock. Now was not the time for that sort of reaction.

"Ari…" Vict reached across and squeezed his shoulder. "Bo let us know what Navigator Broc'tak told him."

"Broc'tak?" Ari looked around in confusion.

"The Green demon who helped you."

"He saved me," Ari corrected.

"And we will be forever grateful to him," Vict assured Ari.

Ari closed his eyes briefly, gathering his strength. "She's disowned me. I've been branded a traitor and banished from Aducia."

Bo hugged him tighter.

"I have no family left."

"Not true in the slightest." Vict glared. "You have me and this lot, whether you want them or not."

"I told you, Little Demon, you have family here." Lo'jat looked pointedly at Ari.

Ari grimaced. "Bo?"

"Yes, Tiko?" Bo nuzzled Ari's hair, relieved to have his mate back in his arms.

"I need to talk to you about something." Ari wrung his hands.

"I'm here to listen any time, Love."

Ari thrilled at the words. "Umm, I'm not sure you want me to say it in front of everyone else." He nervously glanced around at the intrigued looks.

"Is it bad?" Bo asked.

"Umm, I don't *think* so. But I don't know how you're going to take it."

"Tiko, these lot, for better or worse, are our family. They all love us."

"Love Ari, yes. Not so sure about you, you reprobate." Dasa drawled making Ari and Caris laugh.

"You want me to say it in front of them?" Ari blushed profusely.

"Only if you're comfortable, but I don't mind, these gossips tend to find everything out anyway." Bo bit back a laugh at the eager nods from Vict, Dasa and Caris. He narrowed his eyes as Drel'nic and Lo'jat looked on serenely. "You two know, don't you?"

"We do." Lo'jat nodded.

Bo looked at Ari expectantly.

"Don't blame me if you wish this had been private." Ari started to tremble, his nerves going haywire.

331

"Hey, Tiko, whatever it is, it isn't going to stop me loving you, I promise." Bo tried to reassure Ari.

Ari held Bo's gaze, fighting against his nerves. "I know what the markings mean. My mo… Agota was the one to tell me. It's why she disowned me and called me a traitor."

"Ari, are you sick?" Bo's heart rate was rapidly picking up speed.

"No, it's not like that. I'm… that is, I… we…" Ari blew out a huff of breath. *This is hard.* "I'm pregnant," he whispered, his words so low Bo was the only one to hear him. Bo's eyes widened so far Ari was beginning to wonder if they might pop out of his head.

Bo ignored the chorus of voices asking Ari to repeat what he said. "Are you serious?" He studied Ari's face, his gaze darting down to his abdomen and back up. "You're truly serious? You're… we're, it's a… we're… I'm going to…"

"Wow, I don't think I've ever seen a demon quite so lost for words." Drel'nic snickered, earning him glares from about the room.

Bo traced the markings around Ari's hairline. Pregnant. Demonlings. His heart thumped rapidly. *This is what the markings meant? He was going to be a father? His own little demonling? They were going to be parents'?*

"Are you upset?" Ari started to try to get up out of Bo's lap. Bo, however, held him tight.

"I'm many things… stunned, amazed, ecstatic, delirious, overwhelmed, scared, happy, you name it, I'm feeling it, but the things I'm not are angry and upset. Ari, it's a shock, yes, but I'm happy, incredibly happy." Bo kissed Ari for all he was worth. A pronounced cough eventually brought him out of the trance he was in and his focus back to the room.

"I'm dying over here," Vict drawled. "Fill us in."

Bo's wide grin said it all. "Ari's pregnant. We're going to have a demonling."

There were a few beats of silence before anyone reacted.

Caris leapt up and embraced Ari, still held securely in Bo's arms. "I couldn't be happier for you both. A little demonling! You must be thrilled."

Ari shared a shy smile with Bo, whose face was positively alight with happiness. "I am."

"No, my love, we are, we are thrilled." Bo couldn't stop caressing Ari's belly. "I can't believe I'm going to be a father. Frek, what do I do?"

Ari started to chuckle softly. He happened to glance up and caught sight of Vict, who was trying valiantly to stop laughing. When Vict lost the battle, so did he.

"Bo'saverin, you've got a little while to cope with the panic. Stay calm, there are plenty of us around who've been through it before." Vict wiped a stray tear from his eye, still chuckling softly as Bo continued to glare at him. "You aren't the first to be freaked out, and you won't be the last. But despite all your fear, the one thing I can honestly tell you is you will be a great father. Have no fear about that. Your demonling will be loved and cherished. That fear? It never really goes away. There is always something you worry about. No matter whether your demonlings are babes, or grown demons like Dasa here, you will always worry. The type of worry simply changes. From skinned knees before they get their scales, watching them learn to walk, learn to fight, to seeing them grown and go off on their first space mission, watching them navigate the minefield of love. It will always stay with you. But, as much as there is fear, there is overwhelming joy, and pride, so much pride in their achievements."

Vict turned to look at Dasa. "Son, I probably never tell you this enough, but I am proud of you. So very proud."

Dasa dashed away a stray, traitorous tear. "I love you, father."

"Here now, enough of that." Vict grumbled before winking at his son. "I love you too, never doubt that. Ari, your demonling will never want for love. He, or she, will be my grandling. I will declare it fully, the same way I declared you as my son."

Bo was stunned, that would give their demonling the full protection of the royal family. No one would mess with them. "We are honored. Thank you."

Ari eased himself out of Bo's grip, patting him on the arm when Bo frowned. He quickly moved to Vict's side and hugged him.

"Here now," Vict grumbled. "No need for that." Yet he hugged Ari tightly, whispering in his ear, "You have made an old man happy. To see young Bo'saverin happy after so much heartache fills me with joy. You are a special man, Aridien." Vict turned to the Guardians. "I want to thank you. It's far too late, but I never knew. Thank you for saving these two in the ruins when they were younger. My life would not have been the same without my son and young Bo'saverin." He bowed to each Guardian in turn.

"You are most welcome." Drel'nic grinned.

CHAPTER THIRTY FOUR

One by one, they all hugged Bo and Ari, smiles replacing the frustration and anger from the last few hours. They were interrupted by a rapid knocking on the door. One of the guards poked his head around the door.

"I'm sorry to interrupt, but we have a situation that needs your attention, Commander. There is a demon here by the name of Perik, demanding to see you. He insists it's a matter of the upmost importance."

Bo shared a puzzled frown with Dasa. Looking for confirmation from Vict, who nodded, he turned to the guard. "Show him in here, please."

"Yes, Sir." The demon backed out slightly before bringing a demon in, who was wrapped up in a hooded cloak, hiding his face. His face stayed hidden until the door was firmly shut behind him.

"I'm sorry to disturb you after everything that has happened, but I bring word from my father." Perik looked around the room, gulping when he saw Vict.

"Your father?" Bo asked.

"My father is Guild Master Drenk'alic of the Orange guild. He sent me here to tell you Kinesh summoned the guild leaders. He's planning on a guild tribunal. He plans to evict you from the throne by declaring you unfit to rule."

Vict crushed his goblet. "I guess it's better than an all-out attack." He studied Perik. "You'd better tell me everything."

Dasa gestured to a seat, passing Perik a goblet of ale, making sure he had a firm grasp in his shaky hands before he let go.

"I'm sorry." Perik took a long gulp and looked in Vict's general direction, but was unable to meet his gaze. "I'm nervous."

"Take your time, young one." Vict pitched his voice low, not wanting to upset the obviously scared demon any more than he already was.

"We'd gone home after the troubles. I'd locked up the shop early. I didn't want anything to be damaged. I've worked too hard to see it all taken from me." Perik shook his head. "Sorry, I'm finding this hard."

"You're doing great. It's okay," Bo reassured him.

"We were having something to eat. My mother makes some really special xozi squares. Some Reds came to the door, demanded that my father go to see Kinesh for an important meeting. Father isn't one for normally ceding to demands, not from anyone bar you, Your Majesty. For you he would do anything. That's why I'm here. When the Reds pulled laser swords on my mother, he went. He came back about an hour ago and asked that I come see you. Too many people would notice if he went walking about. I'm quite sure there are Reds watching us, or him at least. He asked that I came to you. Even as important as it is, he wouldn't order me. He wanted it to be my choice. How could I not? You're my king, Kenistal's king, the rightful king."

"What was said?" Vict shared a long look with Dasa.

"As I said, Kinesh called the guild leaders together. He used a combination of bribery, cajoling and threats. He wants all the guilds to back him when he goes to the tribunal. He wants, and plans on taking, the throne. He maintained you were an unfit ruler, that you were preventing trade deals, and…" Perik looked around nervously. "Allowing the blood of Kenistal to be diluted by no-horns."

"He means Ari and I." Caris held Perik's gaze.

"Yes, he does." Perik wrung his hands. "He's bringing a battalion of armed Reds with him. They will stay hidden until the last possible moment. He wants them there because he is so convinced you will refuse, no matter what the tribunal says. He plans

336

on attacking to take the throne anyway. There's more." Perik looked around nervously.

"He says that he has an inside source, someone who knows your every move, who knows how you think, how you operate. They've told him what to expect from you. They even told him about the weapon you keep hidden in your throne."

Vict's anger was absolute and palpable. So intense he struggled with a desire to attack something. Grabbing the nearest thing— another goblet— he crushed it before flinging it towards the fireplace. He grabbed his sword, fist flexing around it. The soft whoosh of the laser engaging was the only sound as everyone waited for Vict to gain control of his temper.

Ari's eyes tracked Vict as he stormed across to the doorway and grabbed hold of the handle. But he froze before turning it. Vict's head dropped, hanging so low his horns scraped across the door, leaving indentations as he moved. His fist went to bang on the door, but he obviously thought better of it. He whirled around and stalked across the room, going into the spare bedroom in Bo's suite. The door shut quietly, but seconds later there were muted thumps and crashes. Vict was obviously taking out his frustration on something.

Ari's gaze darted about the room. Caris looked concerned, but calm. Perik's tail was swinging back and forth rapidly, his skin soft, as though he was scared to make any move Vict could consider confrontational. Dasa eased out of his chair, but stopped as an unseen voice whispered in his ear.

"Leave him be, Dasalin, let him get this out and come back to you calmer."

Ari could make out a faint outline leaning into Dasa. He presumed it was Drel'nic. As soon as Perik entered the room, they'd vanished from sight.

Dasa moved to the drinks table and poured sets of quastik, a potent, yet light, fresh and smooth alcohol. Handing them out, he left a large one by his father's seat. He passed a berry crush to Ari with a wink, smirking when Ari pouted.

I'd forgotten there would be no alcohol. Ari frowned, but drank his crush.

It was a few minutes later when Vict returned, looking considerably calmer. "I must apologize for that. There are only a handful of people who know of the existence of that weapon. If Kinesh knows, then it's the ultimate betrayal."

Bo wracked his mind trying to think who knew. "How many people?"

"Who know about the weapon?" Vict clarified. "You and two of my assistants."

Bo considered which Cobalts held the knowledge. "And my second and third in command. That's it. That does not leave a lot of scope for someone to betray us. I would like to say my two officers are innocent, but then that would leave your assistants and frankly, that would leave just as bitter a betrayal as my officers."

"You're forgetting people." Dasa tipped his head back so he was staring at the ceiling.

"No, those are the only people who know," Bo insisted.

"Apart from the royal family." Dasa looked pointedly at his father.

"Well, yes," Bo muttered, "but you can't honestly expect me to believe you think it's someone in your family."

"Can I not?" Dasa stared at his father.

Vict stared out the window to the stars that were slowly appearing in the early night sky, as though he were pleading with them for their suspicions to be incorrect. "I don't want to admit it. I hate that I have to, but… there *are* possibilities within the family."

"Who?" Stunned, Bo didn't know who to focus on, his king or his prince.

"Cousin Meriok, Ekris'tak and Larelk." Vict flicked a finger out with each name mentioned.

Dasa stared at his father. "There is someone else."

"No." Vict pinched the bridge of his nose. "I know you think she's gone bad, but I can't believe she would take it this far."

"Who?" Caris asked, sure he already knew the answer.

"Alenska." Dasa said the word no one else was brave enough to.

Caris, looking around the room, noticed Perik's gaze bouncing back and forth, complete astonishment written all over his face. "Perik. I know we can trust you, after all you came here to warn us, but—"

Perik madly shook his head. "Let me stop you there. I have absolutely no desire to gossip about this. You have all graced my shop, treated me well when you did and never expected anything for free. In fact, you've gone out of your way to be kind. I know you don't consider us friends, but I wouldn't say we are strangers either. All that aside, you are my king, my prince. I could never betray you."

Caris smiled softly in thanks. Looking back, he could see emotions warring across Vict's features. He was obviously deeply troubled at the thought of his daughter betraying him.

"I know why you think that, Dasa, but I have to believe she is still a member of our family. I *have* to." Vict's eyes pleaded with his son.

Dasa signaled to Bo. He would make sure they both kept a close eye on her. If she had betrayed them, she would not get away with it a second time.

"What time?" Vict asked Perik.

"The ninth chime of the ruins clock."

"Fitting. Very well. I think you'd better return home. I don't want you or your father to get in trouble over this. Go with our thanks. Should we see tomorrow and I am still the king, I shall see you rewarded."

"That's not why we did this," Perik insisted.

"I know, and that's why you shall be rewarded." Vict gently ushered Perik to the door. "See him safe as far as you can." He ordered the guards outside.

"Yes, Your Majesty."

Vict gently closed the door, took a deep breath and went to join the others. "It's time to plan."

CHAPTER THIRTY FIVE

Bo lay on his side on the bed, Ari held securely against him. His front was against Ari's back, his cock nestled between Ari's ass cheeks. He was trailing kisses up and down Ari's neck while he gently stroked his abdomen.

"Are you happy?" Ari broke the silence.

"Happier than you could believe. I know it's soon, I know you're still settling in here, but I refuse to be upset. Having a demonling with you is like a dream come true. I have everything I could ever have dreamed of in you and the little one. Please, if you struggle to come to terms with what's happened today, and I know it's going to be hard for you, but please, believe me when I tell you I want this with you."

Ari nuzzled in tighter to Bo.

"Stop that or you're going to make me horny and we don't have time," Bo chastised him.

Ari snorted. "Horny."

"What about it?"

"You said horny and you've got horns, so doesn't that make you constantly horny?" Ari was chuckling so much the bed vibrated.

"Oh, you're getting wise on me?" Bo pushed forward, rolling Ari onto his front. As he moved to straddle him, his back pulled slightly and he cried out. "Damn it! Why do I have to keep getting injured? And why the frek is it always my back? It's not fair, I'm telling you."

Ari's lips started to twitch. Bo was pouting, full force pouting. "Umm, Bo, you're kind of behaving like a demonling at the moment, and a little one at that."

"I am not." Bo's pout got even bigger. "It hurts," he whined.

"Aww, is the big, bad, scary demon all sad?" Ari rolled over so he was facing Bo, squealing with laughter when Bo attacked him, tickling his sides.

"I'll show you a big, bad, scary demon." Bo gently nipped at Ari's skin biting softly. Starting at his shoulders, he soon worked his way down Ari's body, exposing his skin as he worked.

At first Ari couldn't stop giggling, but soon enough his giggles turned to quiet moans. He went to grab hold of Bo's horns, only to be stopped.

"Uh-uh, no you don't. You deserve to be punished." Bo continued to nip at Ari's skin, the green marks thrilling him as they appeared.

"What am I being punished for?" Ari ground out as he grabbed a hold of the covers.

"Hmm, let me see. Teasing me, being mean to me, and, oh, I don't know, I just want to tease you right back and with your skin on display like this, I can't think."

Ari giggled softly. "Are you saying I scramble your brain?"

"You always do, Tiko, you always do."

Ari's heart melted when, instead of biting his abdomen, Bo started to lay gentle kisses all over it.

"It's way too early to start talking to you, but I always want you to know your fathers love you so very much my little demonling, never forget that." Bo winked at Ari.

"You're a complete softie at times, do you know that?" Ari teased.

"Only with you, love, only with you… and now this little beauty." With a last kiss, Bo started to ease lower.

"Bo, are you sure we have time? Shouldn't you be getting ready?" Ari tried to pull him up, his actions useless against such a large demon.

"I can't think of a better way to get ready for a battle than pleasing my mate." With those words, Bo gently kissed the tip of Ari's cock before sliding his lips down.

"Bo!"

Ari's soft cry tore at Bo and filled him with a sense of deep satisfaction at bringing his mate such pleasure.

"Bo, I'm not going to last, you're too good at that."

Bo's grin grew carnal, his fingers softly tracing Ari's balls before moving down to tease his hole.

"Bo, please," Ari whined. "I want to come. I don't want to wait. I want to feel good."

Bo looked up. The desperation on Ari's face was absolute. Now was definitely not the time to tease his poor mate. He redoubled his efforts, his forked tongue dipping in and out of Ari's slit, making him buck wildly on the bed. He fumbled for the oil on the bedside table, coating his fingers and slipping them back between Ari's ass cheeks. He quickly prepped Ari, not wanting him to come too soon, no matter how much he needed it. When Ari was stretched enough, he slipped his finger in deep, finding the first bundle of nerves and tapping it gently.

Ari started to buck wildly. He needed to come so badly. When Bo slid another finger in and then went deeper, to his second bundle of nerves, he couldn't hold back the wild cry that poured from his lips, swiftly followed by a litany of curses that would have made even the most veteran Cobalt blush.

Stunned at the way Ari reacted, Bo teased the second bundle of nerves mercilessly until Ari's body arched off the bed and he screamed in pleasure. He kept up a gentle tease until Ari slowly came down from his orgasmic high. "Love…"

Ari looked up in a daze to see the need on Bo's face. He spread his legs wide. "Take me."

Bo quickly coated his straining and leaking cock in oil, immediately sliding home. "Oh frek, I can't go slow."

"Then don't." Ari caressed Bo's horns, breaking the last shred of his control.

Bo thrust in deep, bottoming out with a cry. "I love you, Tiko, so damned much. You are everything to me. You make me feel like I'm flying among the stars. I could soar with you forever." Bo slowed his pace, stroking in and out steadily.

Ari continued to steadily stroke on Bo's horns. "I love you, Bo, more than I ever believed it was possible to love someone. I cannot imagine my life without you in it. You are all I want, all I need, all I could ever hope to have in a mate, in a husband. My life is complete now you are in it. Whereas all I saw before was a life of heartache, all I see for our future is joy. Joy and love."

Ari's words wrapped around Bo's heart. "You will never leave me. You will never get hurt. I will never let anything happen to you or our demonling."

"I will never leave you, not voluntarily, but the rest... I can't promise that, Bo. I will do everything in my power to stop it happening, but I won't promise."

"I'm going to have to keep you in bed, well satisfied so I know where you are at all times."

"Now that's a plan I can get on board with." Ari blushed.

"And we need to keep going to Perik's shop. I want to see you in just about everything, always."

"Then think on those, take me, and stop talking. I'm horny again now!" Ari growled.

Bo threw back his head and laughed. "Your wish is my command." He picked up speed again and started thrusting in deep, hard and long. It wasn't long before Ari cried out once again, his muscles locking tight around Bo and sending him over the edge with a cry.

Ari fidgeted with the hem on his tunic. It was stiffer than he'd become used to, preferring the loose, flowing style of the tep'rink. As for the leathers Bo had put him in… he loved the fact Bo kept staring at his ass as if mesmerized, but damn, he was hot in them.

Bo stood at attention beside Vict, fighting the urge to yet again stare at Ari's ass. Damn the plan to make sure his mate had a little more protection had seriously backfired on him. Ari looked stunning and delectable. If they got out of this in one piece, he was going to have fun pulling them off. Forcing his mind to pay attention, he scanned the room.

Vict was being deceptively relaxed and glared at Bo to calm down, nodding his head towards a seat. This would only work if they could give the impression they had no idea what was coming. When Bo finally sat, Vict looked imploringly at Caris to talk. These lot really needed to work on how to look normal. They looked like they were preparing to attend a Rite of Ulisian, where a fallen warrior's comrades chant the warrior's Journey to Jekar, the final spiritual home of all fallen demons.

Caris took the hint and started to talk to Ari about his pottery. "I can't believe how well you've taken to it."

"There's something about getting messy that I think calls to my inner child. I never got a chance to try things like that when I was little. I could never be messy, so having an excuse as an adult is perfect. Plus, I get to create things. There's something simple and honest about working with what the land gives you. If even one of my pieces brings a smile to even one person, then I'm happy.

Besides, the potters are great at dishing all the gossip on the comings and goings in the market."

"Like what?" Caris grinned at Ari's enthusiastic response.

"Well, did you know that Heli'sha was discovered sneaking out of the Silvers apprentice building?"

"Really? I bet her father wasn't happy."

"Nevermind her father, her mother grabbed the meat tenderizer and chased her down the street." Ari giggled.

Vict watched on, warmth in his chest at the two new additions to the palace. They'd brought a lightness no one had seen in a long time. Demons were a hard race, but seeing his son, seeing Bo'saverin tempered by these two remarkable men, made him think about opening up his borders more. If he was still king after all of this, he would talk to King Kastain on Landran. It was time to trade more freely. He would even consider reaching out to other carefully selected planets. Diversity would do the demon society some good.

Although he'd been expecting it, Ari still jumped when the doors slammed open. The Cobalts on guard were escorted in with blade tips to their throats.

"What is the meaning of this!" Bo's roar bounced around the room, the vaulted ceilings echoing his words in what seemed like a continuous loop, that slowly quieted down to silence.

Avric'ke, a Red guild officer, stepped forward, a smug, slimy grin on his face. "Vict'arin's presence is requested at a full guild tribunal. Now."

Bo's hand hovered over the hilt of his sword. "King Vict'arin." His words were deadly calm.

The Red just looked Vict up and down slowly before dismissing Bo's words with a shrug. Behind him, heavily armed Reds poured into the room, moving quickly to disarm Vict, Bo and Dasa.

"I'm to escort you to the meeting. Any attempts to escape will be met with force and retribution. Both to the two no-horns here and Princess Alenska."

"Where is my daughter?" Vict rose from his seat, his outward appearance totally calm.

"Held safely at the tribunal. You will see her when you get there." Avric'ke gestured towards the door.

Vict kept a careful hold on the box in his hand. "Lead on, then." He slowly walked towards the door, gently squeezing both Caris and Ari's shoulders as he walked by.

"The no-horns as well. We don't want them trying to get the Cobalts together, now do we? And before any of you think to try, your implants have been disabled."

The group left, surrounded by Reds. Walking through the palace corridors, there were gasps at the sight. Vict tried to send reassuring smiles, but word would no doubt quickly spread as to what was happening. What the average demon on Kenistal chose to do was the one unknown factor in all of this— they could make or break the outcome. Making sure his voice was loud enough to carry to those observing them, Vict asked, "Why the tribunal? What is the reason for it being called?"

Avric'ke laughed. "You're more of a fool than I thought if you don't know the answer to that. By the end of the tribunal, the Purples will no longer be in control of the throne. The Reds will. Kinesh will be king."

Vict heard the frantic whispers racing down the corridor as word spread. Damn fool Red hadn't even considered what would happen if all the demons found out. He caught glimpses of staff quietly activating commlinks. Another mistake the Reds had made. They'd only isolated his, Bo's and Dasa's implants.

Bo's gaze repeatedly connected with Cobalts as they passed them by. He shook his head every time. Now was not the time to attempt a rescue. This needed to play out. One way or another, the Kan'erkit would succeed or fall tonight at the tribunal. It was the only option left. The one that reduced the potential for bloodshed, anyway. None of them wanted a single demon hurt unless it was unavoidable.

CHAPTER THIRTY SIX

Typical. They'd chosen the arena to hold the tribunal. In their arrogance, and complete assurance that they would win, they'd allowed any demons around to take a seat. Word must be spreading fast as demons continued to pour in from all directions.

On the arena floor, the guild leaders were all seated. Kinesh stood holding court. Alenska was in-between two armed Reds, off to one side.

Vict was unceremoniously pushed into a chair facing the tribunal. He simply smoothed out his clothes and waited. Dasa and Bo flanked him, their mates on either side of them. He was pleased his queen had gone off to the mountains to visit relatives. At least whatever happened, one of them would survive the night. He rested his hands on the wooden box in his lap and waited. Perfectly calm.

Kinesh stood, a wicked glint in his eyes as he focused on Vict. "I've called this tribunal as it is time we discussed your ability to lead. An ability that has been seriously lacking of late. You've repeatedly rebuffed all attempts made by the Barin Alliance to consider becoming part of their network of planets. You've rebuffed offers of trade from powerful traders like the Aducians. You've harbored one of their citizens and refused to hand him back when asked, resulting in a violent confrontation that led to the deaths of Kenistalian citizens. Because of that, we have no doubt lost the ability to trade with them. It will take all my powers of persuasion to bring the deal back to the table. But I will do it. I will not see Kenistal suffer for your mistakes. Where is the Queen?" Kinesh frowned, only now noticing she was missing.

Kinesh kept looking at the camera that was broadcasting to the arena. It was painfully obvious he was putting on a performance for the crowd. "I hope you are ready to defend your actions. Although what defense there is for the way you have treated Kenistal lately is beyond me."

Ari was trembling. How Vict could be so calm was beyond him. He guessed it came with being King. A gentle impression of a hand resting on his back finally registered. Lo'jat's calm voice whispered into his ear. "Be calm, Little Demon, all will be well. This is as is meant to be."

"I'm scared," Ari admitted, his voice so quiet Lo'jat was the only one to hear.

"I know, but I would never let anything happen to you. Stay strong. We are here. All of us."

"How many of you are there?" Ari wondered.

"Thirty of us that you will be able to see, more who are here in whatever capacity they can be."

"So many?"

"Ah, Little Demon, we've been growing our ranks with the good and great from Kenistal's past. We will not let the rightful ruler fall. Have faith. Now listen."

Ari turned his focus back onto Kinesh who was still raving at Vict. "Face your charges!"

"Then list them. As for the Queen— she is in the mountains visiting family." Vict's quiet voice was in deep contrast to Kinesh.

"You are charged with destroying a trade agreement for the sake of a no-horn." Kinesh spat.

Vict looked around the arena. "Partially true. The trade agreement, brokered by you and the Red guild, was shrouded in secrecy. When you asked for a contingent to be granted permission to land, it was given. When we asked for a manifest, detailing who was onboard, we were given one. Only it wasn't correct, was it? The manifest listed members of the Trevon race only. Instead Trevons, Aducians and Loperis were on that cruiser. And one Aducian in particular. Agota Kelotian. Aridien's mother."

Vict let his gaze wander over the assembled demons. "Aridien, Commander Bo'saverin's mate. This young man went above and beyond when he was held prisoner by the Loperis to rescue Caris, Prince Dasalin's mate. He piloted a pod, despite being injured, bringing them both, and Veris, back to safety." Vict turned to Ari. "I'm sorry I have to talk about this."

Ari shook his head. "It's okay." He really didn't want everyone knowing his past, but anything that would help Vict was alright with him.

"Aridien was held a prisoner by Agota Kelotian, his own mother. From a young age, he was held in a suite of rooms with no interaction with family, no friends, just guards for company. The only time he was allowed out was when his mother wanted something from him. Do you know what that was? She paraded him in front of select individuals that held power and who were looking for trade deals. She presented him as though he was nothing more than an object to be controlled. She detailed how she'd trained him to be the perfect complement to any important dignitary. How he was trained to host parties, engage in polite conversation, keep guests at ease. Now all of that is bad, but do you know what's the worst thing? Now, remember this was her son… she arranged for him to be married to a senator from the Barin Alliance. He was expected to birth this senator's children, and in return she would get access to trading rights, trading rights I believe are the ones she wanted to barter with us about.

"All of this was arranged without his knowledge, without his input and certainly without his consent. He was shipped off in the middle of the night. Agota could not even be bothered to provide him with proper transportation. No doubt deciding she had spent too much on him already. His transport was attacked by the Loperis. He was taken and held captive. The Loperis planned, we presume, to sell him to the highest bidder at one of their sex slave auctions. Agota considered him property, he had no rights in her eyes. Her own son."

Vict looked around, taking note of how many demonlings of various ages were in the crowd. "Is that something you could ever imagine doing to your own child? To any child? Is that the sort of trader you want to do business with? If she can sell her own son out like that, what would she do to mere business partners? So, Kinesh, to answer your question... I didn't destroy the trade deal, but I offered Aridien sanctuary and asylum, yes. And yes, he is as you so 'nicely' put it, a no-horn. I would like to think any other demon in my place would have done the same. Since when are we a race that would see young ones treated in such a manner? What sort of planet, society have we become if we would stand behind someone who would sell their own child into sexual slavery?"

"You still destroyed the trade deal!" Kinesh blustered.

"No, I did not. All I said at that negotiating table was that any trade that important should be negotiated at the highest level. A trade deal between two planets should always be for the benefit of every citizen and not simply those who bartered the deal." Vict looked around the arena. "You know, I asked the Trevons why they brought Agota with them. For money and because they were asked to. That's all it came down to for them... credits."

Vict held Kinesh's gaze. "The talks broke down when Commander Bo'saverin raised a very pertinent question. How did Agota even know Aridien was here? He was captured by the Loperis, rescued himself, landing his pod on the Hek'rajin. None of that could have been predicted. So how was it she knew he was here? The answer? Someone on our planet, a demon told her. Now... you tell me, Kinesh, who do we know who has open access to talk to other planets? Who else apart from the royal family? You do, Kinesh. You and the most senior officers in the Red guild. I will ask you once only. Did you tell Agota her son was here?"

Kinesh smirked. "Not personally, but I know who did. They had my full support. No lowly no-horn was going to prevent me from trading, and letting her know he was here is what prompted the trade visit. She arranged for the Trevons to come and negotiate."

"That's what it all comes down to for you, isn't it? Credits and deals. You've never cared who gets hurt in the process."

"Why should I?" Kinesh sneered.

"What are the other charges?" Vict sat back. There was no point laboring the argument. Kinesh couldn't see he'd done anything wrong, so he could only hope his words had swayed some of the gathered demons.

"You've allowed security to get lax. Loperis have been found running around the streets, attacking people." Kinesh challenged Vict. "You cannot deny that."

"I do not deny Loperis have been running around the streets of Kenistal. How could I when they have attacked our citizens. Attempted to kidnap Aridien, to take him back to his mother. Again, how did they know he was here? Or were you talking about the Loperis that came on the cruiser you invited onto our planet?"

"If security is so lax, how was Commander Bo'saverin able to take out so many in that first attack, and reinforcements arrive within minutes? How were the Cobalts able to find Aridien, who'd run into a city he didn't know, in a matter of hours? If security is so lax, how did we find evidence in the tech department that all our communications, all our data was being rerouted to your terminal?"

Shocked gasps echoed around the arena. Kinesh himself looked stunned, his skin paling slightly, tail wrapping around his legs before he quickly held it in place.

"Lies! I have arranged no such thing," Kinesh blustered.

"We have proof. It's being held under lock and guard at the Cobalt offices." Bo calmly joined in the conversation.

"You're just his puppet." Kinesh sneered at Bo and Vict.

"There is little I can do to stop you thinking that." Bo stayed calm, refusing to be baited into losing his temper. "There is plenty of evidence. Not only that you have everything routed through your terminal, but which techs are responsible for it. We have evidence of every department and every guild system you have infiltrated. It's not just limited to the royal family and the Cobalts though, is it? You have a digital eye on *every* guild."

Many of the Guild Masters stared at Kinesh in abject anger. They were muttering to themselves.

"You lie!" Kinesh screamed.

"Again I am more than happy to provide the evidence."

"You're in the pay of the royal family!" Kinesh was getting himself worked up into quite a fury.

"Yes, I am," Bo answered. "But so is every guild represented here. Or, had you forgotten that the crown pays each and every guild a stipend from the taxes collected? That the crown pays for each Cobalt who guards them and the planet?"

"Talking of crowns—" Kinesh sneered, a blaze of triumph in his eyes— "We all know our histories talk about the Crown of Horns, about how only the rightful rulers of Kenistal can wear it. If you are the true king, then you should be wearing that crown. But you can't wear it, can you? You don't have it. You've never had it. You can't be our rightful ruler without it."

One of the Guild Masters, Vict wasn't sure who, spoke up. "But you don't have it either, Kinesh. You want to take the throne from Vict'arin, you want the Reds to be the new royal family, that's what all this is about tonight. If Vict'arin cannot rule without the crown, then neither can you."

"Can I not?" Kinesh gestured around the arena. "By rights, there is no one single demon here who could hold the throne. The Crown of Horns has been lost for generations. No single demon, family or guild holds the right to the throne. Therefore, I think it should be done by ballot. I think I, and a few select others, should be put forward as alternatives to Vict'arin ruling. I'm sure we can all agree, however, that I am the best choice."

There were murmurings amongst the crowd. Ari couldn't tell if they were friendly or not. Lo'jat's hand soothed his hair, trying to provide reassurance. Ari leaned into the touch ever so slightly, taking what was on offer. As much as he wanted Bo for comfort, he needed to keep an eye on what was happening around them.

"You know," Vict began calmly. As he spoke, his hands were working at the clasps on the box in his lap. "There is much we can remember and learn from when studying our histories. I don't simply mean the Crown of Horns, I mean the Guardians, the Dawn of the Long Blades, the betrayal that led to one of the worst events in our history. Is this what we have come down to? Repeating our past mistakes? Refusing to learn from the errors of our forbearers? If the majority of our people want a different king, then they shall have one. But, there is just one thing…" Vict withdrew the Crown of Horns, looking at it for a moment, and placed it on his head, the crown sitting snugly between his horns.

The arena fell to a complete silence. Ari shuddered at the eerie atmosphere. It was as though every demon was focused on the crown nestled between Vict's horns. Even Kinesh was rendered dumb in the face of its appearance. Then the murmurs started as slowly the crowd recovered their wits. The murmurs steadily got louder until the entire arena buzzed with conversation. The assembled Guild Masters stared in complete astonishment at Vict, who maintained his seat calmly.

"That's not possible." Kinesh reached out as though to grab the crown from Vict's head. A deathly stare from Bo stopped him. "I would have known if you were in possession of the Crown."

"How would you have known, Kinesh? It was kept secret for a reason." Vict crossed one leg over the other, his tail resting comfortably on top.

"She would have told me!" Kinesh's words once again silenced the Guild Masters, although the crowd still spoke in whispers.

"I think I need to find out who this woman is. Is she the same demon who told you about the weapon in my throne? Who has been funneling information to you? Who allowed you to know what was going on with the royal family? Just who has betrayed me, betrayed my family, betrayed our people?"

Bo scanned the crowd before returning to the Guild Masters. It was obvious few were there completely voluntarily, especially considering Perik's words. Many looked at Vict with renewed respect. Yet, Bo found it a sad testament to how far their society had fallen that it would take the appearance of the Crown of Horns to restore faith in their king.

Kinesh looked about wildly, searching for someone to come to his aid. When none of his allies in this venture stepped forward, he did the only thing he could. He named the traitor. "It was Alenska! She told me the weapon was in the throne. She told me who to talk to gain access to the tech center. It was Alenska who contacted the Aducians. She was in contact with them from the moment we knew of Aridien's existence. They offered a reward for the return of the boy. They offered to help us, Alenska and I, cause chaos on the streets of Kenistal. They suggested we destabilize our society so much that I could sweep in at the last minute and restore order."

Alenska finally broke free from her stupor. "You lie!" She grabbed the sword of the Red stood next to her, surprising him, and charged towards Kinesh. Several Reds made to intercept her, yet seemed reluctant to actually engage her in battle. As they formed a ring around Kinesh, she struck two down, uncaring whether they were killing blows or not. Some of the Reds who had been assembled behind her came to her aid. Less than a minute after she'd launched her attack on Kinesh, Bo was looking wildly around trying to find a weapon. Nothing could have surprised him more than a ghostly sword that suddenly appeared hovering in front of him.

"Use it wisely, young demon," Drel'nic ordered.

With a swift nod, Bo charged into the fray, his scales at max.

Ari grasped for something to hold on to. As before, he was in awe of the way Bo fought, his moves highlighted by the large and ghostly sword he wielded. He watched Red after Red back away from Bo, refusing to engage him, leaving either Kinesh or Alenska to their own fates. No one else in the arena moved, it was as if they had been rendered unable to react. "Dasa, can we do something?" Ari begged.

"I have no sword, and, as much as I deplore her actions, have always worried she has taken up with the wrong people, she is my sister. I cannot bring myself to engage her in a battle that may well be to the death. Forgive me?" Dasa pleaded with Ari.

Ari nodded, unable to speak. When Bo dodged a weapon aimed at his heart, Ari cried out. More and more Reds were pouring into the arena. Suddenly, scores of heavily armed Cobalts appeared from another entrance. They didn't stop until they were by their Commander's side.

"You need help here, Commander?" One of the officers grinned. "How unlike you to get yourself in a bit of bother," he drawled sarcastically.

"You want on farm rotation after this, Jofrin?" Bo drawled, but nodded his thanks to the young demon.

"Eh, it might be worth it for a spell after all this action of late."

"Always the same, trying to shirk your responsibilities again." Bo rolled his eyes, even as he dodged a spear of all things. "What the frek? Who brought a spear?" he yelled out, not really expecting an answer.

Ari gaped as Bo continued to banter with the warriors at his side. Despite their chatter, they were quick in subduing the assembled Reds, both sides of them proving no match for the might of the Cobalts. Less than five minutes after Alenska started on her attack, all was quiet. The Reds were bound and forced to kneel. Alenska was pushed forward by Bo, a sword at her back. When she didn't immediately drop to her knees in front of her father, Bo pushed down on her shoulder.

Vict fought his emotions. Rage battled with sadness. Grief with anger. "You did this?" His words were sharp as he stared down his daughter. "You are responsible for Agota and the Aducians coming to our planet, for the Loperis, for everything? You are the traitor?"

"No, father, that was all Kinesh," she wheedled.

Vict shook his head at his daughter's antics. His soul hurt with how he had failed to raise her in the right way. "Really? Then who told him about the weapon I keep in the throne? Who told him who Aridien's mother was? You have sat in on most of the meetings I held. In fact, the only thing Kinesh doesn't know is about the Crown. That was the meeting where Aridien asked everyone to leave."

"No, he asked me and mother to leave. He allowed Dasa to be there." Alenska spat towards her brother.

"Dasa is a friend, Bo my mate. I wanted them there." Ari found the strength to stand up to her. He was fed up with being treated like he didn't warrant consideration, like he was nothing more than an inconvenience. "You had no need to be there. You are *nothing* to me. I don't owe you any explanation as to what happens in my life, what happens to me. The fact you think you have the right to know these things shows to me, a stranger to your planet, just how arrogant you have become. It is nobody's right to know everything about anyone. Not even a citizen about their king."

"Well put, Aridien." Vict's lips twitched as he smiled at Ari. "Alenska, I have failed you. Failed to show you the difference between right from wrong, of respect for our people, of compassion. I have failed to maintain a strong enough hand when dealing with you. That ends now."

Dasa stopped his father talking. "No. You did not fail in raising your demonlings. I have not turned out the way Alenska has, I have followed your path. I sought to be like you— kind, just and honorable. The only failing in this family is Alenska's."

"Thank you, son." Vict turned back to his daughter. "You will be forced to work, under guard, where I see fit. You are to be stripped of your rights as a princess. You will still be a member of this family, but you will hold no power over a single demon." Vict let out a bone-weary sigh. "I should put you to trial until the people of Kenistal can decide your fate, yet I cannot ask them to do this for me. I cannot put them in the position where they have to order this." Vict closed his eyes briefly, pulling on his years of regal life, refusing to let his emotions out. "You will be de-horned. You will become the very thing you despise the most, a no-horn. I cannot help but feel it is a fitting punishment. Besides, it's the fate that awaits all traitors. I will *not* make an exception purely because you are my daughter."

"No!" Alenska screamed, collapsing to the floor.

Kinesh, now under heavy armed guard, found his bravado. "How do we know the crown isn't a forgery? That you had it struck and shaped to support your false claim?"

Vict stared in astonishment. "Just because that is something you would do, does not mean we would all behave in such a manner."

"Yet you have no way to disprove my allegations. You cannot prove the crown is real." Kinesh smirked, now sure in the belief he once again had the upper hand.

"I cannot prove it is real, no. No one alive could," Vict confirmed.

Kinesh pumped his bound wrists in the air, positive his plans were finally coming to fruition as once again the more skeptical of the Guild Masters looked upon Vict and his family with unease.

As soon as Vict started to speak, a quiet voice stopped him.

"Let me deal with this, King Vict'arin." Drel'nic stepped forward, allowing himself to become corporeal and visible to all. Seconds later, every Guardian in attendance who possessed the ability followed suit.

"King Vict'arin may not be able to attest to and prove the legitimacy of the Crown of Horns, but I assure you, *I can.*" The presence of so many Guardians caused the air to swirl eerily about them. A soft mist dancing around their feet swirled slowly upwards before settling and seeping outwards towards the gathered Guild Masters.

"I am Drel'nic, one of the Guardians of the ruins. One of your forbearers. It is we, as is our right, who allowed the Crown of Horns to be revealed to King Vict'arin. Kenistal has become mired in the same sense of self-importance, greed and personal advancement at the cost of all, that came close to destroying our way of life before. We are in full support of King Vict'arin as the rightful ruler. None should ever doubt he is the true king."

Drel'nic turned his attention to Kinesh. "Did you honestly think we would support the claim of someone who would treat the throne with such contempt? Someone who would attack innocents? Someone who would work against the very people they insist they are wanting to serve? Tell me, Guild Master Kinesh, what do you expect to do if you take the throne?"

When Kinesh didn't answer, another Guardian stepped forward, this one far more imposing than Drel'nic. "My fellow Guardian asked you a question. Do not attempt to play games with us. Do not attempt to lie. Answer what we have asked, or we can compel you to."

Kinesh studied one Guardian after another, each one more imposing than the last. He kept his mouth shut. Nothing he said could work out well where these… apparitions were considered.

Tolik'ek, the Guardian who had spoken, looked briefly at Kinesh before slowly stepping out from the Guardian ranks. He slowly walked around the arena. He stopped in front of a young Red family. He gazed at them intently. "Lo'jat, could you come here please?"

Lo'jat separated from the group and jogged over to join him. "Tolik'ek?" He cocked his head to one side, looking at the young demonling in the demoness' arms. "Ahh, I see." He dropped down into a crouch. "Lady demon, may I ask to hold your demonling? Have no fear, no harm will come to him."

The demoness shared a look with her mate before slowly holding out her son with trembling hands. Lo'jat immediately held the demonling to his chest and began crooning a lullaby. Even the older demons around the family seemed to relax into their seats, as though any lingering aggression had seeped out of them into the atmosphere. Lo'jat let his hands glide over the air above the demonling. "Ah ha, here we are." He concentrated, sending his healing power into the little one.

"Just enough, Lo'jat, remember, not too much. We can't disobey the rules, only skirt them." Tolik'ek warned.

"It's done." Lo'jat gently kissed the little demonling on the forehead, handed him back to his mother and swiftly returned to the other Guardians.

Tolik'ek gently brushed the fine downy hair on the demonling's head. "He had a small heart problem. There was a valve not quite pumping properly. It wouldn't have been picked up at a normal scan. Without detection, it would have been deadly. We can't cure him completely. We may be Guardians, but we are still bound by rules. Lo'jat has done enough to keep him healthy for years, but I would see the medics and tell them what happened. He should only need the most minor of procedures now."

The demoness couldn't speak for tears streaming down her face. The demonling's father bowed deeply to Tolik'ek. "Thank you, both of you. We tried for years and couldn't have our own family. We'd almost given up hope before this one appeared. If we had lost him…"

"You won't lose him. He will lead a very long, very happy life. I promise you that." With a lingering and friendly smile, Tolik'ek continued his walk around the arena.

Once done, he rejoined the other Guardians. When he spoke, his voice carried to everyone there, without the need for vids. "I have studied all those gathered here. I don't mean those on the arena floor, I mean you in the seats. You are the demons who have always been badly affected by the power games of the leaders of our world. I would ask you this. Who do you want to lead you?"

"King Vict'arin!" came the crowd's roar.

"Who will look after your needs?"

"King Vict'arin!"

"Who is always there for you, and if he isn't, then his son is?"

"King Vict'arin!"

"Who should rule Kenistal?"

"King Vict'arin. Vict! Vict! Vict!" The crowd took up the chant as Tolik'ek walked back to the assembled Guild Masters.

"I think you have you answer. The Crown of Horns is real. There are historians on Kenistal who can confirm the legitimacy of the crown. If you need to."

"No! Vict is our king! Vict is our true ruler! King Vict'arin forever!"

Caris gestured for Vict to stand. "Talk to them."

Vict lifted his hands, gesturing for the gathered demons to settle. It took a few minutes, but eventually there was enough quiet for him to talk. "Thank you, demons of Kenistal. I am sorry things have come down to this. It is my failing and my failing alone that I have let the guilds, let certain members of certain guilds, believe they have the right to change the way things are on our world. We don't have a perfect system, no planet does. But, I have always tried to lead you with wisdom and compassion. I have never believed one guild is better than another, and I never will."

Vict let his gaze travel from one group to the next. "I ask this of all of you. My door has always been open to anyone, so has Dasa's and so has Bo'saverin's. But now I must implore you to use them if you have any issues. We cannot fix them if we don't know about them. As far as an Alliance goes, we will not be joining with the Barin."

Caris and Ari both looked towards the Reds, seeing the serious discontent on their faces.

"They are not a good fit for us," Vict continued, ignoring the glares from various quarters. "Kenistal is open to trade with any world who proves themselves to have honor, respect for others and proves themselves to be trustworthy. There may indeed come a time in the future we will be open to trade with the Trevon and Aducians, but they certainly have a lot to make up for before I will allow any trade to be considered. I will also be discussing an alliance of sorts with the Landrans. I know they are not as technologically advanced as we are, but do not let that fool you into thinking they have nothing to offer us. They do. I will be discussing all manner of deals with them. If there is anything you have, whatever guild you are from, that you think may benefit them, then speak to your Guild Master."

Caris coughed pointedly to gain Vict's attention. Vict leaned down to hear Caris talk quietly. "Send them to me. I know what Landran needs and many of them may be apprehensive about going to their Guild Masters, especially after today. I am used to dealing with negotiations. Not trade, but I'm sure Ari can help me out." Caris winked at Ari.

Ari grinned. "I would love to help out. It's justice that the skills Agota taught me can still be used, just not how she intended."

Even a couple of the Guardians chuckled.

Vict looked between his two new sons. "I like the idea. As long as both of you are sure you don't mind taking this role on?"

Both Caris and Ari quickly assured him they were fine. They spoke quietly for a few minutes, going over some of the details before Caris addressed the gathered demons. "If you don't want to discuss trade with your Guild Master, you can come to Aridien or I directly. We may be mated, or about to be mated to those two…" He waved vaguely behind him causing a slight chuckle to run through the crowd— "but we are not demons, we are not of your political system and we will listen to each proposal fairly. We will look at a proposal on its merits only and if we say no, or not right now, we will give you a reason why. It might be that your citrus is not sour enough, or your sugar not refined enough. There could be many reasons. If you would still like to trade with Landran, then we would look at ways in helping you to adapt what you have to what they need."

Caris smiled at the volume of interested faces. "What's more, if there are certain items you want that you know Landran may have, then let us know. We can request that as trade. This won't be solely about making credits. This will be about fostering good relations with our neighbors and entering into a mutually beneficial arrangement. So I ask you all to think about it and get back to us. You don't need to rush, there is no deadline on this. You may not be ready now, but in six months you could be raring to go. If that is the case, our doors will still be open then. This is not a one-time only offer or deal. Any questions, then please, come and see us."

Caris and Ari both returned to their seats. Vict once again looked out over his people. "I still don't know how we ended up where we are. There will be a lot of thinking, a lot of talking and yes, some changes. How many, I don't know. But I thank you for having faith in me, for trusting me to do what is right for you all. Now, unless anyone has immediate questions, I must ask that I be given leave to fully deal with my daughter. She will not go unpunished for her part in this, I promise you. She will meet a traitor's fate and be de-horned. No conspirator will escape justice for their part in this treachery. They will face a full trial. The trials will be public and all will be welcomed to attend. Those selected to serve on the judicary panel will be given the choice of two punishments: death or de-horning. The panel will be tasked with deciding each conspirator's fate. I ask you all to return to your homes. The Cobalts will continue to patrol the streets as they are now, there will still be curfews in place for the next couple of days, but as things ease, so too will the curfews. I ask you, the honest, hardworking demons of our world, to bear with us as we move on from today's events."

Vict took another two steps forward, so he was alone with no guards and went down on bended knee, before spreading his arms wide, palms down in supplication, his forehead resting on the arena floor. No king had ever bowed so deeply to anyone else, certainly not the demons of the world. Those present at the arena knew it would be an image that would stay with them forever.

CHAPTER THIRTY SEVEN

They'd all returned to the palace with little incident, the Guardians providing a slightly ghostly guard of honor as they walked back through the streets to the palace. The whispers surrounding them carried on the wind, and snippets of gossip left them all smiling. They saw neighbors stood on porches talking, people walking home in the same direction from the arena discussing the night's events. If this night did anything, Vict hoped it brought everyone closer together. They had taken a few minutes on the steps of the palace to thank the Guardians. Ari especially lingering in his goodbyes. If it wasn't for them… Vict shuddered at the thought. He forced his attention back to the problem on hand. Vict studied his daughter. "Why?"

Alenska stayed sullenly silent.

"I thought you might be just a little bit apologetic, a little bit contrite over your actions. I can see that is not the case. I'd hoped a quick stint working in the guilds would be enough. I know now it won't. I can only see one course left to me. As well as suffering the fate of being de-horned, you are hereby assigned to the KS Talike. There you will serve out a two year posting as a crew member. Your commander will have full power over you, including the ability to punish you as he sees fit. You are not to use your royal status for anything. Any attempts to do so, any attempts to sway a single member of the crew to your side, will be met with the severest of consequences. If such events happen, you will be confined to the brig and escorted to a neutral planet under armed guard. You will be fully charged with treason in your absense and I will issue the order for banishment. You will not be allowed to return. If, however, you serve your time on the Talike, you will return to Kenistal and face a trial to determine if our society desires to lay out further punishment.

You will be de-horned before you leave, like the traitor you are. There will be no special treatment for you. Sending you away is not for your benefit, but for my citizens. I want to spare them the pain of putting someone from the royal family to death."

Vict forced his emotions back. "I will not have anyone think they are above the law. It breaks my heart to do this to my own daughter, but until you have seen the error of your ways, until you fully understand the chain of events you set in motion with your act of rebellion, you will not be a member of this family. In essence, you started a process that could have killed our entire family. I *cannot* and *will not* take such action lightly."

When Alenska finally went to talk, Vict slashed his hand through the air. "Enough. You've had your chance to attempt to justify your actions. To attempt to atone for all you set in motion. You failed. Now you've found out the full impact of your actions on your own life, you want to talk. No. I won't hear it. You are only doing it now to try to lessen what I have ordered. Enough, Alenska. Simply enough. I'm tired of cleaning up after your messes. You've gone way, way too far this time. You will learn, one way or another, a dose of humility. I hope, if and when you return, that you will return as the daughter I once knew. As a demon who has learned her lessons and is prepared to take any further punishment decreed."

Vict turned to the Cobalt officers waiting patiently at the doors. "Have her de-horned, then take her to the Talike and Commander Emlinka. She is to have full authority over my daughter." Vict handed over a comm pad. "Pass this on to Commander Emlinka, it has a full list of my instructions, but she knows what to expect."

"Yes, Your Majesty." The officers bowed, two stepping up and grabbing one of Alenska's arms each, walking her out of the room as more Cobalts fell in around them.

When Alenska finally realized this was actually happening, she started to scream. Vict was sure she was cursing him and everyone else who'd done this to her, but her voice was so high and warped with anger, he couldn't understand it. When the door finally shut behind them, he slumped into his chair, his hand hanging, his tail listless as it lay along the chair-leg.

Everyone studied Vict, unsure what they could say or do that would help him come to terms with just how badly his daughter had betrayed him. Ari walked over to one of the guards, pulled on his arms until the guard leaned down, and whispered in his ear. The guard's mouth twitched and he nodded disappearing out the door.

Ari went back and sat on Bo's lap, facing forward. He let his legs swing back and forth while he waited for the guard to return. He ignored the inquisitive looks and just kept up a soft smile as he stroked his belly. "You know, I've been wondering…" His voice caught everyone's attention as it broke the silence. "Will this one—" he patted his stomach— "be a proper demon? I mean, will they have horns and a tail? Will they have the scales? Be big like Bo, or small like me? Have my coloring or his?"

Dasa, Bo and Caris all looked at each other. "I truly have no idea," Bo finally admitted. "As long as the babe is healthy, I do not mind what he or she looks like. We could have a little Ari with a tail, we could have a demon with no horns and who never changes their color. It honestly will not matter to me. I will love them the same no matter what. Although secretly, I'm holding out for them looking like you. How could I not want my demonlings to look as gorgeous as…" Bo pursed his lips. "Huh, what are they going to call you?"

Ari stopped swinging his legs. "Um, I had to call *him* father, I won't use that. I quite like pa. it's got a comforting ring to it. Maybe papa, and then pa when they get older."

Bo nuzzled his neck. "It suits you."

"What about you?" Ari tilted his head giving Bo more access.

"Demons always use father. Most older demonlings use it as well, but the younger demonlings tend to use dada, or da. Very similar to your papa really."

"That would make us pa and da then," Ari mused.

"I like it." Bo nibbled at Ari's neck, earning him an admonishment to behave.

The guard returned bearing a massive tray, another two guards behind him. Placing everything down on the long table to one side, they bowed and retreated. Ari jumped up with a big grin. He walked over to Vict and gently took his hand. When Vict's gaze locked with his, Ari's heart hurt at the haunted sadness in his eyes. He pulled, not able to move Vict, but hoping he would get the hint.

Vict slowly rose, letting Ari drag him to the table. He took a seat when Ari just stood there pointing. His lips fought the instinctual twitch at being bossed about by the little demon. Ari stared everyone else in the room down until they all joined Vict at the table. He went to lift the lids of the tray and frowned. Using Vict's leg as a support, he hoisted himself up onto the bench and reached over the table, his glare not enough to suppress the quiet laughter. He lifted the lids with a flourish.

Vict's eyes widened. "Is that Kerin pie? And jodrix?"

"Caris and I tried the jodrix ale, with Deek and Yav. The way it smoked in the goblet, the swirling mix of greens and yellows fascinated me. I just thought, what better way is there to cheer up than kerin pie?"

Vict frowned and beckoned one of the guards over. "Can you dispatch someone to the kitchen and ask for a falblink pie and some grendrix? Thank you, oh and can you have them delivered to Commander Dea'saverin's room in the med wing? We're moving there."

"Yes, Your Majesty. Would you like me to move these trays as well?"

"Yes, thank you." Vict stood, taking Ari's hand, chuckling when Ari stayed standing on the bench seat so he was at Vict's eye level. "Little Demon, I can't thank you enough. This is exactly what I needed tonight."

"Then why are you having it packed up?" Ari bit his lip.

"Because we're moving to Dea's room. I want to be surrounded by the family I have left tonight and that includes him. I happen to know Mac is still there as well."

Caris and Ari exchanged wide grins.

"But…" Vict cupped Ari's chin. "There will be no Kerin and no jodrix for you. You can't have alcohol, remember."

Ari's face fell. "But I love those two."

"Which is why I've asked the kitchen for falblink and grendrix. They are pretty close to the other two, but with no alcohol. That means you and our littlest demon there can enjoy things just as much as we can, and your poor matc won't have a worry attack about anything happening."

Ari looked over his shoulder to see Bo nodding sagely. He giggled, turning back to Vict. "He's going to be a pest, isn't he?"

"Oh, Aridien, you have no idea. Now, come on, let's go and see our wounded." He gently lifted Ari and settled him on the ground, linking Ari's arm through his. They walked all the way to the med wing, Vict leaning down to talk to Ari as he chatted on animatedly about what new items Perik had told him were in stock.

Behind them, Dasa and Bo tried to block their ears— they really didn't want to hear Vict's opinion on it. Caris rolled his eyes and linked arms with Ari, joining in the discussion.

Dea and Mac were quietly talking. The vid of everything that had happened at the arena had been sent from datapad to datapad. Soon enough, everyone on Kenistal would see it. Even the more remote villages had at least one datapad, provided by the royal family, so that they could always contact the city if needed. The last thing either expected was for Vict and everyone else to come trooping into their room.

When Dea tried to sit up more fully, Vict waved him away. Bo walked up to the bed and hugged his brother, hard. "I'm sorry I couldn't be here earlier."

"Shut up." Dea smacked Bo on the horns. "I know everything that happened." At Bo's questioning look, Dea pointed to the Kenistal News Network playing on the vid screen in their room. All of them groaned. "Oh, come on, did you really think no one would get hold of the vids? I have to say you all have style, flair and… something, anyway." Dea shrugged.

Caris and Ari were both hugging Mac, chatting away animatedly about what had happened. Dea watched them inquisitively. "I know I've met him briefly when they rescued themselves, but I do believe that's my new brother over there."

"Ah, yeah, it, umm, is," Bo mumbled. He wouldn't give Ari up for anything, but he really hoped Dea got on well with him.

"Well, bring him over here. I want to get to know him properly," Dea ordered.

"Oh, this is going to be fun." Vict grabbed a large, comfortable seat and dragged it across the room, uncaring at the squeaks it made. When he looked up, everyone was staring at him. "What? I couldn't be bothered to pick it up."

Dasa just shook his head.

"Ari?" Bo called out. "Will you come over here?"

Ari turned, sudden shyness making his feet feel like they were encased in stone. He looked around, as if there was something that would magically hide him. Realizing there was nothing, his shoulders slumped and he walked over, slightly resigned. Reaching out, he grabbed Bo's hand and held on tight.

"Dea, you've already met Ari, but let me introduce him again. This is Ari… my mate and the man who's carrying my demonling."

Ari wanted to melt into the ground.

Dea, having just taken a sip of water, started to choke.

Ari scowled at Bo, climbed onto the chair beside the bed and started trying to whack Dea on the back. Vict, taking pity on him, waved him away and slapped Dea, helping him clear his airways.

"Frek, Bo, warn a demon next time you want to say something like that." Dea continued to splutter, ignoring the group of guards bringing several large trays into the room. He frowned at his goblet. "If you just said what I think you said, I think I'm going to need something a frek of a lot stronger than water."

Dasa was already pouring out jodrix and passing them around. The medic, who'd stepped in to see what the commotion was about, went to say something, but with the weight of combined glares from everyone in the room, he beat a hasty retreat, leaving them to it.

Dea grabbed the jodrix and downed it in one, holding out the empty goblet for another one. "You want to repeat that again."

Bo was still shaking with laughter. Ari tried to hit him in the stomach, but Bo didn't even feel it. Ari scowled and walked over to Dea. "I'm Ari. I agreed to be mated to your brother, although I'm starting to change my mind—" Ari glared again— "and the bombshell he dropped on you is correct. I'm from a species where some men are capable of carrying young. I'm one of them. We didn't know it was going to happen, but yes, Bo and I are expecting a little demonling." Ari blushed so vividly his entire face was flushed green.

"I'm going to be an uncle? Bo's going to be a, a, father?"

Ari nodded slowly.

"Oh, frek me." Dea downed his second goblet of jodrix. Once done, he carefully opened his arms. "Welcome to the family, Aridien."

Ari's face lit up with a smile and he shifted onto the bed so he could hug Dea.

Bo turned as the door opened to reveal Commander Urias. He was all smiles as he saw everyone until his gaze settled on Dea, his arms wrapped around someone. Bo watched as his skin rippled and Urias fought for control. His gaze sought out Dasa's and he subtly pointed to Urias. Dasa's gaze danced back and forth between Urias and Dea, who was still hugging Ari and whispering in his ear.

Urias went to turn away and walk out, but Vict stopped him. "Ah, Commander Urias, good to see you. I've been meaning to thank you for the part you played in rescuing Ari here. We are forever in your debt."

"That's Ari?" Urias asked.

Ari turned around and spied Urias. He jumped down off the bed and walked over to Urias, pulling on his tunic until the demon crouched down so he was at Ari's height. Ari flung his arms around Urias. "Thank you to you and your men. I was so scared she was going to take me back. Then Dea came, and you came, and you all rescued me. I didn't think anyone other than Bo would."

Urias gently patted Ari on the back, making sure to use the same strength as he used with his baby sisters. "You are most welcome, Little Demon."

Bo beckoned Ari over. As soon as he was in range, he hauled him into his lap and settled him there. "Some of us are getting thirsty over here, My Liege," Bo taunted at Dasa.

"Oh, don't you start that again or you'll be wearing your drink." Dasa placed a tray on the windowsill beside Bo, leaving Bo's drink there while he handed Ari his drink. "Try this. That's the falblink my father ordered for you."

Ari stared at the drink; it was smoking just the way the jodrix did. But this time, his drink was an ice blue that seemed to almost glitter in the light. He took a tentative sip. "Oh… oh! This is delicious." He happily sipped away, smiling at Vict over the rim of his goblet.

Bo smiled, sipping his own ale, pleased to see Ari find something else he liked. He could only hope the pie would be that much of a success.

Ari handed his goblet to Bo and snuggled in, happily dozing as conversation swarmed around him. It wasn't until later when a whispered argument woke him, that he realized he'd actually been asleep. Looking around at the empty goblets and jugs, he must have slept through quite the party. Bo was asleep, but still with his arms around him. Vict was crashed out on one sofa, Dasa and Caris on another. The room was fairly dark and he could see that Mac was also out cold. Which meant… Dea.

Dea scowled at the most annoying, frustrating, hard-headed, tail-twisted demon he'd ever encountered. "I'm telling you, you should have left me." He hissed, trying to keep his voice down so as not to wake anyone.

"Frek, Dea, you really think I would have just left you? He was going to kill you, for frek's sake."

"I thought that's what you wanted, Uri? Me out of your life for good?"

"Not if it meant you dying, you krexjin."

Ari could hear the hurt radiating out of both demons.

"Oh, come on, we both know you never wanted to see me again, in any way other than as Commanders in the fleet." Dea must have shifted on the bed because he suddenly cried out in pain.

"Damn it, you stubborn fool, would you just ask when you want help? Why can you never just ask!" Uri helped Dea sit up a little.

"Yeah, because the last time I asked for anything went down so well," Dea drawled.

"That is not the same and you know it. Frek, Dea, I wanted to make it work, make us work, but I just can't do that."

"I get that, I do, but you couldn't expect me not to ask," Dea hissed.

Ari had no idea if that was from pain or anger. Peeking again, he saw Uri reach out to grab Dea's hand.

Dea went to pull away.

"Don't. Please? Just let me have this. Let us have this. I was scared, D, I thought I'd lost you. The heart that was beginning to heal broke all over again when I watched that Red attack you."

"Who's fault is that? *You* walked away, Uri, not me," Dea mumbled.

"I didn't *want* to!" Uri started to pace. "We can't do this, not now."

"We need to have this out, Uri, once and for all." Dea's fist curled into the blanket over his legs.

"We do. Just give me some time to get my head straight." Uri walked to the door before pausing and walking back. He leaned down and gently kissed Dea on the lips. "I'll always love you, Dea." Without looking back, Uri walked out the door.

"You can stop pretending you're asleep now, Little Brother." Dea looked straight at Ari.

"I'm sorry, I didn't mean to listen in." Ari ducked his head.

"No, it's fine, it's our fault. We just never seem to be able to stay in the same room as each other and not argue."

"I don't know much about relationships, but if you ever want to talk, I'll be here for you." Ari reached out and grasped Dea's hand.

"Thank you. Now get some more sleep before I have anyone else in my life angry at me." Dea slid down the bed himself, getting comfy and switching off the light.

"Night, Dea."

"Night, Ari. I'm glad you chose Bo. He couldn't have asked for a better man."

Before Ari could think of a response, soft snores came from Dea's bed. He snuggled in deeper to Bo and let sleep claim him once again.

The sensation of being carried woke Ari. "W-what?"

"Go back to sleep, Tiko. I'm taking you back to our room."

Bo's steady gait was already lulling Ari back to sleep. "Okay. I love you, Bo."

"I love you too, Aridien Kelotian."

"That's not my name. I'm Aridien Hevalis now." Ari's voice was full of pride.

"You are indeed. I love you with all my heart, Aridien Hevalis."

"Love y…" Ari's words stuttered to a stop as the gentle rocking motion sent him straight back to sleep.

"I love you too, Little Hevalis, whatever you end up being."

CAST LIST

KENISTAL DEMONS

Vict'arin Kan'erkit, King

Meklin Kan'erkit, Queen

Dasalin Kan'erkit, Prince

Alenska Kan'erkit, Princess, Dasa's sister

Bo'saverin Hevalis, Dasa's personal bodyguard and friend

Mac'likrit, Warrior, Caris' Personl Bodyguard

Dea'saverin Hevalis, Commander of the KS Hek'rajin, brother of Bo

Veris Lagonis

Ger'astin, guard

 Fre'lix, guard

Kery'alin, Mac's wife

Welin, Pau'tra, Loas'kin, Mac and Kery'alin's demonlings

Commander Tek'grik, head of Kenistals comms hub

Kreklin, captain in the Cobalt Guards

Alk'fin, young demonling rescued by Caris in street

Guild Master Vonk'ram, silver guild

Master Rekmajin, silver guild officer

Warrior Hek'prit, Cobalt, palace guard

Cari'alin, little demonling named after Caris

Pek'rajin, guard on Caris' detail

Caradeicus, guard on Caris' detail

Arak'leik, guard on Caris' detail

Drey'malik, guard on Caris' detail

Ber'ik, guard on Caris' detail

Zev'ar, guard on Caris' detail

Commander Ola'kis, Commander of the KS Zavrinn

Ki'tak, apprentice

Sub Commander Wildarin – KS Hek'rajin

Le'varkin, Demons on board the Loperis ship

Demoness Geristania, seen as the protector of all demons in space

Guild Master Kinesh, red guild leader

Officer Frega, shield tech/engineer

Officer Sand'el, engineering

Urias, Commander KS Zerkin

Jari'nik

Opink'ik, Op'ik, tinker, Grey demon

Kek'tobrin, Cobalt, warrior

Ep'robal, Cobalt, warrior

Amkdren, Demon, doctor

Leyok, One of King Vict'arin's assistants

Yavek, Yav, Cobalt, warrior

Deek'in, Deek, Cobalt, warrior

Ulkrit, cook, owns a restaurant

Oz'ki, potter

Perik, shop owner

Ir'eki, Head potter

Uxalik, previous king

Le'brix, first Purple King

Geriok Hevalis, Bo's ancestor

Drel'nic, Guardian

Lo'jat, Guardian

Jof'ni, Cobalt commanders during the reign of King Uxalik

Ank'tok, second to Bo'saverin

Elik, doctor

Ubrix, advisor

Dof'vik, servant

Helic, servant

Adrik, previous king

Bekrit, Cobalt, warrior

Wol'ir, Cobalt, officer

Rog'vec, Cobalt, officer

Jeek'sin, Cobalt, sub-commander

Fre'dint, Cobalt, warrior

Osk'it, Cobalt, warrior

Vac'lin, head of tech dept.

Fred'ikel, assistant to Vict'arin

Gil'per, professor of astromechanics

Broc'tak, space demon, navigator, Hek'rajin

Vec'as, medic

Drenk'alic, Guild Master, orange guild

Meriok, royal cousin

Ekris'tak, royal cousin

Larelk, royal cousin

Avric'ke, Red Guild, officer

Jofrin, Cobalt, officer

Tolik'ek, Guardian

Emlinka, Commander of the KS Talike

OTHERS

Caris Dealyn, the Terran ambassador to Kenistal,

Aridien Kelotian, Aducian from the Cherion sector

Ambassador Tremont, previous alliance ambassador to Kenistal

King Adran, ancient ruler of Landran, King when Scottish settlers took refuge

Ilician, Bell's brother

Teris, Bell's brother

Kaalen, Bell's brother

Cashial, Hunter's brother, 13

Tren, Hunter's brother, 5

Anawin, Hunter's sister, 8

Quasi, Loperis guard with a love of the whip

Kolean, Aducian guard.

Felexy, Kolean's husband

Agota Kelotian, renowned Aducian trader, Ari's mother

Xerves Kelotian, Ari's farther

Renauld, Hereditary founding senator

Trader Trinke, Trevon

Trader Gevero, Trevon

GLOSSARY

Averis, Havernian Capital city

Away teams, Derant, Polexin and Verox on board the KS Hek'rajin

Bamklin, similar to bamboo

Compcube, computer in the shape of a cube. Four view screens, two input sides

Constellation Orkanris, graceful curving eleven-point constellation spiral

Crown of Horns, braided crown, symbol of Kenistal, ancient symbol of kings

Dawn of the Long Blades, day of the battle between Uxalik and Le'brix

De-horning, one of the most severe punishments without killing someone. Used in cases of treason.

Difray'kin, the seventh moon of Kenistal

Falblink, similar to kerin pie but no alcoholic effect

Fire rocks of Bekresh, used by warriors to train on. A natural assault course

Freklika, Kenistalian strategy game

Gak'rin Ale, dark and smoky

Gosterin, another planet within the Barin Alliance

Grand Council, part of Aducian ruling system

Grendrix, like jodrix but non-alcoholic

Gruhdean, shit

Hablini, an Aducian soup several combinations of meat in it, with lots of blue vegetables, sour

Hid'link, a small ball of meat covered in a spicy crispy crust

Hot stones pool on Acrasisus, rejuvenate his aching muscles, other health benefits. Universe renowned for their healing affect

Iglink, bitch

Interplanetary Judiciary, independent group who oversee complaints between worlds.

Jec'ri'sa, a special serrated dagger given to those who demonstrated true service to the crown

Jekar, the final spiritual home of all fallen demons

Jodrix, smoky ale

Kenistal, the Demon planet

Keric five, emergency interrupts all comms, highest level, reserved for royalty etc.

Kerin Pie, has an alcohol type effect on non-demons

Krackinas Meditation, helps force a demon's scales to return back to their resting state.

Krafic, pack animal

Krasnilik, the rite of passage all demons went through

The Mighty Krenk, Tavern

Krexjin, idiot

KS Hek'rajin, commanded by Dea'saverin Hevalis

KS Talike, commanded by Emlinka

KS Zavrinn, courier class ship taking Caris to Landran

KS Zerkin, commanded by Urias

Lakris, orange reptile, fast and deadly

Landran, Neighboring planet, current home to Dax's Avanti squad

Lenis, Aducian gender, essentially male, but they have the ability to bear children. Outwardly, their anatomy is male, but internally, they carry both male and female parts

Lubrink, cuddly furry feline, small

Magrinth birds, similar to a hawk, giant

Mea decalis, my life

Mek hela, my heart

Mek iban, my fire

Mek tiko, my little warrior

No horn, derogatory comment for a non-demon.

Oblish, honey

Paraglay, lizard race

Parinka, one of the specialty meats of Kenistal, considered a real delicacy. Smoke cured, spicy and rich, the slivers of meat were often accompanied by a robust sauce— Hobrin.

Pik'dorin, a training session with ceremonial poles. The poles are longer than demons are tall. The poles are about ten feet long.

Pits of Raknavul, fire hounds, demonic form of punishment

Quastik, a potent, yet light, fresh and smooth alcohol.

Poko, moth

Rings of Hak'ran, Combat arena, place of challenges, battles there can determine a warrior's status and their rank within the guard

Rite of Ferik, guild selection process held on a demon maturity, their naming day. (Age twenty)

Rite of Ulisian, a fallen warrior's comrades chant the warrior's Journey to Jekar, the final spiritual home of all fallen demons.

Ronix, berry based spirit

Sanctions, leads to shunning. Temporary condition when demon warriors are in trouble with CO

Seelis, shellfish

Seventh moon of Gerabalis, moon of planet closest to Kenistal

Sinka, like silk

Sliva beast, a special type of comp program, like a virus, worms its way into systems

Span, roughly one mile

Techers, those who love all technology, but are good and standard comp systems

Tekrijit, exotic bird, wide wing span, rainbow of colors

Tep'it okri asteliki aps lekis tep'it okri keriset, the might of the soul is stronger than the might of blood

Tep'rink trousers, loose around waist and thighs, tight around the ankles. Small covered hole for the tail

Teo, tea.

Tiki, Aducian, no direct translation, but it basically means beautiful little one.

Toclin, planet

Trevon, planet, neighbors to Aducia

Ulinte, special fiber similar to Kevlar, yet light and durable

Vasic, a klutz

Vekrin, sour fruit which grows in the valleys of Denkran

Xozi squares, made from grains, similar to the rolls commonly found on Alliance worlds, but these were lightly spiced and melted in the mouth. They were the perfect complement to parinka.

Yevtabrin, Alliance planet

Zubrix, a set of rings and poles. It's like a miniature version of the Rings of Hak'ran and Pik'dorin

GUILDS

Amber, academics

Cobalt, guards, protection detail

Light blue, City guard

Pale blue, temple guard

Forest green, pilots, space-faring demons

Grey, inventors, tinkerers

Mint green, creative, artists, chefs,

Orange, manual,

Purple, royal family, only guild or color that is hereditary

Red, money men, politics, elitist

Silver, metalsmiths

Bronze, shops, service jobs, waiters, assistants

Lime Green Tech

MEET THE AUTHOR

Hannah Walker is a full-time mum to two gorgeous teenage sons, and shares her home with both them, and a very supportive husband. They have always encouraged her to follow her dreams.

She has always loved books from her childhood years reading alongside her father, inheriting his love of Sci-Fi and Fantasy. She has combined this with her love of MM romance to write her series Avanti Chronicles, Demonic Tales and Elements of Dragonis. She loves writing about a complex world where the men love, and live, hard.

Welcome to the world of MM Sci-Fi.

UPCOMING BOOKS:

Elements of Dragonis book 2

Delphini book 2

Avanti: Hunter and Bray's stories

OTHER BOOKS BY
HANNAH WALKER

CORIN'S CHANCE

BOOK I IN THE AVANTI CHRONICLES

Posted to some stars awful cruiser, Dr. Corin Talovich hoped to serve his time quietly and get on with his life, but fate stepped in and decided otherwise.

Crashing into an unknown planet was the last thing Corin expected. With only his friend, Lieutenant Commander Tate Riven, by his side, they face the unexplored world and new enemies bravely, leading them to the Derin Clan, where they're welcomed by the leader's son.

Kel isn't sure about the strange men, but he isn't about to send them away, especially when the bond between Corin and himself is something he can't ignore.

When another clan wages an attack, Kel is forced to make some hard choices which nearly costs him everything he holds dear. Together, with their allies, Corin and Kel fight, focusing on the future they desire, knowing failure not only dooms their love, but also those around them. Side by side, they work to destroy the evil threatening to keep them apart and becoming the family both men desire.

TATE'S TORMENT

BOOK 2 IN THE AVANTI CHRONICLES

When a rare day out goes disastrously wrong, the men have to fight for the survival of one of their own. Their actions spark an appearance by the Conclave, leaving the Avanti's future in the hands of those who choose to destroy them.

Tate will give up everything to save his friends, even if it means losing Dariux and a love he never imagined he would find.

With half the conclave determined to punish the Offworlders, they have to rely on new found friendships. The question is, will it be enough to overcome the trouble that seems determined to take them down?

DELPHINI: DAMAGE CONTROL

BOOK 3 IN THE AVANTI CHRONICLES

When Dax and Bell crash land on an unknown planet they only have one objective— find their friends and fellow Avanti. Of course Bell needs to heal up from his injuries first, then they have to work out where to go. Their biggest problem is— they hadn't counted on the world they landed on being quite as large as it was.

Along the way they encounter hostile local warriors, incredible beasts and more than their fair share of problems. It would be fascinating, if they weren't so worried about their friends.

Dax has gone into damage control mode, as the commander of the Avanti it's his job, his duty, to see his friends and teammates safe and there is nothing that will stand in the way.

Bell, the calmer of the two, has finally found somewhere he can let his inner darintha beast be free and he's making the most of it, using his darintha senses to help find their missing friends.

Never forgetting their mission, the two embark on a journey that not only tests them to their limits, but also deepens the trust and friendship that being Avanti is all about. Together, they search for their friends, and fight for survival as only the Avanti can.

ONCE UPON AN OCANIA

BOOK 4 IN THE AVANTI CHRONICLES

A SHORT STORY

After their trip to Berinias is delayed, thoughts turn to both love and the future. Ocania, a day of love for mated pairs, gives the men a treasured day off. But with love in the air, all the Avanti seem to feel the pull, pushing some to go after those they want and try to fulfil their hearts desire.

May your journey be swift and uneventful, may you all get one step closer to your truemates and may good triumph over evil. Remember love conquers all.

DAX'S DESIRE

BOOK 5 IN THE AVANTI CHRONICLES

The Avanti have made their way to Berinias, the capital and heart of Landran society. Not only is it King Kastain's home ground, but it's the seat of the Conclave's power.

Dax finally gets to see Kastain in all his glory— regal, confident, powerful and downright sexy. As events unfold, Dax and Kastain realize everything happening with the Derin, with Martellon, Nestor and Teriva, is linked. Their enemies draw closer and the plots and machinations of the Conclave deepen. They just need to work out who is behind it all and what they hope to gain.

Kastain finds himself turning to Dax, the one person he seems to be able to count on more than anything. The bond between the two leaders is stronger than they expected, and they long for rare times alone so they can explore it. Instead their time is taken up trying to work out which Chieftains they can count on and who is attempting to undermine them at every turn.

When plots and betrayals run deep within the heart of the capital, who will succeed and who will pay the ultimate price?

Bell's Beloved
Book 6 in the Avanti Chronicles

Bellan 'Bell' Nimeri loved Niko Dastria with all his heart. Knowing Niko was his lifemate from the moment he set eyes on him was bittersweet. Surrounded by unknown threats, becoming more than friends wasn't an option. Besides, he didn't think Niko had the same feelings as he did. What's more, Niko would need to accept both sides of Bell's shifter personality, as he and his darintha are a team.

Niko has grown up, preparing to someday take over the role of Chieftain to the Estrivia Clan. His life has been good, surrounded by friends and family, but he's always longed to find his truemate. Meeting Bell is a dream come true, but coming from different worlds, he's not sure Bell is willing to change his life to make things work between them.

Faced with war and unseen enemies, Estrivia battles for its very existence. The two men cling to their friendship, emotions growing stronger until neither can deny what they feel. Finally together and with the world trying to tear them from each other's arms, they face the enemy head on, knowing the only chance they have of finding happiness together is to defeat the ones who would destroy everything they know and keep them apart.

Mission Most Mysterious
Book 7 in the Avanti Chronicles A Short Story

The Avanti are bored.

On a rare and treasured break from all the chaos, Bray decides to embark on a mission most mysterious. Tate has always been known for the practical jokes he plays on his teammates and friends. It's time for some revenge. This time, the tables are turned and Tate doesn't know what's about to hit him.

Faced with confronting his worst fears, Tate struggles to make sense of the odd happenings around him. He swears not only are there ghosts in the palace, but they are out to get him.

Revenge is sweet, but the Avanti know that if Tate figures out what they are up to, there will be hell to pay. Still, watching him get a taste of his own medicine makes the risks worthwhile.

With his sanity on the line, Tate battles with everything in him to combat Bray's mission most mysterious.

DEMONS DON'T DREAM

BOOK I IN THE DEMONIC TALES

Being the Terran ambassador assigned to Kenistal, the Demon home world, is not a particularly easy posting. Caris Dealyn wants nothing more than to get this assignment done so he can continue searching for his missing Avanti friends. But first, he needs to solve the mystery surrounding the last ambassador's disappearance, while navigating the Demon court with all its whisperings of plots and betrayals. It's not such a bad job, if he could keep his attention on work and not on the prince who seems to distract him just by being near.

Prince Dasalin Kan'erkit is busy running the kingdom in his father's absence, but not so busy he doesn't notice the new Ambassador. Caris gets under his skin like no one else before, which is quite a feat considering Dasa's demonically tough scales.

The attraction between them is undeniable, and when events throw them together, sparks fly. They can't get enough of each other. But there are forces at work that wish to keep them apart. In a fight for their survival, the two must figure out which demonic faction is behind the plot and protect not only themselves, but the people they have both vowed to serve.

DEMONS DON'T DATE

BOOK 2 IN THE DEMONIC TALES

Commander Bo'saverin Hevalis, head of the Cobalts, is trying to recover from the injuries he sustained in battle. The enforced downtime is giving him too much time to think, torture for a man of action. The trouble in their sector is weighing heavily on his mind as it seems to be getting ever closer to the demon homeworld.

The only good thing is the strange green-haired man he rescued constantly stealing his attention. There is something about Ari that pulls at Bo in a way no other ever has.

As the two get to know each other, there is no denying the attraction between them. Bo longs to show Ari a life that he's never had a chance to experience before.

Held hostage by his mother, Ari grew up locked away from everything and everyone, only experiencing the world on his compcube and longing to explore what is outside the walls that trap him. Now, living with the demons, he's free to find himself and live his own life and find his passions.

Even as feelings grow between Ari and Bo, enemies lurk in the shadows, slowly working to take down the demon leaders and send Ari back to his controlling mother. Bo will face down any danger to prevent Ari being taken from him, allowing them to start the life they both deserve.

BOOKER'S SONG

BOOK I IN ELEMENTS OF DRAGONIS

Rillian Mascini is one of the most knowledgeable mages in the world. Spending his days and sometimes nights with his nose in a book has taught him magic and histories that few care to remember. He has a passion for dragons that pulls him to learn all he can about them, including their language. He is one of the last people left alive who can speak to the magnificent beasts.

Conwyn D'Aver is squad leader of the Dragon Riders. He will do whatever it takes to protect the dragons and people he has given his oath to serve. Nothing is more important, and when Neela, his personal dragon, is attacked, Conwyn is out for blood. He vows to find the threat and defeat it.

When an old spell book is found that gives a person the power to control all dragons, Conwyn will do anything he can to keep it from getting into the wrong hands, even if that means teaming up with the bookish Rillian to find a way to overcome the evil enemies who seek to gain the power.

Together with the dragons, the two men must find a way to protect everything they both love, but while doing so, they risk losing their own hearts to each other. As their enemies seek to destroy them, they learn that sometimes it takes love and trust to defeat the things we fear the most.

18179346R00232

Printed in Poland
by Amazon Fulfillment
Poland Sp. z o.o., Wrocław